# The Beggars' Pursuit

# The Beggars' Pursuit

## Christian Filostrat

Africana Homestead Legacy Publishers
Cherry Hill, New Jersey

Africana Homestead Legacy Publishers
100 Springdale Road A3 #206
Cherry Hill NJ 08003 USA
E-mail: info@ahlpub.com



Printed and bound in the United States of America.
10 09 08 07      5 4 3 2 1

This paper meets the requirements of ANSI/NISO Z39.48-1992 (R
1997) Permanence of Paper.



Library of Congress Cataloging-in-Publication Data

Filostrat, Christian.
  The beggars' pursuit / Christian Filostrat.
     p. cm.
  ISBN 978-0-9770904-5-7 (alk. paper) — ISBN 978-0-9770904-7-1 (pbk. : alk. paper)
  1.  Congo (Democratic Republic)—Fiction. 2.  Political fiction.   I. Title.

PS3606.I45B44 2007
813'.6—dc22
                                        2007005894

Parts of this novel are derived from real events, and the Motutu
character is a composite drawn from several strongmen, other heads of
state and from imagination. The novel's other characters are fictional as
well. Any similarity between characters depicted in this novel and
actual characters is wholly coincidental. Congo, Kinshasa, Congo-
Kinshasa are interchangeably used for Zaire, which was renamed the
Democratic Republic of the Congo in 1997.

For Dominique

Et la tradition Mandingue dit:
Celui qui vient en ce monde et s'en va sans rien troubler ne mérite
aucun respect.

*Massa Makan Diabaté*

Lumumba: So, OK, you? Or are you among those who believe that the sky will fall because a black man dares to castigate a king [of Belgium] in front of the whole world? No, you don't agree! I see that in your eyes.

Mokutu: Since you are asking me, I will answer with a story.

Lumumba: I hate stories.

Mokutu: It's to go fast. When I was eleven years old, I was hunting with my grandfather. Suddenly, I find myself nose to nose with a leopard. Frantic, I throw my spear and wound it. My grandfather was furious. I had to go retrieve the weapon. That day, I understood, once and for all, that you should not attack an animal if you are not sure to kill it.

*Aimé Césaire, A Season in the Congo*

# Chapter 1

The call came at 11 o'clock sharp that Monday morning, as if the caller had timed it to ring in the ambassador's office at precisely that hour, perhaps from a prearrangement to minimize interferences and insure confidentiality.

Marie recognized the man's voice as belonging to the ambassador's special contact at the State Department. She told the caller that the ambassador was unavailable and offered to take a message. She was surprised when he asked where the ambassador had gone. She replied, "Capitol Hill," reading from the note the ambassador had written down for her, prominently displayed beside the telephone.

"How long will he be away?" he then asked in a tone marked by surprise or maybe annoyance.

"A couple of hours," she told him. After a moment of hesitation, he said thank you.

Marie did not hear the tell tale click of the telephone ending the call, and only when the line had gone dead did she know for sure that the party she only knew as a voice had hung up. Marie shivered from the concern that had washed over her as quickly as she had responded to the caller's questions. Something had happened. Because she could not think what it could be, she was frightened. Her mind churned improbable disasters to the refrain of the security chief's warning that remaining in Washington depended on knowing everything about the ambassador's activities.

Marie loved being in Washington; away from Kinshasa, she was a person of importance, and no one from home who visited the imposing embassy building on Massachusetts Avenue failed to notice how regal she had become. She wore makeup here and spent hours at the hair salon every Saturday afternoon where two stylists took turns braiding her hair in the latest fashion. The queen of the embassy they called her back home. Now, fear was her crown. She debated with herself, before deciding to call the ambassador on his car phone, hoping that he would let slip a tad of information she could use to alert her control in Kinshasa.

---

Washington was no longer happy with the Dictator. In May the State Department had sent William Klingesthousen to Kinshasa on an official mission to speak to him. Klingesthousen was a well-groomed man, anxious that the hair on the left side of his head cover his bald pate just so. He held his blunt nose up, seemingly to keep the contraption in place, giving him a pinched look of disdainful authority.

Klingesthousen was nicknamed "Thug" for his practice of the "New Diplomacy" of bluntness that had come into vogue following the disappearance of the Soviet Union. Soon after arriving on the State Department's ninth floor, he remarked that his appointment signaled that Washington would no longer pooh-pooh irresponsibilities and corruption. Half rising from his high-backed leather chair like a stotting springbok, he declared, "Unless they are good, aid will be rationed — not as before. And don't tell me the Soviets will provide what I won't. That shit don't work anymore. Pass the word: that shit don't work anymore."

———

"I am convinced that Africans are gene deficient; a chromosomal abnormality may be responsible, making you incapable of doing what is right for yourselves or for anybody else," Klingesthousen told the Dictator to his face. To journalists, he said, "I told the president democracy is self-motivating — democracy like virtue is its own reward — democracy is the only way out of the impasse in the region." Heaving his chest forward perceptibly, unconsciously, the biggest boy in the yard. "And I read him the riot act about stability not being democracy. Democracy is what we demand! We will not stand; will not stand" —his hand chopped the air— "for undemocratic rule anywhere. The administration expects these countries to fall into line." A victor flushed with triumph like a glutton his dinner, Klingesthousen expounded his views to the skeptical journalists, mindless of what was sensible.

The Dictator was astonished. No one — especially from the United States — had ever said such nonsense to him. A realist, he was not really offended. Compared to the Belgian colonizers of his youth, Americans, even those like Thug Klingesthousen, were more considerate of Africans. In any case, he had ways of dealing with careerists like Klingesthousen who, he reassured himself, were out to make names for themselves at the expense of dependable but no longer desirable African autocrats.

What, however, did offend the Dictator was that before coming to Kinshasa, Klingesthousen had stopped in Lyauteyville to confer with the president there, a former Soviet client. It was a new act in an old play; the dialogue had altered, but not all the players had changed costumes or moved on. Until Klingesthousen's visit, Washington would not have thought of sending a high-level bureaucrat to Lyauteyville without first securing the Dictator's acquiescence. Was it not only a year ago that the Dictator had arranged for the humiliation of the Lyauteyville President by withholding his agreement for the President of the United States to welcome him to the White House for a photo opportunity?

It had been the Lyauteyville President's turn, as the elected chairman of the Organization of African Unity, to visit the United States. As was customary, the new OAU Chairman had gone to the United Nations in New York to make a speech about Africa and made a quick stop in Washington for a picture with the President of the United States. But for a week, the Lyauteyville leader had cooled his heels in the refurbished Willard Intercontinental Hotel. He took boat rides on the Potomac River, organized by investors interested in making telephone poles out of trees from the luxuriant central African forest, waiting for an invitation to have his White House picture. With time to waste and desperate to show that he had been to the U.S. capital, he had even paid a visit to the mayor, for whom he had to wait forty minutes before a quick handshake. In the end, they told him to go see the vice-president at his senate office — not the White House.

———

The Dictator was grinding his teeth, an indicator that forces were out of his control, the telling sign of fear, soon to be followed by rage. For Klingesthousen to go to Lyauteyville before stopping in Kinshasa was deliberate disrespect; Washington was signaling him as openly as allowable that it was displeased with him. Or was it more than displeasure? And why had Ambassador Sakeseba failed him? Sakeseba's most important job was to advise him of what Washington thought of him every hour on the hour if necessary; and briefing him thoroughly before a meeting with any American official was routine procedure, which Sakeseba until then had carried out in exemplary fashion. The Dictator could almost feel the cane in his hand as he imagined how he would exact his retribution. For reasons the Dictator had not yet fathomed, his ambassador, one of his most competent and trusted aides, had failed to warn him of the brutal reality Thug Klingesthousen had come to Africa to insult him with.

———

When his secretary reached him on the car phone, Ambassador Sakeseba had almost reached his destination in the Washington suburb of Fairfax. Like the exuberant sunshine, Molu Sakeseba felt a special excitement driving through the quiet, lawn-strewn community of King's Park; it reminded him of the lush woods of his Congo's north. Driving in King's Park under the speed limit on a workday, he would recall walking for days surrounded by the tranquility of his woods with only the macaque cries ruffling the peace of the canopies. Even the cries had been a welcome disturbance, enhancing the eternal quiet of the forest — the forest, indulgent, inviting, endlessly patient, welcomed him. That reminiscence never failed to sharpen his excitement at what awaited him shortly in the arms of his remarkable mistress. Squirrels scampered across the road between passing cars, while three crows perched on a rooftop looked on, waiting for the inevitable tragedy to occur.

Usually he stayed in his office on Mondays to talk to his contacts in Congress and the various governmental agencies about what had taken place over the weekend when policy makers made decisions that might concern Kinshasa. But this was an 'off' Monday. He had not been with the woman in the suburb for a while. And State would not announce who would be the new American ambassador to Kinshasa for another month.

He had done everything, spending lavishly to ensure that the Dictator's choice would represent Washington in Kinshasa. Secure that his man would prevail, and by way of rewarding himself for his efforts, this Monday, the ambassador decided that he deserved a few relaxing hours away from the office.

The telephone's ring brought him out of his reverie. His secretary would not have intruded on his outing unless there was an emergency.

"Yes, Marie."

"Your man at State called."

He waited; she would not have called him for that alone.

"He asked where you were, and when you would return. He *never* asked anything before. I thought that was strange. I didn't want to take a chance after what happened in May; maybe Thug is going to Kinshasa again." After a pause she repeated, "I didn't want to take a chance." Concern had given her voice a rasping tone, like manioc being grated for the evening meal.

"Thug Klingesthousen is gone," Sakeseba said, catching his breath, "he's doing Latin America or Asia, telling the people there about their genetic discrepancies." Marie's anxiety hit its peak; she had been right — the trepidation in the ambassador's voice, which he made no effort to disguise, was telling. After a pause the ambassador said, "I'll be in the office in a couple of hours. I'll call him then."

"OK, is there anything you want me to get ready for you?" she asked.

"No," he said, "I'll take care of it." And hung up.

Concerned caller ID would capture his car's telephone number, he started looking for a shopping center where he would find a pay phone to call the man who had disturbed his outing in the quiet suburb of King's Park. Making a U-turn on Sideburn Street, he drove two miles before reaching the shopping center on Braddock Road and the phone in front of the Safeway supermarket.

"What's up, Marcel? You scared Marie with your questions about my whereabouts."

"Well, you were out of the office at 11 o'clock on a Monday morning."

"I am sorry; I should have told you I wouldn't be in."

"About Marie, that's understandable. She was probably thinking about the guy in Kinshasa who paid the price for not warning Motutu about Thug Klingesthousen. Motutu put that poor bastard through one of his shoeshines with the cane. If Marie knew he was now one of Kinshasa's pitiful beggars, she would die. So that you don't become one yourself, I have to see you right away. I'll meet you in half an hour at the usual place."

"Make it forty-five minutes, Marcel."

"That's right. I forgot. You are — what did Marie say? — at the gym, exercising..." the man from State said with a strained laugh.

Molu hung up and ran back to his car. The King's Park woman would wait another day. In minutes, he was back on Braddock Road, heading for the beltway and the District of Columbia.

---

When Molu arrived at the restaurant on Kalorama Street, his friend and a drink were at the bar waiting for him. They shook hands and walked to a table in the back where the light from the bar was less bright.

The friend was 1976 Morehouse College graduate summa cum laude in anthropology, Marcellus Garinaldi, an African American foreign service officer who, like many black FSOs, had served in

Africa. After multiple bouts of malaria, he had requested an assignment in Europe. "Forget it," the director had said to him, "you look better in Africa. Sierra Leone is where you belong." It was a policy commonly applied to blacks.

Molu Sakeseba had befriended him and showed him the ways of Africa when Garinaldi was a junior officer posted in Kinshasa twenty years earlier. In time he had become this African ambassador's most perceptive adviser, using his familiarity with State Department's bureaucratic practices to guide Sakeseba through the diplomatic and foreign policy mazes.

"Relax Mr. Ambassador," he told Molu, concern on his face and in his voice when they took their seats. "I didn't mean to scare you, but after the Klingesthousen fiasco in May — you know, I didn't know what that clown was up to — I wanted to make sure you were in the loop no matter how bad the news."

"What are you talking about, Marcel?"

"It won't be announced for a couple of days, but the new ambassador for Kinshasa was picked at the Assignment Board meeting this morning."

Sakeseba stared at his companion, his lips pursed. "But I thought that decision was at least a month off. What happened?"

"That's what I thought too, but the word came from the front office to get it out of the way."

"So it's not the old man's choice?" Sakeseba said, his voice flat.

Marcellus took a sip from his drink to hide a grimace. With his free hand, he reached into his pocket for the ever-present cigarette case. He did not understand why his friend called the autocrat in Kinshasa "old man." You called your father "old man;" someone you respected you called "old man," but a corrupt dictator? Another African trait he did not understand.

Marcellus was unlike colleagues who made a great show of "knowing" Africa, acknowledging that his understanding of the continent and its people was limited at best. "There is more to Africa than we comprehend," he would invariably say.

From behind a smoke ring, Garinaldi answered that the Dictator's man had lost out.

"God, who is it then?" asked Sakeseba.

"Judd Mosley," Marcellus said, folding his hands on his lap, knowingly, anticipating his friend's reaction.

Molu leaped to his feet, as if an explosive had gone off in his chair. "Mosley? the black man?" he whispered, incredulous, through his teeth, standing over Marcellus.

"Well, he doesn't call himself that. But, yes, that's the one."

"But why?" Molu asked, sitting back down, when he saw the people at the bar looking at him, his face contorted, almost in tears.

"Look Molu, we have discussed this before. Kinshasa is no longer on the A list, where only a white ambassador will do. Why do you think Thug Klingesthousen did what he did over there? He wouldn't have done that two years or even a year ago. And can you imagine that clown telling a European that he had a dead chromosome? Kinshasa is now on the D or C list, who knows? You have to have African American ambassadors, right? This is America, and it's the late twentieth century."

"Second class citizens for second-class countries! Is that what you are telling me?"

"I wouldn't put it that way myself," Marcellus said. But, yes, that's basically what it is. The State Department sends an African American only every five years or so to a European country — and a small one at that. If you are black, get back. You know. They do it behind your back, and you're never the wiser. Not that you could do much about it, even if you knew."

"What's the definition for this shit? Racism?" Molu asked.

"No, it's not like that. It's something that has no name. They are not all rednecks over there."

"So what's your explanation?"

"Diversity frightens most people, in some form or another," Marcellus answered. "This is how I explain our assignment system to my department mentorees. From October to December, those in the market for assignments seek support from people they have worked with. A reference from someone influential is especially welcome. Expected as much as resented are visits to offices to drop off resumes, grovel, and make a pitch for a job. The practice, in this arena, having evolved into a norm to flush out the strongest contenders has degenerated into a support type of system. And since complaints are common if muted, only the candidate whose hand an authority has shaken knows for sure he or she is the anointed one for a particular assignment, while his colleagues — in hopeful ignorance — continue to solicit furiously. I don't want to bore you with more details."

"What's the social corollary of this? Can you tell me that?"

"The social corollary is that perceived abuse leads to anger, which creates a vicious circle. Akin to prison, to wash off the indignities we put up with, we become abusers ourselves. And there is a political aspect to these appointments, too."

"Political, you say?"

"Sure! The Black Caucus for one is breathing down the neck of the White House for more equitable appointments. And at election time, politicians can say progress is being made under their administrations. They don't have to say where they send African Americans."

"This is all internal stuff. Who cares? What I want to know is what's that got to do with Kinshasa?"

"Mosley's appointment is a product of this internal stuff, Molu!"

"They could have picked a second-class somebody else," Molu said, anguish in his voice, "it wouldn't be as bad." His anger no longer all-consuming, his mind was passing in review all the implications of the Judd Mosley appointment to his country. Like a man on a tightrope, he desperately sought to regain his balance. He was hearing admonitions from his ancestors.

"I understand, I understand; but if you want an American ambassador in Kinshasa, it will have to be a black man," Marcellus said, exasperated.

"God!"

"What I told you is for your ears only," Marcellus said. "I brought you a copy of the Task Force Report on State Department Reform. John Leighton was the chairman. You can use it when you talk to the man about the Mosley appointment. All you have to do is read from its findings. Convince him that a dysfunctional organization makes dysfunctional appointments."

"You don't know the old man, do you?" Molu asked. "What you told me does not change the fact that I failed him. It's my fault that he is going to lose face big time. This is one indignity he will not suffer. He knows your organization is dysfunctional; he has been dealing with it for thirty years. But he sent me here because he thought I was the one who would protect his interests — and I failed. And he knows how to deal with failures."

"Wait a minute," Marcellus said, worried. "What are you talking about?"

"I am dead," Molu said. "That's what I am talking about."

"You did what you could — and more," Marcellus said solicitously now. "You lobbied and kissed all the right asses. This is not your fault. Come on!"

"Tell me this, is there anyway to reverse this decision?"

"As long as it's not announced, I suppose so. The man has friends in Congress; you can try there. But I don't think it will work this time; it would be too easy to leak to the media that a congress-

man is standing up for the Dictator of Kinshasa who has got
billions in Swiss accounts. And they are saying he is to blame for
the Tutsi genocide three years ago. For any Congressman, it would
be the kiss of death. Your man is now in the same league as Baby
Doc, Abacha and Idi Amin, you know."

"He hasn't got billions in Swiss accounts," Molu said. "Most of
the funds he uses to pay people off to stay in power — not to
maintain corrupt Swiss bankers who robbed people fleeing genocide. I was with him once at a meeting with European journalists.
They asked him about his billions. 'Tell me where they are?' he
asked them. All they could do was point to villas in the south of
France, Brussels and Switzerland. 'At the most, you are talking
about a few million dollars,' he laughed; 'you said billions.'"

"The perception that he is the most corrupt man in the world is
not a laughing matter, Molu. And this is what the public responds to."

"You don't care that he is corrupt," Molu said, having gotten
angry again. "Corrupt has nothing to do with it; he is no different
today than he was when you were all kissing his ring for favors."

"That time is gone," Marcellus said. "But corrupt does have
something to do with it. If it were just a question of geopolitics,
they would simply discard him like all the others in Africa. But the
fact he is perceived as the most corrupt man in the world makes
him a burden, an embarrassment to be shunned."

"Where would Kinshasa be without him?" Molu asked rhetorically.
"Kinshasa would have been balkanized — Katanga in Soviet hands.
And do you think that Savimbi would have lasted as long as he did in
Angola against the Cubans and the Soviets? He was corrupt then,
wasn't he?"

"He was needed then," Marcellus said, "that's also the difference. But this isn't a seminar on the whorish ways of nations. This
is about you. Motutu is a violent man whose cruelty feeds on his
vindictiveness. He finds disloyalty even in his own closets. You were
lucky the mud from the Thug Klingesthousen farce didn't splatter
on you. I lied to your colleagues at the United Nations that it was
because of your efforts they removed Klingesthousen from the
Africa account. They told the man who must have bought it — you
are still here. You are going to have to use the Leighton report to
explain this Mosley appointment. Call him right away to tell him
what you have heard, and don't fly to Kinshasa until you know it's
secure. Give yourself time."

Molu looked at his friend in silence, as though he would not
see him again and wanted to remember what he looked like. His

mind drifted. He should tell the old man this afternoon about the State Department's decision. But the worst thing he could do was to use obfuscation.

He remembered that his mother always forgave him if he was the one to tell her first the mischief he had committed. Standing on the road from the market, waiting for her to explain what he had done always got him through. Raised by an African mother, he would always be an inveterate optimist.

"Look, Molu," Marcellus said, "this is a friend speaking. I think you could be the future of the Congo; the man has had his day. God knows corruption is not the only way. You seem to forget that 80% of your people live in absolute poverty? And I mean *absolute* poverty. The average Congolese was 53% poorer in 1995 than thirty years earlier. With that river you talk so much about, only 14% of the people have access to safe water. And minerals? Your soil has so much of it, cockpit instruments go haywire during flyovers. Just think what you could do with a country like that and a few honest institutions."

"What are you telling me, Marcel? That I should overthrow the old man? Are you nuts? I wouldn't be a bootleg head of state for anything in the world. I know we need change. I've known it since I left my village. But why think of coups when talking about change in Africa? You don't say that about your country."

"Look, the last time I was at the UN, I met the Senegalese foreign minister, you know, Fatou-Anne Cerusu. I stared at her for both her age and her beauty. She was amused when I just stared at her, so she came over and introduced herself. I have never met someone with a better understanding of Africa in the world today than this woman. Not even Madiba Mandela gets it the way she does. Get in touch with her; she can help."

"I know who she is," said Molu. "She never misses an opportunity to accuse the old man of one thing or another."

"But won't you at least talk to that colonel friend of yours? The military may have a take on this Mosley appointment that we haven't thought of."

"Yea, I'll talk to Freeman."

"OK man," Marcellus said, "it's your funeral."

Molu thanked him for wishing him good luck the way an African would. It was similar to saying "break a leg," a way to dupe perverse fate. He hugged his friend, thanking him for his help, promising to stay in touch.

"I'll take care of the tab," Marcellus said, "you have troubles enough."

# Chapter 2

The selection of Judd Mosley to be the new ambassador to Kinshasa had incited intense debate on the State Department's ninth floor. One member of the Selection and Assignment Board later compared it to declaring creationism to be science. The uncharacteristic ruckus over this one assignment occurred because not all the members knew that Kinshasa was no longer an A list country.

When the Coordinator of the Selection and Assignment Board, a man practiced in procedure and jurisdiction, but acknowledging the debts due to get a job done, heard that the front office had shaken Judd Mosley's hand for Kinshasa, he thought it was a mistake. When he discovered it was no mistake, he immediately suggested they consider his assistant, Brenda Bleding, instead.

The baron of the bureau, Matthew Breeson, (contrarily nicknamed the "Fatman" for his vigorous daily use of the basement gym), called the coordinator. He ordered the coordinator to cease his frantic lobbying on Bleding's behalf. The Fatman was a middle-aged man, appropriately bland-looking and mannered who used self-deprecation and clichés in a not too-successful effort to mask his all-consuming aspirations. He was reputed to have no enemies and aptly went out of his way to give minorities the impression he was on their side. He told the coordinator that the Mosley appointment was a "political" one, meaning that the front office itself had made the nomination. "We are sending Motutu a message that he has been down graded," he said matter of factly. "We want Mosley because we know he won't stray off the reservation and go native on us. And he is not trigger-happy with the "G" word like some people around here. Given the carnage that has already taken place, it is politic to put his face on the president's policy." Still the coordinator had protested.

"Motutu is not going to take it lying down. He rages like a gored bull and he has friends in Congress. His ambassador spends beaucoup time on the Hill promoting his interests. Every time I go up there, I see him. Have you thought about that?"

The Fatman made a reproachful grunt at being reminded of the Dictator's influence. "A dictator will do what a dictator will do! But Motutu is a simple man. He is going to take the Mosley appointment personally, sure; but his pride will be a deterrent to his doing anything about it on the Hill. In any case, I don't think anybody in Congress will stand up for him."

The coordinator stubbornly continued to argue. He knew that he would not change the Fatman's mind, but he wanted the Fatman to report to his fellow gatekeepers that the coordinator had argued long against the Mosley appointment and done all in his power to keep the faith with them. The Fatman allowed himself to be talked into a handshake and agreed that Brenda would be appointed Mosley's deputy. This is something he had planned to do all along; in his eyes, it did not hurt to give this pliant coordinator the impression that he had wrung a concession out of the Fatman. He was good at giving impressions. In any case, Brenda was his protégé and it was time that he pay back a classmate who had given him good service these many years.

She had been from the south attending his university on a scholarship. A tall, handsome woman, the Fatman still reflected how far she had come. He had looked upon her as a true southern belle. Telling her that he was sending her to Africa would cause a scene, he knew, as he recalled her prejudice toward people of color. But he would explain patiently that it was one of those unique opportunities that people in their business did not say no to. He was the pillar on which her career depended, and, in the end, she would agree and show her gratitude. She always had.

Designated ambassadors have the last word in the selection of their deputies. But Mosley was hardly someone who would object to whomever they suggested to him. It would be like a cleric objecting to God.

The gatekeepers had been concerned that nominating blacks to these positions would be another inevitable opening for more of them to compete in an arena where a man's gain must be another's loss.

To make sure the Monday meeting would not degenerate into a mutiny, the Coordinator of the Selection and Assignment Board went to work as soon as he received his orders from the Fatman. He started with his principal ally on the board, William Jeffries, a slight man in a rumpled gray suit — a blunt speaking, old campaigner against minority encroachment. After listening quietly to the coordinator's explanation, Jeffries announced, "This one will be trouble!"

Using Matthew Breeson's nickname to personalize his request, the coordinator said, "The Fatman told me the order came directly from the front office."

"The Fatman is full of shit," Jeffries replied. "The front office is too scared we see it as favoring minorities like this Mosley fellow to do this. No, it's the Fatman's idea. It's the Fatman's buttering up to you know who up there. I bet you my paycheck it's the Fatman's."

"I thought so too, so I checked with the front office," the coordinator lied. "They want Mosley, no ifs or buts."

"I don't believe it! The Judge is too afraid to have one of his own around him. He won't compromise that precious popularity of his for anything in the world. Not even the guy who carries his bags is colored. What's going on?"

"Let's face it," the coordinator answered, "our system is passé; it no longer protects the institution. Haven't you noticed? They aren't coming anymore; they are here."

"I don't care how passé it is," Jeffries said. (He had worked in Naples and had adopted the Italian gesture of putting the fingers together to emphasize a point.) "Until we have something better to replace it with, we defend it. This is not the military here. Integrating America is not our business. Foreigners are insulted when we send them black envoys. At a reception at a European embassy the other night, the first secretary there pulled me aside; he wasn't blunt about it, but in so many words he was asking what they had done to offend us. I didn't know what he was talking about.

'You have sent us someone of a somewhat lower rank,' he said. 'You have not done that before. Have we unknowingly offended you? It must be a misunderstanding that together we can easily correct, I assure you.'

"I said I was not up to date on all our appointments and asked whom he was referring to. This is what he said: 'Don't get me wrong, this person is very gracious… you refer to them in your building as affirmative action hires and usually send them to Africa. You did send one or two to communist countries a few years ago. We are concerned that you have put us in the same class.'

"I was embarrassed and said I would look into it and left it at that. But you see what I am talking about. Our European friends are raising questions. It's not that we have a choice."

"You handled that one badly," the coordinator replied. He got up and went to the window. His back to him, he chided Jeffries,

"You should have defended the appointment regardless of who it is."

"I said I didn't know; I thought that was enough."

"You should have said, whoever it is, we can assure you is qualified and represents the United States of America." He turned and faced Jeffries. "That would have put the ball in their court. What were they going to do, refuse us an entry visa? They can't question or tell us who our envoys should be."

"Now you listen to me," William Jeffries said, his face now an angry red. "Our business is to put America's best face forward. All this first secretary wanted to know is whether or not our policy toward Europe had changed. That's a fair question! So I checked. In theory, it hasn't changed; in practice it's something else, unless you don't think that sending *one of them* over there is a shift. It was one thing to send a minority or two to some communist countries for propaganda purposes, but that's all. We never agreed it would be more than that. As I told you we must defend —"

"But Kinshasa is not that country, and it is not the time to do it," the coordinator said, interrupting Jeffries, but with unusual patience in his voice. "It would be insane to antagonize the Judge right now. The last thing we need is a confrontation that we are sure to lose. Congress is breathing down his neck to implement the recommendations from the Leighton report. We must make him see we are doing everything in our power to make good on these recommendations. To protect the institution, we have to ratchet up the old tokenism policy. That policy has started to show its rot. It is so transparent —Oh yeah! I am not kidding; in the elevator, I heard one of them refer to it as cellophane. You know how they speak! As you said yourself, we have no choice. I want you to tell everyone to put the Principle of Perceptual Consistency out to pasture. It's not to be used anymore. That's an order."

"As long as we limited them to Africa and Communist countries we all understood, Jeffries said. Now you are suggest —"

"Look, Bill," the coordinator cut him off, using his first name in a rare show of collegiality, "forget for a moment, at least, all this; it's not worth arguing about. We have just two days to get a consensus on this Mosley assignment. I need you to get four of the members on board on this. Please!"

"Who is going to be his deputy?" Jeffries asked, having guessed that the coordinator had already worked a handshake deal with the Fatman.

"Brenda," the coordinator answered, pulling at his nose, a wry smile on his face.

Jeffries looked at him, incredulously. "You're sending Brenda to Africa? I don't believe it. She'll catch something."

"She can't stand the cannibals. She won't screw one of them. No, her job will be to watch over Mosley; make sure he doesn't go native on us — not that there is much chance of that. The Fatman told me that in fact Mosley doesn't feel any particular empathy toward Africans. When another slaughter starts over there, he won't get religion and start shouting 'genocide' like that cretin, what's his name, and expect the U.S. cavalry to come to the rescue. If he is awakened in the middle of the night with that kind of news, he is one who simply will say, 'I'll say a prayer for peace' or something to that effect and go back to sleep. In the scheme of things, a pose is no less impressive than a stand; it's a matter of timing." The coordinator ended an always-difficult consultation with a derisive laugh.

"Yeah, right," Jeffries said derisively as well.

The coordinator made a point of showing him respect by going to open the door for him to leave.

---

The next board member the coordinator called to his office was Mattie Tierney, a middle-aged black woman. After years working as a secretary for the Department followed by a job as an assignment counselor, she had made it to the assignment board as a token minority.

Realizing their mistake — Mattie, besides being tall, was also ethical, no nonsense, and, as much as she prayed for divine help, could not resist being confrontational. They had tried to have her removed on the ground that she was not the team player needed for such a job, meaning that she often asked pointed questions about the appointments of minorities and did not always vote the way they expected.

Mattie Tierney also, when making her constant objections, had the infuriating habit of quoting Martin Luther King, Jr., particularly his "Letter from the Birmingham Jail," which she seemed to know word for word. She had "sued their ass" as she was fond of saying and won with damages to boot. Now, besides praying that one of Washington's rickety and fume-spewing buses would hit her, the other members simply ceased to acknowledge her presence. Having the voting majority on the board made ignoring her effortless.

Then occurred the appointment of a minority to the front office—'the first in the nation's history.' Frantically, the members tried to adjust, reasoning that a minority boss would look favorably on the plight of minorities in the Department. That soon proved a chimera; the boss had enough problems just keeping up. And Mattie Tierney had been coming there too many years not to know that the deference paid to her by the other board members on account of the new boss's race would be short lived.

His first week on the job, he made courtesy visits to the various offices including Mattie's. She had genuinely hoped that, given his larger than life reputation and stature, he would not shrink from supporting the Department's minorities. "I have heard what you are telling me, Miss Tierney," he had said, reading her name tag, "and I assure you the days of sending us just to Africa are over." She stood there, unable to speak, awestruck, not believing her ears. He walked out of the office with the assurance that he meant what he had told her. As soon as she sat down, she called her best friend down the hall, "he said 'us' my dear, you know, the way Richard Pryor says it."

"You mean he is a shifter?"

"No, he is not a shifter. How can you say such a thing? You don't expect him to talk like that to them? He does what he has to do. And since he knows where he is from, it's fine with me." On the way to the subway that evening, she had confidently assured her friend that change had finally come to the Department.

She was stunned when at the very next meeting of the board, a rare African American who had spent his career in European assignments was named ambassador, but to an African country. She had raised her voice in protest, quoting King at every turn, and for once had managed to deadlock the board. And she had won. Instead of Africa, they had sent the man to his area of expertise — Europe — albeit to a small and seldom heard of European country, known mostly for its cheap-fare airline.

Now sitting on the opposite side of the coordinator's desk, Mattie Tierney tried to make sense of what he was telling her. His solicitousness was lost on her, but he had achieved a breakthrough; Mattie Tierney, although clearly distrustful, was interested in what he was telling her. She had already heard it was an African American hand they had shaken for Kinshasa. She tried to understand why this change was taking place now. But she was too far removed from where such decisions were made to know they had picked a black as a way of sending a message to the Dictator of Kinshasa.

The Dictator and his country had been demoted. Had she known, she would have been outraged. But lacking this key information, Mattie Tierney ended up being the one whose stand made the difference in the positive outcome of the Monday meeting of the board.

Looking at her with a mixture of apprehension and repressed condescension, the coordinator spelled it out for her: "Miss Tierney, change has come to the Department, and I need your help getting this assignment through at the meeting Monday. We want Judd Mosley for the Kinshasa job. However, some think Kinshasa should remain a preserve for whites only. President Reagan was right to send a black officer to South Africa — look at the difference it made —"

"Judd Mosley is not that man," she interrupted, her voice rising at "man," shaking her head vigorously, indicating she knew well of what she spoke.

"And Kinshasa is not South Africa," the coordinator said mechanically, surprised at the woman's reaction. "In any case, we want to open the assignment pool to include everyone," he smiled. "Can I count on your help to see this through?"

Mattie Tierney was not used to this kind of consideration; it was the first time the coordinator had called her to his office to discuss her vote, and appreciating what she thought was a genuine change, she agreed in the coordinator's office that Judd Mosley should be the next American ambassador to Kinshasa.

---

The coordinator was hopeful; with Mattie Tierney on board, he now felt certain he could carry out the Fatman's order without too much fuss. But William Jeffries's first report was not optimistic; he had not converted a single member. With the second report, the coordinator became concerned. Soon, the Fatman himself got wind that a number of board members in a rare display of autonomy were reluctant to rubber-stamp the Mosley appointment. A committed opportunist, the Fatman possessed the congenital acumen to thrive in an organization where they worshipped process. He called the coordinator to voice his concern. The boss had personally shaken his hand for the assignment of a lifetime, and he was determined not to undermine that because of another "imbroglio Negro," as he called the troubles minorities caused his Department. (Strolling among the booksellers on the banks of the Seine, he had seen the title of one of the great Chester Himes's novels, *Imbroglio Negro*, and, liking the sound of it, had made it his own to use when referring to minority questions in his department.)

"Look," he said, in a voice he made grave to show how serious he was, "if you can't take care of it, I'll have to do it myself. That would not be good. I think you know what I mean."

"We still have the weekend," the coordinator said, "we'll have the vote by Monday."

"Are you sure?"

"I am sure."

"OK, I am counting on you. Call me noon Sunday with an update."

But Monday, the coordinator was not sure all the promises he had made and the threats he had proffered had gotten him the vote.

Two members were waiting for him at the elevator on his way to the ten o'clock meeting. Coming closely, one of them whispered, "We know how to take care of Mosley."

"Not this time," the coordinator said, his voice firm. "There is nobody else for this one, sorry."

"Not even Brenda?"

"No."

In the room, the members except Mattie Tierney were standing in a cluster in the far corner from the door, in apparent disagreement, chatting in excited voices. Usually they murmured among themselves, sitting around the table in the center of the room. The coordinator took his seat at the head of the table and opened his folder. The two members who had ridden down the elevator with him walked in a minute later. One of them shook his head "no" to a member across the table from him. That member looked at his other colleagues and lowered his head. The coordinator called the meeting to order.

"We have five assignments to hand out today," he said easily. "I'll read the names and the assignments." When he had finished reading, William Jeffries, as he had agreed to do, said, "Mr. Chairman, may I suggest we get the most onerous one, Kinshasa, out of the way first?"

"Any objections?" the coordinator asked.

No one spoke.

"Of the names I read for Kinshasa, Judd Mosley is the bureau's candidate," the coordinator said. And looking from left to right at the members, "I have no objection to going along with the bureau's choice." That was usually the cue for the members to nod their heads in approval. But not this time.

"The bureau's choice?" one member asked, incredulous. "This is one handshake that demands a discussion."

"I agree," said another.

"Alright, what is your point of order? Remember, the rule gives the board fifteen minutes of discussion time per assignment," the coordinator said, looking at the member who had spoken first, his displeasure apparent.

"I think Judd is too immature for such an important post, Mr. Chairman"

"Immature? He is forty-two," the coordinator said in correction.

"He means, he is not qualified," Mattie Tierney said, irony giving her voice a metallic resonance, like pots falling from a shelf.

"Alright, he is not qualified either," the member said.

"He will not be qualified until he turns white, "Mattie Tierney retorted. "What's the chance of that?"

"Please, ladies and gentlemen," the coordinator said loudly, wishing he had a gavel to bang. "There is no need for any of that."

"I apologize, Mr. Chairman, but I am tired of hearing excuses to bar minorities from their due."

"Due?" one member asked. "Color should not be a ticket to any due."

"Unless it's white," Mattie Tierney retorted. "But this is for Africa, for Christ's sake, the place where you send 99 percent of African Americans, remember?"

"Kinshasa is not just any place in Africa," another member said, importantly; the United States has strategic interests there. And this board should be judicious in whom it agrees to send there."

The coordinator was tempted to tell the member that the Department had downgraded Kinshasa, and that, in fact, they needed to send an African American there; but not wanting to alienate Mattie Tierney then, he interrupted to say only, "We have to make some changes."

"We certainly do, Mr. Chairman," Mattie Tierney interjected. "Just because a country has more significance as far as our interests are concerned is no defensible justification to keep it off limits to minorities. We tell the people in this building they are to serve anywhere in the world. Long passed is the time, long passed, to show we mean what we say. As you so well noted, Mr. Chairman, we have to make changes."

"Well, yes, Miss Tierney," the coordinator mumbled, surprised and glad she had not quoted Martin Luther King, Jr. at all.

The discussion continued but with less vehemence, as the members paused to read between the lines of what the coordinator and Mattie Tierney had said. William Jeffries furtively gave the coordinator the signal to call for a vote.

"The fifteen minutes have expired," the coordinator said, holding his watch. "Any more objections to sending Judd Mosley to Kinshasa?"

It was Mattie Tierney who said, "I don't think there are any objections, Mr. Chairman."

# Chapter 3

Ambassador Sakeseba rushed back to his car. Not surprisingly, a pink-colored piece of waxed paper, like an omen, was stuck between the left wiper and the windshield. The District of Columbia, America's "Chocolate City," with a bottomless need for revenues, had created a parking-violation juggernaut to raise cash that spared no one. Like most diplomats in the city, Ambassador Sakeseba did not always pay his parking tickets on time. His friend, the mayor, had threatened to immobilize his car with the made-in-France orange-colored boot. But he was joking. So was the ambassador who asked him what he was really doing with the money from all the parking tickets. Unable to avoid the tickets, the citizens of the city, who only had a nonvoting representative in Congress, had started a rumor regarding the mayor's now infamous smoking habits.

When Molu had asked him about the money, the mayor was not amused and had let fly a few choice American four-letter words. As he pulled the pink- colored polythene ticket from under the windshield, Molu reminisced about his friend now in a Pennsylvania jail, a hundred miles away. It was 12:15 p.m. in Washington, 5:15 p.m. in Kinshasa.

Sakeseba pulled fast from the curb and headed down Kalorama Street, then turned right on Columbia Road in the direction of 16th Street. The light had turned amber at 15th Street, but he chose not to send the big Mercedes through; a police station was down the street, and he had no time to explain his diplomatic status if stopped. Waiting for the light to change, he saw a young black man with a piece of board, trying to push something from the sidewalk into the street. Molu rose up from his seat to get a better look. It was a rat. The young man was attempting to push it into oncoming traffic to run it over. The rat had grasped his intent; fighting back, holding its ground, it was refusing to go to its death in the street. The young man whacked at it repeatedly, but the cornered rat did not budge. Whenever the young man renewed his effort, the rat would rise on his hind legs to free his front paws to swat at the board. This spectacle fascinated Molu. Unmindful of his urgency, he pulled over to the curb to watch this drama of rat and man unfold. The young man could have sent the rat flying into the street with one good whack of the board, but a primeval fear was an impediment.

Molu understood that fear. He recalled having experienced it one afternoon by the river back home when the priest had staggered in the mud, his white cassock pulling him down, Molu following him with a club made from the branch of a limba tree in his hand, afraid to strike, praying the poison would finish the old priest off.

Instead of turning onto Sixteenth Street in the direction of his office on Massachusetts Avenue, Molu crossed over into one of the dilapidated parts of Washington and turned right on Georgia Avenue, heading toward the southwest, where Colonel Freeman was a professor at the exclusive National War College in Fort McNair.

The fort's multilayered iron gates faced Fourth Street, just past the posh Carrollsburg Condominium's buildings at the corner of Fourth and M street. The sentry at the entrance took his credentials and called the office of the professor Molu said he was there to see. In short order, the soldier waved him in, and the barrier rose to let him through. He had to drive around the golf course twice, looking for a parking space, finally settling for the last space in a long line of cars facing the College's Theodore Roosevelt Hall. After a ten-minute walk dodging joggers all wearing blue shorts and white T-shirts, he went up the steps. It was now 1:05 p.m. in Washington, 6:05 p.m. in Kinshasa.

"My dear Molu, *ozali malamu?* I am happy to see you," the colonel said. Colonel Max Freeman, a professor of African politics at the National War College was a tall man. His hair, cut short, was completely white, enhancing the paleness of his face and giving him the look of a benevolent, wise magician. When he hugged him, Molu remembered that the look was deceptive; Colonel Freeman was a very fit man.

"You are in trouble, or you wouldn't be here," Freeman said.

"I think so, Colonel," Molu said.

"Let's go into my office, and we'll talk about it."

Molu had met Max Freeman twelve years earlier when the colonel was finishing his career, serving as the American Embassy's defense attaché in Kinshasa. He had spotted Molu, a promising young captain, one of the Dictator's aides.

As they neared his office, the colonel stopped and faced Molu.

"You won't believe what I heard this morning. Do you remember the blind fellow who was with you the first time you came to the States?"

Of course," Molu said. "Of course I remember Abdoulaye!"

"He was just named Niger's Minister of the Interior," the colonel said. "Isn't that something? There is hope for you yet."

Thanks to Freeman, Molu was selected to travel to the United States as one of the Embassy's International Visitors, all expenses paid. For a month he had been part of a group of seven French-speaking Africans flying all over the U.S. with only an interpreter in tow to experience life the way Americans lived it everyday. He remembered being impressed that no one made any effort to make him see America the way the sponsors of this expensive junket might have wanted him to. From Harlem, New York to San Diego, California, Americans — most of them white — had welcomed the group into their homes, greeting each member as they would a friend.

In his mind's eye he saw Abdoulaye — in Seattle, where the Nigérien's sight was restored.

The trip was ending, and they were having lunch in the home of a retired couple. The husband had been an architect, his wife an art history professor at the University of Washington. As customary throughout their visit, this couple had invited neighbors to join them in a meal. Abdoulaye was an administrator at the Justice Ministry then. When Molu first met him upon arrival in New York, he had no idea Abdoulaye was just a percentage away from being considered legally blind. He was the most imposing and dignified man Molu had met. Molu recalled thinking then that not even the president, the Great Elephant, was as impressive. They voted Abdoulaye leader of the group, not because of his handicap, but for the way he held himself, his dignity. He impressed everyone he met — the calm way he had of speaking, and of course his understanding of administrative questions and his knowledge of France's colonial practices in Africa.

The president of Harvard who had been at a dinner with the group when they visited Washington, their first week in the U.S., had him flown to Boston to lecture on French colonialism in Africa to a class of graduate students.

During the lunch in Seattle, a striking woman with hair cut short, who had listened attentively to the Africans' remarks, told Abdoulaye, "I am a surgeon specializing in ophthalmology; I'd like to take a look at your eyes."

"If you'd like," Abdoulaye said in that calm way he had of speaking.

The doctor went outside to get her bag from her car. "Please come to the window, the light is better there," she told Abdoulaye when she returned.

For ten minutes, she examined Abdoulaye's weak eyes.

"I think I can restore 60% of your vision," she announced when she had finished.

"I couldn't pay," Abdoulaye said, moving his shoulders as if to say, "That takes care of that."

"Oh, it wouldn't cost you anything," said the doctor as a matter of course. "I would do the left eye first and have you come back in six months to do the other."

Abdoulaye thanked her and said he would think about it. He then excused himself and went into the powder room to weep. They said very little after that, each person had his own thoughts to deal with, reliving what they had just experienced that day. It seemed a moment to savor, an experience to imprint on their minds.

The Colonel too remembered. He shook his head in amazement, recalling that Doctor Whitehill had operated on Abdoulaye the next afternoon, giving him more than the 60% of the eyesight she had promised.

After that first visit to the U.S., Molu had pestered him for other opportunities to go back to America. Freeman had obliged him by including his name on the list of Congolese or other French speaking Africans sent to the U.S. for training of one sort or another. In three years, Molu traveled to the U.S. five times. He became a favorite of his American sponsors, not only because he had the highest score on the IQ test surreptitiously given the first time he went to the U.S. but also for his genuine fondness for things American — and his ambition. Following a five-month intensive course at a language-learning center outside Washington, he spoke English well enough, albeit with an accent. Other government agencies became interested in him. The complimentary reports about his performance solidified Molu's value to the Dictator and gave the agencies the entrée to the Dictator's inner circle they sought. When Colonel Freeman left Kinshasa for the National War College, he continued advising Sakeseba. It was Freeman who suggested that Molu exchange the uniform for an Yves Saint Laurent suit. They moved his office from the presidential palace to the Foreign Ministry, but Molu remained in contact with the Dictator, briefing him regularly as head of the Foreign Ministry's North American Department.

In early February 1989, following a trip to Morocco, the Dictator asked that the head of the Foreign Ministry's North American Department come to his villa in Gbadolite for a briefing. The foreign minister came in person to inform Molu of the president's request, even knocking on his door, something he had not done the few times he had come to Molu's office. Molu groaned inwardly; Gbadolite was more than six hundred miles from Kinshasa. The minister read the apprehension. "The ministry's helicopter is waiting on the roof for you," he said, smiling, figuring that the Dictator's interest in the North American Department would rub off on him.

At Molu's request, the helicopter followed the Congo River on its northern course for six hundred miles all the way to the township of Lissala before turning forty-five degrees north to enter Gbadolite's air space on the Central African Republic's border. The pilot, a man from Molu's village, expected that out of respect for the elders, his passenger would also ask him to stop for a courtesy visit at their village located near the township of Bumba neighboring Lissala. The elders, understandingly, would not have held them more than an hour. They had time. But Molu said nothing about the village. In eight short years, an unexpected event would remind him of that faux pas.

The Dictator in person came to the helipad to meet him. Driving a Buick sedan, he gave Molu a tour of the villa's ground overlooking the Ubangi River, stopping for the prancing peacocks and for his grandchildren and their cocker spaniel.

Aides frequently visited the boss at his northern residence, but it was unheard of for one so relatively junior to receive this personal attention. Molu gave no outward sign that such attention overwhelmed him. Excellent, the Dictator thought. I need a man pomp does not easily impress; such quality will serve me well in Washington. Slightly blotted, the Dictator's face had an ashy sheen, and he held a white handkerchief in his left hand, which he used to wipe his lips repeatedly, as if to remove fatigue off his face. No bodyguards were visible, but Molu had no doubt they were there. When he had stepped out of the helicopter, one had stopped him for a pat down; but with a grunt and a wave of the hand, as if shooing guinea hens from the yard, the Dictator had stopped the search. Seated on a bench placed there for them to gaze down on the river whose ceaseless rumble served to screen their conversation as well, the Dictator began the consultation as he always did by asking about Molu's family. He was married to a pediatrician whom he had met in Bumba. At the time, she was a Peace Corps volunteer health specialist there. (The Dictator's gift to the newlyweds was an all expenses paid vacation to the wine country of California, including a round trip flight on the Concorde from Paris to New York.) As Molu pulled out his wallet to show the Dictator the picture of a rosy brown-faced girl, the Dictator spoke of his trip to Morocco.

"Truccard, you know, came to Rabat to see me," the Dictator shrugged. He was contemptuous of the man they called Mr. Africa in Paris, the French government's *eminence grise*. "The French are as transparent as the Americans are righteous! He said that as a friend he had come to warn me that Mitterand was about to make a speech. He begged that words directed at authoritarian regimes not offend me. Can you believe these people? They were giving the Nazi salute to Hitler at the 1936 Olympics, and they lecture me about authoritarian regimes. 'This has nothing to do with you,'" the Dictator mimicked Truccard's falsetto. He noted that Molu did not even smile at his feeble attempt at levity. His sycophants would have had a laughing match. "Well," he continued, "he told me France was reviewing its aid allocation, and it was likely that they would be able to give us only 100 million American dollars this year. Last year they gave us 300. When you depend on the interest of strangers — I asked you to come here today to tell me if the Americans would make up this shortfall. I need to know where we stand, and what our options are. I know I can count on you to speak frankly. You know how grateful I am for that!"

"I am sorry, Mokonzi (my Chief)," Molu said, "but with the Cold War at an end, who knows what geopolitical winds are about to assail us. The Soviet Union is withdrawing. Large numbers of personnel at the Soviet Embassy across the river in Brazzaville are going home. Everything is changing for —"

"What is it to us that Russians are going home?" the Dictator said impatiently.

"It means that the American administration can play by its own book now and blame the Congress for having to do so. The thing about the Congress is particularly important when the French cut back on their aid to us. We were using the French money to service our debt to the U.S. If the Americans start to do things by the book, they'll tell us that their Congress won't agree to more money: because under a provision of the Brooke Amendment, they cannot give us more aid if we don't pay the interest on last year's debt to them."

The Dictator took a long breath. "The attention France pays to Africa is more personal. I know them. They need us as an extension of their foreign policy, perhaps even more than we need them. We can use that to make the Americans see things our way. They are not going to cut back, Molu!"

"I disagree, Mokonzi," Molu said sharply. "The United States is not going to side with us against France. Never! They may quibble at the margins; have little family fights here and there, but that's all. The United States has few reasons to care about Africa outside of its greater geopolitical concerns. They operate at a different level from France. Once the Soviets are gone, there is little motivation to play even a marginal role here. As long as it's not the Soviets, they'll be happy to see France or anybody else, become the dominant external power here and fill the vacuum. For the United States, Africa is a European area of influence. It has always been; it's not going to change. The only exception is if Britain engages in a neocolonial squabble with France here. The U.S. would side with Britain, of course."

"American values, *ezali bosoto*, all nonsense?

"I wouldn't say it's *bosoto*. It is real enough — in the U.S. I have seen it first hand. And I am sure that when their values coincide with their national interests — it's like everybody else, interests trump stated values. No one dies for morality. Man's power of rationalization is too great for that. Isn't that what you taught me?"

The Dictator turned from Molu and watched the river. *A bon entendeur salut,* he told himself, if the shoe fits wear it! How kind of the Americans to warn me!

"Where does that leave Savimbi?" he said, seemingly unexpectedly.

After a moment of reflection, Molu answered. "It's the same thing, why should the Americans care about Savimbi now? They no longer have any need for him. He is on his own."

"What do you advise we do then?"

"We alter our alliances, starting with South Africa."

"You think the Americans will drop South Africa too? They are white."

"America has no more need for apartheid. The whites are on their own, just like Savimbi. America had a chance to change South Africa ten years ago, but they were fixated on pleasing the Cubans in Florida and played for time with Constructive Engagement. The Congress put an end to that abomination by imposing sanctions on

South Africa last year. Events have caught up with them. They have no say in the matter anymore."

"What else?"

"I recommend we tighten our security at the borders, especially in the east."

The Dictator made a violent gesture. "I don't care if they kill each other over there," he raged. "They are nothing but trouble to me."

"But if the east unravels, Mokonzi, the chaos will spill over our borders. They don't know where the frontiers are over there, and even if they did, they wouldn't respect them. If we lose control of our borders, anything can happen. If they question our territorial integrity, it's an endless war."

"The Ugandan Tutsis are supporting the Banyamulenge in the east," the Dictator said bitterly. "We don't have the resources to manage another insurrection."

"Yes, we do."

"We do? Where?"

"Through Savimbi."

"Savimbi?"

"Yes!" Molu said, getting up to stand in front of the sitting Dictator. (The Dictator did not mind this breach of protocol; he appreciated aides who were animated and enthusiastic.) "We become the state that provides the support and patronage that Savimbi needs to survive; for, once the U.S. drops him, he can't survive long without weapons and fuel. We can get that for him."

"Didn't you hear me, Molu? We don't have the resources. How will we pay for weapons and fuel to give him? We can't even pay for our own."

"Oh, we won't pay. He will."

The Dictator was exasperated. "Didn't you just say that once the Americans drop him he can't survive? Where will he get that kind of money? How will he pay?"

"With diamonds!"

The Dictator rose and walked a few paces to lean on the blooming sapelli tree he had planted there thirty years ago in remembrance of his ancestors and for luck. He gazed at the river below. "This tree is my most prized possession," he said in a wistful voice, turning around to face Molu. "I can't wait for the rainy season; that's when I harvest the grubs that fall from the tree. I don't have to tell you that I have had the most sumptuous meals imaginable, but nothing I have eaten compares to the pleasure I get feasting on the caterpillars from my tree. I told the wife of the French president that at a state dinner at the Elysée. You should have seen the look on her face. You know Molu, whenever I see a look like that, I feel good about being African. I have the caterpillars dried and stored, hopeful every year that they'd last until the next rainy season; but a year's supply lasts me barely three months. I could get them from the Pygmies near Ouesso — they love them as much as I do — for a few packs of cigarettes. But I don't have the heart to ask them for it; that's all they have to eat during the rainy season, when they can't catch anything else. And they, of course, want tobacco in exchange. They are addicted to the stuff. I had a specialist examine those in the Ituri forest. He told me Pygmies have a problem with tobacco in a similar way various people have with alcohol.

"I don't know why I still call them Pygmies. They hate that name. I have an idea! What about this? In honor of your visit to Gbadolite today, I'll proclaim a decree that they be called by their correct name, *Bambuti*, or better still, *Ba*. As you know, they have many names; but they all start with *Ba,* people. We will call them *Ba*! Agree?"

"Agree!" said Molu excitedly, a wide grin on his handsome red-tinged face.

"The tea I make from the bark of my tree is what has kept me alive. I am sure it will cure what I suffer from now."

Molu had feasted on caterpillars from the sapelli trees in his village and smiled when the Dictator spoke of them. His mother was a practiced hand at drying them to just the right consistency. She rewarded him with a handful at the evening meal if he had been a good boy during the day.

The Dictator returned to his meditation, looking at the rushing river below. He adjusted his mind at various angles. Molu must be right; he would not have argued the way he did about Savimbi without solid information — probably from his American friends to pass on to me. The French would never have done that. It makes sense that if Savimbi loses America's support, anyone who provides him with weapons and fuel would dominate that renegade. He is as hungry for weapons as graveyards are for men. I will manage Savimbi and through him control the diamond rich fields of Angola's Lunda Sul and Norte. The diamonds would put in my hands limitless resources to maintain the patronage system that keeps me in power. I would now have enough to field an army to protect the eastern borders. I could even hire South African and

Belgian mercenaries to help in the effort. I may have enough to arm the Hutus to destabilize the Tutsis who are trying to destabilize me through their kin, the Banyamulenge. Who knows, I could yet compete with and why not obliterate DeBeers by creating my own cartel. The thought of DeBeers made his mouth water with resentment. DeBeers had humbled him a few years back when he had tried to break from their cartel to sell his own diamonds on the open market. A vengeful man, he would part even with his power to give DeBeers one of his "shoeshines" with the cane.

Taking his seat back next to Molu, he asked, "Would it be absolutely necessary to go through DeBeers to unload Savimbi's diamonds?"

Molu understood, remembering the way DeBeers had crushed his benefactor.

"No," he answered, "given who Savimbi is and his predicament, his diamonds will have to be smuggled. That means we can go directly to Antwerp to find the highest bidder, bypassing DeBeers. No, we wouldn't have to deal with DeBeers. But it also means that you will need someone who is absolutely trustworthy to manage the transactions for you. And you should expect losing a percentage from the sale, however small."

"But diamonds would not be enough — for Savimbi?"

"Diamonds cannot replace American patronage and assistance to him; that was his most important asset, if not his most dependable one. What's more, Savimbi's enemies have oil and a state behind them, which they can use to buy or produce more sophisticated weapons. In the long run, oil is not only more respectable, it has greater value and will outsell diamonds."

"Where would we get the weapons and fuel for Savimbi? Have you thought about that?"

"The weapons we get from Czechoslovakia; the oil from Pointe Noire and Nigeria."

"What would the Americans say when we do this? I don't care about the French."

"If they say anything, it would not go beyond public relations; it's a tongue in cheek guideline we are contending with here. We would have a green light to proceed as we see fit as long as we are not blatant, you know, vulgar about it. The Americans, at least, used to understand the necessity of protecting our country's integrity by whatever means necessary."

"What about this democratization ballyhoo from Washington? Would my subsidization of Savimbi cause them to increase the noise level about election timetables and international observers coming here to stick their nose up my ass and monitor what we do?"

"No! The administration is filled with amateurs and even careerists who know nothing about Africa. But they do like to make statements in the *de rigueur* effort to distinguish themselves from the former administration. In any case, we still have the back channels."

"Yes, I have noticed; they are very generous with public statements and formulaic threats," the Dictator said. "But thank God for back channels!"

"That's right! The one thing they may insist we do, Mokonzi, is adopt a pro forma shareholder-capitalism system."

"That's alright with me," the Dictator interjected. "Profit is a controlling mechanism; we would benefit from that. And I wouldn't mind shareholder-capitalism. It's the mindless insistence on democratization that drives me mad. In fact, they use democratization to threaten me. People whose political system is a camouflage for crookedness should not threaten leaders who are doing the best they can with what they have. With what will I create a pork-barrel democratic system here? Rub a lamp? I'll tell you something else that's driving me up the wall, Molu, it's those missionaries. I can't say a word to them before they threaten me with retribution from their supporters in their Congress if I don't agree to let them convert the natives. Natives! That's what they say, looking me in the eye. Natives!"

"This is only a phase — four years is a short time. Politics is not science; it's alchemy and timing. Anything is possible, if we follow a policy of positive duplicity —"

"I don't think there is anybody in the country who understands the Americans the way you do, Molu," the Dictator said, smiling now. "They have spent a lot to train you. Do they trust you, you think?"

"Mokonzi, they trust me only as far as their interest will let them. They appreciate that I am your man."

"Are you?"

"Of course, Mokonzi; without you, I am nothing."

"I can command that you do anything, and you would do it, no questions asked?"

"Of course!"

"I command you to be my next ambassador to Washington. Your job there will be to protect my interests. I don't care if they refuse to renew my visa even for my annual trip to the United Nations, or talk about democratization until icebergs flow down our river, or compare me to my friend Ferdinand Marcos. I can take anything, even death; what I cannot take is dishonor. Remember that, Molu. Please! You will make certain they do not dishonor me. On your way to Washington, I want you to stop at Antwerp to set up the sale of Savimbi's diamonds for me. Report directly to me, you understand, directly to me. Give my regards to your lovely wife. What is the name of your daughter?"

"Nef."

"Nef? That's not African!" said the Dictator disapprovingly.

"Yes it is," said Molu, moving closer, in a conspiratorial gesture, to speak in the Dictator's ear. "We conceived her the night Ella and I spent on a lark in Pharaoh's burial chamber in the great pyramid at Ghiza thanks to a well-placed bribe to the plateau guards. We named her after the Egyptian queen, Nefertiti."

The Dictator gaped at him for a moment, smiling, his mouth opened. Then in appreciation, he laughed, and he could not control his laughter; and a coughing fit made him gasp for air, so that Molu had to slap his back to help him recover. He stood, his face dark red, to give Molu an affectionate slap and to pull Molu's ear lobe. "*Liaka mikua tango ozali na mino*, enjoy life while you can. I am proud to have you as my son," he said, tears in his rheumy eyes."

# Chapter 4

The Dictator heard the ping from the special bell in the library. Excusing himself to his in-laws, he hurried to his private bedroom, furnished on the ground floor years earlier when his need to be alone had grown as he had wearied of his now portly and always perfume-loving wife and her twin. The exclusive fax machine installed there for messages of urgent and personal nature had summoned him. One page was already in the receiving tray. I am slowing down, he told himself. Not long ago he would be at the machine before the first page made it through. No more than six people in the world knew the number of this fax machine. Rigged to the area code of Malta it had so far been foolproof and reliable. He actually recognized the handwriting on the page in the tray.

The informer was a woman at one of America's government agencies. She had intelligence she thought important enough to use her patron's exclusive fax machine to notify him. "Next ambassador to Kinshasa," read the subject line. The Dictator smiled, forgiving the informer for using the special fax machine unnecessarily. Molu has done it, he thought smugly. The informer thinks it's urgent; but to the phlegmatic Molu, this is another day's work. It's not a big deal; so Molu is going through channels, the foreign ministry, to inform me, leaving it to snivelers to show off on my fax machine. Get the right man for the job and that guarantees the results. Those in Washington like Klingesthousen who were bent on making a fool of him, if they knew of Molu's achievement, were now silent. Defeat is the guarantor of silence.

He laughed aloud. His wife, hearing him, knocked softly on the door which, as a matter of habit, he had locked when he had come in. "Are you alright?" she asked. The fax had energized him, and taking a deep breath, he said more kindly than usual, "I will be out soon. Go back to the guests."

At the top of the fax's second page were two photos: the one on the left was that of a middle-aged serious-looking black man with straight hair of an unnatural brownish color. The one on the right was that of a white woman also middle age, of distinctly modest appearance. As he read that the man in the photo was the ambassador Washington was sending him, the Dictator was horrified. "Judd Mosley," he read as he skimmed the page, looking for the words that would reassure him it was not the man in the picture.

His groin tingled, as anger replaced fright. The photos were those of the new American ambassador and his wife. He read the message several times. There were too many details for the information to be inaccurate. No misunderstanding! Molu had failed him. Rage took him in its grip, thinking for him now. He was a cold calculator, and he put all that strength, with a kind of cruel satisfaction, completely in the hands of his overpowering fury.

He picked up the executive red phone and pressed the orange button, the direct line to the minister of foreign affairs. After three rings, the minister picked up the receiver. "You know how much I paid for this phone? Why can't you answer it?" the Dictator asked, hostile. The minister recognized the tone.

"It's my leg, Mr. President, you know," the minister answered apologetically.

"Do you have anything from Washington?"

"Not from Washington, no sir."

"Has Ambassador Sakeseba called?"

"Friday evening. Not since."

"If he calls, don't tell him that I inquired. You understand?"

"Of course, Mr. President."

One key to keeping it short when talking to the Dictator was to use as few verbs as possible.

------

Molu had sold out to them over there who, like the communists, were contending ever since Lumumba's death that he was an unclean despot, unsuited for decent company. "That's why he hasn't called. That's why he hasn't called," he repeated aloud. He would wait one hour before giving his mind to deciding how to respond. But his patience cracked, and, in less than fifteen minutes, he did the unthinkable: he called Dana, the informer, himself. It was 4:30 p.m. in Kinshasa, 11:30 a.m. in Washington. Dana was at her desk.

"Are you sure about the information?" the Dictator asked without introduction.

"Excuse me?"

"The new ambassador. Are you sure?"

It took Dana a moment to realize who had called her. The Dictator waited.

Finally, Dana said, "Yes, sir."

"There is no mistake?"

"No, sir. I was there when they took the vote."

"You are sure."

"Oh, absolutely, Mr. President."

———

"He is not great on imagination," the Belgian colonial sergeant had written about recruit, Hector Stanley Motutu. (He had not yet replaced his Belgian first and middle names with African ones to reflect the new philosophy of Africanness he initiated to go along with the new Kinshasa dress code.) "But he makes up for it by being single minded. In his stubbornness, he is the most arrogant of all our recruits. Once he has made up what passes for a mind, it's impossible to control him, regardless of the punishment — the Colonial Office should get rid of him. If he remains in the army, he will become a thorn in the side of the colonial authorities," the sergeant had concluded.

The Dictator had read that report many times. Whenever he felt beleaguered, he read it again; it was a balm from a soothsayer, reminding him of how far he had come and that there had been no limit to what he would achieve.

———

Over the decades in office, he endured then prospered. In time, he took it for granted that he would recognize the signs that the West was about to stop behaving toward him the way he had become accustomed. But ever since France had reduced its aid to him, he had noticed that the predicted change was taking place at a pace he had difficulty at times controlling. But he had managed. The gullible west had not made it so hard for a crafty man like him to get his way in the end.

Two years earlier, he had feigned reluctance at the establishment of opposition parties and then had let the West persuade him that it was best for the country. He had put his nemesis, the archbishop, in charge of giving the blessing, as it were, to new political parties. The West seemed to have no inkling that he was the one behind the charade. If they did, they pretended otherwise. That was usual; and for a while, that made things well again. In fact, it had been too simple. Better that it had been a more torturous business, he reflected; he would have had more practice at sharpening his knives for the final battle. The naming of that new American ambassador was proof that change had established itself unexpectedly and for good. The alarm he had experienced upon receipt of the informer's message was due to the uncertainty at what was coming next. Control of events was no longer entirely in his hands; he felt lost, unsure the single-minded determination he was famous for would see him through this ultimate challenge to ensure a worthwhile survival.

The patronage system that had served him so well had broken down; the means had swallowed the end, and the pork barrel system had bankrupted the country. It was now just a collapsed pyramid scheme. He couldn't believe how rapacious his clients were — they had run the system to the ground. The big projects of yesterday funded by foreign sources to keep the Kinshasa system afloat were rusting in the tropical sun. He was down to looking for ships to register, selling passports, taxing smokers, and helping tax cheats defraud his state.

Always a ruminator, he was usually these days in a reflective mood and didn't miss an opportunity to tell visitors about his latest economic-cum-political thoughts. When the ping from the fax machine had summoned him, he was entertaining his visiting in-laws — something he was loath to do before — with his latest musings and observations on the most appropriate system for Kinshasa.

The ready audience, most likely clueless, listened mesmerized: "The capitalist system is the most appropriate because it flows from man's inescapable fear of himself and his fellow man. Man's selfishness comes from that fear; that obligates him to care for what he owns. When I was a practicing journalist, I spent a lot of time covering the waterfront. That's where I saw for myself what it meant to be a property owner. The men who worked there used to wash and polish their makeshift wheelbarrows every Sunday afternoon. Why would anyone want to waste water and time washing a wheelbarrow? I once asked that of a man on *Ngobila Beach*. 'Because it's mine,' he answered. 'Why do you always ask inane questions?' That man has been my security chief ever since I came into office — Maka Mgonu." He looked around the room as if he had divulged a state secret.

"Those who practice kleptocracy are against the benefits private property conveys. To kleptocrats, the country is merely a golden-egg laying goose; they have no personal incentive to care for it, since they have no stake in what they steal. That's why they have their greed kill the goose in the end. You would think that they would care for their loot by burying it under a sapelli tree, for example. But being fearless, they just steal more.

"When I initiated Article 15, the 'Be Resourceful' doctrine, what I had in mind was the celebration of fear. Is it my fault if thieves took it to mean 'steal to your heart's content?' I had an ambassador in Asia who sold his embassy. He was resourceful! But what did he do with the proceeds from the sale? He squandered it. He is not in jail today because he sold a building, but because he turned fearless and wasted the proceeds. Had he invested the money, I would have made him finance minister. Fear is a self-regulatory acumen, more practical and, in the end, more effective than any government."

The Dictator stood unexpectedly then hurried to his urinal. Upon his return he said: "Patrice (Lumumba) and I used to have arguments about this all the time. He thought socialism the answer to our future, like God's blessing to mankind. He was mistaken. Like all idealists, he was mistaken. I would say to him, Africans are not different from anybody else; they are as afraid as Europeans are. 'That's why socialism is the answer,' he would argue back the way a somnambulist might. 'They need us to protect them from fear and defend their interests.' No, I would say, they would never cease to be afraid; but if we give them something to care for, their innate fear will do the rest. We didn't work, we argued. Then was the best period of my life. He thought me a good debater, Patrice did. That's the reason I am the one he sent to Brussels to argue with the Belgian thieves for our independence. Who would have thought that Patrice, a naïve bucktoothed, myopic Batetela would be the left's saint du jour?"

# Chapter 5

Molu almost trotted from Roosevelt Hall to his car. He got in and inserted a CD with thirteen repetitions of Bing Crosby crooning *Buddy Can You Spare a Dime* that he had asked Nef to make for him. When he wanted to distract his mind, the CD with the haunting lyrics was the best choice.

Before pulling out of the parking space, he called his secretary to check for messages. There were no urgent ones. That relaxed him a little. He then called his residence to say he had nothing that would delay him. His wife didn't mind if he was late as long as he called to let the maid know.

He headed toward the river to cross Constitution Avenue on Seventeenth Street behind the White House, calculating that it would take him at the most twenty minutes to reach Dupont Circle and Mass. Avenue, the fastest route to his office. But it was five o'clock, and Washington's afternoon rush-hour traffic was reaching its peak. It was 10 p.m. in Kinshasa.

When he got to the river, he found traffic at a stand still. It would now take him at least an hour to get to the office. It would be 11 p.m. in Kinshasa. He no longer listened to the crooner. If only his car could ascend like a helicopter, he mused, as he did every time he was stuck in traffic. He regretted, as his impatience grew, not having gone directly to his office following his meeting with Marcellus — especially after the angry manner he had left Freeman's office. His wife will chide him for his lack of discipline — she will actually say lack of *sang froid* — and what she considered his impulsive African ways of dealing with the world.

I was not wrong, only the way I reacted was improper, he thought. But how could Marcel and now Freeman think of my supplanting the old man? I have never said anything to them that could suggest such an idea. What is it, then? It's that I am the one they know. He remembered that Freeman had said the same thing. That must be it, he thought — nothing else, not anything special about me.

Things were unraveling in Kinshasa; and, of course, centers of gravity were shifting. Marcel and now Freeman were putting the two together and assuming that like a metaphysical benefaction he would answer the Kinshasa riddle for them. How misguided! But

Marcel and Freeman were not amateurs; in fact, few understood the region as comprehensively as they did.

He started to think somewhat clearly again. The snarl-up gave him time to ponder what he would say to the Dictator when he arrived at the office.

———  ———  ———

Molu arrived at 6:10 p.m., 11:10 p.m. in Kinshasa. His secretary as usual had waited for him. He thanked her for staying late and told her to go home. The anxiety she saw in his face made her fear soar. But she could not bring herself to question him; that was too much — too soon since she was a woman whom men in Africa impose upon. Molu went into his office's men's room, then to his desk. After a moment, the light for the line to Kinshasa came on. Marie wanted to listen in on his conversation, as if her life depended on hearing it; but she hesitated, and the window of opportunity closed. If she lifted the receiver after the party at the other end had answered, Molu would know that she was eavesdropping. Unable to chance that, she shuffled a few papers in the file cabinet besides the door in an attempt to be within earshot of Molu's conversation with Kinshasa. It was for naught. She left for the day tied down to an anthill.

"Good evening, Mr. President, this is Molu Sakeseba in Washington. I hope I am not disturbing you, sir."

"Good evening, Molu. No, you are not disturbing me. I was only telling the family what I thought was the best system for the country. I am sure they are happy you called; they were tired of listening to me, at least for now."

"Mr. President, the reason I called is to let you know about Washington's new ambassador."

"They have made the decision already?" the Dictator said, sounding pleased as if he were only waiting for Molu to tell him that it was his choice who had been selected.

"Yes, they have, sir."

"Bob will be pleased."

"I am sorry, Mr. President, they have picked someone else."

"They have what?"

"They have chosen another man, sir."

"How the hell did that happen?" the Dictator shot back but not with as much vehemence as Molu had expected. That encouraged him to continue.

"I am not sure, Mr. President."

"Whom did they select?"

"A career man, Judd Mosley."

"A career man is not so bad. We could have gotten another car dealer from Arkansas. Remember him? But I detect in your voice that there is more to it than that, Molu. Come on with it."

"Well, I failed Mr. President. I know how much you wanted Mr. Delaney for the job. But, yes, there is more."

"Well?"

"Well, as a rule Judd Mosley would go to another African country."

"Another African country?… Oh! He is an American of African descent? Is that it?"

"Yes, sir."

"How the hell did that happen?"

Molu could not bring himself to tell him the truth. Instead, he pulled toward him the Leighton report Marcel had given him and read the passages his friend had highlighted.

The Dictator interrupted him, after a while. "Hell, John is not saying a thing I don't already know. They have been dysfunctional ever since Carter. That's why I only deal with the Pentagon; not only are they reliable over there, they are not the political football that Department is." The Dictator then recited a list of grievances he had endured over the years.

"Yes, sir," Molu whispered, unable to think of anything else to say.

"The bastards! After all we have done for them, they are treating us like any other African country now. And you know what that means! Look Molu, do you remember what we did about South Africa? Why not do the same with this thing. We could have another PR success with it, and turn a disappointment into another achievement."

"I am not following you, Mr. President. I am sorry."

"Think man! They will never be up-front with this, admitting that they send their blacks to Africa as a matter of course. We have the field to ourselves to make of it what we like. And what we like, son, is for people to hear that *we* wanted to be treated like other African countries. We are striking a blow for African unity, Molu. We'll make a big show of that. Those in the know will say, 'they can't beat them, so…' But they'll say it quietly; so it will not matter. Not everybody believed us about South Africa, but many were not so sure, and that was enough to have made the effort worthwhile.

The key to public relations, or propaganda, or whatever you call it, is to create doubts."

The Dictator's ebullience was infectious, his charisma reaching out through the wires, taking Molu in completely in its embrace.

"I see Mr. President," Molu said, excitement infiltrating his voice. "I think you have something here… and since we'll have the field to ourselves, as you said, we will have the last word. I was sick with guilt at having failed to get Mr. Delaney appointed. I know what it meant to you. But this has given me a chance to retrieve… something."

Thousands of miles away, the Dictator pressed his ear against the receiver for every nuance in his prey's voice. He heard what he had been waiting for: emotion clicking into place. Molu is in and sniffing, he told himself. That accomplished, he proceeded to take Molu to every height of possibility and even triumph. At length they discussed how they would rescue success from the defeat the appointment of Judd Mosley had inflicted on them. The Dictator was like a conductor, directing an orchestra made of the entire world, calling the horn section to produce a certain sound for France, the second violin for Belgium, and the woodwinds and brass for the United States. After thirty-five minutes in the clouds, the Dictator sprang the trap.

"I will need a foreign minister, Molu," the Dictator said, as if the statement had proceeded logically from their discussion. "MbuJudda is too ill to handle this turn of events. He has thrombophlebitis in the lower extremities and carries on with difficulty. This is the job for you."

"Thank you, Mokonzi. Thank you," said Molu, almost faint with relief, brilliant sunshine in his heart and voice.

"Good night, Minister Sakeseba," said the Dictator.

———  ———

Had Molu called within the hour following the informer's fax, the Dictator might have arrived at a different conclusion as to the action to take in response to what he believed was another insidious Tutsi-led international cabal to disjoint Kinshasa and unseat him. Having no other credible information to influence his reaction, he took only advice from his impulse to retaliate.

That evening, he gave the cabal Molu's face. It's probably greed that got the best of him and made him fearless, the Dictator thought. Who knows what his American and Tutsi friends promised him? How is this possible? He repeated and repeated. Molu is a

Ngbandi, a kin. How can this be possible? After all I did for him; this is how he repays my lifting him above the men who helped me hold the country together, the men of faith who would give their lives for me.

But Molu's betrayal has given me an unexpected opportunity. The more time he spent deconstructing Molu's treachery, the more dangerous the world seemed to him, and the more tortuous his blueprint for coping with it became. Betrayal is infectious, he warned himself, and will spread if not dealt with immediately and in a way that leaves no doubt that I am still the Great Elephant. If I don't cauterize it at once, every double-crosser will come out to take advantage of this turn of event. I must strike before they make Mosley's appointment public.

In this frame of mind he devised a plan to trap Molu and hand him over to his security chief for the special treatment reserved for the regime's traitors.

This is a job fit for Mgonu's special literary proclivity, the Dictator agreed. We'll see how long Molu can stay fearless! Motutu grew excited at the thought. He pressed the green button on the executive phone to summon his security chief. Almost at once Maka knocked on the door. The man's presence never failed to affect the Dictator in ways he did not care to understand. Maka Mgonu was as tall as the Dictator and massively built from years spent on the waterfront and at the gym he had acquired when brought into the Dictator's service. To accentuate a ferocity look, he shaved and oiled his head and wore custom made dark glasses except in private conference with the Dictator where he always remained standing. The Dictator's wife and her twin sister had complained that Mgonu's wearing of dark glasses in their presence was impertinent. For a while, Mgonu removed the offensive shades when they were near. However, when the Dictator moved to his own bedroom, the eyewear stayed on his face. The black suits and shirts he wore completed the appearance of a malevolent spirit.

A sedulous official, he demanded efficacy from the network of secret service men, agents, informers, beggars and prostitutes he directed. But unknown to the public, whose fear of him had grown to pathological levels, he was a cultured man and a voracious reader. When not working or at his gym, he read constantly works in Dutch, French or English. He delighted particularly in Catholic church history a Belgian priest had introduced him to when he was nine years old, and the *Père Blanc* order took a short-lived interest in his village. On the wall of his library hung a portrait of Girolamo Savonarola that he had commissioned from the Poto-Poto artist cooperative across the river in Brazzaville. It was done from a photograph of the Fra Bartolomeo portrait of the Florentine religious reformer.

The Belgian priest, a Savonarola fanatic, had baptized Mgonu a few weeks after arriving at the village; and, for a few years, Mgonu's name had been Girolamo. The priest, ignoring the parents' and elders' wishes, had bestowed the name of his hero on the boy. Mgonu's father and the other elders argued for four years to make Mgonu give up Girolamo and accept his village's name, Maka. The Savonarola painting on his library wall was an expression of gratitude to his mentor, the priest.

Mgonu had translated Shakespeare's *The Tempest* in Lingala, the lingua franca of western Congo-Kinshasa (Zaire), and had written numerous sonnets, imitating the language Shakespeare had given Caliban whom he admired. His fondness, however, he reserved for the Trinidadian writer, Wilfred Cartey. He had attended Cartey's funeral in 1992 and was seen to scratch his cheeks in sorrow. His hatred, he reserved for the Marxist playwright, Amédé Cerusu. He would have ordered Cerusu's assassination, had the Dictator not explicitly, on pain of banishment, forbidden it. He did not hate Cerusu for asserting in a celebrated play, *A Congo Chronicle*, that the Dictator had murdered Patrice Lumumba. He hated him for saying that the Dictator, Kinshasa's Savonarola, had the mannerisms of a pimp.

A personal librarian maintained Maka's extensive collection of books and maps. He had hired her when he started receiving publications mentioning the Dictator from Kinshasa's embassies all over the world. She was a fixture at book shows in Europe and America.

On his desk, he kept multicolored folders of press clips about the Dictator. No journalist who had ever written negatively about his boss could see the Dictator without an interview with Maka first. And the Dictator valued his written reports; for, unlike the reports of other staff members, his never included interpretations or generalizations.

# Chapter 6

Maka recently had undergone a life-changing experience. His life of service to the Dictator was no longer his undivided raison d'être. His transformation began when he accepted an invitation to dine at the home of the new Hotel Continental's manager and his wife.

Seeking the indulgence and the patronage of the Dictator's security chief, the new manager had invited "Mr. Mgonu" to dinner a week after his arrival in Kinshasa. His wife was an excellent cook, a graduate of the *Cordon Bleu*, specializing in the cuisine of the tropics, he had told Maka expansively. The security chief, whose policy was never to accept invitations unless sanctioned by his boss, had agreed to come. The Dictator hoped that the new manager would be more malleable than the old one regarding the laundering of diamonds. The Continental was a laundering command center to buyers from Hong Kong, New York, and Amsterdam who traveled to Kinshasa.

The manager received the security chief as he would a head of state. His family's small vineyard in Bergerac, in the south of France, had produced an especially delicate-tasting *vin mousseu* that year and he asked Mgonu for his opinion. He then picked up a small package. "I have heard Mr. Mgonu that among your many interests is the study of literature. Don't ask me its provenance, please," he said with a shy chuckle, "but I think this first edition of Wilfred Cartey's *Waters of my Soul* will enhance your collection." Mgonu took off his dark glasses and beamed at the Frenchman.

"A first edition of… I can't believe it! But how did you know Cartey was one of my favorite authors," he said, radiant, genuinely impressed.

"A director of the September Paris Book Fair is a friend. He heard of my assignment to Kinshasa and said that the private librarian of the security chief here was always on the lookout for Cartey's works. I wanted to ensure a good welcome — you know, make a good impression here, so I procured this edition for you. I had hoped you would like it."

Mgonu had interrogated too many people, not to know when someone was lying to him. But he accepted the story and, after a courteous show of reluctance, accepted the gift as well. He opened the small volume and turned the pages to the poem *Song of the Ranchitos.*

The hotel manager handed him a small paper cutter made of ivory with a malachite handle. "It comes with the book Mr. Mgonu," he said in his expansive mode. The security chief thanked him and very carefully cut the pages folded together, late 19th century style, to free the poem he was looking for. He looked at *Song of the Ranchitos* as if at a shrine. After a moment, he closed the book and began to recite it from memory.

I hear ranchitos calling
Calling you and me
I hear ranchitos calling
Begging to be free
I see them
Scale the mountain tops
And mingle with the clouds

He heard the manager say, "Mr. Mgonu, this is my wife Julie." But he wasn't sure he had heard the man accurately. It must be the poem, he thought, from far away.

Maka felt the presence of the woman who had come out of the kitchen when she heard a voice reciting a favorite poem with such reverence. He stopped his recitation and turned to acknowledge her. Her presence stunned him, and his psyche shook like a dog that had just crossed a wide river. A yearning he had never before felt overwhelmed his heart. It was as if the long-ago lost part of himself had stepped out of a hidden doorway to confront him, demanding recognition. One moment he was Maka Mgonu, the feared security chief; the next, he was a man bewildered by a woman.

Julie wore a sarong of silk in tangerine and lime green. Her small belted waist accentuated the bulge behind the opened V of her décolletage, and her jet-black hair, cut short, pulled Mgonu's attention to the smooth exposed bronzed shoulders and the swell of her breasts. Julie was looking at him with a perplexed frown, bemused, as if she had divined his heart. She was the perfection of his books.

"I am pleased to meet you," Mgonu heard himself say as if in a trance.

"And I, you, Mr. Mgonu. When my husband told me that the most feared security chief in all of Africa was coming to dinner, I was incredulous. Then he told me that he had heard of your love for Wilfred Cartey's works, and I couldn't wait to meet you."

Mgonu stared at her. He wished he could escape from the couple's villa. Imagining he was odd-looking in Julie's eyes, he hunched his shoulders in a vain effort to hide his massive torso. He could not conceal his shaved head, so he moved away from the reflecting ceiling light. But he came back into the light when he realized how stark his dark suit made him appear to her.

Quasimodo must have felt this misery when Esmeralda looked at him, he told himself. He didn't want to speak, imagining that Julie would think his accent not French enough. He who hated the sound of the *Negro de Paris'* accent of some Africans now wished he had one. Julie continued to look at him quizzically.

"I find it fascinating that a man such as you loves poetry and Wilfred Cartey's at that," Julie said.

"Yes," he said, in a shaky voice. "Cartey's worship of nature, especially the sea, attracted me to his works. He could have been writing about our sea, our rivers, our lakes and of our woods here," he heard himself say, ashamed of his voice.

———

Julie was a skilled conversationalist, practiced at furthering her husband's career by entertaining and sometime dazzling guests and business associates. She had learned that men never resist talking about themselves. However, she had never met a man like Maka Mgonu, and she was thrilled at his reaction. This most feared of men was having difficulty holding on to his composure — because of her. Her loins were radiantly warm.

Mgonu began speaking again, naming a list of famous men who had been both warriors and great men of letters or poetry lovers. For the first time in his life, he wanted someone to like him for himself. Quasimodo would never manage it with looks, so he recited multiple Cartey poems to a captivated Julie, willing her to hear and not see him.

———

The manager looked on, amused. She is at her best tonight, he thought, entertaining this African oddity. When Mgonu recited the poem about the book of life, being unable to go back to the page where you love because the page where you die is already under your fingers, had brought her tears. These were her hostess's skills at new heights on this balmy tropical evening, it seemed to the manager. He could not see her growing captivation with Maka. She was born in the colony of Guyane, French Guyana, of poor emigrant parents from Southern India, and he, a scion of France's bourgeoisie, had rescued her from certain colonial insignificance. She was too grateful to find anyone else fascinating. This would be especially true of an African who could not be more than a curiosity.

When she returned to the kitchen, her assistant had taken the green papaya soufflé, her signature dish, out of the oven to keep it from burning; but it had fallen and was now a disappointment rather than a triumph. The assistant had already peeled two papayas and had all the other ingredients standing by, knowing that his employer would insist on making another soufflé.

"Mr. Mgonu," Julie called, girlishly, from the kitchen." I want to show you how to make a green papaya soufflé."

"You should see this, a master at work," the manager agreed.

"I know nothing about cooking, but I wouldn't mind learning something about it. Perhaps your wife could teach me."

"This is your first lesson," she said when he reached the kitchen, handing him a red chef's apron, a gift from the great New Orleans' market. "You break the eggs; it's easier to do it with one hand. There… now you try."

Had Julie's assistant not been near to catch it, Mgonu would have dropped the bowl, when Julie put her hand on his. He had never appreciated such a gesture more. And for the first time since the priests had thrashed him to force him to kneel, he prayed for the moment to last. Julie had him beat the egg into stiff peaks and holding his right hand showed him how to fold in the papaya mixture. Mgonu laughed when the assistant took out the golden-crusted dish from the oven.

This is like entering a new world, he said to himself, while watching Julie, who sat at the head of the table, talk about the various hotels her husband had managed and the celebrities she had seen there. No matter how long I live, meeting this woman will always be the defining moment of my life. If the ancestors are responsible for putting her in my path, why don't they also tell me what to do? Why impose this complication on me now? Why? Could this be the cool sunlight they bequest men whose world is ending? This is not a small matter; I cannot compartmentalize it like any other.

But what will Mokonzi say? He need not know, his mind shouted at him. Why should he know everything? A special complication has entered your existence; you have a life now. Mokonzi was never more than a job; you are responsible for turning him into a life. What he did for his living was not a job or a life but what he was. And why I ask would the ancestors deny me a refuge? What I am is my sanctuary. Mokonzi finding me was a blessing. He heard the familiar reassuring gravel voice of the Dictator, "There is no exit, Maka; we are linked for eternity." Mokonzi would laugh, if I told him. "She is a toy, Maka, nothing more," he would say. "The real mistress is immortality; it is the only thing deserving the exertion of men like us — immortality is life's only trophy." Julie's voice intruded on his mental argument; she was describing the time Prince Philip of England had stayed at one of the hotels to attend a birdwatchers' convention.

At the door taking his leave, Maka stood alone with Julie, the manager having gone to the living room to retrieve the book of poems for him. Julie told him that she looked forward to seeing him again. "I hope you will take me up on my offer of cooking lessons," she said with what Mgonu thought were genuine feelings. He nodded "yes," with a strained smile. She waited for him to say how much he had enjoyed meeting her, but he did not want her to remember his voice and did not say anything

In the front seat of the armored Suburban, his bodyguard was giving instructions to the convoy escorting him back to his office in Kinshasa. He sat alone in the back seat, his entire body tingling. A single idea burned in his mind: I don't know how I can be part of her life; I only know I can't stand her being tied to anyone else.

———  ———  ———

"Good evening, Mokonzi," the security chief said, as he took a long look at his boss. "The cares of the world seem to be on your shoulders this evening. How can I be of service?"

"The cares of the world are on yours, Maka; you look like you haven't slept in days," the Dictator retorted, handing him the fax about the new American ambassador. After a couple of minutes reading the document, Mgonu asked simply, "Sakeseba?"

"Yes," the Dictator shouted. "Whether through incompetence or by design, he is responsible. I don't have to tell you what this

Mosley appointment means. It will give an enemy with an entrepreneurial penchant the idea that it is a propitious time to act against me because Kinshasa is no longer under Washington's protective umbrella — just another African country where they send black ambassadors. The opposition has upped the ante, Maka. The Tutsis are probably involved. Whatever it is, unless we counter decisively it will be a nail in our coffin. Dana tells me that they will post the announcement and make it public in a couple of weeks. Can you be ready by that time? It's important that it be at the same time, to make the point that our response is deliberate; that I am not asleep at the wheel as it were. Pressure? They want pressure! I'll give them pressure."

Maka had difficulty believing his good fortune. A few days after the dinner with Julie, he had seen Molu put his arm around her waist at the Dictator's birthday bash at the Continental Hotel. Ever since, he had been dreaming of walking on Molu's grave. Molu's wife had gone to the Mama Mangbetu Hospital as a favor to the Dictator to assist the French doctors the Dictator had flown in to Kinshasa for a minor surgical procedure on his eldest son. Molu had taken advantage of his wife's absence to flirt with Julie. Noticing Mgonu's stern look, she made a gesture with her shoulders as if to say, "What can I do?" Only his ruthless discipline had held him from intervening. In torment, he told himself he would take revenge on Molu. And here, like on the proverbial silver platter, the Dictator was offering him Molu's head. Getting an assassin in place to eliminate him would be an easy and most rewarding assignment.

"Easily, Mokonzi," Maka answered. "The Chileans did it in Washington in 1976. There is no reason we can't do the same. It would be a clean hit."

"In Washington?"

"Well, close by. Sakeseba has a mistress in Virginia. We can arrange for the husband to find Sakeseba in his house. That state's gun laws will do the rest for us."

"Wait a minute, Maka, I don't want him killed! What — ? That will not serve our purpose — another murder of a black man over there — forgotten as soon as it happens. Our policy is to make beggars of those who betray this government. After he has served our purpose, you can do what you want with what's left of him."

"I am sorry; I misunderstood you, Mokonzi. But what you want requires that he be here."

"That's right, Maka, that's right. But I'll take care of that," the Dictator answered.

The security chief looked at him curiously, clearly disappointed.

"I know what will snare his mind." He seemed to be taking delight in the thought.

The security chief looked at him in silence.

"His poison is ambition. I'll dispose of him with that."

Still, Mgonu did not react.

"I will promise him MbuJudda's job," the Dictator said. "Remember this, Maka, no one can protect against himself. If you are going to be ambitious, you should be cunning as well. Molu is not — cunning that is."

"As Sun Tzu said, 'All warfare is based on deception,'" Maka reflected, trying to think how to secure the Dictator's order to dispose of Molu outright.

"That's right, we are at war. And Molu is the first casualty."

"Do you want me to take care of the matter — when you get him here?" Mgonu asked.

"No, I'll do it to him myself — in my library."

"What about your friends in Congress over there? Why not ask them to quash this Mosley thing? You can still punish Sakeseba."

"I thought about that," the Dictator said. "But the days are gone when one call from me would make them hop. Another rejection can hurt as badly. No, we will have to do it here. I even prefer it that way. For too long we have depended on the interests of others. It's time we depend on *our* interests."

"What do you want me to do, Mokonzi?"

"Start your planning. But be careful and don't activate anything until Molu is on the Paris — Kinshasa flight."

"He is going to run," Mgonu warned.

The Dictator picked up a cane lying on top of his desk and holding the handle carved in the shape of an elephant thrust it toward the ceiling.

"Not after this," he said in a choking voice, swinging the cane like a club.

"I will have to inform the hospital to expect a casualty as well then," Mgonu said.

"Please do. But it does nothing for us to have him in the hospital long. He is no good to us there. Tell them two days at the most. It's the streets after that."

"Of course," Mgonu said.

"I want this to be a cautionary tale where everyone can see it. It is not only for self-promotion that they call me the Great Elephant and all-powerful warrior who because of his endurance and inflexible will to win goes from conquest to conquest leaving fire in his wake."

"Oh, don't worry — a cripple in the streets for three months. He is not going anywhere."

"Three months," the Dictator shouted, hitting the desk with the cane.

"What about his wife? What do we do about her?"

"We can keep her or anybody else off balance for three months. After that I don't care. Why are you worried about her?"

"She is a feisty woman. I saw how she ran the Bumba clinic, when a Peace Corps volunteer there. She is not one who takes an 'I don't know' for an answer. She could be a problem."

"I'll talk to her. But if she comes here, you make her disappear. I want that traitor in the streets for three months, wife or no wife."

"I will give this some thoughts and get back to you. It's possible that we may not have three months."

"It's three months or your job, Maka. Choose!"

"… Yes, three months!"

"*Lelo boye*! Get the beggars ready."

"How about his replacement in Washington?" Maka asked. "Have you given that some thought?"

"I told you I was going to throw Mosley back in their teeth. Who is better to do it with than my old Belgian sergeant, Johan Van Kees?

The security chief gaped at him.

"That's right!" the Dictator said, laughing. "They send me a black; I send them a white. If that doesn't make the point, I don't know what does."

"It's brilliant," Mgonu exclaimed. "Will they accredit him?"

"What choice will they have? If they don't accredit mine, I don't have to accredit theirs. I intend to be aggressive toward these people, not conciliatory."

"Does Kees know? He has been in Antwerp for a month now."

"Not yet. As you reported, he has been taking too much from the top, off-loading Savimbi's diamonds for me over there. I want some of that back. Appointing him to Washington, I will make a point, sending a white Belgian crook as my ambassador, and I will make him pay for the appointment from what he has been stealing from me."

"Did he ever become a citizen? He would have to be a citizen. I have to check."

"You take care of that. But it doesn't matter. I am appointing him." The Dictator then looked at his security chief the way he did when Belgians were the subject of their discussion.

"There are many old colonials who have made a good living here," said Mgonu. "We have not inconvenienced them in any way. The citizenship question is something to hold over their heads if and when necessary."

The Dictator knew how his security chief felt about "old colonials." A few years back, Mgonu had gone to a wholesale merchant in Kinshasa to purchase a hundred cases of soda. His men were going to celebrate a successful sting operation against Ugandan smugglers. At the cashier's, he discovered he didn't have the new currency. He asked the owner, a French woman, if he could return to complete the payment of his bill. The woman responded with rage, ranting that all Africans were dishonest, and berated Maka with every invective a soldier could know. When she had exhausted her insults, he took off his jacket and the cap that concealed his shaved head and proceeded to smash the thousands of soda bottles in the warehouse. The next day the French distributor was on the flight to Paris, not because Mgonu had asked her to, but because she was too frightened to remain in Kinshasa.

"I agree!" the Dictator said. "But make sure it is done correctly. Our colonials are individuals too."

"I was only saying —"

"I know what you were saying, Maka. And I agreed. But I wouldn't want my legacy tarnished further by what we do to these colonials. That's another reason I want Johan to be my ambassador to Washington."

"But will it be beneficial to him, Mokonzi? He cares for little other than his pockets. Isn't that dangerous?"

"Johan's life is ruled by fear, Maka. And he has worked very hard for what he has and wants to keep it. He knows that the best way to do that is to obey my orders. Although I agree that the job in Washington is full of possibilities for someone like him, you can be sure I will not confide in him the way I did in Molu. All and all, he is perfect for the job. I want all the gossips at soirées and cocktail

parties to be about this appointment. One day, perhaps
the same person who says that I was the symbol of unity, and that
without me this country would have been dismembered, will also say
that I was open minded enough to make a European my ambassador
to Washington. I hope that person misses the part about Johan being
a crook, a colonized colonist, and an adventurer too.

"People around the world make the correlation between Africa
and inadequacy the same way they make it between black and slavery.
It's not a coincidence that most African American ambassadors are
sent to Africa. Since it is no longer politic to exclude them totally,
they do the next best or worst thing depending on the point of
view. They thought I expected their ambassadors here to be white
because I considered myself superior to other Africans. You know
the real reason, Maka. Kinshasa isn't inferior to other capitals.

"I don't know a European ignoramus who doesn't think himself
better than any of us. I have seen with my own eyes that kind of
thinking in action. A European of the lowest class feels better about
himself the moment a black comes into a room. The Jews had to give
the world God to escape from this, and still look what they have done
to them. People have been anti-Semitic so long they have acquired
a gene for it. If they remain racist as long, they will acquire a gene
for that too. Means to prevent hereditary diseases such as this should
be part of the curriculum at our university. I will talk to the Rector
about it."

The Dictator walked to his desk and picked up a thick document.
"Take a look at the life story of this fellow Mosley, Maka. Dana faxed
it to me with the announcement of his selection. Here is a cautionary
tale for the ages — we have here a man who has worked as assiduously
as you used to on the waterfront to escape from what he is in order
to fit in over there. I am going to blackmail him with this document
when the time comes. If he doesn't behave himself, I'll have it published, not only in Kinshasa but in Brussels and Paris."

The Dictator changed glasses and began reading the document
at the third paragraph. *Judd Mosley was an excellent student at
Centenary College, a small Methodist school outside of Shreveport,
Louisiana. He was one of seven minority students attending the
school at the time. In his junior year, he had an experience that
changed his life. His history professor, a man originally from
Minnesota, asked Judd to do him a favor and take his wife in the
professor's car to a scheduled visit at the hospital in town. On the
way the police stopped him. When the highway patrolman saw*

*that the woman next to Judd was white and pregnant, he went berserk and thrashed him so severely that Judd suffered a life-threatening concussion and remained in the hospital for forty-two days. He had a number of surgical procedures to close gashes and underwent physical therapy to regain the use of his shoulders and arms.*

*During his stay in the hospital, his personality underwent a noticeable change. A nurse said he had a sort of revelation. The first manifestation was a marked hostility toward the black orderlies on his hospital floor he began to exhibit a few weeks after the incident...*

*When he applied for a job at the State Department, they investigated his background for the pro forma security clearance. They questioned family members and acquaintances about him. Sarah Doyle, his mother's sister, reported to one of the investigators that Judd had told her that the thrashing in Shreveport had lead him to recognize that if he was going to survive and be successful in a world run by whites, he had to construct his personality and life accordingly. He had to be where what happened to blacks did not happen to him. He adopted a new aloofness at the same time that he had his hair straightened chemically. He married a white woman of modest appearance and little expectation. But she was intelligent and totally devoted to his success. (A college roommate told one investigator that she had told her that since her prospect of finding a husband of her own race was limited at best, she would marry a smart black man, one looking to marry up.) Over the years, when Judd associated with minorities, it was almost exclusively with those who like himself had married across racial lines — a loose-knit club he founded and guided. On the other hand, the hostility he demonstrated at the Shreveport hospital toward the black orderlies he extended to blacks outside of his club. He frowned on demonstration of black solidarity and opposed display of exuberance or any manifestation that might fan white distaste and arouse further prejudice towards blacks.'*

"This is not a person, Maka. It's a caricature, a cliché, a poseur, a man who has set himself up to be an exception. Can bigotry have a better ally? A model case of Stockholm syndrome, and they are sending him to us!" the Dictator exclaimed, as he shoved the document in his security chief's right hand. "But he is perfect for what I have in mind. As long as we remain devious, Maka, we are not powerless. Deviousness is the great equalizer in an asymmetric world. Sun Tzu anticipated my using deception to grapple with the great powers. These people don't credit us for having brains and so are careless with their power."

———

The reading he had done over the years cautioned Mgonu about his boss's interpretation of history. The Dictator did not let facts compete with his intuitive generalizations, swearing by the psychic gift he said his ancestors had empowered him with. He tailored truth to fit his personal world view, mindless of the contradictions defining his decades in power. But Maka was not able to converse with his boss — he envied Molu Sakeseba's independence and ability to do so — and offer a different view when necessary. Like his boss's in-laws, he was one of the Dictator's favorite audiences. His veneration of Motutu would always be an obstruction; it could not be otherwise. Nevertheless, he had work to do. A meticulous planner, he was eager to get back to his office to set in motion the demise of Molu Sakeseba.

Aware that his security chief had, as much as he tried to conceal it, looked at the door, the Dictator ended the meeting. "Maka," he said, "you have to start your planning. This affair requires caution, and many of the beggars have the mental capacity of twelve-year-olds. Molu must be alive if the proof we want to give of our determination to remain in charge is to mean anything. Dead, he is no good to us. Remember that! Three months in the street! That's not too much to ask. Let's discuss your plan the day after tomorrow. Thank you my friend," the Dictator smiled. Moving toward Mgonu, he reached out and affectionately pulled his security chief's right ear lobe. Mgonu bowed, beaming that the Dictator had shown his appreciation this day, calling him "my friend."

"Good evening, Mokonzi na Bakonzi, Chief of Chiefs, I will not fail you."

When he reached the door, he put on his fierce face and dark glasses and let himself out.

———

The Dictator sat behind his imitation Louis XVI desk and picked up the report Jacques Truccard, the French *eminence grise* on Africa, had sent him through the diplomatic pouch the night before. After reading a while, he exclaimed, "Who is he fooling?"

and dropped the document in the for-shredding tray placed on a small table behind the desk. This was the report Truccard had promised him following the Frenchman's visit to Kinshasa to discuss his government's concern about the situation in Rwanda and the Dictator's eastern borders.

Truccard had proposed an *entente* to ensure the uninterrupted dominance of the Hutu ethnic group in Rwanda, in order to checkmate the Banyamulenges, the Tutsis' kinsmen in the east, who had risen in rebellion against the Dictator. "It is safe to say that the Hutus will continue to control the situation on the ground for the foreseeable future," Truccard had promised in his high-pitched voice. "As long as they do, you have nothing to fear from the Banyamulenge; they are no threat without support from the Tutsis, who pose no danger as long as the Hutus are provided for."

"Then we must ensure that the Hutus are well provided for," the Dictator had agreed.

"Exactly!"

"How do you propose we do that?"

"Very simply, we keep them armed."

"I prefer cash. I'll get them the arms."

"Of course… As long as they have the weapons, procedure is immaterial — as long as they remain master of the situation. That solves the Banyamulenge problem for you, and the Tutsiland — I mean the Uganda one for us."

The Dictator fearing the loss of his eastern province of Kivu, where the Banyamulenge had lived for two hundred years, had agreed and made the Kalashnikov gun market accessible to the Hutus. The *entente* that day opened a Pandora's Box of genocidal proportion in Africa's Great Lakes region.

Since the beginning of the Tutsi reaction against their mass execution, nothing took place in which the Dictator didn't see their treacherous hands. When lightening struck his prized sapelli tree, the trunk's bark shredded as if by a finger of fire, he had seen a Tutsi conspirator. The Tutsis are behind the Mosley affront, he had told his uncomprehending wife and her twin sister. And perhaps the French are helping them now, not unlike the way they helped the Hutus through me. If the French had anyone of color in their diplomatic service, they would send him to Kinshasa to spite me by imitating the Americans. Their contention that the Americans are now aiding the Tutsis is another ruse to lead me astray once more. Who is there to trust? I must admit that after the Hutu disturbance in Rwanda — disturbance, that's all it was. Genocide was that New York Times' reporter's fabrication — the Americans have taken to the Tutsis the way my hippos take to water. They think they can make up for their inaction during the Hutu rampage by pandering to the Tutsis now. The Tutsis purchased Molu through their mutual friends — the Americans — he concluded. Well, they are about to get what they paid for.

# Chapter 7

Molu remained at his desk awash in exhilaration made more exquisite because it followed a day of frantic anxiety. He felt reborn to a place where nothing was out of reach — the perfect future. For a long while, he savored being named foreign minister, his profession's highest position. Unmindful of the hour, in a frenzy, he began to jot down actions he would take to upgrade his ministry — and enhance his country's prospects in the world.

His first step would be to create a truly functioning foreign affairs organization, staffed with genuine professionals wherever he could find them. Such a ministry could never serve the country otherwise. Since independence, foreign affairs, like the other ministries, had not escaped the corruptive influence of the Kinshasa patronage system. An institution where profiteering was excluded would serve also as an example to others, directing them away from sordidness toward honest service. He had heard of the success the Senegalese foreign minister, Fatou-Anne Cerusu, had achieved routing out corruption after just two years at her department, and the impact that had on other institutions in Senegal. The United Nations' General Assembly meeting was in a couple of weeks, he would ignore the ill will between his boss and Fatou-Anne Cerusu and call the minister to request an appointment to discuss what she had done to turn her organization around.

Molu did not admit the likelihood of coincidence; so when he heard the name of the minister for the first time, he also acknowledged a presence at his side. For what purpose is the old priest coming out of the grave? he had asked himself.

His wife rang to check why he was still at the office. "I was talking to the president," he muttered. Still, she chided him for being dilatory after telling the maid he would not be late — another proof to her that Africans were culturally oblivious to clock time. She would probably buy him another watch, in the hope it would break what she considered an offensive trait. He would ask her not to bother.

The call from his wife had interrupted his rumination. He decided that he had better call it a day. Tonight was too important to concern himself with anything other than being thankful for the good fortune that had befallen them. He was anxious to tell her the good news and to discuss their new living arrangements.

He pressed the buzzer, informing his driver he was ready to leave. After a few minutes, the man, who also functioned as his communication technician, rang to say he was bringing up a cable from Kinshasa. The two-line message read: *"You are hereby appointed the foreign minister. Congratulations. Report to the president two weeks from today at 6:30 p.m.."* It was signed, *"The President."* The driver stood at the door grinning. "Congratulations Minister Sakeseba."

"Keep this under your hat, will you," Molu told him in mocked seriousness. "I haven't told my wife yet." The driver's smile vanished; Molu's wife detested him.

Molu pocketed the cable. "Let's go," he said, his joy an antidote to the man's woes.

       ——— ——— ———

"Where are you?" Molu shouted when he entered his residence.

"In the number two kitchen," his wife answered.

Molu crossed the two living rooms of the ambassador's residence. In the second and smaller kitchen, his wife and two daughters were at the table. Their South African cook was serving them.

*"Nayebi bino te. Nabo sani nkombo na te, Mokonzi"* I don't know you. I forgot your name, my chief, his daughter Nef said, as she always did when he came home late.

*"Mbote bokilo!"* Hello beautiful girl, Molu said. He had spoken to his daughters in Lingala since they were born; they were growing up trilingual, speaking English, Lingala and French fluently.

He kissed his wife and daughters on their foreheads and sat down for the cook to serve him.

"Diplomats are supposed to have poker faces," his wife said after he was seated. "You look like a Congo tetra that has swallowed a tsetse fly."

"I couldn't hide anything from you," Molu said.

"Now let me guess," Nef said, closing her eyes and putting her index fingers to her temples in mock divination, everyone looking at her. "You have been named foreign minister."

Molu looked fixedly at her. "How did you know?"

"Mama told me."

Molu turned to his wife, his mouth opened as they did in his village to ask a question. "How do you think, Mokonzi?" she answered, ribbing him.

After a while pondering her question, he said, "It can only be the president. The only other person to know is the driver who brought me the cable."

"Go to the head of the class," his wife told him.

"Isn't he something?" Molu said, impressed.

"Yes, I have to give him that," she answered, irony in her voice. "He is something."

"What did he say? Tell me!"

"It wasn't that much. Just that he needed you there. Minister MbuJudda is old and ailing and can no longer carry on. He said he would put his personal plane at my disposal to travel to Kinshasa whenever I wished; and if I wanted to stay in the residence here, that would be fine. He said that twice, I guess to make sure I heard him. I asked him how long he would need you. He said that the country was going through a rough patch now and at the most two years."

"What did you tell him?"

"Well, I said, with my practice, the girls in school and a baby on the way, I could only be a visiting wife."

"Did he say anything to that?"

"He said it would be beneficial if I came to Kinshasa. I could run the hospital. He would even name a wing after me. I didn't say anything to that. The last thing I need is to take on that hospital. I don't know how I would have felt about this if you had been the one to tell me. But he has a way of speaking that keeps all objections away and makes you feel your troubles are trivial. I wonder what it is."

"He knows his own mind. It's as simple as that," Molu said.

He handed her the cable.

"Two weeks..." She read.

"I will only go to meet with him to see what he wants done and come right back. My plan is to spend half the time here, which, when you think about it, makes a lot of sense. So much of our business is with the United States."

"You are going to need a good deputy," she said offhandedly.

"Yeah! But where do I find one?"

---

When Molu's secretary brought in the overnight traffic to his in box, she found the pad he had left on the desk the night before. After rereading his notes several times, she concluded that her boss was engaged in a conspiracy to overthrow the Kinshasa government.

She went to her office and dialed her control's number at the Office of Internal Security in the Interior Ministry in Kinshasa.

After numerous rings, someone picked up the receiver and she heard, "Mgonu."

The name so took her aback that she reflexively hung up the receiver. But the phone fell from her hand. When she picked it up, she heard again, "Mgonu."

"I was trying to reach Mr. Nkenda," she said.

"Who is this?" The voice was harsh.

"Marie at the Embassy in Washington."

"What can I do for you Marie?" The voice lost its sharp edge, becoming attentive.

"I wanted to report notes that I found on Ambassador Sakeseba's desk this morning. They discuss getting rid of people in Kinshasa and finding replacement for them. I became concerned when I read them. Mr. Nkenda told me to report anything suspicious … I am sorry to have disturbed you."

"No. You did the right thing. I compliment you. I will tell the president of your good work. Fax these notes to me right away. Make photocopies at once and fax them to this number. Then shred the copies. I will be waiting for them. And, Marie, of course, you know not to tell anyone that you have spoken with me. Is that clear?"

"Oh yes, sir."

---

When Molu arrived at his office, he called Marcellus Garinaldi, to tell him of his appointment and to ask if he would be in New York for the General Assembly meeting. He was going to request a meeting with the Senegalese foreign minister. Garinaldi said he would be in New York. Regarding Molu's meeting with Mrs. Cerusu, he said that Molu should speak to the minister alone. That would be the most appropriate thing to do. He would excuse himself once pleasantries were out of the way. About his friend's appointment as foreign minister, he made no comments, not even "congratulations." Molu thought this lack of reaction was due to the suddenness of the news. Seasoned diplomats like Marcel prefer to say nothing when taken off guard. Molu then asked his secretary to call Minister Cerusu. She was in a meeting and would call back. While waiting, he called Colonel Max Freeman at the National War College to tell him the news.

"This is unexpected," Freeman said. "Congratulations; that's truly *malamu*. You are now in a position to make the changes we talked about."

"When I called the president to tell him about the appointment of Judd Mosley to Kinshasa, he recognized immediately that a change had occurred in our bilateral relations. He thought that our current foreign minister was too old and ill to carry on. So he asked me… he told me to …"

"I see —" Molu's phone rang; Minister Cerusu was on one of the other lines.

"Colonel," Molu said, "the Senegalese foreign minister is on the other line. I'll call you later."

"Please do!"

"Good afternoon, Madame Minister. It's very kind of you to call back." The allure of speaking to someone who had known the old priest was irresistible.

"Not at all, Mr. Ambassador, it's my pleasure. What can I do for you?" The cultured lilting Senegalese accented French of the minister was welcoming.

"I saw your name on the list of delegates to the General Assembly next week and was wondering if you could spare me a few minutes of your time," Molu said with a confidence he knew he did not have yesterday.

"You want to meet with me?" the minister asked, surprised. "Certainly, I will be glad to. My assistant will come to your bench in the assembly to show you where I am. Or if you prefer, I'll just wait for you outside the assembly at the end of the plenary session. You can't miss me; I will be the old lady wearing a boubou of dubious blue coloring."

"I'll meet you outside the assembly, Madame Minister. Thank you."

"Not at all. I'll see you then. Good-bye."

The Minister wondered why Molu had not mentioned being named foreign minister. But perhaps that had nothing to do with why he wanted to see her in New York. The Kinshasa Creature, as she called President Motutu, had informed her boss the night before of Molu's appointment. Francophone African Heads of State extended this courtesy to each other regularly. Sakeseba would know soon enough.

———  ———

Coming out of the plenary session of the UN General Assembly, Molu did not miss the six-foot tall, black woman wearing a flowing Senegalese indigo garment inlaid with silver filigree. She was standing very straight next to the beige-colored couch outside the entrance to the interpreters' booths. That's presence! Molu exulted upon recognizing Fatou-Anne Cerusu.

Father Brabant had spoken wistfully about meeting her on his first vacation to Paris in the '30s. She must have been no more than eighteen at the time. The priest was in love with her, Molu had thought. The apple of his eye. If I tell her that I knew Father Brabant, she'll ask me about him. I can always say that he died of natural causes. I would rather not say anything, though. We'll see how it goes. If mentioning his name gets me a better reception, I'll throw it in. A friend of yours visited my village. A friend of mine? Yes, Father Brabant from Belgium.

# Chapter 8

Father Jacques Brabant took his two-week vacation habitually in May to visit his widowed mother in Brussels. In 1936 he took the advice of a colleague to visit Paris. It would be his first trip outside of Belgium. Anticipation at walking the streets of the city of his dreams, of being a boulevardier, filled him with joy. He would spend one week there and the other with his mother. A fellow priest had given him the address of a small student hotel on Rue Vaugirard in the Latin Quarter near the Sorbonne. St. Sulpice lay only two blocks away. Brabant not only would hear the grand-orgue de St. Sulpice, one of the great organs of Europe, but also would play *La Nativité du Seigneur,* a toccata by Olivier Messiaen, thanks to his colleague's recommendation to the choir master.

On an unusually sunny Tuesday morning, Father Brabant took the train to Brussels. He had a two-hour wait before his connection to Paris. After a half hour at the station, he decided to take a taxi to his mother's apartment to tell her that he would be back the following week. Telling her to her face he was on his way to Paris filled him with foreboding; she would disapprove and be disagreeably difficult. He had planned to write to her from Paris to say he would see her a week late but the duty of an obedient son weighed on his conscience.

As expected, his decision vexed her greatly. Her face pale as death, she said between angry teeth, "Paris is far away," in the cold tone that never failed to remind him of who he was. He argued with a whine in his voice that Paris was just three hours away by train. "Three hours, three hours," she repeated.

After a moment of silence, she told him in a rush of words what was bothering her about his excursion. "Paris is the city of sin, full of people who are not Catholics or who are Catholic only of a certain kind." She bobbed her head up and down when she repeated, "Of a certain kind."

When he answered that she didn't know the French, she scolded him as though he were a small boy. She warned him that he was "embarking on a journey not sanctioned by God." He tried to explain that Paris was the most cultured city in the world, but she cursed him and told him he was risking his soul to hell.

"I will say a *pater noster* for you at Saint Sulpice and at Notre Dame," he told her before he opened the door to leave.

"Say it for yourself," she retorted, as she sat in the cushioned rocking chair facing the window.

Brabant returned to the station just in time for the one o'clock *rapide* to St. Quentin. After a short wait, he caught the express to the *Gare du Nord* in Paris. From there he took the metro to the St. Germain-des-Pres station, and following a map his colleague had lent him, walked to the *Hotel Trianon Rive Gauche* on Rue Vaugirard.

He checked in, went up to his room and put his bag on the bed. He immediately left the hotel to discover Paris. It was late afternoon and still warm. Map in hand, first, he walked to Rue St. Sulpice to make sure the Church was there, that he was really in Paris and to have a look at the great organ with the large clock on top of the secondary pipes. Satisfied, he crossed over to Boulevard St. Germain.

At the corner of St. Germain and Rue de Rennes, in front of the *Café Deux Maguots*, a young man of medium height, with thick glasses and a confident smile, was selling a thin newspaper. He was telling the passers by that his name was Amédé Cerusu, and that he was a student in Paris. Many *Deux Magots* patrons queued to buy a copy of the newspaper. Brabant stopped to watch what was to him an amazing scene. Amédé Cerusu was as black as the coal of Brabant's Belgium, and he spoke French with a facility the priest had not heard before. Brabant had seen Africans. Brussels's street sweepers were Africans, but he had never paid much attention to them.

He crossed the street to buy a copy of the newspaper, aptly titled, he thought, "*L'Etudiant Noir*," The Black Student. He thanked Cerusu, who responded with another smile. Brabant had a gift of curiosity and immediately looked for a place to sit to read *L'Etudiant Noir*. A student sheet, as he expected, was crammed with everything its publishers could get their hands on: history, poetry, essays, and letters. However, most prominent were translated excerpts from literary works by the Black American writers, Richard Wright and Sterling Brown.

Brabant dimly appreciated that such publications were *de rigueur* critical of Europe's activities in Africa. Yet *L'Etudiant Noir* offered more. Here was not another black student newspaper fated to last two issues at the most. Brabant noted that this was the third issue, and on the front page the students had printed an office address and the paper's price in the colonies and other cities. The priest recognized the work of professionals.

He then discovered, written in literary French, the contributors' proclamation that they were "proud to be black." At first with fascination and then something like dread, the priest read that revolution was necessary in the colonies. And that it would begin as soon as Africans had achieved pride of race. Taking out his fountain pen, he underlined the last paragraph of the front page essay. It was Cerusu who wrote, *"let's work at being black, certain that it means working for the revolution. Only the strong can make revolution. And only one who is true to himself can be strong."* For a long time Brabant remained at the fountain on St. Germain, where he had found a seat to read the paper. What he read greatly unsettled him. Cerusu's words sounded the way hearing the world was round must have to people who cared about such things in 1543. The more he reread Cerusu's essay, the more he envisaged the end of the world he knew, the world he had taken for granted. He tried to remember the face of any of the Africans he had encountered in Brussels but could not. He thought then of Belgium's colonies. He knew of the riches taken from them — the rubber, the mahogany, the cocoa and the gold, but these commodities were things, not people. The colonies were labels on maps, intellectual constructs, and not real people. What must they be like? The colonies were there, part of another background.

By the time he was satisfied that he had read every word in *L'Etudiant Noir,* he was convinced the end of the comfortable world of European ignorance would occur in the not too distant future. He walked back to his hotel with questions swirling in his head. When he reached his room, he felt compelled to write to his mentor and friend, Abbé Jules Renquin, his old Louvain seminary's rector. There was no writing paper in his room. The desk clerk directed him to the nearest bookstore on Rue Madeleine where he bought stationery. Back in his room, he sat at the small round table near the window to expound on his fears. "This African speaks French like an educated Parisian," he wrote of Cerusu, as if that had a pivotal significance. "And he exudes confidence. Where does that come from?" Brabant then told his friend about the newspaper, and the correlation between revolution and pride of race Cerusu articulated in the pages of *L'Etudiant Noir.*

*"The first thing that occurred to me when I read it was, how long before these ideas infect Belgium's territories in Africa? Were you aware of this? You know as well as anyone that when you lose land, you lose souls. What will become of those poor souls over there? It's only a few*

*years — a generation at the most — since we brought our light to their darkness. Those poor souls! How will the Almighty judge us if we let that happen? We can't just sit on our hands and do nothing. The Socialists and the Protestants will fill the vacuum made by our sloth and ineptness. I beg you to bring this to the board of trustees right away; no one should leave the seminary without an appreciation for the threat hanging over our work in the colonies. Forgive my excitement, but I discern a dire future for the church over there. And don't forget Belgium is a small country. Only our possessions in Africa give us a semblance of significance. Without these colonies we are just a ship-wreck on France's shore to piss on. And you know how much they like to piss on us. Leopold understood this. If we strengthen our mission's organization in Africa, we maintain our presence, even if we must abandon Leopold's legacy."*

Brabant signed the letter with his usual flourish. He was, he wrote, his master's "humble servant." He folded the African newspaper neatly and inserted it in the envelope he had bought at the bookstore, making sure that his letter was the first item his master would see. The sun was setting, but his excitement would not let him wait until the next day to post the envelope. He walked briskly to the post office he had reconnoitered earlier on his way to the bookstore. They were about to close, but a look at his cassock convinced a clerk to accept the envelope and to promise to mail it at once.

---

Brabant returned to his hotel. After a shower he changed into the pair of pants and the shirt he had folded into his small cardboard suitcase. Forgotten was the thought of idling about in the parks and museums of Paris. He set out to find out all he could about the world of the African student who had handed him the newspaper. From Rue Vaugirard he walked down Boulevard St. Germain and stopped at the corner with Rue de Rennes in front of the *Deux Magots*, hoping that the African would still be there, passing out his newspaper. But the student had left.

The priest was not sure what he would say if he had found him. He had never spoken to an African before. He wanted to know at least the student's age. Perhaps he would be less concerned if the student were too young to be certain about anything, recalling that he, himself, had many ideas he now considered outrageous when he was at the seminary. Disappointed not to have found the African, but relieved he would not have to make conversation, he turned back toward St. Germain, walking past Vaugirard, until he saw a group of Africans in front of what looked like a club. A brown *La Rhumerie* sign in very large letters hung above the door.

Across the street, he argued with himself whether or not he should go in. He was about to turn back, when a Frenchman walked to the door, kissed one of the Africans on both cheeks, and went in without any hesitation. Brabant crossed the street and sheepishly slipped into *La Rhumerie*. It was a smoke-filled bar full of Africans and a few white Frenchmen and women. Loud, syncopated music made it difficult to discern any meaning in the hubbubs. No one paid attention to him. Cerusu was at one of the booths in the back. Next to him was another African. Across from them was a young woman whose radiant eyes illuminated an arresting face.

A barman approached him. "We only serve rum here," the barman said. "You can have it with sugar and lime, or you can have it straight. You are new here; I suggest lime and sugar. A glass of Perrier will help cool the sting."

"I will take just the Perrier," said Brabant.

He was too nervous to nurse the Perrier successfully. Moreover, he needed the rum if he was ever to summon the courage to go to the booth where Cerusu was in heated conversation with the other two Africans. After a few minutes, the priest raised his hand to call the barman over. "May I have one with lime and sugar," he said. The barman smiled. After a few sips, Brabant walked to the student's table. He waited until Cerusu looked up.

"My name is Jacques Brabant," he said. "I am visiting Paris from Belgium. You sold me a newspaper this afternoon. I read it. I was wondering if I could ask you a few questions." He had a voice one would stop to listen. Cerusu looked at him in silence, surprised. The priest seemed at ease. And unlike most of the whites who came into the bar, Brabant did not seem to be what the African patrons called a "*complexé*," looking to feel better about himself by rubbing elbows with blacks. When the priest said Belgium, Cerusu thought "paternalist." But Brabant's manner had no tinge of condescension.

"You have changed your attire," Cerusu said, smiling. "This afternoon, you were wearing a cassock." He stood up to shake hands. The priest reddened perceptibly. Cerusu smiled again and introduced his friends. Brabant noted that Cerusu acted with the confidence he had observed earlier.

"This is Fatou-Anne," he said. The priest extended his hand to the young woman. "And this is Zengher," he pointed at his other companion. "Please sit down. Zengher is one of yours — a Catholic. Fatou-Anne is engaged to him. Me, I am a Marxist." The priest sat next to Fatou-Anne. Cerusu was the obvious leader. He spoke very fast, with a lisp and an occasional stutter, in the most refined French Brabant had ever heard. (A few years later, a member of the Academy observed that he spoke so well that God would smile when hearing Amédé's voice. No one doubted that he would be the first person of color to receive a Nobel Prize.) For a while Brabant listened to the confident Marxist resolve problems in a way the priest could not imagine anyone imitating. Cerusu's voice hypnotized him until he recalled why he had sought out the student. This was his chance to learn something about the church's influence in Africa. He thought himself a born missionary; he could not pass such an opportunity to do God's work.

"I read your paper with interest," said the priest in his endearing and polite voice.

"What was interesting about it?"

"Your dialectic between race and revolution, for one thing."

"What I said is simplicity itself," said Cerusu, a bit of the eager student in his manner. "Africa will not free itself until Negritude is achieved"

"Negritude? Is that what you call Marxism in Africa?"

It was Zengher who answered. "Negritude has nothing to do with Marxism. Negritude is simply the expression of our individual shame-free and fearless selves."

The priest said, frowning, "Why do you need to express — if you'll permit me — the obvious? Were you ever unsure of what you are? Why?"

"It's a long story, but quite simple actually," Fatou-Anne interjected. The priest took in the sound of her voice. It held his attention as much as Cerusu's had. "I'll tell you," she said, "to better use us or, if you like, to make us willing participants and auxiliaries in their exploitation of Africa, Europeans made us a negative appendage. Some of us complied. Now escaping that powerless, empty role is an obsession for many of us."

"That's right," Cerusu said, looking at Fatou-Anne with admiration. "We are Europe's sad toys. We are good Negroes"

Brabant went to the question he had waited to ask. Looking at the woman, he said, "How will you make revolution in the colonies?"

Without hesitation Cerusu said: "By taking possession of ourselves. Anyone can make revolution. What makes it difficult in our case is that we are an-ashamed-to-be-black black people. For us to make revolution, we must emphasize both the substantive and the qualitative. That's the reason we are working at taking back possession of ourselves first. That must be our ontological choice. Until we are successful at doing that, we will continue to be Europe's playthings."

"Will the Communists help you?" asked the priest.

Fatou-Anne and Zengher both laughed.

"They are as bad as the subjugators," Fatou-Anne said. Zengher added, "In one way they are worse because they hide that Africa means nothing to them except in Moscow's global world view. They want to dictate to the continent and make use of us for Moscow's advantage. Everything is Moscow, and Moscow is totally against racial consciousness." Zengher looked at Cerusu, expecting him to expand on what he had said. After a while Cerusu seemingly reluctant added, "At the most, we are an ethnic curiosity. The internationalists expect us to be their toys just as the other Europeans do. To them, we are culturally empty vessels into which they pour our history as they see it. It's racism at its worst. They will not help us for what we are; only for what they want us to be."

"I thought you said you were a Marxist," the priest reminded him. "Has the discovery of your Negritude changed your mind?" He noted that Cerusu was losing interest and had become much less talkative. Confessing his ambiguity to the priest had depressed him. But Cerusu answered, "I said I was a Marxist not a Communist. There is a difference. I believe in the Marxist economic plan, for example. And Marxists were not the first subjugators to reach Africa. Now they want to take advantage of the situation. But what else can I be? Another assimilated French Negro? Another toy? Sitting on the fence is not for me. I'll tell you that I may be an ambiguous Marxist, but I am a devout Negritude man. There I have no choice. You should see the masks in my apartment!"

"Masks? What sort of masks?" said the priest. "Is the mask a Negritude symbol? I have never seen an African mask. I'd like to see one. Where could I go while in Paris to see them?"

Zengher said, "The mask is an authentic expression of where we come from. To many, especially in the forest regions of Africa, the ancestors speak through the man who wears the mask. There are some very expressive ones at the *Musée d'Ethnographie*. If you like,

I'll show them to you. I have a class there tomorrow afternoon. I can meet you."

Cerusu arose and everyone followed. Outside, they said their good-byes in the way of friends, the priest thanking Cerusu for putting up with his questions. Fatou-Anne left with Cerusu. Zengher stayed behind to tell the priest how to get to the *Musée d'Ethnographie*. They walked down Rue St. Michel in silence. At the corner of Boulevard St. Germain, the priest thanked the African and said goodbye. The evening was still warm. The cafés along the boulevard were full of mostly young people. The priest continued to walk all the way to Rue Vaugirard, delighted with his evening.

Confusion and fears no longer pressed on his mind. Relieved at what he had learned from the students, he enjoyed his first evening as a boulevardier in the Latin Quarter. Cerusu's ideas are not so threatening after all, he told himself. At the most, Cerusu's Negritude aspiration would be a pressure valve to release intellectual frustration. Everything the brilliant Cerusu had said could be turned on its head. As long as he stayed in his particularism and did not graduate to something larger, an "ethnic curiosity" as he said, he would remain. No doubt, he will continue to lead. And that was good. Through him, Europe will control the colonies."

He dismissed Zengher as a "Frenchman." Had the African not been so black and had he not spoken with that awful accent, he would be taken for a Frenchman. The priest had acknowledged Zengher's faith and had blessed him when they parted. The African had crossed himself and thanked the priest.

Fatou-Anne he did not dismiss so readily. He didn't know why, perhaps it was the direct, unblinking way she had looked at him, or what she had said about escaping one's race, or the look of admiration in Cerusu's eyes when she spoke — whatever it was, he had sensed that it was the young woman who was the real leader, not Cerusu. Now Brabant was confused, for his world admitted no women in leadership positions. In passing, he told himself that she would end up with the dynamic Cerusu and never marry the cautious Zengher. He delighted at the thought that there was a good possibility that Zengher might then become a priest.

He went to bed thinking of his old master at the Louvain Seminary, and of what he would write to him next. Before falling asleep, he gave his mind a few minutes to think about the best way to uphold the church's interests and to do God's work in the poor colonies. The answer came readily enough — his pupil, Roger

Temple; the lad was God's gift for the task. He smiled when he thought how much his mother would approve.

———  ———  ———

The next morning Brabant put on his cassock and left the hotel, telling the clerk that he would have breakfast at a café he had seen last night. But it was too early for a table on the sidewalk; a man with a long white apron was washing the sidewalk with a worn brush. He went inside and stood at the counter waiting to place his order. Next to him was an old man whom he heard ask for a cognac. The priest remembered his mother's aversion to alcohol and, looking at the man said, "Isn't it too early, my son?" The old man did not answer. The priest was not sure he had heard him. The old man's eyes were fixed on the bartender pouring Remy Martin into a brandy glass. His face brightened perceptibly when the barman placed the glass in front of him. He took it with gnarled fingers and savored the amber liquid from the moment it touched his lips. He drank all of the liqueur languidly. "Aaah," he moaned, setting the snifter on the counter. Only then did he look at the priest.

"Ever since Africa," he said in a guttural voice, with no introduction, "I must start my day with this," pointing at the glass. "It's the only relief from the pains which almost killed me. That and the devils over there."

"Africa? What were you doing in Africa?" Brabant asked.

"For the pay mostly and the adventure. The pay evaporated in the tropical sun and the adventure almost lost me my life. Adventure my ass. The Bozambos couldn't wait for me to leave. But I gave them as good as I got, if you know what I mean."

"Bozambos? Is that a tribe?"

"I don't know anything about tribe. They were the monkeys we were stuck with. We didn't say lazy bastards like the Brits did; that took too long, we simply said Bozambos. Don't ask me where that came from, if you know what I mean."

"You worked for the government?"

"No, I was a boss on the Senegal-Mali railroad construction project. They hired us to build the railroad. But those monkeys never wanted to do anything. Singing, and, well, you know what I mean. That's how they were building the railroad — singing."

"Did you ever face rebellion?" asked the priest

"Rebellion? Sure! But nothing we couldn't handle. We had work stoppages, but nothing that I would call rebellion. A man came from Dakar once to try to talk the monkeys into forming a union.

He lasted one day; they found him dead by a new set of tracks. After that, it was quiet. The monkeys were more interested in getting wives than in rebellion. Every time they got paid they got a new wife!"

"And the church? Did you know any priest?" asked Brabant

"Look Father, if you are thinking of going into the conversion business, forget it. The church will never make it, where I was. The Mohamedans got there first. It's perfect for them; they can adapt to the monkeys' ways better than you ever could. Don't worry Father. There is nothing you can do about it. Jesus Christ in person couldn't do anything about it."

The priest turned to the coffee that had come while he was talking. He thought about the masks he was going to see at the *Musée d'Ethnographie* that afternoon. "What about masks? Did you see any when you were over there?"

"The Mohamedans forbid that sort of thing. A man came from Liberia looking for work on the railroad. He was carrying a mask, his totem. He didn't last a day. They ran him out because he had this thing. That's how they converted the monkeys — they took away their masks to make them focus on God, if you know what I mean," he said and then laughed.

"I am going to the museum this afternoon to see some."

"Oh, which museum?"

"*Ethnographie.*"

"That's not far from Avenue Mozart," the old man said. "I have a room there. If you want, I'll walk with you."

The priest put a franc on the counter and walked out with his new companion. On the sidewalk, he introduced himself. "I am Father Brabant, I am Belgian."

"And my name is René Bousquet," the old man said. They shook hands.

"Let's go to the *Quai de Grenelle*," said Bousquet. "We'll cross to the other side; from there it's a short walk to the museum." They walked side by side in silence. After a while the priest said, "Monsieur Bousquet, do you really think the church cannot make headway in Africa?"

"Forget it, Father!" the old man answered, emphatically. "You can never replace the Mohamedans over there. And even if you could, by the time the Africans were finished with it, it would not be much of a church. You would not recognize it. Oh sure, they'll sing your hymns on Sunday and then go make sacrifice to the dead on Monday."

"Then how were the Mohamedans able to do it?" asked the priest.

"I told you. They impounded their masks."

"Monsieur Bousquet, I still have a couple of hours before I have to be at the museum. Is Notre Dame far from here? I promised my mother I would say a prayer for her there."

"If we walk, it's about thirty minutes. By metro it's less than ten."

"Do you mind walking?" asked the priest.

"If we walk to Notre Dame, I will have to take the metro to my place. I can't walk to both. I would suggest we take the metro to the cathedral and then walk to the museum. It's a long walk."

"Agreed," said the priest. "Where do we take the metro?"

"One of the pretty things about Paris is that we have a metro station on every block. I would have died long ago without the metro."

In seven minutes, the metro took them under the Seine to the *Ile de la Cité*. From the stop there, naturally named "*Cité*," they walked up the steps to *Place du Parvis,* the square in front of the cathedral, whose shadow, as if to bid them welcome — or was it to remind them of all it had witnessed in the past eight hundred years — fell on them. Brabant thought that the cathedral was smaller than he had imagined. Perhaps its gothic style or the unfinished square towers watched over by the gargoyles made it appear so. He walked to the center of the *Parvis* from where all distances in France are measured. Bousquet joined him, and they stood in front of the central portal.

Bousquet took the priest's arm. "Builders make cathedrals for men to look up," he explained. "Look, there, the potted plant with the large leaves and the red pods. Then above it, up the left portal, the Portal of the Virgin, is Ecclesia, the statue representing the Roman Church. Notice the crown of victory on her head and how held-high and confident that head is, if you know what I mean.

On the right, above another plant with large leaves and red seed pods is the Portal of Saint Anne. There is another female figure. You see it? It is the same size as the other; her back is arched in the posture of a seductress, if you know what I mean. But notice that her head is bowed in desolate defeat." Bousquet laughed. "And a serpent covers her eyes. Five tablets are in her right hand at her side in a surrender demeanor, and in her left hand, hanging at her side, next to a fallen crown, is a flagged staff broken in three. You see it. This figure is Synagoga, representing Judaism.*" He laughed.

It took Brabant, the provincial priest, a while to take in the meaning of the two figures above Notre Dame's front portals. And when Bousquet told him, "*Attention! Ils sont soupçonneux et méfiants,*" he turned pale and his right hand shot to his mouth to stop a scream. His mother's words damning Jews screeching in his ears, he turned away from the two Notre Dame symbols. Mother Brabant had never met a Jew; she had simply grown up knowing that she should curse them for all ills and troubles. Bousquet, a Notre Dame habitué, standing at a forty-five degree angle from the priest, continued to smile appreciatively. "The world took the Ten Commandments from them. Can you imagine the royalties they are owed?" he said, still laughing. "They will not get a *sou!*"

Inside the great church was as dark as a cave. Medieval, Brabant thought, experiencing an eerie sensation of time taking him back a thousand years, when Europe trembled with faith and his predecessor priests were Europe's masters. His companion stood behind him, his teeth bared, his jaw jutting out, looking toward the candle stand near the Church's east portal, like a pointing bird dog.

Brabant followed the old man's gaze and saw what he was staring at. Revulsion flooded his senses, as though the acrid smell of the guttering candles had sharpened disgust at what he saw. Against a column, behind the candle stand, in the semi darkness, a French girl was kissing an African, hungrily massaging her mouth into his. The priest watched transfixed as the old man pulled out his belt and hobbled toward the couple.

---

*Notre Dame de Paris built between 1160 and 1250 epitomizes *le style français,* the Gothic age in Cathedral building. These colossal structures denote triumph and accomplishment — the Church (Ecclesia) victorious. To underline that victory most such Cathedrals feature a figure denoting a defeated Judaism (Synagoga) invariably blind because Jews had not followed or had betrayed Christ. Ecclesia, the figure consistently on the right of Synagoga is, on the other hand, always portrayed as confident, sure of her way, Christ's agent, the hand of the divine on her head. The ascendancy of Church over Synagogue is the master mason's message. The builders also favored stained-glass windows, frescoes, wood and plaster carvings to portray with various illustrations this victory of Ecclesia over Synagoga. Such depictions fell into disuse when the *Age of the Cathedrals* ended and Renaissance building, which began in 15th century Florence, spread throughout Europe.

Bousquet shouted an obscenity as he swung the belt at the African's shoulders. The girl was the first to react. She pulled away from her lover in a violent gesture and screamed an obscenity. Her voice reverberated through the church nave. She pushed herself forward, daring Bousquet to hit her. He cursed her and had raised the belt to strike her. When the African swiveled to hit him with his right fist, he hesitated, and after a moment of what Brabant thought was fright, instead dashed out of Notre Dame. But the French girl stayed. She attacked the old man with both hands scratching at his face. The old man stumbled and fell on the black and white tiles, mouthing obscenities. Her face contorted, she kicked hard at his right leg and stood over him heaving ragged breath. After a moment, she ran out of the church through the Saint Anne portal.

The priest had not moved. He said a quick prayer and stepped out, leaving the old man lying on the floor. The girl and the African had disappeared. The priest walked to the *Quai de Montebello* and crossed from *Ile de la Cité* to Rue Lagrange back to the Left Bank.

The candle seller helped the old man up. He picked up his belt, cursing, and limped outside, expecting Brabant to be waiting for him. But the priest was gone.

---

Father Brabant walked all the way to the *Musée d'Ethnographie.* On Boulevard Montparnasse he passed the French girl and the African walking in silence together holding hands. No one was paying attention to them. He arrived at the *Champs de Mars* exhausted after his long walk through Paris and sat by the large fountain at the corner of *Quai de Branly.* When he felt refreshed enough to go on, he crossed the *Pont d'Iena* over to the *Place du Trocadero,* arriving at the museum in time to see Zengher get out of a taxi and walk to the large edifice of the *Palais du Trocadéro* where the *Musée d'Ethnographie* was housed. The priest waited for him at the entrance. In the cool vestibule, Zengher gave him a ten-minute history of the museum, explaining that it had one of the largest collections of artifacts in the world, arranged according to geographical regions. "Here you can find anything you can think of on prehistory, anthropology and ethnology," he concluded proudly. They walked to a large musty-smelling room. African masks of all sizes covered the walls. A short man in a black suit stood behind a lectern at the far corner, facing the door. He was alone in the room waiting for people to enter. After ten minutes, he walked over to the priest and Zengher, smiling. "Good afternoon. My name is Théophil Mauzé. It looks like you are going to be my audience this afternoon," he said. "I do a lecture at this time every Wednesday. Instead of my usual talk, perhaps I can answer your questions." Zengher was about to reply, but the priest said, "Do you have anything from the Congo."

"You are in luck," Mauzé said, pointing at three masks on the farthest wall. "The museum has just acquired these Chokwe masks. The Chokwes are a people in southern Congo. The first mask is used for the king inauguration ceremony, the second is a male initiation mask and the third is also used during ceremonies of inauguration."

"You said initiation ceremony. Initiation into what?" asked the priest.

"Initiation into manhood! Among the Chokwes, eight- to twelve-year-old boys are given two years of training on what it means to be a Chokwe. During that time, they circumcise and initiate them into the traditions of the Chokwes."

"This sounds serious," said the priest.

"Initiations are always a serious matter," Mauzé said gravely. "For many groups, it's a matter of life and death as far as their traditions are concerned. Jews have the Bar Mitzvah; the Chokwes have the Mukanda."

"Are there other people with similar traditions to the Chokwes?" asked Zengher.

"Aren't you from the Congo?"

Zengher stiffened. "I am from Senegal," he said solemnly. "Most of us are Moslems, but I am a Christian."

Mauzé apologized then said, "There are hundreds of groups like the Chokwes in the Congo."

"Do they all believe in the same things?" asked the priest.

"If your question refers to the role African masks play in the various societies, yes," said Mauzé. "The mask is a conduit between people and their ancestors. It also has many other functions, and not all masks are used for ritual ceremonies."

"You mean they worship these masks, or… they worship their ancestors through these masks?" asked the priest.

"No, absolutely not," Mauzé said. "There is no ancestor worship in Africa, nor are there idols to ancestors. There is a general belief that ancestors visit and speak through persons who wear the mask. And certain groups have interpreters who accompany the wearer of the mask to explain the message from the ancestor. People relate to their dead relatives the way they do to their living ones. The ancestors are full participants in the life of the community. And because the living believe the spirit of the dead can intervene in their daily lives, they are careful not to offend. You may say that people treat the dead the same way they treat the living.

"So, it's not a religion?" the priest said in a relieved voice.

"When it comes to Africa," said Mauzé, "Europeans do not differentiate among what they call 'ancestor worship,' religion and superstition. It's all *Tintin au Congo* to Europeans. But you'd be surprised to know that most ethnic groups in Africa believe, for example, in the God of creation, not that different from Christians. Families, clans, and so on, have their own totems for the ancestor to whom they trace their origin. And like the Catholic clergy, they have their priests and other go betweens."

Zengher said, "So masks are very important to these people."

"That's what it sounds like," the priest added.

Mauzé took a long breath and after a moment of reflection remarked, "You take away the mask and you create a catastrophic disruption and damage to all that is traditional in many parts of Africa. It would be like uprooting an entire group. You would create a huge vacuum in the people's lives."

The three stood looking at the masks of the Chokwes in silence. None could ignore that these cultural implements were not in the Congo but on the walls of one of the world's great museums.

They thanked Théophil Mauzé and walked out of the mask room. "I want to put the mask room experience behind me directly," Zengher said, sighing. "My friend Sandaga is waiting for me," pointing at a small man weaving unsteadily across the avenue. "He is in my class. I better go before he falls in the street."

"Last night, your friend called you Zengher. Is that your first name?" said the priest.

"It's my last name."

"What is your first name? I would like to bless you, using your baptismal name."

"Léonidas, but my friends call me Léon," the African said with a shy smile.

The priest watched the African cross the *Place du Trocadero* to join his friend.

What a cautious man! he thought. You have to pry every word out of him. Brabant had dabbled in the new science of psychology and had read Le Bourget. And, although he would not admit it, he fancied himself a decipherer of people's inner motives. His mother had reprimanded him for frequently trying to interpret her friends' motives.

I wonder if he is that way because he is African and French, he asked himself, as he stood watching Zengher cross the plaza. What a struggle that must be, to be both at the same time. He can't be both at the same time! And not knowing exactly when to be one or the other, he uses caution as a protective mechanism, a buffer. It must be like that; men who are of two worlds are prudent by second nature. What about the women? I wonder.

He could see the metro sign from the museum's sidewalk. At the ticket window, he asked for directions to the St. Germain Station. He had no transfer to make and in a short time he was back on the boulevard with its hundreds of cafés full of young people, including Africans. He noticed Africans everywhere. They didn't exist before, he thought; now, I can't take a step without seeing one. He walked to his hotel. After a quick shower, he sat in his underwear by the window to write to Jules Renquin. He wrote without break for forty-five minutes. He then put on his one pair of pants and shirt and walked to the post office to mail his letter.

Brabant continued along the boulevard. At the intersection of Rue de Rennes, there was Cerusu handing out his newspaper to the *Deux Magots* patrons. When he saw the priest, he said good-naturedly, "Good afternoon, *Monseigneur*. Did you make it to the *Musée d'Ethnographie?*" The priest nodded, yes, and told him that with Zengher's help he had now an appreciation for African masks. They went into the café, stopping to admire the statues of the two sitting Mandarins above them — the *Deux Magots*, decorating the central column. They then sat at a booth facing the boulevard. "The French seem really interested in your paper," he told Cerusu.

"Yes, Africa is *a la mode* here. They have gone gaga over black Americans, too. The French are attracted to the exotic these days. What I fear is that it will never be more than amusement.

"We must reach an equilibrium. You see, if we remain exotic, they will never take us seriously. On the other hand, if they take us too seriously, they will become frightened and unload us before we have a chance of making the most of the colonization experience."

Cerusu was about to say more when Zengher's friend, Sandaga, came into the café. Sandaga weaved a pattern to their table. He was slurring his words.

"Zengher received news his father has died. He is on his way to Marseille to catch the *Medée II,* the first boat to Dakar. He asked you to do him a favor — continue the French lessons he was giving Fatou-Anne."

"Sure, I'll be glad to," Cerusu said. "Would you like to sit down?"

"No," Sandaga said. "I have to go find Fatou-Anne to tell her that Zengher is on his way home."

He turned to leave, but changed his mind, took a step back to the table and picked up Cerusu's beer. He drank thirstily, and walked out without a word. At the door, he gave the glass to a waiter. The two men watched him leave the café.

"He is a great poet," Cerusu told the priest. "I would compare him to Rimbaud; that's how good I think he is. The problem is that he thinks he is Rimbaud and must live like him."

"Rimbaud was not a poet for very long," the priest said. "He was just twenty-one when he put his pen down and wrote no more. This fellow looks older."

"That's because he drinks," Cerusu said with a wry smile.

"The church can help him," the priest mused.

"I went to the Catholic mission school," Cerusu said. "Very seldom did I hear the priests mention the name of Jesus Christ. Why is that? Isn't Jesus the way to salvation in your faith?"

"God is too far. There is no salvation without the church. The door to Him is the church. We were talking about salvation for your colonies a few minutes ago. You think that you can achieve it through integration. I think that's an illusion. The salvation you are looking for can be found through the church. As Augustine said, "God has made us for Himself, and our hearts are restless until they rest in Him.""

"We can't wait for your kind of salvation. It's in this life that we must reach it. That's what I like about the Communists. They have done away with illusions."

Damn the French, the priest thought. To Cerusu, he said, "But the church is permanent."

"That's what I am afraid of," said Cerusu.

"Let me ask you something," the priest said. "Would it be possible for me to talk to your friend Fatou-Anne?" That took

Cerusu aback, and he looked at the priest for a long moment. "You had me fooled, Father."

The priest reddened. "It's not what you think," he babbled. "I just want to talk with her, to get a woman's point of view on what we have been talking about. That's all."

"I know. I meant that you are very perceptive. Excuse me, but I didn't think so before. I don't know what you are looking for, but whatever it is, talking to Fatou is smart. I'll ask her to come with me tomorrow afternoon. When she is with me, I sell more newspapers." He shook hands with the priest and went to the cashier to pay for the beer Sandaga had consumed. At the door, he waved to the priest and went out.

The priest had noticed the shine in Cerusu's eyes, when the African said "Fatou." Is that what love is? he wondered.

Damn the French, he thought again, as he watched the African walk up Rue de Rennes.

———————

The hotel clerk handed him his key and a letter from Jules Renquin. In his room, he sat at the corner table to read.

*Dear Jacques,*

*I just received your letter, and hasten to send you this short note to make sure you get it before you make it back to beautiful, sunny Belgium. I can't tell you how excited I was to read that you had stumbled on African students in Paris. Ever since that socialist mad man, Léon Blum, became prime minister and brought in the era of the so-called "Popular Front" in France and its colonies, I have been thinking of the Congo. It's fine for Blum to want to socialize the world; he is a Jew. But for us, you are absolutely right, what happens in the French colonies will influence ours. Remember my course on the impact of the French Revolution on the European Church. The anticlerical rampage did not spare us then! A century later, we are still paying the price here. It is high time we look at the church's interests in the colonies; we have been complacent too long. I mentioned the colonies at the last board of trustees' meeting a couple of days ago. They don't get it. They remain ignoramuses. They tell me that we Jesuits are too good for African colonies, and that we should let the second class Dominicans, the Flemish ones at that, take care of Africa. That it is not going anywhere. When you return to Louvain, let's contemplate this question together. Like you, I fear for those poor souls over there. But I fear even more for Holy Mother Church. Fortunately, we are all in the hands of God, Summus omnes in manu Dei. He will not let the church for which He sacrificed his only Son perish. I don't agree with you though that we will lose souls. My sense is that the Africans will create their own cult, using the true church to mask their real intentions. What is left of Holy Mother Church after the Africans have finished cannibalizing it will become reactionary and corrupt like it was in Europe not that long ago. We have a duty to God to help them find and keep the true faith.*

*Your mother called. She is worried that Paris will pervert your soul. I told her that you were doing God's work, converting the heathens. She thought I was talking about the Jews. She has been listening to that raving Austrian on the radio.*

*Talk to as many Africans as you can while there; they are the colonies' future leaders. Get all the information you can, and come see me.*

*In Domine Patri, etc.*

*Jules R.*

Brabant could always count on his friend's humor and straight forward good sense. His notes were never more than two paragraphs long. Once he had asked him the reason for always writing short letters. Renquin had answered that he had read somewhere an aphorism by the French philosopher Pascal. Pascal was asking a correspondent to forgive him for not having the time to make his letter short. Renquin's method was to make his letters brief, to give the impression that he had taken great care in composing them, when in fact he had spent very little time on each. He was a letter-writing devotee, composing a hundred each day, always with a variation of the same introduction.

---

Brabant remembered that he had not eaten that day. He kneeled at the foot of his bed and gave his mind to prayer, offering his hunger in sacrifice. But his mind wandered. After a moment, he gave up on trying to pray and dressed in pants and shirt, his boulevardier attire. The night clerk, who was meeting him for the first time, told him where in Paris other than the boulevard he could have a good inexpensive dinner close to a promenade spot.

But the clerk had misunderstood his request for directions. Thinking that Brabant had asked for the location of a red light district, he had shown him the way to Pigalle on the metro map. The moment Brabant walked out of the Pigalle metro station, he knew the purpose of the place. Women of every race and size, all dressed in tight-fitting skirts, were standing every two meters or so as far as he could see.

Mechanically he crossed himself and started to walk back down the steps to the metro platform. A black woman in a tight-fitting green skirt was standing on a step below him, blocking his way down. He excused himself and moved to the other side. Playfully, she stepped in front of him, while touching his crotch.

"I'm dying of thirst," she told him in the embroidered accent favored by newly arrived colonials to copy the Parisian way of speaking and which the French had long ago labeled, *the Negro de Paris accent.*

"I have to catch the metro," he answered, a tremor in his voice.

Laughing, she took his left arm and spun him around toward the street. "I'll buy you a cognac," she said, steering him to the café nearest the metro's entrance. They sat at the bar. "Jerome, two cognacs, the best, right away," the woman told a short balding man behind the bar.

"You are causing me to miss my train," the priest muttered.

The barman knew the ruse and had two drinks in front of them in record time.

"Drink!" she told him with a frown. "You'll forget about the Metro and everything else."

"I can't forget about the metro."

"You will; it's not even eleven o'clock yet."

In the damp hotel room, the woman was undressing. "I haven't much money," the priest apologized in a low voice.

"How much do you have?" the woman asked, annoyed.

"Two thousand francs. That's all," he muttered, putting two large bills on the nightstand on the right side of the small metal bed.

"I'll let you see my breasts for that much."

He didn't answer.

"What do you expect for two thousand francs?" she said angrily, having blocked the door.

"I want to see all of you."

She looked at him suspiciously. "You are not one of them, are you?"

"One of them?"

"Police photographer."

"No. I just want to see what an African woman looks like."

She was a thin woman; but she had very large, firm, round breasts that seemed to cover her entire chest. The nipples were two blunt fingers pointing at him. And for a moment, they reminded him of the Victor Hugo poem in which a man barricades himself behind thick walls to fend off the eyes of his conscience. But he was struck that the tips of these nipples were not pointed, but square. And for reasons he would never understand, that fact enabled him to watch in silence, as the woman, naked, did a pirouette in the middle of the room. He sat on the bed, hearing the pounding in his chest, his manhood alive; he wanted in a deep, profound way to touch those two extraordinary mounds of luxuriant black flesh.

Too soon, she had put her clothes back on and had left the tiny room, pocketing the two thousand francs without a word. After a moment, he followed. On the sidewalk he glanced up and down, looking for her, but she was not there. His hunger forgotten, he took his time walking back to the Pigalle metro station. He was terrified, his mind screaming at him, certain that those nipples would become forever the eyes of the conscience Hugo had warned about.

When the priest arrived at his hotel, the night clerk gave him his key and was surprised that instead of a 'thank you' with a knowing smile, Brabant glared at him with a stern, reproachful stare. They must have rolled him, the clerk thought. No man who had a good time would look so glum.

---

At dawn the priest slept. In his dream he was sitting on the hotel room's metal bed, and the woman in a tight-fitting skirt was pirouetting like Salome in the middle of a very large room. He recognized it as the African masks gallery at the *Musée d'Ethnographie.* In the middle also stood the lecturer, who held an object in his left hand, smiling broadly. The woman danced around him over and over. Each time he moved to caress the large breasts with his right hand, just in time she passed him, just out of his reach. Finally, he handed her the object. She stopped pirouetting, but continued to sway in front of him, while he stroked her breasts methodically. Still dancing she placed the object on her face. She then left the lecturer's groping hands and moved toward the priest. Her face was still hidden from view, until it was caught in the light from one of the ceiling projectors. He saw then that it was a Chokwe mask, and that it had his mother's face.

He woke up, desperate for penance. At the seminary, Jules Renquin had prescribed that he memorize Augustine of Hippo's *Confessions* to recite when a significant act of contrition was called for. "Seek for yourself, O man; search for your true self. He who seeks shall find himself in God," Augustine had written. Composed in 397 A.D., *The Confessions* is Augustine's autobiographical account from decadence to the acceptance of God. The priest as was his wont had done Renquin's prescription one better and had memorized the entire text of *The Confessions* and could recite it backward. This he now did, with fervor; not in a French translation that he knew but in the melodious Latin original. It was afternoon when he finished reciting Augustine's mea culpa.

Although he did not "find himself in God" as Augustine had promised, he had achieved a semblance of peace and self-redemption. Still, to make sure, instead of the usual 'amen,' he closed his act of penance, saying, "forgive us our trespasses, as we forgive those who trespass against us. And lead us not into temptation, but deliver us from evil." Finally he recited his favorite psalm, *"De profundis clamavi ad te, Domine: Domine, exaudi vocem meam,"* which he repeated five hundred times.

------

Dressed in his black cassock, he left the hotel. He took his time walking to the *Deux Magots,* thinking of the letter Renquin had sent him and the questions he wanted to ask Fatou-Anne. Talking to Zengher and Cerusu had raised in his mind the question regarding the type of education Africans were receiving in Paris. How does it help them or France for that matter? Would that kind of education ever serve the colonies? What is France up to — what about God? he asked himself. Agricultural development is not served by that type of education — constant questioning and circular and pointless analysis. Where does all of that lead? He wanted to discuss these questions with Fatou-Anne. (He felt certain that the African woman would tell him in better detail more than her friends had.) In meeting the African students, he had stumbled into an image of the future of the colonies in Africa. God had let the light of understanding shine through to reveal what lay ahead. It was now Brabant's cross to carry His salvation to those poor souls there. Brabant now understood what Renquin meant by 'information.' His master wanted a serious assessment of where the colonies were headed, so that he could form a blueprint for the action the Belgian Church would take there. *Appello ad Christum...*, the priest prayed fervently. I call on Christ for the answers that will lead to the advancement of His church.

God had changed the world for him, making him travel to the French capital, and putting in his path three future leaders of a continent in need of him for its salvation. He was eager to be up to the task. Less than a week ago, Africa was not even a dark void to him; now, he was on a journey of its discovery. He marveled at God's mysterious and marvelous ways. Reciting Augustine's disquisition had revived his spirit, and his self-contempt was not as heavy to bear. It had eased the terror he felt following the Pigalle experience.

As he turned onto St. Germain, he saw Fatou-Anne and Cerusu arriving at the *Deux Magots*. They were holding hands. He called to them, and they waited for him to cross the wide boulevard to join them. Cerusu said, "Here she is, Father. Good luck! I have to go pick up my newspapers. I'll join you shortly."

"Thank you for coming, Fatou-Anne," the priest said to the African woman with feeling. "I am grateful for your time. Since I arrived in Paris, I have heard a great deal about Africa from your two friends. Yesterday, Cerusu suggested that I speak with you. It's my impression that he feels that you are the one who can give what I have heard a certain direction and perhaps put into a Catholic context where the Francophone colonies are headed. But, may I get you something to eat, drink? I am starving; I have not eaten all day."

She studied him and after a moment said, "I will speak with you Father, but only if you are honest with me. I don't understand this interest of yours in the colonies. Why?" They went into the café, the priest holding the heavy metal and glass door open for her. They both ordered *croque monsieur* and espresso. The café was empty, and they sat at the same booth by the window that the priest and Cerusu had occupied the day before.

"You are a very beautiful girl, Fatou-Anne," the priest said. "All African women are beautiful, I guess," he added in a strong self-deprecating tone, surprising Fatou-Anne. She could no longer suffer hearing that praise especially from white men. Only an odd sadness in his voice prevented her from walking out of the café. Instead, she smiled, lowered her head and asked, "What do you know about African women, Father?"

"I saw one in Pigalle, last night," he answered. "That's as far as my knowledge goes."

She looked at him in silence for a while. "Is this a confession, Father?" she said finally.

"It's not what you think. I said 'saw;' nothing else."

"Saw? In Pigalle, you saw?"

"Yes, only saw."

She was surprised that the priest's gray eyes glistened when he repeated "only."

"I am sorry to hear that, Father. Men like you need to experience women fully. In a few years, you will not be able to find a priest to give the last rites in France and, I am sure, in Belgium. And the reason is that you don't have women in your lives."

"What do you mean?" he asked, startled.

"I mean that it's senseless — no, suicidal — to exclude women from your life, Father. That's what I mean," she said heatedly.

"I have taken a vow, you know."

"What kind of celibacy, if you'll excuse me, finds you in Pigalle, Father?"

"Pigalle was an accident. I never meant to go there."

"But when you got there —" she didn't finish her question.

"You mentioned France and Belgium, but what about Africa. Are they so different in Africa?" the priest asked.

"Many in Africa join the priesthood not because of a voice on the road to Damascus, but as a means to get an education and to join the rank of the respected. The way young men join the army in France and probably Belgium. The Red and the Black, remember? Priests in Africa take mistresses, or 'second offices' as we call them, and no one thinks less of them for that. And they have more children than anybody else," she said with a little laugh. "In that sense, they are more advanced than you are. The day may come when you will have to go to Africa to find a priest to give the sacraments in Europe."

"A couple of days ago, I spoke to an old man who had worked on the railroad in your country. He told me that the church had no future in Africa," he told her, impatient to change topics.

"Léon, a devout Catholic, feels the same way. But tell me why the old man thinks the church's future in Africa is bleak."

"Islam! He thinks the Moslems are in a better position to gain converts than our church is."

"He is right. For one thing, Islam is closer to the people than the church can be. The fact that the church has never acted independently of the colonial authorities has made the people weary of its powers and influence. They cannot quite trust it, if you see what I mean. And the intellectuals are of course looking elsewhere for answers to solve our problems. Amédé looks to Marx, and Léon has found the priest-paleontologist, Theillard de Chardin, to rekindle his faith with a convoluted theory, although the Vatican doesn't look kindly on priests like de Chardin. For myself, I don't care for a God with a proclivity for suffering. Preaching suffering to Africans is like peddling ice to Esquimaux. But I was born in a Catholic family; I have no choice. If I had, I would be a Moslem.

The priest sat back in his chair, thoughtful. "What should the church do, Fatou-Anne?"

"Pretend that Africans are not just a subjugated people. Can you do that, Father?"

"What do you mean?"

"Get a dispensation to meet the needs of Africa not the needs of Europe," she said laughing. "Stop taking your orders from Rome. Take your orders from the people over there. Live with them. Being white doesn't pose a problem, you know."

They ate in silence.

"What about this Negritude ideology? Where does that fit?" he said when he had finished his sandwich.

"Between us, Father — just you and me, this is what I think about it: Negritude is another of our illusions, nothing else but a way to rationalize that we are a conquered people. Negritude is our way of accepting the fact that we are France's auxiliaries to do with as it pleases. We say pretentiously that Africans have something to offer in our colonial relationship with France, but we can't wait to look for creams to lighten our skin, pinch the nose of our children to make them straight, and adopt the Negro de Paris accent, hoping that the French will think that we are one of them. They have us, Father; all the talk of Negritude does not change what we have become. The people in the African villages don't dissert on Negritude; they live what is left of their lives under European colonization. Happy are those who never had any dealings with the French authorities!"

"I am rather fond of the Negritude idea," the priest said, laughing sheepishly. "To me it means acceptance, yes, acceptance — an existential acceptance, if you like. Look closer, you also find that it means the willingness to participate in creating your own destiny on what remains of what you call a conquered people.

"The course of history is irrevocable; what God has written, men cannot change. The practical person makes the best of what is. Rome conquered Gaul; and today, I am in a café in Paris talking to an Afro-Greco-Roman young woman who speaks French better than 99.99% of the French. Well, as Voltaire would say, this is '*le monde comme il va.*' But do your friends know that you feel this way about their romantic ideology?"

"No they don't. They don't know how I feel about it. Not yet. It is in the gestation stage. But Amédé is very astute; unlike Léon, he knows how far this concept can take us. The problem for him, as I see it, is that he is a Marxist, and it won't be long before he becomes a card-carrying Communist. Once that happens, he will be lost to any African aspiration.

"He thinks that Negritude will solve his dilemma of being an African under French rule, and that he will remain a free spirit able to decide always for himself. He is wrong; time is not on our side. Do you know, Father, we are the only people who instead of looking to free themselves from a moment of historical deficiency create concepts to adapt to it. When you have become the plaything at somebody's party, as Amédé likes to say, and you don't run for your life, you have no destiny, Father. Democracy could have been our salvation; I believe that. Unfortunately, corruption —

"Corruption?" the priest interrupted her.

"Hear me, Father. Pursuing ideas like Negritude coats our destiny with the worst corruption imaginable. I say this knowing that we are denying ourselves the strength of what we are. Whether out of desperation or whatever, we are also giving up the opportunity at democracy, permitting an elite to withhold the franchise from the rest."

"I don't understand," the priest interrupted her again. "What elite?"

"The French have made an elite of those who accept them as the masters of the moment. Like all elites, ours looks after its interests — normal enough. But democracy is not one of them. Our elite also vetoes all mention of industrialization. All the French had to do was to give the monopoly of peanut farming to one of our Brotherhoods, to seal our fate. A few make money, while the rest rot. Not very original, but it works every time. A hundred years from now, we will still be peanut farming. That is if we have not ceased to exist altogether."

"You are so much unlike your fiancé. I was with him yesterday afternoon. He is generous with his purse, but a miser with words.

"That's true; unlike Amédé, Léon doesn't talk much, unless it's about de Chardin. He keeps what he has to say for his silly poems about black women. As for me, I always talk too much. That's what I like about being in Paris, Father, I can talk. Back home, they permit a woman to talk as much as she wants only with other women. If we had the vote —"

"What would women change if they had the franchise, Fatou-Anne?"

"Independence!"

"Independence… for Africa?" he said wincing. "I am sorry, I didn't mean to sound incredulous, but every thing I have heard about Africa… well you know what I am trying to say."

"I know, Father. In truth, the obstacle is not that a white man is skeptical when he hears independence in the same breath with Africa. It is when Africans themselves become dubious at the mention of the word. I believe that freedom is the only thing that will rescue us from the colonial pit. Justice lies there! Even then, it may take a thousand years before Africa is completely out of it. The pit that is."

So this is what French education has wrought, he thought to himself, awed by her. Satisfied that he had maneuvered the conversation in the direction he wanted, he asked, "Are you getting the education you need here?"

"Yes, Father, I think I am. Thanks to the Popular Front, a couple of women from West Africa have the opportunity to come study in Paris. The Popular Front was a godsend. Forced labor is less severe in our part of the continent. We can even form trade unions and some of us have become politically active. Imagine that!" She smiled. "But I must admit that socialist style assimilation has opened doors that were unthinkable just a year ago. I am going to be a high school teacher, Father. Here in France I am getting the best education available to do that."

"Do the French know what they are doing?" the priest asked with a grin.

"The Popular Front is not the French," she answered coldly.

"What do you mean?"

"The Popular Front is a social experiment. Prime Minister Léon Blum is a Jew. Someone not unfamiliar with forced labor. But like all experiments, no one knows what the results will be. I can tell you that in Africa the French trading companies and the Brotherhood want Blum dead. I would not bet against the moneyed interests, if you know what I mean. As for me, I light a candle for Léon Blum whenever I can.

"Now Father, tell me what this is all about. I have done the talking. I have answered your questions. Now it's your turn. Why this interest in Africa? Are you planning to take residence over there? The women are beautiful!" she said with a chuckle."

"That's a thought," he said sheepishly. "But in all seriousness, if I had not come to Paris, I probably would never have learned about Africa. That's true! When I read Amédé's newspaper my first day here, I thought of the Belgian colonies. Then I met this old man who told me about the precariousness of the church over there. If I have an interest, it's that the church survive, and that His seed not die there. As you know, France is Belgium's older brother. We tend to look to France, in spite of all the jokes, for leadership. I thought that understanding the aspirations of French colonies would give me an insight into ours."

"Father, Africa is not a monolith. The Belgian colonies are as different from the French ones as Belgium is distinct from France. In fact, except for the fact that I speak French, I would be lost in the Congo. However, I don't doubt that the French colonies will influence what unfolds in the Congo. In meeting Zengher and Cerusu, you have met two future leaders of France in Africa. And what they told you, I am sure they will try to achieve. But you should remember what I said: in the end it's France, and France alone that will decide what we become. Here is Amedé now, and he doesn't look happy."

Amédé Cerusu came into the café with a somber look clouding his face. "They have confiscated the newspaper," he announced. "They accused us of fermenting resistance at home. What did they expect? That when we had a voice, we would just kiss their ass with it. What else is there for people like us but resistance? Excuse me, Father, it's just that I'm pissed off. This is the third time this month that they've halted our press."

To calm him, Fatou-Anne said good-naturedly in a teasing tone, pointing at the priest with a movement of her chin, "He went to Pigalle last night." Then with a wink, she said, "He saw an African woman."

Cerusu laughed uproariously. "I thought the term was 'know', not 'saw.' Good for you, Father. I think I'll become a Catholic now."

"Now what happened with that damn newspaper?" Fatou-Anne asked.

"Why do you always call it 'that damn newspaper'? I don't understand you. That bastard Molineau came to the press about an hour ago, to tell Jojo that the minister had put another interdict on the paper, that's the third this month.

To the priest Cerusu said, "The last time we thought it was for good. But the minister is in love with Fatou, and we were allowed to print again. I think this time we've had it. And we were doing so well, too. If this harassment can happen with the Popular Front, imagine when it is somebody else. The French traders must have complained to parliament again."

"I'll speak to the minister this evening," Fatou-Anne said. "I'll explain that you are harmless poets. I'll even tell him that your only aspiration is to be worthy of France. I don't think he wants to be known as the man who closed the press on Voltaire even if this one is from Africa."

"Did they give you a reason for shutting you down?" the priest said. He felt his heart miss a beat when Fatou-Anne said she would go to the minister.

"Molineau, the minister's messenger, only said 'for fomenting resistance.' Resistance to what I don't know."

"Was Fatou-Anne joking when she said she would speak to the minister?" the priest asked in a disapproving tone.

"No she wasn't joking." Cerusu answered hard. "Look Father, when you are in our shoes, walking in a straight line is a luxury; we have so few options, you know."

"I wonder," the priest said, his tone sad, "why compromising one's integrity is an option at all?"

"Because we have no choice," Cerusu answered heatedly, looking at Fatou-Anne with disbelief in his eyes.

The priest did not respond.

"My virtue is not in any danger, Father," Fatou-Anne said. "It's a game that we play."

"I am glad to hear that," the priest said. "I hope you make the rules of this game."

Cerusu rose to leave, and Fatou-Anne followed him. Suddenly, the priest felt very alone. He rose, too. "I'll walk with you to the corner."

"Thank you, Father," Fatou-Anne told him, "we have a lot to do."

At the corner of de Buci and St. Germain, the priest shook hands with Cerusu. "You have taught me a great deal. I think meeting you may have changed the direction of my life," he told the student in a flat voice. He then hugged Fatou-Anne. "I'll never forget you," he told her. "*Amici mei benedictus... in domine patri et filii et spiritu sancti,*" he said softly, blessing them. *Deus vobiscum...*

The sun was still high in a rare blue Paris sky. The priest wandered dispiritedly toward St. Sulpice to pray. He saw the fountain where he had sat his first afternoon in Paris to read Cerusu's newspaper and nostalgically went there to remember Fatou-Anne. If she is right, he thought, recalling her words, there is no telling how far any movement will take these colonies. He began to draft a mental report to submit to Jules Renquin upon his return to Belgium. Well aware that he only had a few anecdotes and opinions to go on, he told himself that even if he had not spoken with the three educated Africans, he would be unequivocal about the type of education the church should advocate for the colonies. It was cruel, he thought, to educate Africans as if they were Europeans.

Besides the teachings of the Catholic Church, they should learn modern agriculture methods to feed themselves. The inevitable surplus would of course go toward creating a capitalist democratic society. That in itself would go a long way to stop any drift toward autonomy Africans in the Belgian colonies might fancy in the years ahead.

He caught a contradiction in that idea. By its very nature a liberal colonial power like Belgium seeks to create *grosso modo* a reflection of itself in its colonies, planting the seeds that eventually cause the natives to opt for autonomy. The French have already done that with Fatou-Anne; but she is ahead of them, thinking of independence.

He thought dejectedly of what Fatou-Anne had said about being a Moslem if she had a choice. He promised himself that he would try to learn everything he could about Islam in Africa. He couldn't put a finger on the reason he now thought that religion was the key to controlling the colonies, except for the fact that like God himself religion was permanent. The church couldn't continue to take Africa for granted; from what he had heard, the Moslems were the most proficient at converting the natives to their ways.

How they did it so well might give him a lead into understanding them better. It was paradoxical that he, a member of the Society of Jesus, founded to convert the Mohammedans following the defeat of the Moors in Spain, was now thinking of studying their methods of conversion in Africa. But since he had no doubt that understanding the Africans should become a church priority, it made no difference where the lessons came from.

At his hotel, the clerk on duty directed him to the National Library. He had decided that after an early morning visit to the Louvre, he would spend a few hours at the Paris library. He had in mind to create a bibliography on Africa, as an addendum to his report to Jules Renquin.

After prayer and a quick shower, he dressed in his pants and shirt and left the hotel. He had rushed out of the lobby hoping the clerk who had gone on duty an hour earlier would not notice him. Seeing the clerk had reminded him of his Pigalle adventure. He sighed deeply and walked blindly for a while reciting his favorite psalm, "*De profundis clamavi ad te, Domine...*" Instead of walking up toward St. Germain, he decided to explore a bit, hoping that he would eventually reach Boulevard Monparnasse, which he had taken a couple of days earlier on his way to the *Musée d'Ethnographie.* It was less crowded and gave him a better appreciation of what Paris must have looked like at the end of the previous century.

He also wanted to think about his report to Renquin and strolling always helped him organize his thoughts better. Once his mother had tied him to a chair to cure him of his habit of walking while studying. He had been so distraught that he couldn't memorize even one page of his lesson. She had relented. He crossed Rue de Rennes and continued on Vaugirard and was rewarded; for not too far in the distance was the wide Montparnasse Avenue. He turned left when he reached it and walked more slowly, mindful of the ancient buildings on both sides. Reaching the Montparnasse Cemetery, he paused for a long while, reading the names on the well-kept tombstones. Back on the boulevard, he went in the *Café du Coin,* where he hoped the *croque monsieur* would be as tasty as the one he had at the *Deux Magots* while listening to the African woman with the sparkling hazel eyes.

Inside the café, in a dark corner, sat a French girl and an African. At once, Brabant recognized them as the Notre Dame couple. He took a seat next to their table. They had been arguing.

He heard the African say, "That's because you talk too fast, that I don't understand." And she said, "Don listn so slow, an you ca undstand." After giving his order to the waiter, he turned to the woman who was puffing fiercely on a *Gitane*. "I saw that old man strike you with his belt in Notre Dame the other day," he told her hesitantly, apology in his voice. "Oh yu enjoy tat, dee yu?" she said drunkenly in the argot from St. Denis, north of Paris. Toothless, she smirked and was seized by an uncontrollable smoker's cough. Brabant looked on expressionlessly. Then he mumbled an excuse and rose to leave. He would be on the next train to Brussels where his mother awaited him, where confusion was never the rule.

Mother Brabant approved of her son's pupil, Roger Temple, for the mission to the Congo. Roger's training was thorough, taking nine years. But Temple was in the Congo less than a week when the Africans had him killed. Father Brabant took matters into his own dedicated hands and followed his favorite novice to the northern Congo.

The Africans never connected Temple with Brabant. To them all priests, Flemish or French speaking, were of one mind — the colonial mind. The Africans had other connections to make: independence, for instance, which was right on top of them like a stampeding herd of elephants. Had they made the connection, they might have spared Father Brabant; they were a forgiving lot — been content to let history, which their oral tradition told them reached back to the beginning of time, have its way with him.

# Chapter 9

Minister of Foreign Affairs, Fatou-Anne Cerusu, was seventy-nine years old, but she could have said fifty-five, and no one would have doubted it. Molu looked around to see if Marcellus Garinaldi was near and hurried to where the minister stood.

"Minister Cerusu, it's kind of you to give me a moment from what I know is an extremely busy schedule."

"It's a pleasure to meet you in person, Mr. Ambassador," she answered, liking him.

"Thank you! My president named me foreign minister last week — in fact, the day before I called you to request a meeting. I wanted to take the opportunity of the General Assembly meeting to ask your advice about my new job."

"Why didn't you tell me when we spoke that you had been named foreign minister?" Her smile seemed to suggest an awareness of things to which neither Molu nor anyone else was privy.

"Well, I didn't know whether my boss had informed your president yet. I remembered his reaction when someone disclosed an appointment that he had not yet made public. There was hell to pay."

"I see. Surely you know what I think of President Motutu. I have spoken against him publicly on several occasions, most recently at a meeting of the Organization of African Unity. I am persona non grata in Kinshasa. If he knew we were meeting, there would be hell to pay. Yet you seek my advice. Why?"

"I read how the ministry of foreign affairs in Senegal changed when you took over. I wanted to know how you got the job done. To a great extent, it's because I know what you think of Kinshasa that I sought to speak with you."

"In that case, I can be blunt," she said. "I much prefer to be blunt. Let me say that as long as you have that man as president in Kinshasa, I don't see how change is possible. It would be like expecting snow in Dakar. You can expect, but — you see what I mean. A part can be different from a whole, and I suppose that a foreign affairs ministry can be sheltered from the goings-on of the government it is part of. But — I hope you will forgive me when I say this — I think that decay reaches too deeply in Kinshasa. And it is so because the head of state is who he is. My husband wrote a play —"

"*A Congo Chronicle*, I know it well. No person or anything distressed my president as much as your husband's play. But the Lumumba affair was decades ago. Is that when you gave up on Kinshasa?

"Lumumba was not just an affair, my dear minister. His murder reverberated throughout Africa. Since then, the rule of law has not counted for anything in most of Africa. Killing Lumumba made the rule of one man possible. That man's whims have brought Kinshasa and, to some extent, Africa to the pass we are in."

"Perhaps I made a mistake —" Molu said, getting up.

"Perhaps you have," Cerusu said in a kind voice. "You asked me to tell you how I implemented change at my ministry. I don't know what you expected to hear. But whatever it was did not include change the way I understand it."

"I was hoping that you would tell me about change at the ministerial level," Molu said. "I cannot do anything about the rest of the government. That's beyond my reach. You know that."

Minister Cerusu, still seated, looked up at him for a moment. "How in the world are you going to transform something like a ministry without taking into account its power source? A ministry is a mirror image of the government of which it is a part. But yes, I understand that it is not in your power to reconstruct the whole government. So you said. Alright, if you sit down, I'll tell you what actions I took. I don't want it said that I did not give advice when asked for it."

"Thank you," Molu said, sitting back down.

"Like every ministry that was created by a colonial power, mine was dysfunctional. It had to be redesigned to reflect our needs as an independent nation. The first thing I did was to identify seven of our best diplomats who also had significant work experience in other African capitals. They were seconded to Cheik Anta Diop University in Dakar where they were tasked to identify bright students interested in the diplomatic service. Also, I changed the entrance exam, to decrease emphasis on France. In this way, we could better identify good candidates who also had an African world view —"

"But Senegal became independent in 1960," Molu said, interrupting the minister. "Why did it take so long for your ministry to adjust to your autonomy?"

"Minister Cerusu smiled. "Because a ministry is a reflection of the government of which it is part. Our first president, Léon

Zengher, except for his color, was a Frenchman. As long as he was president, France was our government's alpha and omega. Léon, you know, couldn't see his soul without a French prism. When Daoud became president, he asked me and the other ministers to become Senegalese."

"I see," Molu said. "As I told you, I had heard about the changes you implemented, but I wasn't aware of the reasons for the changes."

"Bureaucracies have cultures that can be influenced like everything else," Minister Cerusu said. "I don't know anything that functions in a vacuum. How you expect your ministry to do so, I don't know; that smart, I am not."

Molu avoided her question. Instead he asked, "What about the old diplomats, the colonial era ones?"

"I offered them a generous retirement package. No one is left from that school."

"What about budget? Do you get a fair share?" Molu asked.

"We are fighting secession in our southern region. Consequently, the defense department gets the lion's share of the resources. But we make do. Our important resources are perspiration and a small cadre of talented diplomats. We spend most of our time lobbying foreign governments for financial aid, and we make appeals to halt the flow of arms to the southern rebels.

"Your government has been selling them arms for twenty years. Colonialism is not the only reason for underdevelopment and the miserable impasse we are in today, you know. But I have restrained my people from engaging in tit-for-tat against Kinshasa. It would be simple — and who could say we are not justified — to arm the rebels on your eastern borders in retaliation for your arming our southern rebels. After the genocide inflicted on them in Rwanda, the Tutsis could do anything, *anything,* in the region, and the world would call it justice. If your president were in our shoes, he would have armed the Tutsis long ago. However, we have refrained from doing so because it is neither in our interest nor in Africa's. Instability and unintended consequences go hand in hand, as you have observed. A debacle along your eastern borders would put the whole region to the torch. The consequences could be colossal for all of us, not just the people in the area. Your president denies that he sells arms to our southern rebels. Denial is a way of life with that man; it is true he has much to deny. The whole world knows he sells arms to Jonas Savimbi in Angola, but he denies that as well. His words are not worth that fancy blue paper he writes them on.

"Recently I was in Luanda, Angola. Half of the children I saw there had a limb missing from having stepped on mines. You have two daughters, I understand. Think of them as victims of Savimbi's mines. Those mines spare no one.

"This is not an ultimatum, Mr. Minister, not at all, not at all. But the time may come when we are not able to control the situation in our country. Before that happens, we will open a second front, to relieve the pressure from our south. This second front may very well be your eastern borders. The Tutsis are awaiting our answer. They know your weaknesses; they can't wait to get their hands around your regime's throat. If your province of Katanga was worth Lumumba's life, I don't see why half of my country would not be worth your eastern borders, and who knows what else."

Molu looked at Minister Cerusu in stunned silence, his black face a few shades paler. After a while, he said, "So that's why you agreed so readily to meet with me. I was wondering about that." He chuckled nervously.

"As I told you, my people and I spend a great deal of time soliciting foreign governments for assistance. You are the new foreign minister of a government that sells arms to the rebels who want to break up my country. When you called me, I already knew that your president had named you Kinshasa's foreign minister. I asked around about you. I needed to know whether you would be a genuine foreign minister or another pawn the Kinshasa Dictator uses for his musical chairs to stay in power. Almost everyone thinks highly of you. 'He is smart and decent,' they all say. An old beggar like me does not turn down an opportunity to talk to someone like you.

"They also say that you are loyal to your boss. I took a chance that you were more smart and decent than you were loyal to such a boss. That's the reason I have been blunt with you. You are an African; so you have given your ears in courtesy to an old woman, even if she is rude and speaks carelessly about a man to whom you owe your station. And perhaps as a smart and decent African you will use your new office to do something other than what keeps that man in power. Can you imagine how it would be if all of us worked together for positive change? I know it is retro to speak of Pan-Africanism. But as a student of Cheik Anta Diop, Pan-Africanism is in my blood."

"Speaking of Pan-Africanism," Molu said, wanting to channel the discussion in another direction. "I thought that I would also ask for your overall assessment of the continent. As ambassador in Washington, I focus entirely on bilateral relations. I have not spent much time on African affairs. Marcel Garinaldi told me that not even Madiba Mandela understood our situation as comprehensively as you. But perhaps you don't have the time or the inclination to speak to me anymore."

"Garinaldi exaggerates. Mandela is the man of the century. Me, I am only an old woman who has seen the baobab bloom too many times. But yes, I have the time, and I certainly have the inclination to speak with you, Mr. Minister. I did not send my deputy to this General Assembly meeting because I wanted to talk to you myself. I am here because of you.

"You ask for my overall assessment of Africa. Well, here it is. What superlative would not apply to Africa? Some days, I am convinced the ancestors have turned against us, when I hear the violence HIV is inflicting on us. But as bad as AIDS is, do you know that it is nothing compared to the environmental ravages taking place throughout the continent today? Yet people talk about AIDS; they do not talk about the environment. The desert used to expand inches per century; now it's miles every year. Then, I hear of an uplifting success somewhere and I take heart again. When it's bad, I remind myself that I did not expect to see South Africa free in my lifetime or even my grandchildren's. If anyone had told me that I would one day dine with Mandela, I would have said he had too much palm wine. In truth the Cold War —"

Molu cut in, "HIV is a poisoned well, Minister!"

"I am not saying it is not," Fatou-Anne said. "The difference is that in time man may come up with a vaccine against it. But what single thing could solve the degradation of our environment?"

"You were speaking of the Cold War."

"Yes, the Cold War. Its end is the best thing that could have happened for us. As much as I wish it were still on, for the support of the western powers in arms and logistics against the southern rebels, I see the end of the Cold War as a gift from the ancestors. That has enabled us to graduate from pawn to beggar. I am sure you recognize the difference between the two. A beggar has opportunities however slim to control his surroundings. He can even choose to refuse alms from someone he thinks unworthy, as long as he is alive. But a pawn is a casualty whose choices are limited to taking only paths of least resistance.

"In our case, we took handouts and just waited, expecting more. We turned expectation into a way of life, like Pavlov's salivators. Some of us even created Expectation Ministries to administer the handouts and competed for the title of donors' darling. Foreign aid was our Sisyphean rock; it never got over the top — it was never enough. You understand? And if you looked closely, you saw that we had become an unstable reflection of whoever's handouts we were taking. For a long time we went along with the idea that being poor was inimical to being free — one reason Africa was synonymous with low expectations. I once had the brilliant idea that we could feed our people if we did what North Korea has done — blackmail the world. Now the handouts have gone with the Cold War. *Gone with the Cold War,* one of my young diplomats sings. That has empowered us. The path of least resistance is now the exigency to survive. Necessity was always a harbinger of wisdom."

"Yes, but — what do you yourself do?" Molu asked.

"You have *not* been listening. I told you that I spend a lot of time seeking aid from rich countries. Now, however, we compete, negotiate and transact, not just administer what it suits the donors to grant us. Beggars have choices; we are masters of our nights.

"I read a great book on the plane, on my way here. I want you to have it. It's by my friend Aminata Sow Fall, *The Beggar's Strike.* It is a story about a group of beggars; what they achieve when they become masters of their nights. I hope you will read it."

"Yes, I will read it. Thank you," Molu said.

Minister Cerusu said, "If you remember anything of our meeting today, I hope it is that 'crushing truths perish from being acknowledged,' as my old friend Camus would say."

"Crushing truths perish from being acknowledged," Molu repeated.

"Africa," Fatou-Anne continued, "has been the poster child for helplessness for so long that we forget that, ever since the Sahara region began changing into a desert, we have been under pressure from other civilizations. However, these civilizations are gone, and we are still here. I could give you a laundry list of what ails us, but I prefer to take advantage of your regard for my age to speak of what is possible, instead of our endless woes."

"I'm grateful for your words," Molu said. "I don't know how fast I can make changes. But I will remember what you said to me today. I will remember, I promise you, I will remember.

"I hope I can keep an open channel to your ministry; talk to you every day if necessary to resolve our differences. I do not believe that the president will look over my shoulder to the extent that I will not have a free hand to make the necessary changes. He pretty much let me have my way in Washington even when I made mistakes I know he considered costly.

"I have not said anything to Marcel Garinaldi yet, but I plan to ask him to come to Kinshasa to help me run my ministry. He has decided to retire. They told him that Sierra Leone is where he belongs, so he is retiring. I want him to be the behind-the-scenes operative whose only stake is my succeeding to reorganize the ministry. I mentioned it to the president, and he agrees wholeheartedly that it is a great idea; only a foreigner can be trusted in that position.

"The president, in fact, has consented to everything I have asked to make the foreign ministry an effective institution. I am very encouraged by that. Now, I look forward to pushing ahead the minute I get there. The way I see it, we cannot afford to have people angry with us anywhere, and I will do everything in my power to mend fences."

"That sounds fine."

"The first thing I'll do when I take up my post next week," Molu said, "is visit African capitals to initiate the kind of dialogue that will leave no doubt that Kinshasa is a good neighbor. I accept your point that we are not helpless."

"That sounds very promising," Minister Cerusu said but without much conviction. "I — everyone — will respond in kind, I assure you."

"You have been candid with me," Molu said. "Let me be candid with you. It was I who suggested to my president that we sell arms to Savimbi. I looked on the business as an opportunity. Somebody would have done it; there was too much money in arms in the region. I thought, why not us? Plus that gave us a most envious vantage point."

Fatou-Anne looked at him a long while, her lips pursed. She then closed her eyes for a moment, perhaps in acknowledgment of his frankness, or in despair at the ways of men. She did not say.

When she spoke again, her voice had a deeper resonance. "I don't know if odd is the proper word — about your appointment. Late on the night you and I spoke about meeting at the UN, your president called to tell us about your appointment. I made some inquiries about you, including a talk with your friend Garinaldi. Everyone should have such a friend. I am the one who asked him not to be here this morning. I needed to talk to you alone. He understood.

"Well — I found out that the man Washington is sending to Kinshasa as its new ambassador is cause for great embarrassment to your president. I also learned that he has spent a great deal of time discussing this appointment with his underlings, especially his security chief, that brute, Maka Mgonu —"

"I can explain," Molu hastened to interject, interrupting the elderly foreign minister. "We believe that the sending of an African American to Kinshasa is a signal that Washington has shifted its policy towards us. My president thinks that because I have spent a great deal of time in the U.S. and have numerous contacts here, I am in a good position to handle this shift in policy. And as you are aware, the current foreign minister is ill. I wanted the job; I am eager to be on the world stage. Being ambassador, even to the U.S., has limitations. However, as foreign minister —"

"But what has your being named foreign minister to do with Mister Mgonu?" She slapped her hand on the table. "I can understand discussing this appointment with one's associates, but Mgonu?"

"I don't know that there is a connection, Madame Minister," Molu said slowly, surprised by her reaction. "Perhaps the situation in the Great Lakes region or the attempted coup a few months ago has something to do with Mgonu being near the president more than usual. Mgonu is devoted to the president; I am grateful for that. He has even saved his life — almost died in the effort. The president does not go anywhere without him. In fact one of Maka's less outrageous names is *Lomposo ya Mokonzi*, president's skin."

"You don't think it's relevant then?" Minister Cerusu asked, clearly puzzled by Molu's lack of concern.

"No, frankly, I don't see the relevance," Molu said. "I appreciate your candor — but no — there is no relevance."

"I am concerned because I wouldn't want to lose you," Minister Cerusu said, with emphasis on 'lose.' "Having someone in Kinshasa we can work with is very important to us. Strategic, in fact! Our southern rebellion robs us of time and the resources we could spend on so many other needs. I hope you will consider how counterproductive your selling arms to the rebels is for all of us. Let me add that we have excellent rapport with all the international financial institutions, not just the Exim and World Bank. We can support your case for loans to make up for the loss of arms sale to these rebels."

"Thank you! What you told me will be one of the first items on my agenda."

"Tell me, Mr. Minister, why is Kinshasa so opposed to an African American ambassador? In Senegal, we have had two truly outstanding American ambassadors. One of them was an African American, Professor Mercer Cook. He even translated Cheik Anta Diop's works into English."

"Oh, it's not that we don't consider them outstanding. Most of the African American diplomats I have worked with are made of superior stuff. Look at Marcel Garinaldi! But why shouldn't they also appoint African American diplomats to Europe? Most of the few African American ambassadors are in the sub-Saharan region. Sending them to Africa is no coincidence, although one tried to explain to me that it's because there are more countries in Africa. I didn't argue. I understood his embarrassment at having to defend his own appointment. Such attitudes spill over into policies. We have made it clear that Kinshasa would not be a party to any of it. But things have changed; our wishes no longer have the weight they once had. It was my failure not to hold the tide."

"A mistake your president would consider costly?" Minister Cerusu asked.

Molu chuckled. "I am not sure that it is my mistake; but it happened on my watch, and I consider it my failure. I do!"

The old minister did not speak at once. Reflectively, she watched the delegates go back inside the hall of the General Assembly. I must have missed something, she thought. Or is it my usual fright of the Kinshasa creature? Ambition is not a bad thing. It's the young's responsibility to be ambitious. But something tells me this one young man is letting ambition blind his good judgment. God, I hope I am wrong. After a moment she said, "Some of them are."

"I am sorry?" Molu said.

"Mistakes. Some of them are costly. I was at a conference in Europe two weeks ago; an African American was there. A very knowledgeable diplomat he was. I suggested he come to Senegal. He told me that's where they wanted to send him at first; but because his area of expertise was Europe, he requested a European assignment. I told him I was sorry to hear that because we needed diplomats like him in Africa."

"He is one of less than a handful in Europe," Molu said.

"Even today?" Minister Cerusu asked.

"Oh, I am sure that in some respects it is different today! Leadership does make a difference. But to change a bureaucratic culture takes a special kind of effort — leadership alone is not enough."

"Having lived under the French boot most of my life, I speak from experience," Minister Cerusu explained. "I am not saying the French were the most egregious of our colonial masters. The Belgians and the Portuguese were. They did not bother with pretence. If Europe were to colonize Africa, pray it would not be by one of its dregs.

"When you see a person of African descent on the world stage, I mean one with genuine influence and power, he or she is almost always from the United States. You have more Brazilians of African descent in the diaspora, but even at the end of the twentieth century, these Brazilians are still trying to figure out what they are. I met one almost of my color, who could not wait to tell me that she had European ancestry. I offered to buy her a plane ticket to Mississippi. Do not expect a black-skinned Brazilian with economic or political influence on the world stage any time soon."

She continued as she smoothed the wrinkles on her boubou.

"Perhaps this is not the perspective your friend Garinaldi wants to put against the rejection he has suffered; having been on the receiving end of a racist policy here, it would do no good for him to hear that his luck would be worse had he been born somewhere else. Garinaldi knows his story is distressing because he is aware of what is possible here. Somewhere else, his question would be an absurd non sequitur. Tell him for me that he is lucky; he's won the lottery, as far as his birthplace is concerned. I have no doubt his knowledge of history will guide him to the correct answer to the many riddles to the race question."

"I will tell him that," Molu said.

"The race question as it pertains to the diaspora fascinates me," Minister Cerusu sighed. "I remember an article Ambassador Mercer Cook wrote about blacks who were flocking to Paris after the war to escape American racism. The French thought black Americans widely exotic at the time. I saw for myself the fuss around Miles Davis there. 'It's for my horn,' Miles said, the way only he could say it. Cook cautioned blacks not to take their minds off the work at hand, and not to shirk their American responsibilities. But why aren't Americans of African descent more supportive of Africa, Mr. Minister? You are married to one, what does she say?"

"Many are, many are supportive of Africa. Marcel Garinaldi went to jail for protesting against apartheid," Molu answered with marked reluctance.

"Many? I read that a black aide — no less — advised that Clinton creature not to use the word genocide for Rwanda. An election was the reason. Support for the policy of extermination denial was widespread, I understand. You don't think succeeding administrations will have a problem with the word genocide, do you? I mean — when the next wave occurs."

Molu was uncomfortable. He had heard the question many times. It was he who had advised Motutu to fortify the country's eastern borders. However, the Dictator had gone further and implemented the Belgian policy of divide and conquer in reverse. The Belgians had favored the Tutsis. The Dictator fortified the more numerous Hutus. The Hutus' enterprise to cleanse Tutsis from Rwanda came indirectly from Molu's advice. This was one more remorse to live with. Why should African Americans do more than Africans for Africa, he asked himself.

"Black Americans have their own issues to resolve," he said. "Before they try to save us from ourselves, they must strengthen their gains here. How can it be otherwise? How can it be otherwise? The African proverb, 'they are not going to be nobler than the king' is true.

"I have to say as well that those who are in position to give support to Africa do so readily, even when the return on their time and effort is meager. I am certain that as they resolve their issues here, they will increase their support. However, Africa will have to show them some success. Race is not the catalyst to everything African. My wife reminds me of that almost everyday. It is our fault African Americans in general fail to work for Africa. It is one thing to support dispossessed kin; it is another to respond to never-ending disasters. Maybe the ancestors will arrange for more Mandelas."

It's time to end this interview, Minister Cerusu thought.

"You are young, Mr. Minister," she said, putting her right hand on his left arm, a troubled look on her face. "I understand why you are dejected. Believe someone who has lived through this century, we are making steady headway. Day to day, it may not seem that we are; but I can tell you that it was much worse under colonialism, much worse. I don't care that statisticians allege that South Africa was more prosperous under apartheid. We only had ignominious, absurd death under colonialism. Of course, it would have been more beneficial for us if the Cold War had not intruded on our independence initiation. Busy being Pavlov's salivators delayed the rewards of self-government. But that forced us to understand a simple truism."

"What is that?"

"I thought you knew: we are on our own."

"Yes, I agree," Molu said. "If we have learned anything, it is that we are on our own. How could we have thought otherwise all these years?"

"I told you. We were the experts at taking the path of least resistance. Thinking for ourselves was too hard; so we believed hollow slogans and bought shoddy goods. Now, if you don't mind let's talk a little substance, shall we?" Minister Cerusu smiled. "How de we join forces to get the African Growth and Opportunity Act enacted in the American Congress. Our apparel industry desperately needs a shot in the arm."

---

Some delegates gawked as the old minister walked into the hall of the General Assembly on the arm of the Kinshasa ambassador. At diplomatic gatherings, she had called the Dictator "Satan's water carrier." Watching the pair chat during the stroll toward their seats, onlookers wondered if once more Fatou-Anne Cerusu's formidable mind and power to convince had not achieved the impossible. Molu was pleased the delegates saw him in the company of Africa's *grande dame*. It gave Kinshasa a modicum of face, when the news from home was so dire.

After the murder of Patrice Emery Lumumba, the only prime minister ever freely elected, Kinshasa became a pariah from the international community. In a futile effort to make Lumumba's aura his own, the Dictator had raised statues of the martyred prime minister and had named streets after him everywhere in the country.

"Would I do all that I have done to memorialize Patrice if I had had a hand in his assassination?" he would ask foreign journalists who questioned him about Lumumba's murder. Despite the propaganda in the equatorial heat, Kinshasa had aged like a decrepit courtesan who plies her wares in the last house on the last street at the end of town. In his play about Lumumba, Fatou-Anne's husband, Amédé Cerusu, had called the Dictator a *maquerau*, slang for pimp. Afterwards it was impossible to look at the Dictator and not think of that moniker. At the *Quai d'Orsay*, officials didn't refer to Motutu as president or dictator, but simply as *le proxénète*, the pimp. The label suited, not from the Dictator's strut, but from the for-sale signs stuck at his country's borders when he seized power following the slaying of Patrice Lumumba.

---

Flushed with success, Molu returned to his seat in the hall. On his priority list of delegates to confer with was the foreign minister of Lyauteyville. The minister was the uncle of the president, a colonel who spent vast sums at the Pierre Cardin *maison de couture*. The shy, tall man from Lyauteyville had just reached the podium to introduce his nephew's annual address to the Assembly. Such pro forma speeches bored Molu. He paid no attention. He opened the book Minister Cerusu had given him, and reading the first paragraph became enthralled in the tragedy of the beggars.

Someone coughed, and Molu looked up. At that moment, he heard the Lyauteyville speaker say that Israel could be compared to Nazi Germany and Apartheid South Africa. Stunned, Molu looked around. His mind repeated "Nazi Germany, Nazi Germany…" The Libyan delegates were smiling broadly. The American ambassador had turned red.

Molu glanced toward Fatou-Anne Cerusu. She turned to look at him and, shaking her head, put her index finger to her temple. Either the Lyauteyville man had gone mad or the Libyans had written his speech for him. Molu felt deep resentment at the Lyauteyville man's remark. He was sure it would reflect badly on every country in Africa, most especially on Kinshasa.

Arriving in Washington he had inaugurated an internship program to give students an opportunity to learn about his country and Africa. One of the intern projects was to determine benefits of diplomatic relations with the Jewish state. The findings impressed Molu. Following the 1967 Middle East War, African governments had followed — to the detriment of their populations — the Arab countries' direction and turned their collective backs on Tel Aviv. The Israeli expertise in desert management, for example, was lost to the environmentally challenged continent.

# Chapter 10

While Molu listened attentively to the Lyauteyville foreign minister's speech, the exclusive fax machine across the Atlantic was informing the Dictator of Molu's meeting with the Senegalese foreign minister. His anger abated, he no longer ground the molars on the left side of his jaw. Then he summoned his security chief to his library.

"He is getting audacious, even insolent," the Dictator said, sounding like an injured defendant. He handed the fax to Maka Mgonu. "Everyone has heard her diatribes against me. Why is Molu flaunting his treachery so? What has gotten into him?"

"Like most of our enemies, he underestimates us. That's why he is not more careful and why he has signed his death warrant."

"Death warrant?"

"His undoing, Mokonzi."

"I am not sure that Molu is careless. Delusional, perhaps. But careless, I am not sure," the Dictator said.

"Then it's possible that he has a solid offer on the table and is building alliances for when he makes his move. It may also be a question of making sure his logistics are in order."

"His move? What are you talking about, Maka?"

"It's clear to me now, Mokonzi. Do you remember that note Sakeseba left on his desk the dull-witted secretary found and faxed to me a couple of days ago? His meeting with the Israelis and the Cerusu woman give credence to what I have been thinking: he is plotting a coup."

"A coup? A coup, Maka? Anyone but you, I would say has lost his senses for imagining… He would have to have the Americans with him for that. We have no intelligence of his plotting with the Americans?"

"Well, he met with Marcellus Garinaldi and Max Freeman the same day, within hours in fact."

"No, if the Americans were involved, it would not be through these two; they're just friends. I wouldn't trust friends; the Americans won't either. No, Maka, it's something else! I just can't put my finger on it. In any case, his fate is sealed. Nothing has changed."

"I beg your pardon, Mokonzi; until we know for sure, we should be ready in case it is a coup."

"What do you have in mind, Maka? Molu hasn't had any exchange with the Tutsis. Where are you looking?"

"No, he hasn't. But who knows what he discussed with the Cerusu woman. I may not have a report for a number of days. When she returns to Senegal, our contact at her ministry will be able to get the information from the young aide who travels with her. We know that she has had numerous contacts with the Tutsis. And my contact at her ministry reported that she threatened to help the Tutsis to counter our weapon shipments to their southern rebels. I'd suggest you give the green light to eliminate him outright."

"No! He is more valuable to me alive. Have I not explained that to you? This hasn't become a personal matter, has it Maka?"

"No, Mokonzi, of course not.

"But there are still too many unknowns, too many of his activities that are unaccounted for. We must try to derail his plans."

"Keep him off balance, you mean?"

"That's right."

"How?"

"We make him move. It's more difficult to plot when moving."

"Excuse me," the Dictator said suddenly. He stood, weaving and lurching slightly until he grasped his heavy cane, the one with the handle carved in the shape of an elephant. He dragged his right foot as he walked to his urinal, closing the bathroom door after him. In a moment, Maka heard a groan, but stayed where he was. It was important that he not assist his chief; it would be an acknowledgment neither man was ready to make.

"You have given me an idea, Maka," the Dictator said when he returned to his desk, his face still drenched in sweat from the effort to urinate. "I have wanted to open a front in the United Arab Emirates for the sale of Savimbi's diamonds. I will have Molu leave Washington early to take care of that business for me. It should keep him traveling for at least four days. And if necessary, I can have him make a stop in Geneva as well. There wouldn't be anything unusual about such a request. When I named him ambassador to Washington, I had him stop in Antwerp for a similar purpose. He wouldn't be the wiser."

"That's a great idea, Mokonzi. Leave it to you to come up with such an excellent idea."

"Flattery I don't need, Maka. Time I do need. I am beginning to feel that time is something we have very little of. I can't take a pee now without feeling *nazali mabe na eloko mingi*, if you know what I mean. And I keep hearing an ancestor blabbering about what Patrice was put through. So, please give me time, not flattery.

I want this operation to proceed as planned. Molu cannot escape. The ancestors may not have understood about Patrice, but they will about Molu. I only wish I could send the hag where he is going. That would be fitting. What about Johan? Is he ready? Everything must be synchronized, Maka. Will he be in Washington when that fellow Mosley gets here?"

"Yes! For the past two weeks, Kees has been spending every day in briefings at the foreign ministry. He will be ready, Mokonzi."

"The submission of credentials must be synchronized as well," the Dictator said, shaking a finger for emphasis. "I will not schedule for Mosley until they have accepted Kees."

"I do not believe they care who Kees is. If they do, they have not manifested it. No one has said anything over there about his race or his past."

"But I care! And that's what counts."

"Of course."

"Now what about Mosley's wife? What have you found out about her?"

"She is devoted to her husband and is an asset to his career. She is totally innocuous, except perhaps for a compulsion to please. She is a compulsive pleaser."

"You disappoint me, Maka. All you have to report is that she is innocuous and likes to please? What are her appetites, man? Is the bedroom a strength or a weakness with her? Surprise me, Maka!"

Mgonu took a moment to answer. "She is a shaker and a screamer," he said.

"Is that all?"

"It wouldn't be particularly difficult to arrange something with her, Mokonzi."

"Interesting! Why is that?"

"She likes the bedroom, but he doesn't seem to," he answered.

"Now, why didn't you mention that?"

"I am sorry! It's only that I was afraid you would give my department the assignment."

The Dictator looked at his security chief dumbfounded. He started to laugh, but stopped when his coughing became uncontrollable.

"From her picture, I gathered you were her type," the Dictator said between mirthful coughs. "But if you know a man who can take care of this, take care of it in every way, give him the assignment. We had an ambassador's driver who bellied with the wife.

Insert a smart driver in that residence; history always repeats itself. She is the kind who tries harder. Good! If I were in better shape, I would do it myself. But whoever it is, don't forget to bring me the video. Something tells me it will come in handy."

114

# Chapter 11

Fatou-Anne Cerusu had slipped into dejection. After hearing the Lyauteyville foreign minister's harangue about Israel, she slumped in her chair, her eyes closed. The young aide next to her looked furtively toward her. She was the oldest person he knew. Although he believed that her energy sprang from a magical well, he was always on the lookout for a break when her strength failed. She sensed her aide's reaction and raised her right hand to reassure him. Must I go to my grave suffering disappointments like these, she asked herself. Not even a demented anti-Semitic ass would compare Israel to Nazi Germany!

What pathology is at work here? She asked the ghosts of her ancestors she was certain were always at her side. Next week the Lyauteyville president is to deliver a speech to the United Nations. And this year, he expects they will receive him at the White House. Now that his foreign minister has mouthed such idiocy at a United Nations' podium, not even the Saudis will invite him in. And for what? If only this could be contained to these fools! But people think Africa is a village; that man's idiocy will splatter over us all. I'm sick of Africa's capacity for suffering. Now I must try to minimize the damage. I had better call Zvi right away.

* * *

"Zvi, Fatou!… have you heard?"

"The Lyauteyville foreign minister?"

"You know?"

"My colleague at the UN told me yesterday that the Libyans had gotten hold of his speech and were making changes. We tried to tell him, but he wouldn't listen. He didn't even review the speech before reading it at the podium. It's probably only after he read the line about Israel that he realized what he had just said to the General Assembly. He's the president's uncle. Nepotism is not known for putting emphasis on competence, you know. But don't worry about it."

"The wire services are already having a field day with this imbecility, Zvi, and you say 'don't worry about it?' After they mention his name and where he is from, everything else is Africa. To these people, it's not a Lyauteyville idiocy; it's an African one. 'Don't worry about it,' you say? Honestly, Zvi."

"OK, Fatou, as the Israeli ambassador to the United States, I'll issue a press release making your point. I'll do it right away. You know, this is such outrageous nonsense that we in Israel are not that affected by it. But the White House is not going to receive the Lyauteyville president next week, no matter what we say. We are not going to make this an issue, but others will. As you well know, our interest is to work in Africa; this may be the set back the Libyans intended. Speaking of the Libyans, how did your meeting go with Ambassador Sakeseba?"

"I didn't mention Maka Mgonu's possible Libyan connection to him, if that's what you mean. I didn't see the point. All that man sees is a foreign ministry carrot hanging in front of him. But as the saying goes, a fool and his ambition are soon parted. I am sorry to say that because I like him — I like him very much."

"That was a mistake Fatou; you should have told him."

"I disagree, Zvi. We would have unnecessarily compromised… what should I call it? And we are not a 100% sure of the Mgonu connection. I think we have more belief than analysis from our source at work here. I for one doubt that there is a working connection. That creature Mgonu, like poor Molu, is totally beholden to Motutu. One of the things that struck me in talking to him is the extent of his loyalty to Motutu. Even if I had told him, his fealty and ambition are such that he would only have shut his mind to doing any business with us. As it is, we now have an open channel to him."

"I think it's his funeral, Fatou. The Libyans are mounting an offensive of some kind. The Lyauteyville man's speech today confirms it. I left an urgent message to Sakeseba. I was going to tell him about Mgonu. He will call me when he returns from New York. Do I tell him about the Libyans?"

"No, don't tell him! We would lose him for sure if you tell him that. If I am wrong… well… his destiny will play itself out to the sordid end. If he is worthy, he will more than survive. Mandela he won't be, but who is asking for another miracle?"

"Even Moses needed some help, Fatou."

"You told me Moses was a myth."

"For a seventy-eight year old work horse, you have quite a memory! I was going to say elephant memory but I didn't want to offend you."

"Thank you! I'll call you before leaving New York."

"Look, why don't you come to Washington? Katy asked about you, and if I tell her that I did not ask you… well, you know. Come down at the end of the session; you'll do *Shabbat* with us. I'll invite whomever you want — what about that World Bank director you've been trying to see? And I owe the wife of the vice-president a return invitation. You could invite her to come to Dakar. She would stay with

Daoud's wife. That would be a nice touch. Just come down. One more thing, Martha is upstairs doing a project on Cheik Anta Diop; you could give her some pointers."

"What about the director of McDonald's franchising? Could you invite him, too?

"McDonald's?"

"You remember the one on Avenue de la Paix? I was in Paris recently and had breakfast there, espresso and brioche. The best I ever had. I would like to invite McDonald's to open a stand in Senegal."

"Are you alright, Fatou?"

"Can you get him or her?"

"Well, if I cannot bring Moses to the mountain, I'll bring the mountain to Moses."

"It's Mohamed, Peace Upon Him."

"Right!"

"Let me know."

"Alright — I'll have Katy call you."

---

Molu had hurried back to his office in Washington, after his secretary had phoned to tell him the Dictator wanted him to call.

"His secretary said you should use a secure phone," Marie said.

"Secure phone?"

"Yes! And she said it twice."

Molu could have used the secure line at the UN's Kinshasa mission, but he was suspicious of the representative. The man had been Molu's colleague at the foreign ministry's North American Department in Kinshasa and was a known security service operative. He had made no secret of his resentment when the Dictator named Molu ambassador to Washington. He must have thrown a fit, Molu thought, when he heard I was the new foreign minister. He will be the first to go once I am installed, he promised himself. After a brief moment of indecision, he had written a note of regret to Fatou-Anne Cerusu and had flown back.

It was 5:30 p.m. in Washington, 10:30 p.m. in Kinshasa.

---

What could it be now? he mused, sitting at his desk, battling to compose himself before placing the call to Kinshasa. He could think of only the foreign minister position. Could something have gone wrong with that? Is it possible that the old man got one of his crony U.S. senators to rescind the Mosley appointment? That would mean rescinding the foreign ministry position as well. I am nothing if not an insecure optimist; he scolded himself, as he always did when anxiety was battering him.

He had never gotten used to the way secure phones distorted voices and was tempted to call Kinshasa on the regular line, but the Dictator had specified a secure phone. With reluctance, he activated the device, pushed the red button on the bulky equipment and waited. Almost instantly, he heard the loud distorted voice of the Dictator.

"Hello."

"Hello, Mr. President, this is Molu Sakeseba in Washington."

"In Washington? I thought you had gone to New York to attend the meeting of the UN General Assembly."

"I did, sir, but came back when my secretary phoned to tell me you wished to speak to me on the secure line."

"Why didn't you use the phone in New York? We have one there you know."

"Yes, sir…"

"You don't trust our man there?" the Dictator laughed. "You did what I would have done. In fact, I was expecting that you would—counting on your remembering how to interpret my directives. Now listen, I have a task for you, something that you have done for me before; nothing big, except that you have to leave Washington right away."

"Right away, Mr. President?"

"Listen!"

"Yes, sir."

"You are to assume your foreign minister duties in five days. I need you to stop in Abu Dhabi on your way here to arrange a front similar to the one in Antwerp. I am having some difficulty disposing of the Savimbi diamonds there, and I need an alternate as soon as possible. My situation is becoming precarious, Molu; my finances are in worse shape than the World Bank reported. But once you have set up shop the way you want at the ministry here, you can go back to Washington to take care of any unfinished business. Your replacement will not mind, I assure you."

"Who is the contact in Abu Dhabi, Mr. President?" Molu asked in a sobered voice.

Even through the voice-distorting mechanism of the secure phone, the Dictator could hear that Molu was unsettled.

"You don't know him; it's not anybody from the embassy. He is a Pakistani national who has a number of businesses in the souk, the largest one in artificial flowers — someone who has handled things for me very successfully in other places. He has proved more reliable and less greedy than Johan Van Kees. But stones are a special commodity, and I must secure his work. That's your assignment. Your going there will prove how serious I am about establishing relations there. And you will have to approve the operation, if I am going to trust him with stones. It will not take you more than three days. If your evaluation of him or of his operation is not positive or if you feel that security is weak, fly to my chalet in Geneva and await further instructions.

"Our situation is precarious, Molu. The Tutsis are taking advantage in the east. I do not exaggerate when I say that unless you are successful in this assignment, being foreign minister will not be worth the janitor's job. Do you understand?"

"I do, Mr. President."

"Good, I knew I could depend on you. Now, when you are through passport formalities, go to the Golden Class Club in the Abu Dhabi airport. Our man told me he would be there to meet you. He will drive you to his office to show you his ledgers and discuss procedures and logistics. If you feel good about this man — if your sense is that we can trust him — then you can fly to Sharjah up the coast to see the bank president there. Listen carefully to the offer, evaluate the bank; see if the president is a man we can do business with, financing the diamond exchange. Use your nose.

"He is to give you a check as a good will gesture. But if he doesn't, don't ask him for it, just abort and go to Geneva. Without the banker, we have no foothold there. And I am wary of the authorities; it's not Antwerp where we have many friends. The contacts arranged for me were at a low level, so I am asking you to be skittish; at the first hint of something wrong, leave. In any case, agree to nothing under 50 percent; but don't haggle over every carat — this is not Antwerp — and say that you will have to discuss their offer with me before proceeding to the delivery steps.

"He will invite you to feast on lamb mishoui. Decline! We don't want these people to think that we mix business with pleasure. If you have the check, fly to Al Fujayrah to see Sheikh Mustapha bin Omar at the Emirate bank. Unlike Antwerp, I'd like to have two bankers, with the option of using one or the other as necessary. Keep them guessing when and where I am laundering the stones.

This is not the most secure procedure, but it's the best I can devise now. A third banker would be better. Perhaps the Pakistani can help. If you have a positive sense of the man, mention bankers to him and take note of what he says. When you are through, fly to Cointrin International in Geneva. Our man there will have his driver meet you and take you to our bank to deposit the check. You are to brief our agent on every detail of what you accomplished in Abu Dhabi. It would be best that you not commit anything to paper. But if you have to, do so only after you have left the Emirates. I don't have to tell you why this security measure is necessary. And, of course, when you get here, you will brief me as well. Do you understand, Molu?"

"Yes, sir! I wrote all your instructions."

"*Ozali moto malamu*! Memorize the information and shred it."

"Yes, sir! When am I expected there, Mr. President?"

"Sunday evening."

"The day after tomorrow?"

"The day after tomorrow."

"That leaves me little time, Mr. President. If I had known, I would not have gone to New York. There is still a great deal to do before I assume my new duties."

"I understand; but as I have made clear, this is an urgent matter. Once this assignment is completed, you can return to Washington. One more point, Molu. Use your regular passport for this trip; a diplomatic one may only serve to broadcast your visit. In any case, entry formalities are a simple affair in Abu Dhabi."

———  ———  ———

The security chief asked, "Why Geneva?"

"Maka, I am beginning to think you are losing your wits. Unless he is debriefed on the way here, how do I get the Abu Dhabi information from him?"

Not understanding, the security chief stared with a puzzled look.

"Tell me this, Maka. When Molu arrives in Kinshasa, what will you do with him?" the Dictator asked.

"I will have him brought to your library here, Mokonzi."

"Directly! Correct?"

"Correct!"

"And what do you think I will do? Wait for him to give me the Abu Dhabi information ?"

"No, of course not. You are sending him to the hospital, a cripple! You're saying that unless he is debriefed in Geneva, the Abu Dhabi information will be lost."

"That's right! I must be losing my wits too; I almost forgot to tell him to go to Geneva," the Dictator said sotto voce, getting up to go to his urinal.

———  ———  ———

Molu went to the window and peered into the distance. Does anyone ever think straight when chaos rules? he asked himself. He called his wife at the hospital. But she had already left for the day. I won't tell her about Abu Dhabi, he decided. That would cause her to worry, and I don't need any more confusion now. But she will still worry; she is an avid newspaper reader.

Unless the situation stabilizes, I won't have a country to represent, and foreign minister will be a frivolous title. Without doubt, the first task is to come up with some kind of arrangement with the Tutsi power. But if the situation is as dire as the old man says, doesn't it make sense to make an adjustment on the ground? Was the president saying that conditions had reached a point beyond face saving arrangements? If that is so, why is he saying once I have established myself at the ministry, I can come back to Washington to take care of any unfinished business? Doesn't he need his foreign minister in Kinshasa to help him manage the situation?

He went to his secretary's desk to look for the number of the Senegalese mission in New York. The Rolodex was crammed with numbers and addresses dating back to the first secretary who had sat behind the desk, but the number he wanted was not there. He called his residence; Nef would know how to get the number. When she came to the phone, "*bokilo, pesá ngái*… the telephone number of the Senegalese mission in New York, how do I find it?"

"How long have you been in this country?"

"Nef, not now, please!"

"I thought you were going to tell me that you are an ambassador, not a secretary."

"I am a foreign minister now."

"Even the president of the United States knows to call information when he needs a number."

"What is their number?"

"411. Mom wants to talk to you."

"I can't talk to her now. I'll call back."

"Oh boy!"

"Thank you!"

Had he known that tracking down Minister Cerusu would be such an elaborate affair, he would not have started the search. After multiple calls to New York and Washington, and one to the minister's daughter in Paris, Molu finally reached Fatou-Anne at the residence of the Israeli ambassador in Washington.

"I am terribly sorry to disturb you, Madame Minister. I talked to my president a few minutes ago… without going into details, I'd very much appreciate it if you'd arrange a consultation for me with the Rwandan ambassador here. I was close to the former ambassador; but since our disagreement several years ago, I have not had any contact with the representative of the new power in Rwanda."

"You mean tonight?"

"If possible, yes."

"I understand that you have met the Israeli ambassador; he would be in a better position to do what you ask. He works in this town."

"This is an African matter, Minister. I only need an intermediary introduction."

"I see! Give me a number where I can reach you."

"Thank you."

———  ———  ———

Molu settled at his desk for what he expected would be a long wait. On his pad, he scribbled some observations in preparation for his talk with the Rwandan. After no more than a few generalities, he concluded that he had nothing concrete to say. At least, I will tell her that as the new foreign minister I intend to do all in my power to make up for past misunderstandings. It's not much! She might hang up on me when I say that, he was concluding, when the phone rang.

"I am sorry, she will not talk to you," Minister Cerusu said without preamble. "I am not sure I should tell you this; I don't want to exacerbate an already unfavorable situation, I have seldom heard such bitterness. Things are too raw for talk, I suppose. After what has happened…"

"Could the Israeli ambassador arrange it?"

"I thought about that, and I asked her. The answer is the same. I gather talking to her is your idea, and I told her that. May I make a suggestion?"

"Please!"

"When you get to Kinshasa, cease all, and I mean all activities against the Banyamulenge Tutsi people in the east. If your president refuses to go along, resign — and Mr. Minister, get out of there at the first opportunity — you have a family."

"Thank you."

"Good luck."

Molu stared at the ceiling, stunned. I should not have gone that route, he thought; it was a terrible blunder. That's what you get for being an impulsive fool. Thank God the minister told the Rwandan the request was my idea. If she had said it was the old man's… Pensive, Molu paced the length of his office. What do I do now? After a few minutes, he walked to his desk and called Marcellus Garinaldi. The voice-mail answered. He asked his friend to call him at home regardless of the hour. He then buzzed his driver and turned off the lamp on his desk.

At home he found his wife in bed, reading, waiting for him. "Have you had dinner?" she asked, when he came into the bedroom.

"I am not hungry. Don't worry. I spoke to the president this evening," he told her, taking off his jacket. "He wants me to leave Washington early."

"Early? Why?"

"Because he wants me to stop in Brussels to talk to the bankers."

"Bankers in Brussels?" she sneered. "You have been independent for more than three decades and you still go to the *colons* for your coins."

"Please don't start. First Nef and now you."

"It was just a reminder," she answered, hearing the frustration under his voice. "How was New York? Did you see Minister Cerusu?"

"Uh, huh."

"Well?"

"One day I'll write a book about her; I have never talked to someone as wise as that woman. If Africa were a union, she would be the president."

"Not Mandela? Wow! I'd like to meet her."

"I talked to her about an hour ago. Guess where she was?"

"At her hotel in New York! It's late!"

"You'll never guess. She was at the residence of the Israeli ambassador!"

"The Israelis! What does that mean?"

"I wish I knew!"

"But why did you talk to her there? What's the connection?"

"The president told me that the Tutsi power was taking advantage of his financial difficulty. And — you know what an impulsive fool I am — I thought that the old woman could arrange a parley for me with the Rwandan ambassador here. So after going around the world, starting with Nef, I finally reached her at the Israeli's. I couldn't very well ask her what she was doing there. Maybe she had gone there to make up for what the Lyauteyville foreign minister said about Israel this morning at the UN."

"Yeah, I heard! There is no hope for you people!"

"You people? You people? That's where Nef gets her attitude from — the Rwandan ambassador told Minister Cerusu no; she will not talk to me."

"She wouldn't talk to you? Wow!"

"That's what I said!"

"What are you going to do?"

"I don't have a clue! Minister Cerusu suggested that when I get to Kinshasa, I should cease all activities against the Banyamulenge in the east. But that's not up to me. That's a decision for the president."

"It may be too late anyway. Hasn't he killed them all?"

"No, he hasn't killed them all. Anyway, they are an ally of the Tutsi power that's rampaging in the east."

"You have been in Washington for eight years; you don't know what the situation on the ground is. Reading reports is not the same as being a participant. Once you get to Kinshasa, you will have to ascertain for yourself what the situation is really like."

"Don't you think I know that?"

---

Molu's private phone rang. "It must be Marcel, I asked him to call me here. I'll take it in the study."

"Remember it's late."

"It's always late!" he muttered, walking out of the room.

"Hi Marcel! Yeah! I saw the Libyans smiling broadly when he said it. But that's not why I called you. Let me put it this way — I don't mean to be dramatic — we have reached a major turn in our existence as an independent country. I need your help."

"I don't think we should discuss sensitive information on the phone," Garinaldi said. "How about meeting at the usual place tomorrow."

"Earlier this evening, the old man asked me to leave early. I am going the day after tomorrow. Couldn't you come to the residence tonight? I really need your help."

"OK! But it will take me forty-five minutes to get to McLean from the Washington ghetto."

"The Gold Coast is now a ghetto?"

"How long have you been in this country?"

"Never mind! Come when you can; I have all night."

# Chapter 12

The Israeli ambassador stood next to Minister Cerusu, listening to her talk to the Rwandan ambassador. When she was about to hang up, he whispered, "Why don't you invite her over?"

Covering the mouthpiece, she answered, "It's your residence, Zvi."

"Ambassador, the Israeli ambassador would like to speak with you," the minister told the Rwandan.

"The Israeli ambassador?" she asked dumfounded.

"Yes! He is an old friend. I came down from the General Assembly meeting to see him. He wants to say a few words."

"Does this have anything to do with what the Lyauteyville foreign minister —"

"I'll let him tell you."

"Good evening, Madame Ambassador, this is Zvi Ben Nun."

"Good evening! Shalom!"

"Shalom Alakem! I could not help hearing Fatou's conversation with you. May I make a suggestion?"

"Mr. Ambassador, our bureau in New York issued a press release, denouncing what was said about Israel this morning at the General Assembly."

"Thank you! But it's not about that."

"It is to talk to Molu Sakeseba, then. The answer is the same, no! As much as I would like to accommodate someone whose country's surgeons were of such great help to us and with whom I have much in common, it is no. We don't discuss genocide. We try to stop it."

"Of course! But that's not what I was going to suggest either. I wanted to invite you to my residence here."

"Tonight?"

"Yes, I'll send a car."

"What is the purpose of your invitation, Mr. Ambassador? I don't understand."

"I want to take the opportunity of Minister Cerusu's visit to discuss my country's position regarding the situation in the Great Lakes region."

After a long moment of what he assumed was hesitation, she said, "What is the address?"

The Israeli gave it to her.

"I'll be over in my car. You will inform your protective service of my arrival?" she asked.

"I will meet you at the gate personally."

"Thank you."

———

"I think we can do business with her, Fatou," the Israeli said, enthusiastic after hanging up.

"I think so too. But what are you going to tell her, when she gets here? This is not going to be a discourse on genocide, is it?"

"And why not? Is there enough *Shoah* awareness in the world? Since when?"

"I am sick of awareness Zvi! People talk about awareness only after extermination has taken place. Or, haven't you noticed? You should instead devise a way for people to identify with others, a way to put themselves in somebody else's skin. How about that? Since man is not predisposed to suicide, that might work. Awareness hasn't."

"Man is prone to commit suicide and more, Fatou, and not always through ignorance. When that blood lust is on him, he kills all life. But I don't envisage broaching the subject with the Rwandan ambassador unless she brings it up. I want to share with her my sense of Sakeseba. The fact that Rwanda can do business with him. Her country is too small to take on a giant like Kinshasa. They need someone there they can do business with. That's Sakeseba."

———

She came alone. The Israeli secret service officer at the gate checked her identification, searched her car, and then informed the residence that the Rwandan ambassador had arrived. The Israeli ambassador, accompanied by two guards, hurried to meet his guest. He walked with her in silence to the residence and into the living room, where Minister Cerusu and his wife waited. The Israelis greeted their new guest formally. She insisted on an embrace from the Senegalese minister and sat down next to Mrs. Ben Nun opposite the Israeli ambassador and the Senegalese minister, who sat on a sofa beneath an oil of a Jerusalem panorama.

Minister Cerusu noticed her friend staring at his new guest. She lowered her head and said for his ears only, "You are staring, Zvi."

"Oh, I am sorry," he said when he heard, as if awaking from a dream. "Please excuse me. Looking at you, Madame Ambassador my mind digressed to the argument about what Pharaonic Egyptians looked like... you are in every museum in the world and on every tomb wall in Egypt. But I am not telling you anything you have not heard before. Again I apologize for staring."

"His mind is prone to wander, and at the least opportune time," the ambassador's wife said gently. "I have had to apologize for him more than a few times."

The butler came in to take the new guest's order.

"I am not offended at all. I saw the 1950 movie, *King Solomon's Mine*, in which there is also mention of Tutsi cattle painted on tomb walls in Egypt. And yes, I have heard of the Nefertiti look. Morphotypically, I suppose it's possible. Why not? So what if she was a Batutsi? Whatever ethnic group she belonged to, she was African. As you well know, the people we call Egyptian called their land, Kemet, the Black Land. Only doctrinaires imagine that Egypt evolved in a regional and racial vacuum.

"And since I am in a beth Israel, let me add that I have also read that Batutsis are descended from the Jewish tribes of Dan and Judah. Mr. Ambassador, there is almost as much nonsense told about my ethnic group as there is about the Jews. And just as with the Jews, the nonsense was used for extermination purposes. Everything, in fact, was used to differentiate us, to turn us into the 'other,' if you see what I mean. Once a group becomes an 'other,' the next act follows. It's an axiom." She had made a quotation mark with her fingers, at *other*.

"There are few autochthonous inhabitants left in the world. In the case of a Lilliputian area called Rwanda, the Twa is the aboriginal occupant. Both the Batutsis and the Hutus migrated from somewhere else to settle in the Twa's area. Need I tell you that over the centuries we have intermarried, Twa, Hutu and Batutsi? No! Whatever we were before we arrived in Rwanda, we are all Bantus now, speakers of the *Kinyarwanda* tongue.

"But *otherism* had its way with the Batutsi, and an issue was made of his non-autochthonous status. Colonialism is responsible for this. Colonialism continues to govern our lives, taking Africa from the Africans. That's the real crime against humanity. Until we are rid of its foulness, Africa will keep on suffering. You have not seen the last attempt at extermination on the continent."

"You said colonialism?" Minister Cerusu asked, wanting to hear from the Rwandan ambassador a better articulated, less acrimonious view of a question close to her heart.

"Yes, colonialism! Africa's curse!… first the church, which is as inseparable to the Belgian colonial order as ink from paper. Then the French assumed the colonial mantle and made Hutu nationalism acceptable. Ethnic cleansing of the Batutsi is a by-product of that nationalism."

Katy Ben Nun noticed Minister Cerusu looking at the ceiling in disgust. She hurried to ask a question of the Rwandan before her friend began one of her famous monologues about accepting one's responsibilities.

"Why would the French be involved?" she asked.

"That's the question! But only a forensic psychiatrist can answer that precisely. Whatever the answer is, it is the source of our sorrow. France's neocolonial policy in Africa is to maintain what it believes is a balance between the territories carved by the British and those created by France and Belgium. France, for example, sought the dismemberment of English speaking Nigeria, to decrease its influence in West Africa, where lie most of the former French colonies.

"With some variations, the policy was replicated in the Great Lakes region. English speaking Uganda was France's target because of the large number of Batutsi refugees who had fled there following various periods of slaughter. To counter a Batutsi Anglophone influence, the French expanded their support of the Hutus with defense treaties. We have had slaughters from both sides over the years. But a 'final solution?' It was colonialism that provided that option."

"You spoke of the Twa. Who are they?" Mrs. Ben-Nun asked. "Until you mentioned them, I had never heard of them."

"The Batwa, the Twa people, are an ethnic group very much like the Bambuti, the Pygmies of northeastern Congo. Over the centuries, they became part of the area's racial *mélange*. Figures I have seen put what remains of them at just above 1 percent of the Rwandan population. I don't believe they number more than thirty-five thousand. At one point, they sided with the Batutsis against the Hutus and suffered accordingly. The 1994 one hundred-day holocaust affected them particularly hard. More than any other group in our country — a fourth of them lost their lives."

"Where does Kinshasa fit in this 'colonial' equation?" The Israeli ambassador asked, beginning a line of questions he hoped would lead to a discussion about Molu Sakeseba.

The Rwanda ambassador laughed. "As a famous playwright wrote, 'the Kinshasa Dictator is a 'pimp.'"

"My husband tends to overstate his descriptions," Minister Cerusu replied caustically.

"But he has described Motutu correctly," the Rwandan said. "But to answer Ambassador Ben Nun's question: Kinshasa was an intermediary that fed the killing machine — almost a million died. But Motutu's days are numbered. There is a race to see who will pull his plug first: our forces or ill health. I believe we'll both get him at the same time. Doctors in Geneva tell us that he lives on borrowed time."

"That's one of the things I wanted to talk to you about," the Israeli ambassador said softly. "Fatou — Minister Cerusu and I agree that you should give Molu Sakeseba a look."

"Mr. Ambassador, we distrust everyone from the Motutu regime. Everyone!"

"Please listen," Minister Cerusu intervened. "He is not of the same cast of mind as Motutu. I had a long discussion with him in New York. He is naïve. Do you know what he wanted to see me about? A way to eliminate corruption from his ministry. But he is upright, and I believe that with his intelligence and level of energy he can play a constructive role. At some point you will need an intervener, someone with whom you can treat, unless you plan to govern Kinshasa yourselves. And as important, you will need someone who has the interest of the region at heart because he understands that it is the only way his country can come through all the disasters of the past few years. If you lack such a person, France or some other foreign power will impose someone whose hands may not be as clean — certainly someone who does not look at the region the same way! More than three million have perished. A million more are in line. I strongly advise you to consider Molu Sakeseba."

The Israeli lifted a hand. "I am an outsider. But that does not mean I have no stake in what unfolds there. *Tikkun olam* dedicates us to repairing the world. And our borders are not that far away. Not today! My country wants to make a contribution — play an instrumental role. When he was named foreign minister, Sakeseba called me to say that he wanted our development assistance. He was very open. I wanted to pass that on to you. I want all the cards on the table. You should be informed.

"I agree with Minister Cerusu that someone like him should be allowed a role. What we say here this late evening does not obligate you to anything, anything at all. But perhaps you will pass on what we said to your government. Will you also tell them of his attempt to contact you? Personally, I fear for him. When things are falling apart like they are in Kinshasa now, the innocents are carried away with the guilty."

"Anyone can easily turn development assistance into weapons, Mr. Ambassador, said the Rwandan. On a regular basis medical supplies are sold to purchase Kalashnikovs. This is a moribund, desperate regime inclined to all manner of evil. But yes, I will tell my government what both of you said this evening. And that ambassador — foreign minister, Sakeseba wanted to talk to me. I gather he doesn't know of your demarche?"

"No, he does not know," Minister Cerusu said. "He asked only that I contact you on his behalf. I am sorry you could not accommodate him. But yes, this evening is our idea."

In her car, the Rwandan ambassador reflected on the evening. I can't believe it, those two outmaneuvered me, manipulated me — the Rwandan thought angrily while pulling out of the residence's parking lot. They even threatened me! Oh, they were polite about it — 'perhaps you will pass on what we said to your government. Will you also tell them of his attempt to contact you?' If I don't tell Kigali about their demarche, they'll find a way to do it for me, making me look irresponsible. What choice do I have now? I have to see Sakeseba — get that out of the way.

"So what do you think?" the Israeli ambassador asked.

"If they are all like her, he doesn't stand a chance," Minister Cerusu answered.

"Who?"

"The Kinshasa dictator. What about you Kat? How do you see her?"

"She is bright and she is ambitious. In a few years, she'll be the first African woman president."

"I hope not," the minister said, her voice deeper. "The last thing we need is another heartless president. Something about her temperament bothered me. She is too detached, too mechanical. So much so that she reminded me of the saying about bacon and eggs. For the bacon, the pig is committed; but for the egg, the chicken is only involved. She is the chicken."

"Bacon and eggs? I don't know what you are talking about. I think she is too full of herself," the Israeli ambassador reflected, kneading his empty glass, a sign he wanted it refilled. "Talking to her on the phone, I thought she would be someone we could work with. But now, I think Fatou is right. She is like Sakeseba, but without a heart."

"Without a heart, what vision can you have?" Minister Cerusu asked him. "Did you notice that she said nothing about putting an end to the slaughter? Wouldn't that be a priority? For me it was striking she mentioned nothing of the ongoing death in the jungle and camps. Maybe that was her way of telling us something about the objective of her government."

"Do you think they intend to pursue the war? To what end?" the Israeli ambassador asked.

It was his wife who answered, "To create a buffer between themselves and Kinshasa. What else?"

"You noticed she didn't respond to my question regarding governing in Kinshasa," Minister Cerusu said. "They may have more than a buffer in mind… or the buffer together with somebody to replace Motutu."

"Who?"

"It could be a number of people. He has been there over three decades and has had plenty of time to make many enemies."

"But who in particular?"

"There is this warlord, Jean-Luc Nundu, whom central casting would classify as a gangster — the Americans like him. Now if you'd excuse me, I'm going to bed. The last time I stayed up this late —"

"You still want to be up at six?"

"I don't know that I have a choice."

# Chapter 13

Garinaldi arrived at Ambassador Sakeseba's residence in forty minutes. "What's so urgent that it couldn't wait 'til tomorrow?" Marcel said. "I had to give a 'yes sir' to a cop from West Virginia. Did you ever see a deputy that didn't have a fat ass? Ever since I read *The Grapes of Wrath*, I've been asking that question. I missed the exit and then took a wrong turn. A patrol car flagged me. You know the routine for a black man around here after midnight. This is not the first time they've stopped me in this area. I pulled to the side of the road and waited eight minutes for the cop to get out of his car. I was rushing to get here, so I said, 'Yes, sir.' He told me I was too old to drive in what he considered a reckless manner. I was glad I was driving the Volvo. Had I been in my old BMW, I most likely would have spent a couple of hours, if not the night, at the police station. A black man in a BMW — drugs."

"I am sorry you had to go through that. They know us and our cars. They don't stop us anymore; I have diplomatic plates. But what would you like to drink?"

"The usual. Now, what's so urgent that I had to come here tonight to be reminded that the U.S. is the only country in the world where profiling is a sport. Do you know how many security clearances I have?"

"Many. I can only guess. You need a clearance for permission to go to the bathroom from what I understand of your procedures. Look, I talked to the old man earlier this evening. He wants me to leave early for Kinshasa."

"Why? What's up?"

Molu lowered his voice. "Remember, our diamond concern in Antwerp? I told you about it. I set it up eight years ago on my way here. The old man wants me to set up a similar operation in Abu Dhabi. I didn't want Ella to know. I told her I had to make a stop in Brussels."

"What do you know about the Abu Dhabi diamond market?" Marcellus asked.

"I am just a mediator, Marcel. My job is only to ascertain the trustworthiness of the people who will handle the stones for the old man."

"Molu, this doesn't make sense! I can understand Antwerp — not that I approve — you know the place — But Abu Dhabi? That's a new world for you. It's like setting up a *comptoire* on the moon."

"Look — take it easy — what I told you is for your ears only. I am not handling the stones myself. Not even in Antwerp did I see the stones!"

"If it's the U.S. government you are referring to, don't worry; they'd think I'd lost my mind, if I told someone what you were up to."

"OK! Now to business. I have a job for you."

"Diamonds! Didn't you hear what I just said? And what do I know about diamonds?"

"No," Molu laughed, putting a hand on his friend's shoulder. "It's much more prosaic than that. I have big plans for the foreign ministry. I want to create a working institution, Marcel, one that will do real work. The country is sliding into chaos, and the factotums are passing out jobs like in the old days. I won't get to first base with these bureaucrats. No, for the country to survive, and for my title to have real meaning, I need someone there I can trust to help me run the ministry. Someone beholden to no one but me. No obligation to third cousins no one knew ever existed. No bribery. No cash. Nepotism is the lead in the hold of a sinking ship."

"Nepotism is not the only weight countries like yours carry, Molu. If you succeeded in plugging every hole in that ship, you would not make it sea worthy.

"I know! But that's where I can make a start."

"Molu," Garinaldi said exasperated. "I would think that administrative trivia would be the last thing on your mind right now. The Tutsis control your eastern region and giving no sign they intend to stop there. Your focus should be on that. Administrative —"

"I tried to make contact with the Tutsi power through the Rwandan ambassador. She refuses to talk to me."

"They don't have to talk to you — they hold all the cards. You will have to do much more than make telephone calls. I have no evidence that your president is serious about coming to terms with the Tutsis. He seems to think they are just an inconvenience. He is still carrying water for the French. How does that help? Somebody had better tell him the Tutsis are not going away! Somebody has to prevail on him that he has very little time.

"That's your job. You are the foreign minister. Instead of going to Abu Dhabi to launder diamonds, you should go to Kigali or wherever to sign a cease fire. Think Molu! If you were president, what would you do?"

"I am not president, Marcel. I am only the foreign minister. Right now I am trying to enlist a deputy — you— so that I can do what he recommends. It's because the situation is dire that I need your help.

Your friend Minister Cerusu told me what you just said. But it's like saying, 'there is nothing to be done. Don't even try.'

"Maybe you didn't hear me, so I'll say it again: we are going under, Marcel. Telling me that we made every mistake known to man, and the devil doesn't change that. The old man has given me the opportunity to do something about those mistakes. I want you to come with me, man! I want you to be my deputy."

Garinaldi gaped at his friend. After a while, he said slowly, his palms in prayer, "How can I be anyone's deputy in a country other than the United States, Molu? You are not making sense this evening. Get hold of yourself and think things through. I can help you think out of the box. I am good at that. We can even go to a think tank in Washington for research and advice."

"Fine, we'll go to a think tank — when we have the time. I spoke to the old man about bringing you in. He understands and thinks it's a superb idea. I even spoke to your friend Minister Cerusu about it. She also thinks it's a capital idea."

Incredulous, Garinaldi gaped at Molu.

"I have no one in Kinshasa I can trust," Molu pleaded. "God knows I need someone, if I am going to make the changes that you, yourself, told me have to be made. I cannot do it by myself. You told me that too!"

"I think I understand why such an arrangement would be attractive, Molu. There would be no pressures on me to meet social or political expectations. But have you considered the level of resentment a foreigner would incite in such a position over there? The whole structure — those third cousins who stand outside the door of the foreign ministry would be incensed and murderous. You may not remember the guy who was your president's right hand man in the '70s, Bisengimana Qwema. A foreigner. He didn't last. How long would I last? Come on! I'd be too scared even to consider such an offer. Especially where it's getting to the juncture when it's every man for himself."

"Yes, I remember Bisengimana Qwema. He was the old man's chief of staff, a Tutsi. That's why he didn't last. An American would be different. I didn't think I would have to say this — having an American there would enhance our image, and —

"Wait a minute," Garinaldi interjected. "You think my appointment would give the impression the United States is standing behind Kinshasa? I am sorry, man, but one error will not compensate for another. The United States has turned the page on Kinshasa. That's why they are sending Mosley. The Tutsis are calling the shots in

Washington now. This White House is making up for eight-hundred thousand dead Tutsis. It's a guilt trip for a president who could not say 'genocide' in an election year." Garinaldi put a hand on his friend's shoulder. He was almost in tears. "I am sorry, man."

"The image idea was an afterthought, Marcel. It cannot hurt to give an impression that you have the superpower in your corner. I told you the reason I wanted you for my deputy. It's the truth! If having a retired American official burnishes an image, what's wrong with that?"

"Nothing, except that it won't work. And I don't know about this retirement thing — I was going to tell you. I have an offer to go to Burundi."

"What does that mean?"

They offered me Burundi."

"So?"

Garinaldi didn't answer.

"You? You who rage all the time against blacks being assigned to Africa on account of race. You're considering going to Burundi?"

Garinaldi looked at his friend in silence.

"It's a test," Molu said. "To shut you up. The minute you say, 'I take it.' They'll say, 'you fraud.' And they would be right."

"They haven't said that yet."

"You are serious? You're going to do this? You're not a fraud!"

"Well, I am considering it."

"Well, don't! There is the foreign ministry of the second largest country in Africa to run. And you wouldn't be a token there."

"You just told me I would be there for show, to give the idea that the U.S. is supporting Kinshasa."

"Oh, come on, Marcel! I told you it was an afterthought — an icing on the cake, you know."

"I was reading Frederick Douglass's autobiography the other night. He says that his appointment to the office of Minister Resident in Haiti was an honor. That inspired me. I thought, if such a person as Douglass could see it that way, who am I to discredit an appointment? Was Douglass a fraud?"

"I cannot answer that for you, Marcel. If you can live with yourself, subsidizing — what did you call it? a diversity-adverse system — by participating in it —"

"You don't understand."

"Isn't that what frauds always say, 'you don't understand?' Good night, Marcel. I still have much to do. Thank you for coming."

"Come on, Molu."

"Good night!"

"Sure!"

―――――――

Molu emptied his glass and walked back to the bedroom. His wife was still reading. "What are you reading?" he asked in the tone of voice he used when he wanted her to ask, 'what's wrong?' But she had her no nonsense face on, and she just looked at him, not in the mood to cater to his idiosyncrasies that night.

"Marcel is a fraud," he said, sitting at the foot of the bed to remove his shoes.

"A fraud? You mean he is not what he appears to be?"

"You remember telling me that I needed a deputy? Well I offered him the job. I even spoke to the president about it. He thought it was a superb idea. Minister Cerusu thought so too. But Marcel, he gives me a line about people being offended by a foreigner in that position."

"Well, that's true, isn't it?"

"Of course, it's true! But only to some extent. The rabble that passes for a bureaucracy in Kinshasa, of course, would resent having a foreigner for a deputy foreign minister, someone who is not a part of the patronage system. In that position a foreigner would mean the end of the system because the link between the bureaucracy and the man at the top would no longer exist. That's what I want. But that's not the only reason I want him for the job. He is an expert in foreign relations and public diplomacy. Having someone like that, not obligated to any person or any faction in Kinshasa, would help a great deal. He would help me take control of the events that are pulling us under."

"What does Marcel say?"

"That concerning myself with administrative matters at a time like this is frivolous. He doesn't understand. He tells me that the people he rails against have offered him the ambassadorship to Burundi. He is considering it. He was going to walk away, retire, fed up with his agency's policy of sending blacks to Africa on account of race. The guy is a fraud. I can't believe it, but it's true."

"What made him change his mind?"

"He tells me Frederick Douglass was appointed to Haiti."

"And that's why you are calling him a fraud?"

"They dangled a little carrot in front of him, and he fell in line. Isn't that what a fraud does?"

"And what did you do? Don't tell me! You ran. Instead of finding out what his needs are, how you can work this out, you got up the way you always do and walked out on him. If you lose him too, you lose your best friend. Did you stop to think that in the business you are in there is no one you trust the way you do Marcel? What are you going to do now?"

"What can I do? He is going to Bujumbura. When he said he is considering it, he means he has accepted. What can I do?"

"You can call him in the morning to apologize. Send him a note. Whatever! Something! Explain to him again why you need him in Kinshasa. Even if he goes to Burundi, have you thought that it is right next door to Kinshasa? He may help you from there. I don't imagine there is much to do in Bujumbura."

"OK, I'll call him… If I told you I were hopeful, I would be lying."

"It's too hot in May," Julie told her husband. "It's best I go next week."

"But Martiale will be here next week. How will it look if you are not here?"

"Another one I have to be especially nice to? Do you ever think how tired I get of this? Being especially nice to your associates?"

"Isn't that what wives do? And wasn't a transfer to Abu Dhabi your idea?

"Where is your brain?" she hissed, turning to face him. "If Kinshasa is as hazardous as that, why would you want Martiale to come here? Tell him that you'll fly to Paris to meet him at headquarters. And since you need to create in his mind a graphic correlation between how dangerous it is here and your request for a transfer, telling him that it is too risky to come to Kinshasa. God!"

"Why must you always refer to my brain every time we have a discussion? The hotel is the safest place in Africa; that gorilla Mgonu is there every day. He literally lives there."

"Aren't you the one who told me to be especially nice to him? I have noticed you don't say African. Why is that?"

"If you were white —"

"Here we go! I was wondering when we would get to that."

"I was only saying —"

"You were only saying that you were color-blind when you signed on the dotted line on the marriage license," she said in a tone empty from constant use.

"OK. OK. You go to Abu Dhabi next week, and I'll tell Martiale that it's best that I go to Paris to see him."

# Chapter 14

The security chief heard the telephone ringing. The select-ring system a German firm had installed in his office warned him it was Sakeseba's secretary on the line. Maka Mgonu, a mystification devotee, practiced answering the phone only after the fifth ring, maintaining that it served to disorient the caller, making it more likely that the person on the line would talk more readily, aiding in an interrogation when necessary.

"Hello!"

"This is Marie, Ambassador Sakeseba's secretary. I am sorry to disturb you. I found notes on the ambassador's desk when I came in this morning. I wanted you to know."

"Read them to me."

"Rwanda ambassador must know —"

"Are you sure?" he interrupted her.

"Yes, sir. I was reading from the notes."

"Very well, Marie. Proceed as before. Fax me the notes right away!"

"Yes, sir."

The security chief immediately called the Dictator on his private line. "I think we have the smoking gun, Mokonzi."

"What are you talking about, Maka?"

"A fax from Washington. Could you give me a couple of minutes."

"My next meeting is not until two. I am free until then."

---

Dutifully, at 6 p.m., the security chief's administrative assistant secured the special fax machine in his boss's office and ensured it was in good-working order. That afternoon, the chief asked him to check the equipment again. Marie's faxes always rolled off the machine within minutes of her calls, but ten minutes had elapsed, and the machine remained silent. He waited. On one of his training trips to the U.S., he had enrolled in a yoga breathing class. He did the ten long, ten shallow exercises the instructor had taught him to alleviate his anxiety, which now constantly coursed through his body, like a current.

He was sure that Marie had handed him Molu Sakeseba's head when she began reading from Molu's notes, and he berated himself for having interrupted her. Like a novice he had let his excitement at the gift being presented to him cloud his judgment. He waited. Meanwhile, he breathed ten long, ten shallow breaths. After another ten minutes, he called the Dictator's personal secretary to say he was delayed.

Since he had met her, the hotel manager's wife obsessed him and had turned his world into a maelstrom. At the PTT, Kinshasa's telephone company, one of his most reliable operatives, Soeur Angélique, a nun he had sequestered from the International Criminal Tribunal for the prosecution of persons responsible for the 1994 Rwandan genocide, was assigned to tap Julie's home phone. On one of the recordings, he thought he recognized Sakeseba's voice, but he was not certain. He was more eager to admit that it was Sakeseba's voice than he was willing to confess that Julie was having an affair with Sakeseba.

The machine had recorded a short conversation, ending with a muffled "I'll see you then." Julie clearly could be heard responding, "I need that."

Mgonu sought release from the incertitude the tape created by looking for more ways to be rid of Molu. The stress made him frantic. He had three times tried to explain to the Dictator the merit of finishing off the man he now called his rival. But he could not articulate his reasons convincingly enough to change the Dictator's mind. It would take a Molu Sakeseba to accomplish that. Nothing would deter the Dictator from making Molu a beggar — unless Mgonu could bring him the proof that Molu was conspiring with the Ugandans and the Tutsis to depose him. Only then would he order an outright elimination. Mgonu would never contemplate an unsanctioned assassination; he feared the Dictator's disapproval. What he sought was the statutory "proceed" from the Dictator's lips.

He called Soeur Angélique and instructed her to phone Marie in Washington for the status of the fax she had promised.

A moment later, Danielle, the Dictator's personal secretary, summoned him. "But the fax hasn't arrived yet…" Mgonu began to explain.

"Mokonzi said to come," the secretary told him curtly. "He wants to see you before his next appointment."

Mgonu knew not to quibble with Danielle. She had the ear of the Dictator, giving her license to loosen her cruel nature on whomever she disliked. She wore an aura of invincibility, which she exploited with harsh efficacy.

Before going to brush his teeth, a ritual preparation for meeting with the Dictator, Maka nodded to the administrative assistant. The man then rang the security chief's driver and his personal-security details for the short drive to the Dictator's residence.

"The fax hasn't arrived," he said when the Dictator came out of the lavatory. "I waited a few minutes. One of my people is still checking."

"What did she say that made you believe it was the smoking gun, Maka?" the Dictator asked, a towel in his hand.

"She said she had found notes on his desk. I asked her to read them to me. When she read, 'the Rwanda ambassador should know,' I stopped her to ask that she fax the notes at once."

"Rwanda ambassador? Is that all? It could mean anything."

"The secretary has been dependable… and the problem is not with the fax equipment. One of my people is checking to find out what happened."

"Rwanda ambassador," the Dictator repeated. "Could it mean that Molu is in contact… I need that fax."

"At least we know he is communicating with them."

"Do we? Unless we see his notes, it could mean anything. You must understand Maka, if we are wrong and have him killed outright the way you have been intimating, we miss a god-sent opportunity to demonstrate how far we are prepared to go. Besides being counterproductive, there is no sophistication in a direct execution, Maka. Not my style! No, Maka, he is infinitely more valuable to us alive. Now, if he is conspiring with the Tutsis against me, that's an entirely different matter."

"I understand, Mokonzi," the security chief said earnestly. "But the notes his secretary is faxing me are the closest thing we have to the proof he is involved with them. I understand that we lose something by not having him alive to use for the statement you want to make against the Mosley outrage. But why take a chance? It might be too risky."

The Dictator gazed at his security chief for a long while, assessing the desperation in the man's attitude toward Molu and wondering where he had gone wrong. "Didn't you tell me that making him move would destabilize his plans? Until we have your smoking gun, I am going with that. Between now and Thursday he will be traveling constantly. No, Maka, it's too risky to pass on the opportunity to show our enemies what kind of reprisal we are capable of. When Mosley comes out of his residence in the morning, I want the beggar, Molu Sakeseba, to be there to greet him.

"Let me ask, Maka. Are you afraid? Do you sometimes wonder what the future has in store for you if I am driven from office? Could you live in Kinshasa after all you have done to keep me in power these three decades? Remember what happened to Anastasio Somosa? I am asking these questions to remind you that unless we respond to the Mosley outrage with the retribution it deserves, we might as well shout from the rooftop of the tallest building that we have ceased to be of any account. And what good is telling our adversaries that we are finished? I will give no quarter; I expect none from the parasites who want to sit here. Is that clear, Maka? Is that clear?"

He began coughing and sat behind his desk. He noticed the red light on the signal panel underneath the desk: his secretary had an urgent message. At the first opportunity, he excused himself to his security chief and lifted the receiver.

"I think this is urgent, Mokonzi," the secretary told him. "Molu Sakeseba is on the line from Washington. He is angry. He said that unless he speaks with you he is not leaving Washington."

"Let me speak with him." He signaled to his security chief to pick up the earphone attached to the equipment.

Wanting to give the impression that he was in excellent humor, the Dictator shouted Molu's name when he came on the line. "MOLU! What has happened? Danielle tells me that you are angry — that you are not leaving Washington. Molu, really! One of the qualities that always impressed me about you is how calm you always are. Aren't you a Ngbandi, a kin?"

"Yes, sir."

"Well, we Ngbandi are deservedly known for our calm. You should learn to control yourself; an impulsive nature is a ticket to an early grave."

"Yes, I should, Mr. President. I tell myself that frequently. But how can I succeed when I find out that my secretary, my secretary Mr. President, informs on me directly to Maka Mgonu —"

"Wait a minute, Molu, what are you talking about?"

"Would you like to speak to my secretary, Mr. President?"

"Molu! Your tone! You forget yourself."

"I am sorry, Mr. President, I mean no disrespect."

"Tell me what happened."

"Yes sir! Because I have so much to do before my departure for Abu Dhabi, I came to the office earlier than usual. I looked for my secretary and found her making copies of notes I had left on my desk last night. She told me that she was acting under instructions from Maka Mgonu himself. When I leave notes on my desk, she calls him, and he gives her instructions to fax the notes to him. She has been doing that ever since she arrived here."

"Molu, this is my fault. After Nkondo sold the embassy and pocketed the proceeds, I asked the Diplomatic Security Service to monitor my ambassadors. It never occurred to me they would include you. They are not known for their wits over there. I am sorry! This is a bureaucratic mishap, nothing more. They probably file what your secretary sends them and forget about it. Maybe they throw it in the trash can. I have never seen your notes."

"But, Mr. President, she reports to Mgonu directly."

"Oh, I don't know. It's possible that she calls; and when the phone rings, he answers if he is nearby. How can it be more than that? They are somewhat informal over there, you know. But let me ask you this: what are you doing leaving notes on your desk at night, Molu? That's where the breach of security is! We are lucky it was only your secretary who forwarded your notes to the security service. Whom should I censor, Molu? My security service, your secretary or you? I hope you will not continue this practice when you have assumed your functions here. That kind of transgression is unacceptable, Molu."

The Dictator heard silence at the other end and smiled. His tone fatherly now, he wished Molu a good trip to Abu Dhabi, Geneva and Kinshasa.

"I have placed a special order for our favorite fresh palm wine to welcome you home and for the ablution. We will drive together to your office, to perform the ceremony in front of your desk. Together we will call on our Ngbandi ancestors to remember their promise to us."

"Thank you, Mokonzi. That is thoughtful of you."

The Dictator slowly replaced the receiver and looked at his security chief. "There are places where such incompetence is a criminal offense — but at least we know what happened to your fax."

"I am to blame; I didn't follow procedure, rushing the operation. I should have listened to all she was saying before asking for the fax of Sakeseba's notes. I admit that she didn't behave very competently when she was discovered. Our people are usually quicker on their feet."

"Yes, but we have the answer to what was preoccupying us. And Molu has no idea we are on to him. That's clear! Not forewarned is not forearmed. Fine!"

"Pardon me, Mokonzi, but we still don't know for sure what his plans are."

"Yes we do! He is flying to Abu Dhabi, Geneva, and then to Kinshasa. His call puts to rest any doubt there might have been about that. Now, Maka, I hope the men you have picked to keep him boxed in when he gets here are better prepared than that secretary."

"I have vetted all of them personally, Mokonzi," Maka said, his voice dreary from depression. They have even rehearsed how they will keep him in that street. One of the men will carry a vial of morphine in case it becomes necessary to drug him."

"That man should be careful; I don't want Molu so drugged up he is not conscious. What about the journalist?"

"Once he is on the street, the journalist will be told to go see him. Two of our photographers will go with him."

"*Ambassador now Beggar on Kinshasa Street* will be the headline, right?"

"Right! As soon as he is on the street, we'll notify the media, TV, papers and the tabloids."

"Do any of them know who it is I am sending over?"

"No!"

"Until he gets here, keep a tight lid on this operation. Don't let your guard down. On your way out, ask Danielle to come in."

Danielle didn't go in immediately. She gave the Dictator a few minutes to use the lavatory and wipe his face that was these days always drenched in sweat following his use of the urinal. After ten minutes, she went in without knocking. The Dictator was about to sit behind the Louis XVI desk.

"Well?" he asked.

Taking a small tape from her pocket, she walked behind the desk, bent over, and pulled out the second drawer from which she lifted a small portable player; she fitted the tape in. Without a word, she placed the machine on the desk in front of her boss, pointing at the play button as she did so. When she had left him, the Dictator pressed the button. After a few seconds of static, he heard Molu Sakeseba's voice. "Hello, good afternoon. May I speak to the lady of the house, please."

"It's me you fool," a sardonically accented voice answered.

"Julie, my love, how are you?"

"Troubled! I miss you like you are the only person on earth. If that isn't enough, that creep, Maka Mgonu, shows up every place I go. That man should be in an insane asylum or a cage."

"Has he bothered you?"

"No! It would be easier if he did. He hardly says a word. He just looks at me from behind his dark glasses — he shadows me everywhere I go. Him or his people. It's the worst situation I have been in. My simpleton husband thinks it's a good thing to have the security chief watch the hotel and the house in these troubled times. But it's hell!"

"Listen, my love! I have to be in Abu Dhabi in a few days. Meet me there."

"In Abu Dhabi?"

"Yes, there we can discuss our future… and I need to see you… we'll have three days."

"I'm dying to see you… wouldn't it be better to meet in Juan Les Pins, you know. Three days? I will tell my husband that I am leaving him. Have you told your wife yet?"

"No, not yet! It has to be Abu Dhabi; I won't be able to go back to Juan Les Pins for a while. Abu Dhabi gives us the place we need to discuss what we are going to do."

"I understand! I'll find a way to get to Abu Dhabi. Give me —"

The Dictator pressed the stop button, shutting off the machine. He had heard enough. "So that's what it is!" He murmured to himself. But his delight at being privy to such gossip was fraught with worry. Maka is enthralled! he told himself. That's a terrible thing for any man! And for me! Without a functioning Maka, I have no fortifications. Molu is just doing what men who have it easy with women do.

That Julie must be an imbecile. Maybe that fool is considering leaving his wife and children. If only I had the power to make Julie respond to Maka's boorish advances!

Should I eliminate her? That would solve the problem with one simple blow. I would not hesitate if I were sure Maka would not suspect me. A bewitched man is as unpredictable as a mamba.

But it may be the only way. It's clear he knows or suspects that Molu is involved with this woman; that's why he wants to spit on his grave. How long before he knows about this Abu Dhabi tryst?

Soeur Angélique is a most discerning woman for bringing this matter to my attention. I need Molu to open Abu Dhabi for me. And I need Molu, the beggar, even more, to make my enemies cry 'ruthless' every time they pronounce my name. I need that fool!

If Maka gets a whiff of this woman's plan to meet Molu in Abu Dhabi, I'll have to remove him at once. I don't have a choice.

The nun would handle Maka for me. How many did she kill in the Rwanda rampage? That a woman can wield a machete for days like that — unbelievable!

Who then would I get to be my security chief? The impressive nun? That may be too brazen! But foul times call for foul measures.

# Chapter 15

When she sat down at the small round table where Molu had been waiting, the Rwandan ambassador took a handkerchief from her elegant handbag and blew her nose exhaustively. She then focused, with undisguised animosity, her eyes on Kinshasa's new foreign minister. Her look was so full of reproach that Molu felt it — actually felt it — as he would a flame.

In her clipped masculine voice, she began, "I called you because you got me boxed in by two old pros who made me promise that I'd tell my government of your effort to contact me. My only reason for seeing you —" She paused impatiently when the waiter brought the double espresso she had ordered when she came in.

"I am sorry, but it was imperative that I speak with you," Molu said, the moment the waiter had turned his back, eager to placate the European mannered Rwandan woman sitting across from him.

When his deputy, who was sitting in for his fired secretary, told him that the Rwandan ambassador was calling, he could not believe his ears. He invited her to his office, but when there was only silence, he offered to go to her embassy. No answer to that suggestion either. Finally, sounding exasperated, the Rwandan told him in her clipped voice that she would be at the Starbucks on Seventh Street, in Chinatown, at 11:30 that morning. If he wanted to talk to her, he had better be there at that time. His driver had rushed him to Chinatown. Arriving early, he had ordered a cup of American coffee and had sat down at the one empty table next to the café's front door to wait.

She walked directly to his table after placing her order at the counter. He stood up when he saw her approaching.

"Your regime is moribund. It will expire, in a few months, if not weeks," she said with a precision that unnerved him, without preamble. "Nothing you tell me can change that. Minister Cerusu insists that you are a decent man. If that's true, you should have nothing to do with Kinshasa, least of all become foreign minister, the regime's spokesman."

"I have made plans to travel throughout the Great Lakes region to diffuse the misunderstanding—"

"Misunderstanding! Is that your word for extermination?" she said, almost shouting. "What that Cerusu woman calls decency is idiocy or worse!"

"As I was saying, Madame Ambassador, I will make it my purpose to resolve the conflict between us," Molu said hurriedly but with a calmness that surprised him. But he had no choice. "I will go to any length to do that."

"Your regime is in no position to go to any length, Mr. Sakeseba. It has no length to go. And who would believe anything you might say? To save your failing regime, you are prepared to make any overture; self-preservation is your only motive now. Well, it's too late! If I were speaking for my government — which I am not — I would tell you that if you leave and that dictator of yours declares what is left of Kinshasa an open city, we would let you escape with your life. That's more that was offered to any of us."

"I was not aware that anyone from Kinshasa had participated in what you call the 'extermination.'"

"Are you patronizing me because I am a woman, or because you are another ignorant fool, Mr. Sakeseba?"

Molu bowed his head. "Neither!" he said after a moment staring at the table. "I don't know that any of us was involved. That's why I said what I said."

"Who gave those damn murderers the AK-47s used during the hundred days?"

"My understanding is that the Hutus used machetes and very few firearms," Molu answered softly.

"Presidential guards aren't armed with machetes. Gendarmes aren't armed with machetes. Soldiers aren't armed with machetes. The Interahamwe militia aren't armed with machetes. General Bizimungu wasn't armed with a machete. No, Mr. Sakeseba, the Hutus were armed with AK-47s from your regime."

"Arm merchants are not from any particular country, Madame Ambassador . If our quarrel is about the sale —"

"Quarrel?" she said sharply, interrupting Molu. "You insist on paring your regime's responsibility in the extermination of almost a million. How much are the French paying you?"

"I don't know anything about the French. I have taken money from a few people who wanted to conduct business in Kinshasa; the French were not among them."

"You know damn well what I mean!"

"I know that as Kinshasa's foreign minister I am to do everything possible to achieve peace in the Great Lakes region. That peace is the only thing that can safeguard our integrity — for all of us, including Rwanda. That's the reason I asked Minister Cerusu to arrange an interview. I was hoping you would pass my intention on to your foreign minister."

"I have told you: you are wasting your time."

"Then, why have you told me to come here. I can have better and cheaper coffee in my office."

The question dumbfounded the Rwandan. Was her silence hesitation? Doubt possibly? Molu was not sure. Perhaps it was an opening to try to diffuse her hostility.

"The extermination was not due to sales of arms, Madame Ambassador," he said as if he were walking on glass, not looking at her, his course set. "Had the UN not withdrawn from Rwanda that April, how many of the massacres would have taken place? And isn't it true that those you consider your friends asked the UN to leave? Kinshasa could not have done that.

"And as the world knows, the killers used radio extensively to advocate and then encourage the massacre. Kinshasa did not have the capability to do that.

"These same friends rejected the 'genocide' designation of the massacres. Without that designation, the international community would not intervene. So you had more massacres."

Molu turned to look at the Rwandan, to see what effect his words had had on her. To his surprise, tears were running down her angular cheeks. Molu kept his eyes on his still full cup. In his mind, he once again looked down on the great river from the helicopter flight to Gbadolite. The River of Adversity, the river of our lives, he told himself is like the continent itself, surging endlessly, seemingly to no purpose. If only it could linger a while.

"I apologize, Mr. Sakeseba. Your mentioning the radio broadcast brought back difficult memories. What you say is a matter of record. Maybe you don't know the part about our 'friends'..." She saw a flash of recognition on his face.

"Africans have no friends, Madame Ambassador." Molu rushed to say. "Didn't you know? We have many pimps, but no friends."

"These so-called friends, they knew who the murderers were," she insisted; "second-level bureaucrats even talked to them, with cries for help in the background. Some of the bureaucrats joked that Clinton would punish them."

"As my daughter Nef would say —"

"Nef? That's an extraordinary name."

"We named her after the Egyptian queen, Nefertiti."

"Nefertiti?" She smiled. "Yes — Your wife has her practice at Children's Hospital in the District, I was told."

"That's right. I met her when she was serving in the Peace Corps in Bumba, not far from my village."

"I will tell my government of your intentions — what you said about the Great Lakes region. But what I told you is undeniable — for us to live, that president of yours must go. With Jean-Luc Nundu in power, our chance of survival is exponentially greater."

It was Molu's turn to be dumbfounded. At length he said with feeling, "Jean-Luc Nundu is a criminal!"

"The Americans don't think so!"

"Oh, God!"

"You're going to tell me the Americans conduct their African policy on the cheap," she said with a shrug. "Whatever — it's their policy! Don't think you would be telling me anything I don't know. External events have little effect on the Americans."

"Nundu sells slaves in Southern Kivu," Molu said.

"As I told you, the Americans have given Nundu their blessing." The Rwandan ambassador leaned over the small table, her jaw pointed at Molu. "Tell me that you will remove Motutu, and I'll personally fly to Kigali to tell them of your plan."

"Should we be discussing the removal of a head of state in a Starbucks?" Molu asked with a little laugh.

"It's as good a place as any. At least I am sure it's not compromised. It's my feeling your office is."

"If it is, I don't know it. But there are lots of things I don't know."

"What does that mean?"

Molu didn't answer directly. "So you say the choice is between Nundu and me?"

"I didn't say that. But what I will say is that if the choice is between you and Nundu, you win with me. I know his record. And if you say the word, I'll tell Paul. I think he would agree."

"Your president?"

"Yes, Paul Kagame."

"I can't say that," Molu said. "What I can say is that I will do everything I can to make things right between our countries. This madness can only spread, doing neither of us any good."

"The Hutus won't agree with you. Nor the French."

"Maybe the Hutus are betting that time is on their side. Killing is not the only method, you know! Population replacement is just as effective as genocide, only more time consuming. Their number guarantees that they can wait you out. Instead of thinking of replacing my president, why not consider an alliance between our countries." Molu's voice gained confidence as he left the territory of emotion for more secure facts of political reality. "We need your help to solve the Bunyamulenge crisis. I think my president would agree that if you help us we'll reciprocate in kind."

"Even if you could, which I truly doubt, the French would not agree. For them the conflict is colonial and greater than any one regime. The slaughter is secondary. Something that can't be helped. They too have their African policy."

"Don't worry about the French," Molu said.

"How can we not worry about the French? Who do you think is behind the Hutu nationalists? Who do you think is the facilitator?"

"Let me answer you with a little story. Do you mind?" Molu said. "Speaking to Minister Cerusu, made me understand what her husband meant by Africans being the 'clown' — or 'the fool,' I am not sure — at the carnival of others.' My village's Mokonzi understood how destructive colonialism was going to be for us. He had perfect foresight. He tried ruse to protect the village from the Belgians.

"It would have been better if he had protected the village from us. It was we. We let the Belgians impoverish the village. I can see how simple it was to do it. The first time my mother accepted a can of cooking oil from them, we lost our cohesion. We lost the spirit that gave us identity and made us worthy to be unique. After that, it was as if death not life was telling us where we were in this world. The ancestors must have gone somewhere else; they no longer knew us. Mokonzi died badly; he knew.

"Most days, I think of the Great River. Nef calls it the Disaster River because I told her that the river is a metaphor for our lives. It never gives us a break to rest and assess where we have been and where it's possible to go. We slipped our mooring and have been looking for it ever since. Some tell me that it could not have been otherwise for any African, and that it is pointless to implicate history. I don't know."

She no longer looked at him as she did when hostility was driving her. To Molu, she appeared uncomfortable now, and he wondered why? Was it because of what he had said about the Great River? "This business can't be a *jeu d'esprit*, a parlor game," she then said in a new, deeper voice, full of emotion. "The 'Hundred Days' was not a spontaneous act of people frustrated from years of Batutsi dominance. It was planned. *It was planned!* The Hutus had lists with victims named. Many in the international community were aware… When I get back to my office I will cable the foreign minister with a copy to the president advising them of what you told me," she said as she stood up. "Perhaps I will get to meet your family one day."

The three other customers in the café that early afternoon saw two tall Africans hugging one another. The man had tears running down his round face. *Likamboté*, they heard him say. He was speaking in a language they did not know.

# Chapter 16

Forty minutes before his 7 p.m. flight, Molu walked to the Continental Airlines counter in Washington's Dulles Airport, excitement in his steps. Arriving in Frankfurt at 9:05 a.m. the next day, he would have a four-hour layover. Fortunately, his deputy had secured a transit visa to enable him to spend a couple of hours at the Kinshasa embassy before his 1 p.m., seven-hour flight on Gulf Air 4 to Abu Dhabi. He would not get there until 9:20 in the evening.

He had dressed entirely in silk — dark blue suit, blue shirt and matching tie. Coming down to breakfast with him that morning, Nef asked him why he was dressed in such fine clothes. Before Molu could reply, her mother answered that it was important that her father, who was going to be Kinshasa's foreign minister in a few days, make an exceptionally good appearance wherever he went, but especially if he was going to Europe to trade with the *colons*. To Nef, *colons* meant Belgium. Her father was going to Brussels.

When his wife had bought him the blue suit, she had told him that it was critical that Africans show well. "Our status imposes on us the obligation to try harder," she had said, pointlessly he thought. "*Pour ceux qui font la pluie et le beau temps,*" she had explained in French, to the powers that be, "black is synonymous with poverty and all that entails.

"I wish you were more like Judd Mosley; that man understands that sort of thing perfectly. You noticed how aloof he is. Even his teacup, he lifts aloofly. I was embarrassed I hadn't ask Emma to get the most expensive tea from London. His *Negro de Paris* French accent is a testament to how dedicated he is to being aloof.

"And he didn't even smile at my joke, the one about being pregnant with Nkosia. You don't remember? I told him that I gained so much weight I looked like a fire engine. The only difference was that I didn't sound like one. I usually get a laugh with that one, but not from this man — he has given up on familiarity for good. I don't think that even the president will call him by his first name."

Molu laughed, remembering Mosley's insistence that they speak French. "You think he does *it* aloofly," he asked. "You know — with his wife? If she were my wife, that's how I would do it."

"Whatever! She gets more than I do; that's one thing we can be sure of," she had answered, glaring at him.

"You want me to be aloof? OK, I'll be aloof," he had answered quickly, recognizing the turn the conversation had taken.

When Nef asked whether he was sick, he had told her that he was feeling fine, just practicing acting aloof. His wife was not amused.

Getting dressed that morning, he kept thinking about Julie. He wanted to look his best when they met in Abu Dhabi a few hours from now. Surely, she would notice that he had spent time on his appearance to look his best for her. This was one way to show how much she meant to him, how seriously he was taking her. "Women are angels until taken for granted," the Dictator had explained the day Molu had introduced the woman he was to marry to him. He tried not to think about the lovemaking and passion for Julie that would be unleashed in a few hours.

The roped-off area reserved for first class passengers led him directly to the Continental Airlines' counter where a flustered clerk entered his name in the computer. His driver had gone ahead of him and placed his boss's small suitcase on the airline scale. After a few seconds, the clerk retrieved his boarding pass from under the counter, which she handed to him following a cursory check of his passport. Molu thanked her and turned to say goodbye to his driver for the last time. "*Kendéke malámu, tokomónono na nsíma, Mokonzi*" the driver said, hugging his departing boss. "*Íyo, melesí, melesí, nayókité, tokomónono na nsíma,*" Molu answered, surprised at the man's show of emotion. They shook hands. When he got to the car, the driver looked at what Molu had put in his hand. It was a small canary diamond.

As soon as he could pry his mind loose from the daydreams about Julie, he reflected on the meeting at the coffee shop in Chinatown. He was still astonished at how the tone of the meeting had changed and how it had concluded. He tried to recall the moment when the Rwandan ambassador, who had come, he was certain, to have her biases affirmed, thawed and listened to what he had to say and altered her hostility.

Upon returning to his office, he called Minister Cerusu in New York to give her the news. The Minister, recovering from her surprise at the unexpected report, told him that he had been given a unique opportunity and suggested he lose no time in contacting his counterpart in Rwanda. Molu had asked her to act as an intermediary. She agreed. As expected, she reminded him of his promise regarding Kinshasa's sale of arms to her country's secessionists. And she had again been generous with her wisdom. "The ancestors have an inherent interest in your success," she had said to encourage him. "If you don't prevail, who will venerate them?"

He then dined with his wife at *La Jardiniere*, their favorite French restaurant on K Street in the west end. Ecstatically he told his wife about his meeting with the Rwandan ambassador. However, Ella was not convinced Molu had achieved any kind of breakthrough. And she was furious when she learned what the Rwandan had said about Jean-Luc Nundu, the warlord. "Wait a minute, wait a minute," she had interrupted. "You mean they've picked a replacement for the president?"

"That's what she said. But, of course, there's a world between wishing they had Nundu in Kinshasa and making it happen," Molu replied.

"And who's going to stop them from making it happen?"

"Oh, come on! They can't just walk in and crown someone president."

"And why not? Don't the spoils belong to the victors? What makes Kinshasa different?"

"You don't understand. Affairs of state are more complicated than a patient walking into a doctor's office. The relationship of forces gives affairs of state a dimension involving too many interests for it to be as simple as that."

"Do you know you have a tendency to speak balderdash when you are on the defensive?"

"Balderdash?"

"Ezalí bosóto," she explained in Lingala.

"Bosoto! Rubbish?"

"That's right. What you said was rubbish. Or maybe you think you can patronize me with *affairs of state?*" she asked, her lips pursed, her nose turned up, her voice deeper.

"What I was telling you is that the international community has a stake in this. Kinshasa is too important —"

"The international community, in Africa? Another of your glorious illusions? You worry me!"

Molu knew how it was and kept his eyes on his plate. "Look, this is my last dinner here for a while. Let's order," he said after a while. "I heard Giorgio has a new concoction, a froie gras in a crepe with chestnut sauce. Everyone says it's the best thing in Washington."

"I'll order in a minute. Wasn't Nundu the one who kidnapped two Americans in the '80s?"

"Yes, in '75! He is a slave runner too. But the Rwandan ambassador said that the State Department likes him."

Ella scrutinized him.

"Look," Molu said, "don't worry. The Tutsis are far more interested in an alliance with us than in championing a criminal from Kivu. The president will get the French on board to support a policy of cooperation with Rwanda. As for the U.S., they have no real interest in this. I'll take care of it. I have a plan, and I am sure she will help."

"She? Who? Minister Cerusu or the Rwandan ambassador?"

"Both actually! Now can we eat?"

His wife was not convinced. She had more questions, but he repeated what he had told her, afraid that if he told her the plan in detail she would find a fissure in it to criticize. So Ella was left with her disquiet, agreeing only to invite the Rwandan ambassador to meet Nef at their residence. Her salad and tournedos were left untouched; and as soon as he had finished, he asked for the check. They did not greet the owner as they had in the past.

During the drive home, neither spoke. Both preferred that evening the sound of one's own thoughts. Ella looked at the passing traffic; she knew that whatever the question, her husband would make his explanation fit any course he was contemplating. The driver also was quiet, for the boss's wife was in the car. As was her wont, she was annoyed about something, and he wondered what it could be this time. Ever since, the ambassador's deputy had told him what *proxénète* — the name she gave him following the visa business — meant, he thought it prudent to keep her at arm's length. He had concluded that she was like every other African American woman he had met.

He had married an African American so that he could obtain a visa to remain in the United States. The ambassador's wife found out about this "crime," was outraged and demanded that her husband fire him at once. But the ambassador had deflected his wife's indignation and kept the man in his service, after scolding him for seeking the visa on the same day as the marriage ceremony.

The driver's new wife had sought an annulment immediately when the authorities contacted her and explained that her husband had lied about a prior marriage. Not fully understanding, the woman was told pointedly, "He has a wife and three children in Kinshasa, dear. That's what he wrote on the initial application to come here. Bigamy is against the law in the United States." As far as the driver was concerned, "They all thought they were too good for Africans."

# Chapter 17

Motutu called his secretary to his study to tell her what he wanted done with the wife of the Continental Hotel's manager. Danielle looked at him, seemingly pensive. In fact, she had no opinion about the matter; but to give her boss the impression she was an active participant, she looked at him for a few seconds as if reflecting on the feasibility of what he had told her. When satisfied, she nodded her approval. She then stood and for a few moments waited in case the Dictator had something else in mind.

In her office, Danielle phoned the nun who had enchanted Motutu, the latest of his great finds. Resentment in her voice, she told Soeur Angélique to travel to her house at nine o'clock that evening. She could have picked a better time; but why make it easier for the nun? She felt a thrill, telling Soeur Angélique, who rented a one-room shack in Kingasani, one of Kinshasa's *bas-fonds*, that her house was in Gombé, the city's affluent suburb on the southern bank of the river where the regime's elite had their guarded residences.

Soeur Angélique would have preferred to stay at home that evening to nurse the cold the incessant tropical rain had imposed on her. But the request had come from too high up to consider not going out. If she was to reach town on time, she had better get to the corner to catch the taxibus, whether it was raining or not.

The taxibus followed no set schedule, departing from the corner only when every seat, including the space on top, was occupied. No matter how much the people grumbled, it left only when the operator could squeeze no one else in. But this day, Soeur Angélique was lucky; the driver had concluded that the downpour and the late hour would impede his being able to cram his vehicle no matter how long he waited. He would try to make up the shortfall on his return trip.

The nun stood at the corner with eleven other passengers for a little over an hour when the van pulled up. To the surprise of everyone, the driver announced that he would go as soon as they were on board. True to his word, once he had shut the passenger door and pulled himself up into his seat, he left the corner, racing down the muddy, potholed road at breakneck speed. Soeur Angélique made it to the drop off point with time to spare.

Buses did not travel to the center of town but stopped at the periphery from where passengers walked whatever distance to reach their destinations in Kinshasa. Soeur Angélique walked the six miles to the Continental Hotel, the only location from which she could catch a cab for the trip to Gombé.

Seated at a kitchen table, a green-plastic glass of tap water sweetened with a pinch of sugar in front of her, she listened astounded at what the Dictator's secretary was asking her to do. Never mentioning the Dictator by name, the secretary explained that their business entailed the eradication of "another cockroach." Pausing at the word to make sure her meaning had sunk in, the secretary repeated, "A cockroach — it's a matter of fact, she looks like a cockroach; I have seen her. She doesn't look any different from those you eradicated in '94."

The nun continued to look straight ahead, her hands on her lap, the glass of water in front of her. That late morning in April she was listening to radio Mille Collines, and the male voice was saying that the Tutsis, the same people her Benedictine Convent was hiding, were the *inyenzi,* cockroaches. She called the Interahamwe militiamen to force the *inyenzi* out of the convent, but it was not because she thought that anyone was a pest to be exterminated by fire. Did she know the militiamen would use the gasoline she gave them to burn the people alive?

As if in a dream, she heard the secretary say, "She is the wife of the Continental Hotel's manager. Her name is Julie. We want her to disappear for at least a week. But it would be best if she were never found. We would prefer if it happened on the way to the airport."

The nun had looked up at the mention of airport. The cemetery where she prayed was in Mikonga on the road to Ndjili International Airport. The nun's movement irritated the secretary. "She has a reservation on the Air France flight tomorrow," Danielle said in a tone that left no doubt the nun had no say in the matter.

Danielle picked up her purse and extracted seven twenty dollar bills from her billfold and set them down next to the water tumbler. Soeur Angélique was relieved to see that they were giving her real money and not the discredited local currency no one trusted.

"This is for the taxi and whatever else you might require," the secretary said, more pompously with every word. "Is there anything you don't understand?"

Soeur Angélique shook her head, "No."

"Now to the most important detail," the secretary said. "This must be done without Mgonu's knowing about it. That's very important."

Soeur Angélique was about to stand, but when she heard the instruction about Maka Mgonu, she sat back in the chair and gaped at the secretary.

"Without Mr. Mgonu knowing?" she said weighing every word, fright in her voice. "How is that possible? This woman has bewitched him; he is insane about her. If he is not doing it himself, he has one of his people shadow her all the time."

"We know that," the secretary answered. "We plan to have him occupied during the time she is on the road to the airport."

"But what about his people?" she challenged the secretary. "And how can you keep something like this from him?"

"What can he say if she has an accident? An accident is an accident. Anyone can have an accident. We will distract Mgonu; you take care of whoever is watching her. We don't care how you do it."

The nun shifted her expressionless gaze to the kitchen window, her face set.

"What do you think I meant when I said she was a cockroach?" Danielle said, angry that the nun had questioned her. "Do I need to remind you that the International Criminal Tribunal has a few words to say to you? You make her disappear the way I told you; if you ask me, this is more important to you than it is to us — she is a menace."

Soeur Angélique didn't think an answer was necessary; the secretary didn't want to be bothered about understanding Maka Mgonu. After a few moments, she put the money in a pocket inside her bosom and stood up to leave. Thirst parched her throat, but nothing could entice her to drink the water in the green plastic glass.

The moment the nun had left her kitchen, Danielle threw the glass into the sink, splashing her new pink Italian marble counter.

"Hutu zóba!" She cursed in disgust.

---

Soeur Angélique prayed for a cab. She saw many large, armored cars but no cab or any other vehicle that might stop for her. For a moment, she regretted not having donned the brown and beige habit. She had thought of it, but had given herself the excuse that she could not very well have gone to the secretary's house dressed like that. A nun might have received certain consideration an African woman on foot would never get in Kinshasa's fashionable neighborhood. But who would stop for a maid here and at this hour? Her "should have" moment was interrupted suddenly, when she heard one of the residences' guard lewdly offer to relieve her of her undergarments. But she might have imagined things because her Lingala was still approximate.

She realized the danger she was in when the guard left his gate and followed her saying repeatedly, "Boní?" How much? If he detected she was a foreigner that would be a *carte blanche* to do whatever he wanted to her. She pressed on, walking as fast as her stumpy legs would go. She didn't slow down even when she heard someone call the "boni" man. When she felt secure enough to look over her shoulder, she saw the man walking back to his gate.

She didn't know how she would make it home. She longed for a floor to sleep on and forget. By the time she got to the hotel's taxi stand, it would be midnight. It's possible that a driver would take her all the way home for ten dollars. But Danielle had given her only large bills. No driver would give her change, certainly not in dollars, for a twenty dollar bill. She contemplated parting with one, but reconsidered; a black woman speaking French and paying with dollars would be robbed if not killed. For another moment, she thought of walking back to the secretary's house, but gave up on the idea, unable to convince herself that she would be welcomed. Besides, if she retraced her steps, the "boni" man might fancy that she was coming back because of him.

Stalked by shadows, she walked steadily, fright lengthening her strides. Fortunately it was downhill, and soon she walked in darkness, Gombé's extravagant incandescence no longer lighting the road. She had given up on making it home; instead, she would walk to the PTT communications compound where she would sneak into one of the trucks parked there and stay until daybreak. If she had to use a twenty to bribe a guard, so be it. The probability was that he would be on the other side where the women from La Cité congregated at night; but if not, she would wait until his round had taken him behind the building. Once the way was clear, she would steal into one of the trucks parked to the left of the entrance.

She had concluded that what Motutu's secretary had asked her to do was her death sentence. Maka Mgonu's wrath would have no bound when he found out. No human being could be as beguiled by a mere mortal as Maka Mgonu was by this Julie! The man's mind must be in the hand of a spirit that she had no intention of challenging.

Harming Julie would be a mad undertaking, certainly not something Soeur Angélique should involve herself with if she wanted to live. Since she had seen the Tutsis die like sprayed locusts that bright Tuesday in April, living had become a desperate obsession for her. No! She would not defy whatever was at work between Mgonu and Julie. She also dismissed the notion of warning Mgonu. Not able to think of another option, she prepared to flee.

Soeur Angélique had been alarmed by Julie's last telephone conversation with Molu. She had arranged to give the tape to the Dictator's secretary, expecting that Motutu would impose a simple solution that would favor his security chief. He was the one who had rescued a simple nun from the clutches of the International Tribunal and had even found a job for her in Kinshasa. I should have gone to Mr. Mgonu with the tape, she cried inwardly, passing in review all her regrets, while she walked from the effulgent Gomé to the totally dark P.T.T. compound's parking lot.

At dawn, no one paid attention to the large woman slipping out of a parked truck and joining the throng on Boulevard du 30 Juin, heading for Ngobila Beach on the river. For an hour she remained at the dock among the crowd gathered around the ticket booth, waiting to buy passage on the ferry to Kinshasa's sister city, Brazzaville.

Brazzaville's few tall buildings rose cramped together like soldiers standing in defiance of Kinshasa, the metropolis across the water. Brazzaville's skyline was built just for Kinshasa to gaze at. For a moment Soeur Angélique's attention stayed on a powder blue-colored building, shimmering in the tropical sun of the new day. How fine it would be if it were a church, she told herself. She then contemplated the river curling lazily around the bend toward Malebo Pool until she became dizzy. She watched the water hyacinths that paved the river, counting their blue-purple flowers. The earth-colored water turned into the April graves as far as the eye could see, and she adorned them with the flowers. Someone watching at that moment would have noticed that she had become very pale.

Soldiers were everywhere, and each time one came near, she was convinced it was to take her away. But like the cripples, the soldiers were lured by the prospect of sharing the breakfast of those among the passengers who had something to eat. Partial to boiled eggs, the soldiers, like the gulls, were insatiable as they picked at the scraps. The cripples scavenged, making the most of the fear people felt toward them. It made no difference how repulsive and frightful they were to the passengers waiting for the ferry; like everyone else, they had to eat.

When boarding she had one last moment of fright: a soldier stood next to the ticket agent by the gangway, checking passengers' papers. Mechanically she gave him the special PTT badge the security chief had obtained for her. The soldier looked up, impressed. Once on the ferry she walked quickly to the stern to await departure. She walked to the bow once the boat had left its berth and made its turn, heading for Brazzaville, its stern in Kinshasa's face.

She found a seat next to a woman as large as herself and settled down for the half hour crossing. She must have said something or cried out when she dozed off, for the woman was now standing in front of her, gripping her shoulders, shaking her awake. She opened her eyes. The woman whose chest was in the nun's face was clad in a T-shirt too small for her large bosom. "I survived the Kinshasa-Brazzaville Ferry" was emblazoned in English in fading, bold letters across the T-shirt. "*Melesí, melesí,*" Soeur Angélique thanked the woman.

She used what change she had to pay for two *kàwa na mabéle* from the coffee vendor. On the other side, she paid a twenty-dollar bill in lieu of the mandatory Congo-Brazzaville visa to clear customs. She then joined with the woman who had awakened her on the boat, and together they followed the disembarking passengers in the direction of town, disappearing.

# Chapter 18

The press officer stood in front of Brenda Bleding's desk to receive his instructions regarding the arrival of Ambassador Judd Mosley that evening. He was not like a soldier standing at attention, but he was on his guard, fully aware of the deputy's negative feelings towards him. He had made the mistake of reminding Brenda that protocol called for the ambassador to say nothing to the media until after he had presented his credentials to President Motutu.

In return, he was receiving a tongue lashing. "I don't care what protocol says!" Brenda declared furiously. "Ambassador Mosley wants to make a statement on the tarmac, and that's how it's going to be." She slapped the desk with a notepad for more emphasis. "Your job is to see to it that there are enough journalists at the airport to ensure that his statement is widely reported in the media, not to tell me about protocol. Don't you know that Americans never lower the flag in a parade? Now, let's get something clear right here! If your plan is to make me look bad in front of the ambassador because you resent my getting a job you think should have gone to you, look again."

Brenda had a certain way of speaking that never failed to surprise. She clipped her words in an effort to disguise her southern accent; but she was not always successful, especially when excited, tired or under the influence. With her guard down she deteriorated into a clownish Mae West — without a sense of humor.

The press officer laughed and said good-naturedly, "Brenda, press officers don't get deputy jobs. And when was the last time a black ambassador had a black deputy. As to planning to make you look bad, nobody can make you look bad. Haven't I gotten you the most complimentary press coverage of any chargé in Africa? And yet here you are accusing me of planning to make you look bad. What's going on here?"

"I know what you have been saying behind my back."

"I have been saying something about you?" the press officer asked, surprised. "I have never laid a word on you. If I ever say anything, it would be to sympathize with you. You are a poor white woman from the South; I am a poor black man from the South. I know what you have to deal with to get ahead —"

"Poor white woman? You better go back to where you got your information and ask for your money back."

"OK, Brenda! Have it any way you want. I understand. Now, to the business at hand — do I have to draft something for Ambassador Mosley for his arrival or has that already been handled?"

The press officer waited a moment for an answer. When none was given, he laughed derisively and walked out of the deputy's office. Closing the door, he heard a muffled, "little black twit." He was about to go back to answer the slur, but then let it go. He had reached the jaded stage of his career and his sense of futility was now too strong.

If he ever had it, he had lost it, the temperament to thrive within such an order. Nothing he said, or did for that matter, would alter anything. It struck him later that he had changed, and the recognition that he had lost what he considered the best part of himself depressed him even more. To become soulless was his punishment for maturing into another careerist, like those for whom he always expressed contempt.

He was in Kinshasa only because he couldn't get an assignment elsewhere. And as long as he stayed in his place, he could count on making a living and be promoted faster than others. That was the unspoken understanding. As long as he remained where he belonged. When he had enough in the bank, he would leave to do what he really wanted.

His concern was that drug traffickers or other high-sea pirates would storm his sailboat one night in winter when he would let the wind take him back to St. Pierre where Mt. Pelée was keeping watch. He would then anchor to write the story of what he had witnessed during the '94 Rwanda genocide. Brenda here, pirates there? If that was the choice, Brenda mattered but little.

———

Within minutes of the press officer's call to his media contacts, the security chief was informing Motutu that the Americans had upped the ante once more: Mosley was going to disregard protocol and talk to the press before he presented credentials to the head of state. Silently Motutu cursed Molu for letting one more humiliation befall him, his benefactor. At first the Dictator considered declaring an emergency that would shut down the airport, leaving Mosley's plane circling central Africa. But he reconsidered, deciding instead to forbid all journalists access to Ndjili Airport.

"Even the foreign ones?" Mgonu had asked.

"All of them!" he stormed. "Threaten them, deport them, just make sure nobody except Petit Pierre is there. This makes it even more important that we take care of Molu as agreed. Everything is set for Thursday night, right?"

"It's all arranged!" the security chief answered. "There has been no change since the briefing yesterday. Everything is in place."

Mgonu's call had jogged his memory about the hotel's manager's wife. "If the nun is as impressive as you say," Danielle told him with a little laugh, "it should go well." At another time he might have laughed with her at being reminded of his predilection to put his faith in strangers like the nun. He was eternally thinking that he was one person away from finding the one with a magic wand to help him solve the problems of his day. But Mgonu's call about the American ambassador and what he might say to the press reminded him that he was running out of the magic that made him the 'Great Elephant who because of his endurance and inflexible will to win goes from conquest to conquest leaving fire in his wake.' These thoughts put him in a frame of mind that demanded he find an outlet for his resentment.

"If it doesn't go well, you will sleep in her shack in Kingasani tonight," he told his secretary in the distinctive tone he reserved for those he was about to discard. It was a tone which the secretary had noted had been in too much use lately. To Danielle's distress the plan had not gone well. Soeur Angélique neither reported at the agreed hour nor could be found anywhere in Kinshasa. For a moment, Danielle considered asking the security chief on some pretext to look for the nun, but she couldn't think of anything reasonable that would not make the distrustful Mgonu suspicious. At the end, she had to call the airport. The customs officer at the departure gate informed her that Julie indeed was on board Air France flight number 718 to Paris.

She did not have a choice really, fearing the consequences of failure as acutely as she did. This one little failure, she told herself, this one little malfunction, after all these years — "*elle est avec les ancêtres*," she told the Dictator. She is with the ancestors, her lie as well modulated and well timed as all the information she had given her boss over so many years.

From the top of the stairs, Judd Mosley noticed that instead of a crowd of journalists jousting for position on the tarmac to get a better feed for what he had to say, his deputy was shouting at a short balding black man who kept his eyes on his shoes, like a naughty boy bearing a reprimand. Seeing the ambassador, the deputy shoved the man aside and walked quickly to the bottom of the steps to welcome her boss. "*Likambote*! Welcome to Kinshasa, Mr. Ambassador," she said, flying open her arms in a show business hug meant to convert a stranger to an instant bosom friend. She kissed him on both cheeks.

"Thank you, Brenda. *Melesi*! It's good to see you again."

"Oh my God! You speak Lingala like a native. I heard that you were brilliant —"

"I just know *melesi* and *malamu*," Mosley said. "That's the extent of my Lingala."

"It's a simple language! With that Harvard brain you'll know it in a few days."

"I understand that Lingala is like Brazilian, great only for music," Mosley said, meaning that learning Lingala was not on his agenda. "I'll get by with my good French. Now, shall we go meet the journalists? Are they waiting in the diplomatic lounge over there? I don't see TV cameras. Drew insisted that I read this statement when I got here."

"Yes, well, I am afraid not, Mr. Ambassador. This is the embassy's press attaché," Brenda waved a hand in the direction of the man she had been shouting at earlier, who had approached them from behind. "He is not the most dynamic press officer I have met," she added under her breath, but loudly enough for the man to hear.

"You are the most dynamic deputy I have met, Brenda," the man said. He turned to Mosley. "Good evening Mr. Ambassador, welcome to Kinshasa. I am sorry but there won't be any reporters here this evening, sir. President Mututu has forbidden them to come."

"Wait a minute, you are American! I thought you were a local."

"In a sense I am, sir, but from South Carolina," the press officer said with a wink in his voice, seeking to establish a sense of ethnic familiarity with a fellow African American.

But Mosley's expression, friendly a moment earlier, slammed shut, and he no longer looked directly at the embassy's media man. The press officer cursed inwardly. He had dealt with Mosley's type before and had the scars to remind him that ethnic antagonism was too often a "family affair." Mosley waited for his wife to emerge. (He had not wanted her to be part of the media show, so she was to remain on the plane until he had read his statement on the tarmac.)

He had read the disappointment in the media man's face and thought, got you, you scrounger. Got you. They walked toward the building topped by a long-ago broken 'Salon Diplomatique' neon sign, Mosley, speaking only to Brenda who chatted nervously. The press officer tagged along, apprehensively, weighing his transfer options and thinking of boats and of the welcoming harbor under the volcano of Mt. Pelé.

The diplomatic lounge was empty except for a slender man in a white double-breasted suit holding a gold-headed ebony wood chief's cane in what looked like a crippled left hand. Taking his hat off and bowing stiffly when the Americans entered the lounge, he announced, "I am Citoyen Nganga, the protocol chief. Welcome to Kinshasa," he said in a tone the press attaché recognized as deliberately unfriendly.

When he spoke, his right thumb rubbed a gold watch chained to his vest. "Journalists ask silly questions and importune our guests. We do not want to give a bad impression, you understand! And since we know that newly assigned diplomats never want to start their tour in our country on the wrong foot, we make sure there are no reporters here when they arrive." He looked at the Americans sternly, enjoying the performance he had been told to give that evening.

"Have you ever been told that you look just like Aubelin Jolicoeur?" the ambassador 's wife asked with the undisguised intent to put the man in his place.

"Ah, Madame is an aficionada of Mr. Graham Greene's oeuvres," Nganga answered with the same objective, surprising Mrs. Mosley that he knew who Jolicoeur was. "Yes, the president even calls me Petit Pierre — affectionately, you understand. But I am sure Madame is not suggesting that because Africa is as black as Haiti we are comedians here."

Nganga then turned military style to the ambassador, giving Mosley's wife his back. "The president will see you tomorrow morning at eleven o'clock at his office in La Cité de l'OUA," he said. "The car from the protocol motor pool will be at the embassy at ten-thirty to take you to him. We appreciate punctuality," he concluded with a meaningful smile in the direction of Mosley's wife.

"What an awful little queer," the ambassador's wife said when the man had left the lounge, her face a mottled, angry red.

"I think the journalist fiasco ticked them off," Mosley said evenly. "Well, Drew wanted a statement read, and he is the boss. They'll learn to live with that."

"They are touchy when it comes to the media," the press officer told him tentatively from where he stood in the back. "If you want to see foreign journalists, I can ask them to go to your residence or meet with you at the embassy."

Mosley did not respond to him directly and instead told his deputy, "I'll see the journalists at another time. Right now, we want to go to the residence; it's been a long day. Have the driver pick me up at eight tomorrow. You will accompany me to the presidential palace, Brenda. But I'd like to know what the president has in mind before I see him."

Brenda was about to get in her car when the press officer called out, asking for a ride back to town. "I also want to know if you could arrange to curtail my tour," the man said. Brenda noted that he didn't laugh when she told him that she would see what she could do.

When Mosley arrived at the embassy the next morning, Brenda told him that the scheduled appointment with the president would not be the get-acquainted sort of meeting they had anticipated. Instead, he would merely present his credentials. Apologizing effusively, she explained that she had been given this information only as Mosley was pulling into the embassy's driveway. (She didn't tell him that the press officer had warned her the previous evening that something like this would happen.)

Mosley rushed back to his residence to put on formal attire as protocol demanded. It had been the first item hung in the closet the evening before. He had bought it, thinking that he would use it for the pomp. The entire embassy staff in their Sunday's best around him. The president's entire cabinet, including the new foreign minister he had impressed with his French, champagne glasses in hand. All together, Americans and Africans, they would raise their glasses in a toast to his presence in Kinshasa. Now, instead, he was going to a rushed affair, where from the look of things, there would not even be a ceremony.

Because they would have been late had they gone back to the embassy, Brenda called the marine guard on duty to ask that he tell the driver from the protocol office that the ambassador had gone to the presidential palace in an embassy car. Remembering the chief of protocol's demeanor at the airport, she thought it wise to tell the guard to apologize to the driver for the inconvenience.

From Gomé they drove west of Mont Ngaliéma and the city center, where Motutu had his palace in the Cité de l'OUA. (Heads of state built at remarkable expense a city usually on the outskirts of their capitals to host summits of the Organization of African Unity. The Dictator built his for the 1967 summit.)

Brenda wasn't sure what answer to give when Mosley asked if business was always conducted "in this manner" in Kinshasa.

"I have been here only a couple of weeks, Mr. Ambassador; I don't know," she said, telling herself that it definitely was not what the Fatman had promised her. "This is also my first experience in Africa. The press officer is the most knowledgeable person at the embassy on what makes this place tick. By the way, he asked for my help to curtail his tour."

"When?"

"ASAP."

"I mean when did he make the request?"

"Yesterday. On the way back to town from the airport."

"That's fine! Curtail him. We don't need a media operative, especially one who can't get a couple of reporters at an airport to hear what the American ambassador has to say. I have never cottoned onto the idea that anyone can go anywhere the way State Personnel thinks. This man has no sophistication, no political sense. He's harmless, but his type grows mustaches with their resentment. I'd rather not have him around.

"In any case," he continued, feeling more confident as he always did after speaking negatively to a white associate about a black person, "I don't care for the press; they are nothing but a pain, practicing gotcha gossip on our backs to fill the coffers of the entertainment industry. I'd put them all against a wall and shoot them if I could. He wants to curtail, that's fine. Do all you can to make it happen."

"In all fairness, sir, Washington made the request for the journalists at the airport at the last minute. And from the little I have seen here, if Maka Mgonu, the security chief , says no journalist at the airport, it's no journalist at the airport. Consider also that we may not get a replacement; Kinshasa is not a garden spot with a line of bidders waiting to come here."

"Brenda, we don't need a media operative here!" Mosley said with finality.

"OK, sir, I got you."

"Alright then. Help him curtail. He is not someone I want on my team anyway."

———

The man who had so irritated Mosley's wife at the airport was at the door of the vestibule to welcome the visitors to Motutu's offices. The palace may have been made of marble, but the Dictator, reputed to have billions in Swiss banks and to live in phenomenal luxury, had a definite fondness for plastic fixtures. When Danielle came out to usher Mosley into her boss's presence, she found the American ambassador shaking a vase, saying to his deputy, "there is nothing here that is not synthetic."

Marshal Motutu, breathing shallowly, was slumped in a chair behind an ornate desk; he may have been asleep. At his right hand lay a heavy cane with the handle carved in the shape of an elephant, the only item on the desk. The room itself, although brightly lit, was in all appearance a replica of the vestibule. After a few minutes a tall, muscular man, dressed entirely in black walked in from a door concealed in the wall and bowed stiffly to the visitors before taking his position at the right of the desk slightly behind the Dictator.

Motutu looked at the man for a moment and then turned his gaze on Mosley and Brenda, seemingly surprised to see them. Mosley sat frozen in his seat, his eyes on Motutu, asking himself why the intelligence reports regarding the Dictator's health had been so incomplete; for if ever a man had the right to say 'look upon my face and despair,' Motutu was that man. His face incandescent, the inflammation caused by the battle waging in his body consuming him, the Dictator burned with a fever. Hebetude had not yet settled in, but it was close. Brenda waited silently, a notepad on her lap, prepared to take down every word spoken there that day.

Motutu slowly began to focus. For a while his eyes were fixed on Mosley's brownish-colored hair, studying it. After a moment of what seemed indecision, the muscular man walked to the Dictator and spoke in his ear. "Thank you, Maka," Motutu said in a barely audible rasp.

"Maka was just telling me… you have, of course, met Maka Mgonu, my security chief, I believe? Maka was telling me that at this very hour Johan Van Kees is presenting his credentials in Washington," the Dictator said with a chuckle that made him cough and then gasp for air, which drew a look of concern on the security chief's face.

Mosley waited a moment for Motutu to recover, and said, "That's right Mr. President, good morning, Mr. Mgonu. Let me thank you, Mr. President, for allowing me to present my credentials so soon upon my arrival in your wonderful country —"

"A speech is not necessary, Judd." He pronounced it Jood, an offensive word in Ngbandi. The Dictator lifted his right hand, resentful that Mosley sounded so poised, having hoped that the last minute scheduling of the credentials presentation and the two-hour wait in the junk-filled vestibule would fluster the American. During the wait, Judd could overhear the French ambassador speaking to Motutu in a loud voice. After a little over two hours, the Frenchman had come out, giving a perfunctory nod in the Americans' direction. "Or is it a lecture about the rewards of democracy and the rich getting richer," Motutu continued. "You are among friends; you are spared the drudgery of lecturing today. If you hand over the envelope that will take care of the presentation.

"I insist on strict reciprocity between countries; it is only fitting that my ambassador be presenting his credentials at this very moment. I am sure you have heard of Johan; he may be a crook, but he is my crook. That means he will serve us both well. You can assure your superiors that he will continue Kinshasa's policy of no-questions-asked cooperation. And if I know Johan, he will make our bilateral even better; the man's bottomless font of creativity never ceases to astonish even me."

Mosley walked to the desk and reverently placed the envelope containing his credentials in front of the Dictator. "Thank you," Motutu said, sliding the envelope to the left corner of the desk. "You are now the American ambassador to Kinshasa. If that was you life's dream, I am happy for you.

"Tell me Jood, how do you get your hair that way?" Motutu asked. "What do you think Maka? Jood's hair would make me look at least twenty years younger, and I would start a trend among African heads of state. They copy everything I do."

Mosley made no reply. He had wanted to read the statement prepared for him to give to the press at the airport, but the truncated credentials presentation had prevented it. He had looked forward to telling Drew that he had one-upped the snotty Dictator, but it was Motutu who had once again been one step ahead of him.

No one spoke, waiting for Motutu who, after a moment of head-bowed reflection, said plaintively, "Jood, Kinshasa has been a faithful ally, no? Not even the Brits have been better. You will find no record of my ever refusing America a service, even when doing so turned me into a stench in the nostrils of the so-called civilized world. And you know why? Because I believe in the promises Americans made to me over the years. Was I wrong? No?

"Then why did one of your high officials, a man with a foul name to go with a fool's face come to my home to tell me that Africans are chromosomally deficient. No, don't argue. That man sat where you are sitting now and took his pleasure telling me that I had a missing gene. Me, after all I have done, I am called a degenerate. You look like you may have some African blood. What do you say to that man?"

"Mr. President, I assure you that... did not represent the views of my government. I assure —"

"Cut the crap, Jood! You don't believe what you are telling me anymore than I do. Now let's get to the matters that matter. But first you must tell me the name of the lovely young lady you have brought with you and who has so assiduously taken down every word we have said." Mosley, both sullen and confused, made the introduction.

"Welcome to Kinshasa," Motutu said, beaming at Brenda. Mgonu gave a hint of a smile when the Dictator turned to tell him in Ngbandi what he thought of the ambassador's deputy. Looking back at Brenda he asked, "I'd like to know why it's the French commercial attaché you have taken up with? Why not one of our young men here? There isn't even one that attracts you? It's not that you too think we are gene deficient, do you?" Brenda smiled and without hesitation said curtly, "I don't think of genes at all, Mr. President. And as to the French commercial attaché, he is a friend." She looked in the security chief's direction. In his brief to Motutu before the meeting, Mgonu had mentioned Brenda's liaison with the French bureaucrat. Professionally he was offended that his Mokonzi had used the information so cavalierly, and, it seemed, for no purpose at all, not even to embarrass the woman. Then, too, another agent had reported that Kenlugu, Motutu's son, had taken a shine to Brenda and at a reception at the Belgian Embassy had importuned her mercilessly. Brenda harked back to Julie whom Molu had shamelessly pestered at the dictator's birthday bash not too long ago.

"I am getting mixed signals from Washington, Jood," Motutu was saying. "On one hand they insist on stability here, but then they insist that I make prime minister a corrupt politician who wants to overthrow the constitutional order. Why do they want more disasters here? Talking about disasters — what about the Tutsi invasion in the east? Washington thinks that by cheering the Tutsis on now the world will forget the Tutsis were told when they were being slaughtered that, 'It will be better the next time around.'

"Yeah, I was surprised when I heard that; I didn't know they were Buddhists in Washington. Buddhists do not have missionaries in Africa insisting on native conversion," Motutu said, his voice rising. "You people are always insisting.

"Anyway, I see all these things, and when I add them up, I conclude that Washington doesn't like me anymore," the Dictator said tearfully, shaking his hands in front of his face, seemingly to beat off something frightful. Brenda, writing furiously, glanced at Mosley who stared in apparent astonishment at Motutu.

"The problem now," the Dictator said, tears now running down his face, "is that conflicting pointers are fueling a dissident movement that is destabilizing the country and fueling the disturbance in the east."

"I am sorry, Mr. President, for any misunderstanding. Without you, this country would have been torn apart and the region where all the mineral resources are located would have fallen into Soviet hands. I assure you Washington is grateful for all you have done to help us win the cold war."

"Come on, Jood! You can do better than that. Even the man who said Africans were incomplete knew enough to tell me that. I don't want another speech. What I want to hear is that Washington will do what is right. What is honorable."

"And what is that, sir?"

"It will reinstitute my visa — for me and members of my family. But most importantly it will give me the helicopters I need to put an end to the disturbance in the east. What difference does it make where the helicopters come from? France makes the best, and, of course, they are cheaper than yours — that way your Congress doesn't have to be involved."

"Mr. President," Mosley answered, disapproval in his voice, "Washington is not going to give you American taxpayers' money to buy helicopters from France."

"Things have changed!" Motutu said. "When you needed my help the American taxpayers were the least of your problems. I even had one of your officials tell me the American taxpayers were the most understanding in the world. They were sheep, he said." The Dictator turned around to look at the security chief , as if to say,

"Right Maka? You were there when the official said that." Mgonu nodded grimly.

"Mr. President," Mosley said, taking out the speech from his breast pocket, "Washington recommends the immediate start of negotiations with the AFDL, Alliance of Democratic Forces —"

"What?" the security chief said, his voice a scalpel, taking a step as if to snatch the paper from the visitor's hand.

"That's alright Maka; Jood does not know the situation here; he only arrived yesterday," Motutu said soothingly. "He doesn't know that over there they are Communists calling themselves Democratic Forces. He doesn't know that among them are people planning to break Shaba from Kinshasa."

Leaning on his cane, the Dictator stood and walked with surprising ease albeit slowly to the sofa and, putting a hand on Mosley's knee, sat next to the American ambassador. "Jood, I need your help to convince Washington that I am the only person who can prevent a deluge here."

"Mr. President, Washington is not going to intervene in this region. Washington will only guarantee your safety and that of your immediate family," Mosley said, glancing at the security chief. "A dignified retirement wherever you and your family desire would in our view be the best solution. Of course, as a citizen of this country, you have the right under international law to live here in peace. Let me also say that your possessions here and abroad will not be touched by anyone but you."

"Jood, please, it wouldn't take much — the helicopters and a few marines. Surely your intelligence services have told you that."

"Washington will not get involved, Mr. President," Mosley answered, sympathy in his voice. "What I told you is as far as we will go in this matter. Why not sit down with the AFDL? I heard that the South African President has offered his help to get the negotiations started. I assure you the dignity of your office will be preserved in every way. And the movement that you started here would survive."

The Dictator didn't respond, but looked at his security chief, who gaped at Mosley his face an angry mask.

Motutu pushed himself up from the sofa leaning on the cane and shuffled back to his desk. Presently, two large, middle-aged women, evidently identical twins, came through the door the security chief had used and, one on each arm, marched the Dictator out, saying in unison, "What did we tell you, Papa, it's time for your rest." At the door, Motutu freed himself and turned to the visitors, "The ALF team reports that we have oil in Shaba, Jood," he said, shaking his head for emphasis. "Make sure to write that down, Miss. There is oil in Shaba." The Dictator's voice trailed off and he looked at the floor, surrendering to the fatigues of fever. The security chief followed, stopping in front of Brenda. "I apologize," he said. He then stood in front of Mosley, shaking a finger in the ambassador's face. Mosley recoiled, fearing that the security chief was about to pull his ear. "If you make a fool of us, you will hear from me," Maka told him, meaning it.

---

Mosley and his deputy sat alone in the Dictator's study.

"So those are the famous twins?" Mosley asked in an unsteady voice.

"I guess so," Brenda answered. "I didn't realize they were so heavy. Perhaps fleshy is a better word. Pictures show them slim and youthful."

Mosley walked to the desk and put the speech on top of his credentials. "This will serve as an aide mémoire. Maybe he will read it and understand what I was trying to tell him. History has turned the page on the authoritarian concept. The game is up. Unless he makes a deal with the AFDL, he'll not make it out of here alive.

"Did you know he was in as bad a shape as that? The reports I have seen made no mention of his health. When we walked in the room, I thought he was in prayer. He had that inward look. Then I saw him more clearly. We better tell Washington that he is on his death bed."

"He has been staying in his villa in Gbadolite on the border near the Central African Republic," Brenda answered offhandedly. "I had not seen him until today. He must have flown down to receive your credentials, or maybe to see the French ambassador. Something must be up. Until the new foreign minister arrives, I doubt that any of what you told him will be looked at. I have requested an appointment for the foreign minister to see you the moment he gets here. I would suggest you give him a copy of the speech when you see him."

"Thank you, Brenda. I hope we have better luck with the foreign minister. If we don't, we'll have a mess here. The French are the only one with the stomach to prop up Motutu. But if we let them have the upper hand here, they'll prop up the Hutus in the east as well — and you know what that means. You know, between

Hutut and Tutsit or Tutut and Hutsit, I am never sure which one is which."

"Yeah, more massacres! Of that, one can be sure. Our tour in this country will be an interesting one."

"More ridiculous than interesting, I would say. All that bureaucratic hand wringing for Rwanda! We knew we couldn't do anything about it. So now it's not in any of our interest parameters. I don't want it on my agenda."

"You are right. In the case of Mututu, I have heard that he uses the divide and conquer method very effectively. Washington may have to send representatives of all the agencies he has been dealing with to tell him to his face that the game is up."

"I don't want anybody else to come here to talk to him," Mosley answered; "that's my job; he is my responsibility. I don't want anybody else to see him. The foreign minister, I am sure, will help. Now let's go back to the office to get your notes transcribed. I'd like to have them in Drew's hand by close of business Washington time today, so that he can see how well I have done dealing with this man. By the way, how do you think the meeting went?"

"Very well! I was impressed with the way you told him he had to sit down with the AFDL people. Can you believe that security chief, though?"

"He is thinking of his skin. The president, he can go into exile wherever he wants, except the United States, of course. But a man like Mgonu, where can he go? Which soul would wish Charon well after crossing the river? I thought it interesting that he apologized to you. I supposed that was for telling his boss about your friendship with the French commercial attaché?"

"Yes, I am sure it was. He was embarrassed that Motutu not only brought that up at a meeting like this, but made so much of just an acquaintance. That's all it is, you know, just an acquaintance. Nothing more. I want to make that clear. Couldn't the president arrange something for Mgonu? A million here or there can make a great deal happen."

"I don't know. I think it's every man for himself — *sauve qui peut* — it sounds better in French. Once Mgonu realizes that, the debacle will follow swiftly. At our next staff meeting, we should discuss the question of security for when that debacle occurs. In the meantime draw a list of whom at the embassy we will evacuate. The press officer's name should be first on the list just in case Washington has a problem finding a replacement for him and balks at a transfer."

Danielle came in to clean up and was surprised to find the visitors still in Motutu's office. She called the protocol chief whose job it was to show the visitors out. Citoyen Nganga showed the two Americans out, standing in the doorway, pointing at their car.

The Dictator dismissed his wife and her sister, thanking them for rescuing him from a disastrous meeting with the American ambassador. He had expected Mosley to be cowed, but understood why the American ambassador had taken the opportunity of the presentation of his credential to raise the AFDL question. That did not prevent him from being furious that his security chief had not warned him that Mosley would make a pronunciamento out of the AFDL question. That Mosley had done so could only mean that Motutu's "friends" in Washington had definitely turned the page on him, expecting an imminent collapse of the administration in Kinshasa, regardless of where Motutu stood or what happened to him.

He had miscalculated. Not fully understanding Washington's predicament following the 1994 decimation of the Rwandan Tutsis by Hutu nationalists, he had fancied that the Americans' failed response to the slaughter would cripple U.S. standing. Had the Dictator, himself, equivocated between Hutu and Tutsi, and not backed France so openly, he would this day be in the role of wise mediator and proclaimed savior for all to hear. The old days would have been back in full swing, and a million or more would have lined Kinshasa's Lumumba Boulevard to show how grateful a people could be when they had such a wise man for a leader. Money from abroad would be pouring in as before, the IMF in the lead, begging him to accept one more loan at an ethereal interest rate. For a moment, he wondered if it would not have been wiser to have kept Molu in Washington for a few more days, to rally the supporters he just might have left over there. But he dismissed the thought; the urge to revenge himself on Molu was more powerful than any momentary consideration.

Molu was the reason he had come to Kinshasa. He had braved the six-hundred mile helicopter ride from his Gbadolite hideaway, not even once taking a look at his beloved river below, to be on hand for Molu's arrival. Maka had pleaded with him to remain in Gbadolite, swearing that he would not inflict on Molu greater harm than the Dictator himself. "I beg you, Mokonzi," the security chief had told him, "consider that there are more important things for you to worry about than Sakeseba. He is trapped; he cannot escape."

"You are a pain, Maka," he had answered, not unkindly. "How many times do I have to tell you that out here it matters who does what to whom? If I listen to you, how long do you think before it is known that it wasn't I who had done it to Molu? I ask you? And what will it mean? Sometimes I wonder if you don't shave your brain when you shave your head. Or is it that you don't think I am strong enough to make the cane do what it was born to do — by me?"

The hours tortured his patience, but his excitement grew as he practiced swinging the cane, hitting an invisible Molu, thrilling the twins who followed him with hungry eyes, making incomprehensible chatter, anticipating what was to come, bargaining and cursing each other, but praying he would have enough for both of them.

They had changed their dresses and splashed themselves with his favorite perfume in the places he liked. They anticipated the feel of the cane with the elephant-shaped handle, hoping it would work its magic and bring back the old days. Their shouts would echo through the palace and smiles would brighten faces of attendants as one twin and hopefully both would cry out and Eros triumphed. Everyone except Danielle who fantasized about her Mokonzi and dreamed she had him to herself alone.

And Petit Pierre, his face flushed, would, in his most endearing imitation of *La Cage aux Folles*, gambol up and down the central staircase screaming, "Papa is back in the saddle." After all, it had been a long time since the Great Elephant had made his "importance" felt.

# Chapter 19

Brenda called Washington from her residence rather than the office. Refreshed after a swim in her pool, she had dinner that the French commercial attaché had prepared. The fare included what Brenda judged to be a "highly acceptable" Blanc de Blanc brut that set off well frog legs from the Niger River prepared in Moroccan olive oil, salted Avignon butter and a ton of garlic and parsley.

She woke early to call the Fatman at home. It was two in the morning in Kinshasa, 9 p.m. in Washington. She usually timed her calls so that the Fatman answered. This evening her timing was off, and the wife picked up the phone. As brusquely as she dared, she told Brenda that her husband had not yet arrived from the office.

"Does she have to call you at home, too?" she then asked, after hanging up.

"She" the Fatman knew meant Brenda. Still he asked, "Who?"

"What other woman calls you at all hours? I asked you to tell her to stop."

"She is in the eye of the storm in Africa. If she is calling here, it's because it must be important."

"You people wouldn't know important if it hit you in the face," she told him, referring to an ongoing argument between them. "Tell her not to call here anymore. That's not too much to ask! And while you are at it, tell her to hold her breath the next time she thinks something is so important that she should call you here," she concluded on the way to her bedroom.

Not having a reply that wouldn't exacerbate a difficult situation and bring on more barbs from his wife, the Fatman closeted himself in his study to return Brenda's call.

When she heard the phone ring, Brenda heaved the commercial attaché off her and reached for the receiver on the nightstand. She tried to disguise her panting by covering her mouth, but she had to remove her hand after the Fatman told her twice that he could not hear her. "I am sorry — it's that I had to rush to the phone," she explained.

"Jeanne said that you called… it must be serious. What's up?"

With frantic waves of the hand, Brenda indicated to her lover that it was a personal call and wanted him to leave the room. However, he continued to caress her, mouthing, *"raccroche,"* hang up, as Brenda tried to sit up and bring the sheet to her chin. She kicked him, but he would not let her go. Her desperation surged; the fool was imposing himself between her and the only man she knew with the means to further her ambition. She would not be able to talk to the Fatman until the next evening, unwilling, as she was to call him from her office, where she could be overheard.

She kicked at the Frenchman again, but this time he held both her feet, immobilizing her. On the phone, the Fatman was calling to her. Finally, she pretended that she had an "African connection" and could not hear him. "If you hear me," she shouted in the receiver, "I'll call you back at 5 o'clock your time. What I have to tell you is urgent."

Her heart was pounding. She was so angry that for a while she was unable to speak. When the flood of invectives came, the Frenchman knew that she was through with him. His pride forbade apologizing to this uncouth American woman or begging her forgiveness. Yet, as he unlocked his car door to leave, he admitted to himself that he had been wrong to assume that Brenda's nature was limited to her aggressiveness in the bedroom. If he lived a hundred years, he would never have a woman like this one again.

When everyone had gone to the cafeteria, Brenda placed a hasty call to Washington to remind the Fatman that her call to him would be at ten Kinshasa time, 5 p.m. in Washington. She then told her driver to be ready at eight to take her home.

Crises are the crucible in which great diplomatic careers are made. Only during emergencies do the media and government agencies pay attention to a capital no one has ever heard of. For a short period, such capitals become as the Fatman told his wife, "the eye of the storm," drawing attention and becoming a center of interests that advance careers not previously contemplated. The media descend like locusts converging on a millet patch.

Brenda had not failed to appreciate that the crisis about to break in Kinshasa was the one that would give her the headlines she craved, ensuring both promotion and title. With the constantly amused press officer at her beck-and-call, there would be plenty of headlines! That man was a natural. Probably because he was black, she thought. He knew where everything was in Kinshasa, and he had an affinity for the media that seemed, yes, innate.

Not for her, the dime-a-dozen ambassadorships in some black country the State Department meted out to minorities and to the women who knew better but had to settle for less — always for less. No, a minor ambassadorship would not do for someone with her ambition and drive. She was too "big;" she had too much potential for an insignificant posting. Turkey, Germany, that's where she belonged.

First, she had to neutralize Ambassador Mosley. Her call to the Fatman was to begin the process.

From what she had heard about Mosley, she had accepted that he was another affirmative-action hired hand she would readily marginalize. The Fatman had allowed that she — not Mosley — would be running the show in Kinshasa. "The accolade would be yours," he had said, "more so for the fact that you are a relatively young white woman enduring great hardship in the middle of black Africa." But the meeting with the Dictator earlier had dissuaded her. Mosley had handled Motutu surprisingly well, adroitly even; demonstrating, Washington would say, that he could be trusted to stick to Washington's gun over a policy and not let go regardless of the other side's well-placed arguments. If Mosley were left untouched, he would be Kinshasa's success story. Who would remember the note taker?

Maka Mgonu sat at his desk downtown listening to the taped conversation between Brenda and the Fatman. This was intelligence that demanded a reaction from his boss, but he wasn't sure how to proceed. Thirty-six hours earlier, he would not have had any doubt, but he was panicked by the way his boss had used the intelligence regarding the liaison between the ambassador 's deputy and the French commercial attaché.

In fact, his Mokonzi's whole demeanor at that meeting had given him sweats. "*Il a perdu le nord,*" he has lost it, had become his refrain in thinking about his boss. Who knows? The Dictator might change his mind and insist on disrupting the carefully laid-out plans he had put in place to welcome Molu Sakeseba into the underworld of Kinshasa's beggars. "Let her do it for us," he could hear Mokonzi say with that pleased look the Dictator reserved for his brilliant ideas. "The ancestors are helping us, Maka; that intercept is their sign. Where is your brain?" Mokonzi, who had recognized faster than a macaque could climb a limba tree that the Mosley appointment was part of a concerted effort to overthrow him, would let down his arms on a whim. "*Il a perdu le nord!*" People who could no longer focus behaved that way. Mgonu had seen it many times before.

Although Brenda was unequivocal regarding the disastrous situation in the Great Lakes region, the crux of the intercepted conversation was her petition to the man at the other end for help to supplant Mosley in Kinshasa. Like all coups, this one also would be an internal affair.

The security chief was surprised at Brenda's vehement fabrications about Mosley, but that did not move him to act. However, after some deliberation, he decided that as much as he disliked the American ambassador, a "trafficker" like Brenda should not remain in Kinshasa either. Maybe the ambassador and Brenda would kill each other. But it would not do for Motutu to be disturbed by somebody else's attempted coup; that was another country's domestic concern.

In any case, Danielle had called to report that shouts could be heard in Mokonzi's special room. "The twins are in heaven," Danielle had said, not hiding her bitterness. More reason not to tempt fate with the American embassy's internal affair. A session with the twins might unhinge the Dictator further, and he might let Sakeseba slip on one pretext or another.

As regards to Molu, from the beginning Mgonu had doubts about Mokonzi's plans to add Julie's tormentor to the number of Kinshasa's panhandlers. In the security chief's opinion, Mokonzi's rage against Sakeseba was based on personal disappointment rather than on "it's necessary, no matter what."

Motutu had written Kenlugu off when he discovered his first son's preference for less than presidential behaviors. He had turned to Molu for filial reassurance and, despite the hedonist's independent penchant, had placed him on that special pedestal dictators reserve for their favorite son. Maka's resentment was palpable whenever he thought about Mokonzi's feelings toward Sakeseba. Molu's imminent ruin in no way alleviated that bitterness. Nothing would.

Kenlugu and Sakeseba are two of a kind, he had told himself. How is it that Mokonzi thinks that Sakeseba is different? What kind of explanation could there be for that?

In the end, he convinced himself that the intercepted telephone call had no immediate value and put the tape in the largest drawer in his desk, together with other items he had labeled "Metaphorical Discards." Then he remembered his one "friend" at the American embassy.

"If you can hold onto your courage with ten fingers and come to my office, I'll have something for you that you'll find interesting," he told the press officer over the phone. He was pleased when the man said without hesitation, "I'll be there."

"Good," he answered. "If I am not here when you come, my secretary will give it to you."

"I can be there in half an hour. It's always good to see you."

"I'll see you then."

Unlike the others at the embassy who shunned him, the press officer had actually gone out of his way to befriend him. Their experience with boats and waterfronts had cemented what both would admit was a transitory friendship. However, among people for whom any friendship was as rare as an honestly procured flawless diamond, even a transitory one had value.

The press officer walked into the security chief's building without once being stopped. "Gorillas," as the men who worked there were called, most with shaved heads, wandered in and out of offices flimsily built of the cheapest plywood. Twice he was bumped into, followed by cursory apologies. After a third bump, he realized that he had been checked for hidden weapons. Neither the sophistication nor the humor behind the search surprised him. He was laughing when the security chief, in person, opened the door of his office to let him in.

"Good morning, Mokonzi Mgonu. I like the way you have your guests searched," he told the security chief, laughing when he entered the office. "No one would believe it."

"I am glad you approve. You are one of the few to realize that my people have searched a visitor as thoroughly as if it were an official pat down. To the people who venture in here, the more comfortable we make them, the more cooperation we receive. You notice there is no "abandon all hope ye who enter here" sign on the door. But I know what people say about us. As a proponent of mystification, I approve. We let abracadabra, rumors and incredulity work in our favor. We don't have Hollywood, so we make do with incredible stories about us.

"However, no one has ever been tortured here. Torture is a waste of time, meaningful only to the psychopath who uses it. I must admit, though, that I have always thought it a good idea to let people underrate us by seeming to be in disarray. Even if we were the most organized people in the world, Europeans would still think us genetically incapable of precision and neatness. One of your bosses told Mokonzi na Bakonzi that Africans were gene deficient. I am sure that's what he was referring to." The press officer laughed.

"We need surprise as much as mystification," Maka added. "I am sure I mentioned during one of our chats that my true master and first author is Sun Tzu."

The press officer tried to remember where he had heard the phrase "true master and first author" but couldn't. Mgonu had a habit of making impenetrable remarks. "Well, you know I don't believe the crap about Africans being in tune with nature," he said.

"Yes, Europeans want to believe that Africans are structurally incapable of adapting to the technological age," Mgonu added.

The press officer chuckled and said, "You're right. I am not going to tell you in which country they found a bug in the ambassador's desk; but because it was a Francophone country, they thought the French had put the damn thing there. No one thought it could have been a local job. I knew better."

Mgonu also chuckled, then picking up a small package wrapped in aluminum foil he said, "I have something I think will interest you. It's a tape someone brought me — of a conversation between your deputy boss and someone of obvious influence in Washington. She initiated the call from her residence here. I thought it could be useful to you."

The press officer recoiled, as if his surprise had been a jolt. "Did you listen to it?"

"Of course! But the tribal nature of the comments offended me, so I stopped after a few minutes. It's no state secret I am giving you here. I just thought that something of this nature might be more useful to you than to us. Perhaps it will make up for blocking the journalists at the airport. I know your boss was not pleased."

The press officer would have liked to spend some time in the security chief's office. He had many questions. But Maka didn't ask him to sit down, nor give any other sign that he wanted him to linger. The press officer had never learned to impose himself like Brenda. He thanked the security chief and hurried the way he had come. The halls were clear. In fact, he saw no one until he reached the parking lot.

In his car he listened to the tape several times, but didn't know what to make of the conversation between Brenda and the man she called "Matt," certainly Matthew Greeson, the Fatman, State Department mandarin. What was odd was not Brenda's request; rather, it was the Fatman's reaction. For example, what did Greeson mean when he said, "He's an instrument of policy, the face the administration wants to stamp on its policy toward Africa?" That Mosley's face was on the coin of the realm and couldn't be touched?

The press officer had been in this business too long not to know how quickly they could discard the Mosleys from the diplomatic service.

Yet, the Fatman had sounded sympathetic toward Mosley. "He just got there, for Christ's sake. So what if he didn't handle Motutu the way you wanted. This was only a first meeting. In any case, the man who can manage Motutu is not yet born. Give him a chance," he almost pleaded with Brenda. "Look, I'll see what I can do. Right now I can't go up to tell the boss this man is a dud when he's only been in the country a couple of days. Give me some time to set it up." Brenda had thanked him, "I am counting on you, dear," she said.

"Yes, but right now stay the course. That's your ticket to what you are asking me, Brenda. Stay the course! I can help you only if you stay the course; that was our understanding," he warned and cajoled.

Distrustful, the press officer concluded that the Fatman had not acquiesced to Brenda's request only because Kinshasa was heading for certain disaster, and Washington wanted a face like Mosley's on the front page.

Now, there was the question of what to do with the information on the tape. When he handed him the package, the security chief had quoted an African proverb about a snake in a hut. He had laughed when he understood what Mgonu had in mind. It would take more than an illicit taped conversation to put him in Brenda's bed. But why not use it to get what he wanted most — a transfer out of Kinshasa.

He now knew Brenda and the Fatman were more than colleagues, quarrelling over an impossible handshake. The top spot in Kinshasa was one thing "Matt" couldn't procure for her with the snap of a finger. However, transferring an insignificant press officer out of an African capital was entirely another matter. One word from the Fatman and he would be on the next plane to wherever. One nod from Brenda — Feeling the excitement at that possibility, he headed back to the embassy to confront his "deputy boss."

———

The heavy tropical rain felt like the warm blanket he wished he'd had when he was growing up, so he opened his window to breathe the momentarily clean air. Not even the maddening traffic on Boulevard du 30 Juin, an avenue as wide as Paris's Champs Elysées, dampened his confidence that Mgonu had given him the key to what he wanted most. His euphoria soon changed, however. The traffic's slow progress made him a witness to scenes that gave him pause, and his buoyancy seeped away. He had never seen so many troops in the capital. Their dirty uniforms were a sign they were arriving from the field. Discarded uniforms littered the sidewalks. While people sauntered at a normal pace, the soldiers scurried. Three stopped the battered gray Peugeot 505 in front of him. After a few harsh words the driver jumped out, his hands hanging limply at his side. Realizing that this action would spread, the press officer tried to escape the traffic by following a vehicle that had jumped onto the sidewalk. Soon other drivers followed, and the sidewalk became a way beyond the soldiers' reach. But suddenly the way was once again blocked, when a stylishly-dressed white woman abandoned her Renault, blocking the path. He maneuvered back onto the burning asphalt, found an opening, and gunned the car forward.

In the confusion, he crossed over to the other side of the railroad. Too late, he saw that he had entered La Cité, the *bas fond,* where the majority of the capital's residents scraped out a living. Strangers who entered were seldom ever seen again. Certainly there would be more desperate soldiers in La Cité than anywhere else in Kinshasa. He looked for a place to turn around, but the one way alley was too narrow. A demanding crowd had begun to assemble on the driver's side of the car, pressing him for "change." He could feel the motion as the car began to rock when the crowd heaved its collective weight against it. He could not move forward. He had heard of crowds in La Cité doing unimaginable things to strangers, and, for a moment, he regretted not having his affairs in order, concerned, as he habitually was, that his daughter would not know about his boat. There would be no inheritance, and he thought that was a waste. Eventually someone would sort it out, but he wasn't quite sure who. He doubted his daughter would.

Amongst the crowd, he saw two shirtless young men, pressing against the windshield. For a reasons he could not identify, seeing them reminded him of Maka Mgonu and he recalled the phrase the security chief had used less than an hour ago: "… hold onto your courage with ten fingers …" On impulse, he shouted to the two men, "Get into the car." He wanted them to show him the way to Matonge. His boldness took the crowd aback. His apparent lack of concern that the car was surrounded made them hesitate, shattering their cohesiveness. They parted to allow the two young men to move closer to the car.

When they got to his door, he grinned puckishly and cried, "Matonge!" The men laughed. Nightlife and Matonge were synonymous. But they didn't let go of the door handle until he produced two ten-dollar bills.

"Where is a policeman when you need one?" he said aloud, thanking Maka Mgonu in a silent prayer. The man, who had squeezed into what passed for the back seat in a Porsche 944, answered in fluent French, "You have no need for the police when you have dollars." Surprised at that response, the press officer laughed.

Like a gate opening, the crowd parted to let the car back out of the alley. The man in the back seat said he would guide them around the uncharted reaches of the monstrous Cité to the night-clubs in Matonge on the other side of the Marché Central.

"I saw some soldiers on my way here. What's going on? Is anything wrong?"

"Wrong?" the man in the backseat repeated, in an incredulous tone. "Finished is more like it. The men don't want to fight; they have not been paid." He waved his ten-dollar bill. "This is what they want, real money, not those *zaires* — the government's worthless crap. They'll fight for whoever gives them real currency. But Motutu's people have pocketed it all, so the soldiers won't fight. My brother is in the army. He came home yesterday and told me that the Tutsis are killing everyone in sight. How is he going to fight them? He hasn't been paid in five months."

"Is pay the only problem?" he probed, showing friendly curiosity that a stranger would display.

"You must have just gotten here, not to know that the Tutsis are on a rampage through the countryside. They want to take over the whole country and are slaughtering everyone on their march to Kinshasa."

The press officer made a greater show of being uninformed. "I have heard something about that. But you are right, I just got here. You think the soldiers would fight the Tutsis if Motutu gave them dollars, though?"

The man sitting in the front said, "No," in the deepest voice the press officer had ever heard, a profound, hollow bass. When he looked at him, surprised, the man said, "Not even the whites, the mercenaries, will fight for money, no matter what color it is.

Mututu is getting ready to leave with his family. I am going to be one of those who welcome the Tutsis to Kinshasa."

"The tall ones will never get to Kinshasa," the man in the back seat said. "France will send the *Paras* to protect this capital. I don't like the Tutsis. I don't like France either, to tell you the truth. But between the *Paras* and the Tutsis, I'll take the *Paras*."

"*Paras* — oh, paratroopers!" the press officer said.

Not stopping to reply, the man in the front seat blurted out, "Fool! Only a pseudo African would say such a thing. What you heard from the brother there," he said, glancing at the press officer, "is what's wrong with Africans. They think a European — even a cheap one — is always better than an African. They think that nothing will alleviate the problems — you know — self-inflicted problems like corruption. The day Motutu replaced the national bank director with an African, there was a run on the bank. They blame the Europeans for what is iniquitous in Africa. But then they pray that the Europeans won't leave. Anyone who wants the *Paras* is brainwashed! Brainwashed! You know where *Paras* practice their skills? On the head of Africans. That's where! There is nothing *Paras* like more than to decapitate Africans — simple execution isn't enough!"

"I am not brainwashed," his companion in the back seat answered. "I am only going by what I have experienced. That's what an empirical existentialist does. You, my brother are a fuzzy-brained idealist; you live in the clouds, where everything is the way you wish it to be. Me, I'm a realist. Lumumba is the only one who didn't steal from the people! But that's probably because he didn't have time before Africans killed him."

"Europeans killed Lumumba," the other man said. "Africans didn't kill Lumumba."

"Africans killed Lumumba. AFRICANS KILLED LUMUMBA," the man in the back seat shouted. "And they didn't need Europeans to tell them how or when to do it."

"I'm going to smack you when we get out of this car so that once and for all you know that Europeans are the enemy, not Africans."

"You go smack the tall ones that are coming from the east. They're going to be here soon enough. They'll think that you are a Hutu and massacre you before you can say hello in Swahili. They think any black who doesn't look like them is Hutu they have to kill."

"If you were them, you would do the same. We all would. Revenge and hate are built into our hearts." He sucked his teeth to emphasize his exasperation that the obvious had to be stated. "I think the Tutsis have a special power. It comes from the fact that there aren't that many of them compared to us — only about three million. Think about it. If you kill five hundred thousand, like the Hutus have done, you've done a lot of damage. They fear annihilation! They are so terrified of disappearing, they wipe out everybody in front of them to make sure they survive. Motutu is a fool! It was a fool's idea to attack the Tutsis. Now they are coming on Kinshasa, and I am going to be there to welcome them when they get here."

He turned to his friend cramped in the back seat who was stirring uncomfortably as the tires crunched the gravel beneath. "And it's not because I cheer for the first winner to come along. I like the Tutsis the way I liked Muhammad Ali — for winning while standing up for something. These Tutsis are what Africans should be: precise, direct, disciplined. They take care of their own. If they don't, they know they're history."

In the silence that followed these comments, the press officer asked, "Are you guys from *science po*, political science students?"

"We were until Motutu's hatchet man closed down the department," the man with the basso profundo voice replied.

"Motutu's hatchet man? Who's that?"

"It's best you don't know. The crowd back there was friendly, compared to how frightening he is. That man is so wicked he has people picked up at random and taken to a fortress where they're tortured for his amusement. He's a dog who guards the gates of hell.

"Some people saw him with his three heads on the day he had an entire village near Mbuji-Mayi wiped out because he thought that a man from there plotted against his master. No one could leave. They were all burned alive. That place doesn't exist anymore. Not a trace! It turned out there was no plot. Just a drunk in a Matonge bar saying where he would like to put the Great Elephant. The tall ones are the only ones who can end his rule. That's what I am talking about. And I am going to stand there and wait for them as long as it takes to do to him what he's done to thousands."

The man in the back seat said, "Tutsis are elitists. They have a superiority complex. That comes from their centuries of dominance over the Hutus. If the French let them get here, they're going to treat us the same way they treated the Hutus. You know how much they prize their cattle. They're going to turn us into milk drinkers.

The Hutus killed so many in '94 to get out from under them, that's why. Who wouldn't have done the same thing if he could? The only way for there to be no slaves is for them to kill the masters."

"That's true," the man in the front said. "The tall ones will be our liberators; they will free us from Motutu and his Cerberus."

"What are you guys talking about?" the press officer asked as the argument paused. "I read that the man leading the rebellion against President Motutu isn't tall but looks like me."

"You're talking about Jean-Luc Nundu," said the man in the back seat. "He is just a front for the tall ones. They don't want the people here to know they are imperialists, so they are using Nundu. Once they have seized the area around Kivu in the east, they'll have a foothold to pillage the entire Congo. We are going to start drinking milk from Tutsi cattle soon enough. Watch!"

The sun was setting. Each absorbed in his own thoughts gazed at the thickening vegetation while they traveled the worn road to Matonge.

"It's not like that at all," said the man in front, breaking the silence. "It's an alliance between Nundu and the Tutsis. They are helping Nundu take power. They are not going to spit him out. And he will help them against the Hutus. The Hutus are devoted to killing them all, so Nundu and the Tutsis joined forces to stay alive and promote each other's interests. Africans have some sophistication, you know!"

No one spoke. The argument had spent itself, no doubt to be reprised at another time. The words well honed by then would gush from the lips of the two friends as events from the Great Lakes region to the Atlantic Ocean unfolded. In any place but Africa, these events would be called a world war, involving as they did nations on three continents.

At the height of the argument, the press officer determined that his transaction with Brenda would have to wait until he had written down his passengers' contentions. He wanted to sift through the cant and identify politically useful facts buried inside the disagreement.

As he drove, he mentally reviewed their words, trying to be casual as he asked for clarification when he could not remember one point or another. All of this he did automatically — out of habit.

Policy architects use information collected by field officers like him to set courses of action between Washington and other nations.

One of his jobs was to pull together data and reports for analysis, although the evidence showed that very seldom did it work that simply.

Human intelligence, "humit" to the professionals, was not in vogue. But because he was good at gleaning information from people, he did it more often than most.

The value of reports from the field fades from the reality that "all politics are local." He had experienced that dictum in action in countless ways. Unless a report coincides with the viewpoints of key Washington-based staff, it ends up in a crosscut shredder. Early in his career, someone had explained to him the dog-chasing-its-tail principle. Process has more value than a likely result derived from the exercise.

Despite his ruminations, he was a professional, and he reminded himself that reporting the latest news was an essential part of his job. Whether or not what he reported mattered, they were paying him to do it. In any case, what were the chances that Mosley would approve and give clearance to the musings of a street man?

After he met Mosley at the airport, he had called Sid Greenblatt, his mentor in Washington, to discuss his options.

"Mosley, Judd Mosley?" Sid had cried. "Get out of there. From what I know of you, I can tell you that you're in danger. Mosley's mission in life is to show that he isn't to be affiliated with blacks just because of his skin color. One way he does that is by screwing little brothers like you. If you marry a white woman, he might see you differently. Your best bet is to call in favors, get ill, or do anything short of dying and fly out of there. He is a sick man! He will hurt you and live to tell the tale with promotions and titles. They love him here for being demanding, as they call it, toward minorities — particularly towards blacks. His type is not unique to people of color. There're some Jews who think I am too forward with my protests, or for having a brother like you. Take the advice of the *"Desiderata"* and stay away from people like Mosley, 'they are vexations to the spirit.' *A chaser bleibt a chaser,* a pig is always a pig. That man will leave his mark on you. And resentment will become more of your life's blood."

He answered that he would seek a transfer. However, after he had hung up, he reconsidered what Greenblatt had said and was less certain that Sid was right. Ambassador Mosley was indeed sick, but his mentor's diagnosis was wrong. Mosley wasn't fleeing from his color — he was upholding it, like a proud banner. The press officer's grandfather had been the same way.

There are "blacks and niggers," a comedian once declared. Mosley was black. Every person of color who didn't adhere to his values were niggers who lowered black people's standing in all aspects of life. They should stay in the ghettos, their uncouthness a wall of demarcation between them and him. That he had included the embassy's media man in that other category was not surprising. The press officer was a street man who found comfort in a crowd of other blacks. Mosley would suffocate in such a crowd and lived in fear of street men. The press officer wouldn't know how to be condescending to a black man. Mosley's impulse was the reverse.

His grandfather was an old man who hated old people for being "aged." Papo had a simple way of escaping his age: disparaging the old. He would make deprecating comments, especially if someone could hear him. "That man there should be in a nursing home; he has no business being at a concert," he would say. "Look at him. He can't even lift his feet off the ground."

But now Maka Mgonu had come along to rescue him with a conversation on a tape that spoke volumes about Mosley's illusion of superiority over other blacks. Mgonu would not have believed that Mosley's behavior towards the press officer had anything to do with the media fiasco at the airport. Indeed, if the press officer didn't need the tape to compel Brenda to get him transferred, he would present it to Mosley with a note: "This is what they think of you!"

Could he use the tape to ingratiate himself with the ambassador? Would Mosley be grateful if he presented him with this proof of his deputy's treachery? The press officer dismissed the thought. Sure, Mosley would be embarrassed, but he wouldn't welcome him as a brother.

He just hoped that Brenda wouldn't draw the same conclusion. She was the type who would dare him to go to the ambassador with the tape. He could hear her controlled twang, baiting him, "Go ahead, you little black twit. See how far you'll get." He was certain that Mgonu would have considered it a waste to use the tape only as a mean to pressure Brenda into helping him transfer out of Kinshasa. But that was his decision. He was no longer among those who viewed crisis as a road to opportunity.

# Chapter 20

Impending disasters don't affect nightlife, and Place Matonge throbbed. Although still early, terraces and nightclubs were crowded, the music, all in Lingala, loud. The press officer pulled up in front of a terrace, attracted by a *Au Fil de l'Eau*, With the Stream, painted on the side of the building. "I am buying you a Primus (beer) and then I must be off," he told his two passengers, getting out of the car. At the bar, the argument started anew when the man who had sat in the back seat told one of the barmen that soon he would have to stock fresh milk for his tall customers. That was his cue to leave. "I'll come back later if I can," he told them. "If you are still here I'll buy you another Primus." The man who had sat in the front was declaiming the impending liberation when the press officer got back into his car.

He drove south to bypass the great Marché Central where he figured more soldiers would be congregating. He reached the neighborhood outside of Ndjili Airport and its outsized cigarette billboards. Rounding the *Monument aux Martyrs de L'Indépendence*, he marveled as always how tall the monument pillars were — made even taller by the television towers crowning them. For a moment he thought how like his reports the monument was — a meaning-less symbol that no one looked at anymore. People walked by the shrine heedless that it had been built for a purpose other than to be a Kinshasa traffic signal.

---

The thirteen-year-old car's air conditioning strained to cool the muggy, dusty air. Once again, he thought that no one who had suffered malaria and had an allergy to dust should be assigned to such a place. Although a few chose to be here, his options had been more circumscribed. However, a few days ago, his mentor had told him that the token innovation that had been put in place had begun to bear modest fruit. More minorities were entering the service. The economic recession had been a recruitment boon. "Soon they will have London and Tokyo as options to choose from," Greenblatt had noted. "Serious options? No Sid. They will continue to be the 'so-that-you-don't sue-me, I'll-listen-to-your-request-option.'" They had argued over how long before the "be-loved community" would dawn. And he regretted having cursed

Sid. He still would be driving a cab in the District of Columbia, if it were not for old Sid.

----

But there was a redeeming feature to being in Kinshasa. Here he could experience a people's joy unlike any other country in which he had lived. He was awed because he didn't understand that a people who scraped an existence the way they did here had so much relish for life. Could it be that the less you have the more you cherish what you have? Condition did not bind people here.

Most of the affluent people he had encountered over time had little enthusiasm for life. For what it brought them, yes; but not for life itself, not for its own sake. He never spoke about the condition of the people, fearing that he would sound as if he were drunk on sentimentality. He had only a superficial appreciation for the African story. He knew that was so because his own experience told him that he didn't know them and couldn't understand them, certainly not comprehensively. And since there was nothing he could do for them, he said nothing.

What would he do to ameliorate their living condition if he had the means? he had asked himself rhetorically many times. He could never give himself a satisfactory answer, except to agree that if the African woman would be unbound that would free Africa from itself. He did not say what he really thought; he made expressions when people were around, some listening, and he had to say some-thing for them.

The tour of duty here was two years, barely time enough to glance at who the people were. Hello, goodbye, that was the extent of the interaction between interlopers like himself and the people here. His colleagues like to say they were in the goodbye business. But that was an excuse for the superficial life they lived in places like Kinshasa. Others, the French, for example, made a career of serving in one country. And, of course, they used the appreciation gained over time to their greatest advantage. It was a kind of rule.

Imposing an answer would not do. That he understood. What then? Africans must come up with their own solutions. He prayed, whatever their answer, that it would not include becoming mindless consumers. But he was afraid they would.

In the supermarket he had watched a woman wander through the aisles until she found something to purchase: a small eraser. Not because she needed it; but because that's what she could buy, evidently experiencing a kind of satisfaction. "I always wanted to buy something," she told him. "That's all I could get." He wanted to give her money to buy food but thought that she would not be judicious in her purchases, so he picked a cartful of basic staples for her and paid for it. When he went to retrieve his car, she was in the supermarket's parking lot selling the lamb he had bought for her to a well-heeled woman.

He was one of the few Americans who ventured outside of the embassy compound. His colleagues shopped at the commissary and would not once taste dishes from an African kitchen. Even for him, not all African dishes appealed to his sensibilities. His first taste of monkey stew was not bad, until they served the rice, and he saw to his horror that the wizened, roasted paw of the monkey had been placed on top to be used as the serving spoon. The paw looked like the baby hand of his daughter. He passed on the dish and was never again as venturesome.

His colleagues would not speak a syllable of the country's language. They didn't have to; the Africa they saw was cramped between residence and office. Weekends they spent at home. The video club was always crowded Friday afternoons.

Aid was administered in Kinshasa in the same manner as it was elsewhere, like a bureaucratic postscript. Officials had no need to know what the culture could accept; underdevelopment was the culture. He had seen that, perhaps except for the Canadians, no nation gave with more care, although not with the most generosity. But the aid was confined to another process — how much was given, not how much was achieved.

"We have given a billion dollars worth of aid to this place," a well-connected official had told him. "But can you see even a million dollars worth of development here?" He asked if corruption was responsible for the dismal return on the investment. "No," the woman had answered. "In essence our aid is based on a non sequitur, that is, not on any premise that we'll make progress in a place like this. It's something we do, it's a job. And nine times out of ten, we are like firefighters. We respond only after an alarm is set off, usually late. I'll tell you an open secret: to us, the underdevelopment you see out there, it's an abstraction. There is no human face to go along with our aid." He thought of saying that it sounded as if international aid officials were the development trade's weekend warriors, just extras in a B movie; but he bit his tongue. He had been impressed by the way she spoke, and had tried to say, "i.e.," like her several times. A look from Brenda at a staff meeting had put an end to the parroting experiment.

———  ———  ———

Presently he headed west to avoid the downtown area and Boulevard du 30 Juin. To reach his destination in Gomé, he would have to go through la Cité de l'OUA and turn northeast to bypass the more congested areas and potential trouble spots. He had noticed even more troops drifting in from the southeast.

He removed his ID card from his wallet before he got to the embassy's gate when he spotted the marine from Texas who had a "by the book" demeanor since the new ambassador had arrived. In reply to the press officer's question about the deputy, the guard said that she had left for the day. However, a minute later the guard was at his office door. He had forgotten to pass along a note Brenda had left for the press officer. How could something like that be a coincidence? And for a moment he speculated that the security chief was playing a double game and had warned Brenda about the tape. But he dismissed the idea.

"If you come back to the embassy tonight, pass by my place when you leave," Brenda's note read. For a while, he turned over in his mind all the possibilities of what the note could mean. Why would Brenda who would never have invited him to her residence be doing so now? His transfer? That must be it; she was as eager to see him gone as he was. Impatient to hear the good news, he picked up the phone, although he knew he would not have a dial tone. But without the least hesitation, the line hummed the clear signal. He dialed and heard a deep "oui" from Brenda.

"I got your note," he said cautiously, expecting a terse, "pack your bag" reply from the prickly deputy. Instead, in a voice he had not heard before when addressing him, Brenda cajoled, "I want to discuss something with you. When can you get here?"

"You mean it's not about my transfer?" he asked, his tone caustic.

"Yes and no. But this is something that needs to be discussed in person. I'll tell you when you get here."

———  ———  ———

The embassy's top people also had their residences in Gomé, and a fast drive in the deserted residential area of plush villas got him there in less than fifteen minutes. How long before the troops find their way here, he wondered when he drove by the guarded mansions of the regime's barons.

Two guards were at Brenda's gate. When he pulled up, one of them called to another inside. He took the press officer's ID card and a moment later opened the gate. Brenda was standing on the veranda, her arms crossed below her ample bosom, waiting, the door open behind her. A tall woman, she stood, her legs apart, wearing a white cotton dress appropriate to the tropical night. She signaled with a nod that he should go in.

"Please sit down." But he remained standing, as if that would make her tell him that much faster that the transfer order had come through.

"Sit down!" Her tone was forceful but still friendly. "I am not going to bite you." There it was, the voice she had used when talking to the Fatman, the voice on the tape in his pants' pocket pressing against his thigh. "Can I get you something? Cognac maybe? I have a bottle of old Armagnac that you might like? It's an eau de vie, like grappa, that a friend gave me."

"I know Armagnac, Brenda. Cognac would be fine. What's the news about my transfer?"

"I'm getting to that. But first let me get the drinks; I don't have Maurice tonight."

She came back, holding two glasses between the fingers of one hand and the cognac bottle in the other. They could have been in a college dorm room, settling in for the evening, in all appearances, friends.

The press officer followed her with his eyes. He detected an unfamiliar nervousness in her movements. Why is she so antsy? he asked himself.

"Is it when you are nervous that you laugh or is it the other way around? Loosen up," she told him, making an effort, herself, to hide her own edginess.

"I'll laugh once I hear about my transfer," he answered. He waited, silent, for her to pour his drink.

"I don't know where to start, so I'll start with this question, would you like to work with me? Notice I didn't say for me."

"If it's somewhere else, sure," he said, making her understand that as long as there was a transfer, anything was acceptable to him.

"Let's be frank, you don't want a transfer because you hate Kinshasa. It's Mosley you want to get away from. I have seen how he treats you."

"For the record, I have had malaria twice since I have been here. That's my official reason. They'll understand that I don't want to wait until I am carried out of here to transfer."

"But Mosley is the real reason, and between us, I think he's going to be recalled in a short while. They won't name somebody else to replace him, leaving me to act as the interim. I want you to help me run this place."

"Help you run this place? You mean like your deputy?" he made a face and turned to look at her.

She changed position on her sofa, finally tucking her feet beneath her thighs. "This is no time for administrators," she answered earnestly. "It's time for press officers. If you become my deputy, there is no chance they would send us someone to replace you. In any case, I wouldn't want somebody else for press officer; no one handles the press the way you do. We would both benefit, with you remaining press officer. I have contacts in Washington that would ensure they take care of you. In the next few days we're going to have lots of action here. Once that's passed, I'll get you the best job there is in London with a promotion to go along with a transfer."

He didn't answer at once. He had seen Motutu's soldiers in the first stages of becoming a ravaging army against its own population. If the man in the back seat of his car had been right about Tutsis slaughtering Hutus, there was a world of misery out there. He could only imagine what had befallen the people between the Great Lakes and Kinshasa. And this was the place this woman said would be his chance in a lifetime?

"I'm not interested," he told her. "I have the right to ask for a transfer. That's what I am going for."

"Look! If I didn't put it to you right, I'm sorry. But consider that they may refuse to give you a transfer, until they find a press officer willing to come out here to replace you. That's what they're going to tell us, you know. You have to stay until they find a replacement for you."

"If that's the case, if I am stuck here anyway, why this production tonight."

"Because I need your help to make something of myself here." She had blurted that confession out, and now she studied him to judge his reaction. There was none. After a few seconds, she said, "You know everything there is to know about the media — local and international. I need you to use that for me. Work them on my behalf. In return, I'll get you what you want — Kenny."

He laughed. "Kenny? What happened to 'little black twit?'"

"I said that because you called me a white trash. I was offended. I am sorry."

"I never called you white trash. I said you were a woman from the south."

"You said I was a poor white woman from the south. And what does that mean if not trash? if you'll excuse me? I know the code words just as well as you do."

"Then why aren't you concerned that I'll go to Ambassador Mosley with what you just told me?"

"Mosley doesn't think much of you. It wasn't your fault the journalists were not there. I told him that. But he loathes you. In fact he thinks worse of you than the most racist southern cracker I know. You'd think that it would be to his advantage to support a fellow black. I don't know why he dislikes you the way he does. You are after all his kin, race wise. Until I saw this, like everybody in the Department, I thought that you people were a tight-knit group with a common interest, conspiring retribution against us; and unless we dedicated ourselves to holding what we had, it was only a matter of time before you ran the place."

"We should carry a sign around our necks," the press officer said, 'we will not do unto you what you have done unto us.'"

"In any case, if you are smart," Brenda continued as if her interlocutor had not spoken, "you'll go consult that witch doctor you've been seeing — I know about that — and ask him to do something to advance Mosley's departure from Kinshasa. You may have to stay here for a long while — with him in charge. Don't think you don't have a choice other than being between a rock and a hard place. That's true only if Mosley doesn't go. I am asking you to join forces with me, to see to it he is on the next plane. He is no friend of yours; I don't care what color he is."

"What are you saying now? That I should help you get rid of him too?"

"It's in your interest! How can I make it plainer? You are going to be here, at least for a while. It's best if he is not here at the same time you are. Don't you agree? Well? You're looking at me as if it doesn't matter to you if he stays. That man will ruin you, if he can help it. The media can do it for us. What goes in the New York papers about Kinshasa matters to the decision makers."

The press officer looked thoughtfully at his empty glass. Brenda refilled it.

"Hey, who cares about color? The enemy of an enemy is first a friend. It's as simple as that," she told him, confident that she had gotten through to him.

Then unexpectedly he asked, "When you call Washington, which phone do you use?"

"The one in the bedroom. Why?"

"I want to see it."

"You're not going in my bedroom!"

The tone of his "OK!" closed the subject. He stood up. "I better be going. I told two guys at a bar in Matonge that I'd drop by."

The deputy remained seated, looking at him, debating what to say. "If that's what it will take to consummate a deal between us, I'll do it. I'll have to empty that bottle though. I've never been with a black man before."

The press officer looked at her at first dumbfounded, then very sad. "You mean you'd have sex with someone who disgusts you for this?" he waved his hand to encompass the room, as if that were symbolic of her ambition.

"How do you think I got here? I have a figure men like. The thing is I always have to be more or less stoned to go through with it."

"I only want to remove a bug from the telephone you use to call Washington. Nothing more. There is a listening device in there."

"A listening device?"

"Yeah, a listening device!"

"How do you know?"

"I'll give you the answer they give in the movies: I heard some people discussing your telephone in a bar in Matonge. How is that?"

"Who would have put it there?" Then she remembered something. "That bastard! I should have guessed. The French are worse than the Soviets! When you sleep with dogs —" He didn't respond to that remark, as much as he wanted to tell her that Africans were as capable as anybody else of looking after their perceived interests.

She showed him to the bedroom. From the doorway, she pointed to the telephone on the nightstand. He was about to sit on the foot of the bed, but what she said about having to be liquored up had offended him. He remained standing and unscrewed the mouthpiece. A chip slipped out into his fist. Brenda saw him put it in his pants' pocket.

"I wouldn't want anybody to listen in on your conversations, especially the one to Matthew about my London assignment," he said, as he passed her in the bedroom's doorway.

She gaped at him, her face drained of color. "I gather we have a deal," she said at length. "We may not be from the same side but we are looking from the same vantage point."

"We are from the same side, Brenda, but we are not looking for the same thing. You want the world; me, it's just a fair shake. So let's say we have an understanding. I'll be long gone before people like me and people like you have deals. How about discussing strategy? What will Washington need to pull Ambassador Mosley out of here?"

# Chapter 21

Ambassador Mosley's wife was having the time of her confined life. Maurice, the driver, was the reason. Everything Maurice did proclaimed that he valued her for herself. To him she was not an American, a boss, or a person of a different race. She was a woman to be worshiped. The way he opened the doors of the car and the house made her feel as if she were the president's wife. The word Goddess crossed her mind when Maurice looked at her.

If he came to take her on an errand, he brought her flowers he evidently had picked himself. He couldn't buy them; he was a poor man, he had explained, and had several jobs, including one moonlighting as the butler for Ms. Bleding, her husband's deputy. He also brought her starfruits he had picked. Tears sprang to her eyes one morning when she noticed how meticulously he washed them before presenting them to her. He looked so serious.

Even venturing into the madness of that unbelievable Marché Central was a pleasurable experience with Maurice as her bodyguard. Leaning on him, feeling the taut muscles, was very often the treat of her day. She just knew he would risk his life for her. And he was so handsome! Tall, with features like a Moor's, his skin smooth as a black pearl. His hair was soft — sitting in the back seat of the official car she wondered how it could be so black. She had asked him not to wear his chauffeur's cap. She wanted to see his hair.

Had the dispatcher told her that Maurice was unavailable to take her on her ever more frequent errands, she would have killed the interloper. When he was scheduled to pick her up, she would dress in a white *pagne* and fuss about the way she looked, something she had not bothered with in years. Her husband was pleased that the driver had become so devoted to his wife. Behind such devotion, clearly, was respect for who he was.

The day she saw him naked was the brightest, hottest since she had arrived in Kinshasa. He had helped the gardener that afternoon and was showering outside the servants' bathroom. She had stared, remembering Junction City, Kansas, when she was a little girl and the multi-colored ice creams her father bought her on the oppressive days. He looked at her and moved his head slightly to indicate she should go inside — for him. As he walked through her bedroom door, she lowered the blinds.

Ambassador Mosley was taking the Thursday evening flight to Paris with a connection to Dulles the next day. Washington had asked him to come on consultation. That was not an unusual request. Ambassadors serving in crisis areas often visit headquarters to brief policymakers and discuss interests and strategies.

In Mosley's case, Brenda thought otherwise. She was convinced that Mosley had been summoned home to be told he'd been reassigned. Although she refrained from calling the Fatman to check if that indeed were true, she had reasons for so much optimism. A number of coolly critical articles had appeared in U.S. newspapers and journals from reporters who had began to rent rooms in the Kinshasa Continental Hotel, lured by the pungent smell of another great killing. These reports suggested that Washington didn't have a firm hold on events unfolding between the huge Great Lakes region and the Atlantic Ocean. The word "clueless" was sprinkled through the accounts, giving pause to the Washington readers who cared about such things.

The press officer had drafted a number of reports from what he had heard from neighbors, soldiers, men on the street, and even two ministers about the cumulative effects of the disturbing news from the east. None of his reports had cleared Mosley's desk. The ambassador loathed alarming Washington with reports that events were drifting out of control in his area. They might think him not vigilant enough or simply incapable of managing things. He would prefer to be born, like his older brother, a thalidomide baby, than be thought incompetent. That obsessed him, and he wrote himself notes about his fear. When his deputy questioned him about the uncleared reports, he replied: "Too alarmist, they are too alarmist. Washington will think the world is ending here. I don't need that. What about his transfer? That's one thing I cleared — on the first day I got here. Why isn't he out of here? He keeps writing this babble. If I cleared them, they'd think we are a bunch of Ebonics speakers here. Have you looked at them?"

"I don't know what Ebonics is, Mr. Ambassador. As to the reports, they look OK to me. But of course, I don't have your standards."

"If I clear them, it's my name on this crap. In any case, I don't believe we need to upset Washington with fantasies about Tutsis killing Hutus or vice versa. That's old news! Our job here is to watch what Motutu is up to. Nundu should be allowed to come in without us missing a day at the office. A leadership vacuum is unacceptable. I want to see Nundu on that presidential podium. That's what I care about.

"This press officer should've been out of here, and yet we are discussing his incomprehensible reports. Washington would really think I have lost it if I cleared this stuff. You were going to take care of it. When will he be history?"

"I don't know, Mr. Ambassador. Washington has not responded to our request. I was on the phone earlier with personnel. My sense, as I told you the other day, is that they won't agree to a transfer unless they have a replacement. No one has applied."

She was hoping he would say that he would look into the matter when in Washington on consultation. And she had tried to arrange an appointment for him to see the Fatman, but that didn't work either. Matthew Greeson refused to be in the same room with a man he was going to hang for her sake. Matthew a coward? How could she think such a thing? She was beginning to fear that Mosley had nine lives.

---

When he looked in her direction, she shook her head, "No." Mosley would not clear his reports. It was lunchtime, one of the few times he had gone to the cafeteria, usually preferring the local fare and the opportunity to be among the people who frequented Kinshasa's street luncheonettes.

"What's Ebonics?" Brenda asked.

"African American English! Why —" his mouth stayed open; he pivoted to look away, as if that would help him focus on the revelation.

"You mean like jive?" Brenda asked.

"Yeah, something like that," he said between his teeth. "So that's what it is — I am going to kick that…" He put his tray back on the stack at the end of the queue and turned for the door. Brenda went after him and grabbed his arm.

"Kenny, don't be a fool," she told him in an urgent whisper, her eyes wide. "You touch him and that's it. The password in this transaction is 'yes, sir.' You know damn well what I mean!" He gaped at her uncomprehendingly for a moment.

"You know what I am going to do?" He told her when he could focus. "I am going to tell every reporter I meet what his wife is up to. I know the whole story. It wasn't my business before. Now it is. I'll show them Ebonics! I'll see you later."

A colleague who passed him in the hall heard him say, amazement in his voice, "That son of a bitch!" He stopped, shook his head, and repeated, "That son of a bitch!" In the cafeteria, she asked Brenda, who was as customary sitting alone at the table nearest the door, "What's the matter with Ken? I saw him in the hall, muttering, 'son of a bitch,' to himself."

She could have been addressing the deputy in an African language, so unlikely was Brenda to respond to her annoying interruption. But the colleague stood her ground, her large presence insisting on an answer. Afraid the woman would actually sit down, Brenda looked at her as if to ask, who said you could address me? Then looking back down at her plate, muttered, "Who can understand these people?"

---

VIPs don't use the lounge to wait before boarding their planes. Because facilitators take care of the airport formalities on their behalf, they arrive at the last minute, often chauffeured to the foot of the boarding stairs. The plane would even wait from a few minutes to an hour for some VIPs.

Ambassador Mosley's man at the airport had the formalities out of the way early in the afternoon. It would be a couple of hours before he made his radio call — the telephones were often out of order, and cell phones were not yet available — that the plane was boarding. Normally the plane would wait past its departure time so that Ambassador Mosley could get to Ndjili Airport. But the plane taxied down the runway a few minutes early and couldn't or wouldn't be recalled to the gate. The tower was acting under orders from Maka Mgonu that no plane that had left the gate could be recalled that day. Two days earlier, the security chief had briefed the Dictator on a number of issues, including the driver's progress with the ambassador's wife.

"He reports that he already has been with her several times, Mokonzi. She is an eager participant," he droned clinically.

Mototu chuckled. "How is she? What did he say? Come on Maka!"

"He reports that she is eager, shouts what sounds like obscenities. But he has to use the Chinese stimulant on himself to perform. Alluring she is not. It's a job."

"If it's just a job, then you must not wait. You can arrange for Jood to find them easily enough. You said he is catching the flight to Paris Thursday evening. Why not get it done then? There is symmetry in that Molu arrives Thursday as well. Why not settle all our accounts in one day?"

"Do we let him know we are responsible?"

"Who?"

"Jood!"

Motutu turned over the question in his mind. "No need!" he finally decided. "He is smart, he'll figure it out himself. And I don't know if I want to be remembered as another Richard Nixon, a president who used dirty tricks. What about the deputy, has your man done his job there as well?"

"Yes! He has placed the device in the phone. So far our only intercepts," he lied, "are her conversations with the French commercial attaché and with her relatives in the States. Nothing of value. I am beginning to think that calls that would be of interest to us she places at the office."

"Well, you have an intercept there, haven't you."

"No, not there... exactly."

The Dictator looked at his security chief quizzically. There were things he would rather not know. It was enough that they understood each other.

"I wonder how humiliating it will be for him to find his wife with our man," he mused. "What's his name across the river enjoys doing it to his friends, enemies, everybody. And he does it himself. A real stud! At least we have some class and get an agent to do it for us. We are sophisticated, Maka."

<hr>

When his car turned onto the tarmac, the plane was taxiing to the runway for takeoff. If he could get someone to call the tower, they would ask the plane to return to the gate. The driver pointed at the ground crew walking back to the terminal. Mosley waved his hand urgently in their direction, and the driver raced toward them. In the time it took Mosley's electric window to roll down, the car was beside the crew.

"I am the ambassador of the United States" he told them, pointing at the flag on his car's bumper. "Would you please tell the tower that I am terribly sorry?"

At once, a woman with a radio placed the call. It was minutes before someone answered, and to Mosley's dismay, he could hear the woman begging, telling whomever was on the other end that it was the ambassador of the United States who was missing the plane. As she pleaded, she extended her hand as if to stop the majestic 747 moving slowly into position for take off.

Mosley remained in the back seat, listening to the roar from the plane's engines getting louder. He watched as the plane, reverberation from its engines shaking the terminal, rumbled down the runway, and, after a long run, lift off. He got out of the car and watched the plane leave him on the tarmac.

"Let me speak to the tower," he told the woman with the radio.

"They said they couldn't call the plane back," she told him.

"Who was that you were talking to? What's his name?"

She told him.

Mosley, pedantic as always, struck his favorite pose: I am the super power's plenipotentiary. "He will hear from me. He will never set foot in the United States. Tell him that for me. And what's your name. I saw what you tried to do for me. I am very grateful."

The plane had disappeared into the thick air. Ambassador Mosley had no choice but to get back into his car. His radio call to his embassy made *au clair* was heard by a number of listeners.

"Birdsong this is Chieftain, over." Brenda heard the call on the radio that was a fixture on her desk. She was Birdsong.

"This is Birdsong, over. Are you calling from the plane?"

"This is Chieftain. No, I missed the plane. Tell DC, and arrange for me for tomorrow's flight. I'll be home if you need me."

"This is Birdsong. Will do. Over and out."

The guards were not at their post at the ambassador's front gate. The driver waited a moment, then got out of the car to look for them. Having experienced the ambassador's restiveness, he went through the door to open the gate himself. The woman's cries Mosley thought he had heard became louder. As the car moved toward the house, the missing guards came running toward the driveway. Mosley noticed that they had emerged from the back of the house, in the direction of the bedroom he and his wife used. The cries were distinct now, unmistakable, a woman, in the throes of sexual exaltation. The guards had been eavesdropping or watching.

Mosley didn't wait for the driver to open the car door. He ran into the house as if to catch the thief in the act. The bedroom door was open. His wife, naked, her pale skin blotched purple, her limp breasts two-topmast pennants flapping in the storm of her crazed motion; she was hanging on, braying like a frustrated mule, shouting the same word over again. She was astride the driver she had used since arriving in Kinshasa. He had his hands behind his head. And his eyes may have been closed. Mosley's resentment upon seeing that the driver had his uniform on was telling.

The man alerted by the slamming door pulled himself up to get out from under the woman who rocked back and forth, her movement uncontainable. She held onto him, her shouts more urgent. She saw him look in the direction of the door and partially turned her head. Her husband was staring at her. But he was not seeing her. He was recalling the stuck dogs he had thrown rocks at as a youngster. Nausea overwhelmed him. He could not vomit enough to expunge his disgust.

His first thought after the cleansing was how is this going to look? He could give the guards money to keep their mouths shut, and he turned in the direction of the living room where his own driver, averting his eyes, was standing, waiting. He ordered the man to bring the guards into the house. After a while, the driver returned. Alone. The guards were nowhere to be found.

In Matonge that night, the press officer heard about Mosley's wife and the driver. He felt a kind of shame he could not readily explain. At the airport, an arriving Molu was bent over with laughter when he was told. A village thief did not move as fast as the tale of the American ambassador who missed his plane and returned home only to find his wife astride her driver.

# Chapter 22

The Abu Dhabi International Airport, a small, circular shaped facility is well-appointed. As in public areas in other Muslim countries, the colors green and blue predominate. Molu cleared customs with an alacrity seldom experienced in all his travels. In just a short time, he was at the door of the Golden Class Club, where all passengers have access to the installation's meet-and-assist accommodations. He had not followed the Dictator's instruction to use a regular passport.

Even with official credentials, an African diplomat cannot be confident the world will extend the guarantees established by the Vienna Convention to him. Engraved in Molu's mind was a rainy day in February the previous year during a stopover at London Gatwick Airport. He was enroute to a Brussels conference regarding oil exploration in Muanda-Banana at the estuary of the Congo River. Arrival formalities were routine. He sailed through customs and, minutes later, was ensconced at Le Méridien Hotel within the airport. The next day, however, the mood had changed. The officials made light of his diplomatic status and searched his suitcase thoroughly. It was as though Article 30 — *"his papers, correspondence and... his property, shall enjoy inviolability"*— of the Vienna Convention did not apply to him.

The practical reason for traveling as a diplomat was a regular passport required an affidavit of sponsorship from one of the people he had come to see in Abu Dhabi. He had considered asking the Pakistani to be his sponsor but was not certain the merchant could oblige. So, despite vagaries in official treatment, the *de jure* entrée the diplomatic passport bestows made him disobey the Dictator.

As Molu entered, a tall lanky man wearing a "khandura," Abu Dhabi's national dress, stood and, formally addressing him as Ambassador Sakeseba, introduced himself. He had the suspicious, darting eyes of a man constantly on the alert; but he also possessed the dignity of a man whose faith in God was absolute.

Molu looked at the photo ID the Pakistani flashed in front of him and nodded. That was the assent to proceed, and a second man appeared to pick up Molu's bag. "He works for me," the diamond merchant said to Molu, "one of my sons."

They walked into the warm, dry, night air. A sedan raced to their side. Molu was about to sit behind the driver, but the merchant asked him to move to the other side. Concerned, he asked about Abu Dhabi's security. "Is it problematic?" Aware of the subject Molu was raising, the man shook his head, no. Molu then asked about the distance to the city center, saying that he had another appointment later that night. However, his companion remained silent. He did not want to talk in the car.

The merchant's business was in the well-lit Mussafah industrial zone outside the city's center. Encircled by the desert, the area had the appearance of a lit city on a barren planet. After fifteen minutes, Molu was certain that the circuitous drive and numerous checkpoints would never end. Then, the car stopped abruptly in front of a metal warehouse. Molu could hear crackling noises as rivets in the structure cooled down after a day in the blazing sun. The driver sounded his horn. A guard came rushing out, looked inside the car, ran back to his post and opened the metal entry door.

Molu stepped out of the Mercedes and realized he was in an enormous storeroom. From what he could see, the merchant specialized in the import of artificial flowers. Crates were crammed in the storehouse from floor to ceiling. Clearly, this was an operation of some magnitude. For Molu's business, such a display of goods denoted access to full-scale capital.

The merchant walked back to where his guest was examining the stockpiled merchandise. "We do over five million American dollars worth of business per month in this region," he said with pride, gesturing in the direction of an upstairs suite of glassed-in offices. "Our friend knows that we have what it takes. We can accommodate any quantity of the item he privileges us to handle. And he should have no concern for security and or privacy," he said, as he shook his head forcefully. "Let me show you some of our numbers. I also had a folder prepared that includes letters from two banks in Europe and one in America. You will recognize some of the names, I'm sure."

In a comfortable office, sitting on a leather sofa, a half dozen folders on a coffee table in front of them, the merchant, in a methodical and precise way, took Molu through the maze of his operation, taking every opportunity to underline that the "client" should have no apprehension regarding the stability of his business. Molu had no training in this field and understood little of the complexity. However, the merchant's enthusiasm for his operation and his knowledge of the diamond market entranced him, and he found himself following with interest, for a time forgetting Julie at the Continental Hotel.

"We will take all the borts you can give us," the merchant explained. "This region's oil industry is in constant need of that type of industrial diamond. You have most of it. I even heard that you found deposits in the north. Being from that area, our friend should be pleased. I visited him in Gbadolite once, and took a tour; I was amazed at how much development there was in that area — no one can touch him there. There is no reason we cannot have a long and very profitable partnership. I am at his service.

"We will also take all the other industrial grade diamonds you have to trade, carbonado or ballas. However, we have a small request. We would appreciate your considering us also for the gem-grade ones, the high quality ones, the ones you bring from Angola.

"Price and privacy wise, we can do better here. Antwerp can no longer provide the privacy our friend has a right to expect. The bad news out of Sierra Leone and Liberia has damaged the district near the railroad where you trade in Antwerp. This has cramped every-thing over there and reduced prices. He should consider moving the Antwerp *comptoire* to this region.

"This is not a formal request, you understand; but I think this is something to consider. How much longer can he continue to trust them in Antwerp, as we all did in the old days? Trust was the constitution we lived by. We can no longer say that. I hope you will lay out this plan to our friend. The people here are serious. He will not regret it."

The merchant sat back to assess Molu's reaction to his words. And he ordered more tea.

Over the third cup of tea, the merchant told Molu he knew a banker in a neighboring country who could accommodate transac-tions of this magnitude. Molu beamed and shook the merchant's hand; he was the man their friend was looking for. But the dia-mond dealer was unsure Molu favored him as much as Molu said he did. It was well past midnight when the man concluded his presen-tation and walked his guest to the waiting car.

"Is there anything else I can show you? Anything at all?" he asked solicitously.

"I don't think so," Molu said with care. "You have shown me more than I expected to see. I can understand why our friend thinks so highly of you."

"Are you sure?"

"Yes, I am sure. If I have failed to convey my satisfaction let me assure you that I was most impressed with the details of your operation. Our friend has had dealings with you in the past. He knows you. What I have come here to ascertain is the reassurance he is looking for. You are a serious man." Nevertheless, the man looked at him, unconvinced.

"Is there anything else?" Molu asked. "I better go check in, or the hotel will wonder what has become of me."

The merchant hesitated, seemingly not sure how to express what he wanted to convey to his guest. "It's that — usually in transactions of this nature — the intermediary demands a fee, which I assure you I am prepared to discuss. This you have not done. You haven't said anything about a commission. Forgive me — it's that I am uncertain."

"I understand," Molu said with a shrug, "I assure you I wouldn't be loathe to tell you if business was not possible between us. Our times are too valuable for charades. Trust, as you so aptly said, is the most important ingredient in the way we conduct our affairs. Regarding a commission, our friend has already done much for me. This is my job. Representing our friend is my job."

"I'll have to accept that explanation," the merchant said with what may have been a smile, extending his hand to Molu. "Please don't forget what I said about the high quality gems."

"I'll remember. I won't be the one to handle the transactions themselves," Molu said when the car door was opened for him. "But I hope to see you again."

# Chapter 23

When he saw her, Julie was coming into their room from a late night swim, a wet aquamarine-colored T-shirt clinging to her hips above low-cut black bikini briefs, "Continental" in black letters emblazoned across her full breasts. In one step, she was in his arms, and pent-up desire washed over them. He lifted her, removing the T-shirt, to carry her into the room. Had his life ended at that moment, he would have gone to his grave, content. After they had their fill of each other, they were voluble, making plans and promises. He was going to cable his wife that their marriage was at an end. Julie in turn explained that she had left her husband a note telling him that she was divorcing him.

Between meals, lovemaking, and the time Molu spent on the Dictator's business outside of the hotel, they justified themselves to each other. The walls of the hotel made them feel safe, and their fervor for one another made them optimistic. Their passion for one another was a fresco against the clouds on the suite's ceiling.

Julie was a French citizen and would fly to Paris to wait for Molu. Surely, she could get a position with a perfume shop or *haut chic* leather boutique. (In fact, it was at a perfume shop where her husband had first seen her and been smitten.) At first that pleased Molu. There was a romantic and yet sensible sound to her working in such a place. Then he thought of the possible headline, "Kinshasa Foreign Minister's Beautiful Indian Wife Shop Girl in Paris," and wasn't so sure Mokonzi would approve. They talked about what it would mean if she lived incognito in Paris, agreeing that it would leave her free to work and provide a modicum of protection from the regime's political opponents. After a gentle debate, Molu concurred with an ironic smile that it would be a shame to deprive the *haut-chic* quartier of *Rue du Faubourg Saint Honoré* of the presence of such an exotic beauty.

Perhaps it would be better if Julie came back to Kinshasa with him? After all, one had only a short single life to live. Why miss even a minute by being apart? Upon returning to Kinshasa, once ensconced with the Dictator, Molu would tell him about Julie. He had an understanding heart. "People would never know that Mokonzi has a romantic soul," he told her. "He will smile on our union, and that should be all the protection we need."

"I don't know! That security man scares me," she whispered with a glint of terror in her eyes. "He is always staring at me from behind his dark glasses. He is like an undertaker waiting for a person to become a corpse. I told you he has his men follow me sometimes. When I left Kinshasa, his men were everywhere. I also saw soldiers. On my way to the airport, they were taking off their uniforms. The man who drove me to Ndjili said they were escaping from the people from the east. You know, the people the president was having trouble with? What will we be going back to there? What about a job at the UN? You mentioned the UN before. UNESCO is in Paris, how about there?"

"Mgonu is not as scary as he looks," Molu assured her. "It's just a façade to unnerve people. He is very successful at pretending to be Mokonzi's evil genius. Then, too, he has overeager bureaucrats working for him. And maybe he suspects your husband of one thing or another. There is always talk about what goes on in that hotel. But once I've explained to the president how it is with us, everything will be fine. I wouldn't mind working at UNESCO. But that's for when I am retired. Right now it's modest compared to the office I am entering. If I have you to come home to — The UN can be for after we have settled in Paris… later. In any case, for UNESCO or any UN job, I'll need the president's approval." She looked away from him, not convinced Kinshasa was safe; he was refusing to admit how it really was over there, she thought.

He flew to Sharjah after lunch. Julie came along. "I can't be in Abu Dhabi and not see the Gold Souk," she told him, aghast that he could think such a thing. Her voice was one he was becoming familiar with — a mixture of childish seriousness and grown-up exasperation. She called the desk to reserve a seat on his flight, to discover that Molu had chartered a plane. She fell into his arms laughing when she heard. It would be very simple, she said. From the Sharjah airport, she would take a taxi to the souk and then return to the airport where she would wait for him. He didn't know how to dissuade her. He tried to explain the nature of the trip in the context of his new position in Kinshasa, but he was not at all persuasive.

Sharjah was business that did not call for her to accompany him; more than that, he also was at a crossroad, having begun to experience discomfort at being seen with her. He tried to dismiss the feeling. The effort to manage the uncertainty made him restless. He tried to rationalize, telling himself that being seen with such a striking woman was to his advantage; but that was a momentary antidote. What had brought this on? Was it the hotel staff's reticence to serve them promptly? Was it the look in the waiter's face when Julie had walked into the dining room at breakfast? It was a look of horror, so pronounced Molu turned to see what had so affected the man. He told himself he was imagining things, but he then made excuses for having their meals in the room.

And to ease his anxiety, he looked for mixed-race couples the few times he was out. He saw many Arabs with whites, but no black African with anybody else. He thought he saw an Indian with an Arab, once; but he wasn't sure of that either. With his wife a couple of shades lighter than he, he never felt any apprehension. But that was in Washington. His uneasiness was real, whether it was driven by imagination or not, it was real to him. He wanted to be somewhere else.

His paranoia made him irritable, more so when he mentioned his concern to Julie. However, he spoke in such a roundabout way, that she could not understand what he was trying to ask her. He just didn't have the courage to be clear. He could not say, does it bother you that we are not of the same race; and that people react to us with question marks in their manner? Julie herself did not seem to notice. He took to wearing a robe in the room to cover his blackness that contrasted to the stark white walls of their refuge.

She noticed the change in him, but it took her some time to discern their racial difference as the cause. The two times they were together in Kinshasa, he flaunted their affair. She repeatedly cautioned him, but he persisted, so pleased was he that she was his. There, she was his pennant that he wanted to wave ostentatiously. However, in the Emirate, she was no longer his trophy. He made little excuses to be either in front or behind her in public. He would leave their suite before or after her. She could not understand why he was different here. Only by eliminating other causes did she stumble onto the racial difference. She was flabbergasted. Why is such a plus thought a negative, she asked herself. And why here, not in Kinshasa? She thought of confronting him. "Listen, my parents were Dalits. In Guyane, we were Coolies. People there treated us worse than their pigs. So my love, I am not inexperienced where bigotry is a challenge. Your planet is my planet." She knew it was not that simple; but it would be something to grab onto, something to help them explain their fears to each other.

On the plane, he still wished he had been able to go alone. It bothered him that he felt that way; that he could make love to Julie with such lustful abandon in the room, yet be fearful of what others thought of him and of her — an African and an Indian together. His mind arched back to the sense of futility he had experienced many times: no matter what high ideals one ascribed to, if they did not stand the test of sweat, they were deceptions. Mokonzi was right. Man did things out of fear and not out of high ideals. Such that man needed to deceive himself, or he would go mad by the time he reached puberty.

What would the Dictator advise him to think? Ella would get back at him by making sure he'd not see Nef, Nkosia, and the baby. Of that, he was convinced. Somewhere, in all he had said to Julie, of the plans they had made, was that dreadful thought. He had this feeling shaking its finger at him, "Remember your children."

He reached for Julie's hand. "Why don't you come with me?" he asked. "I want to impress them at this bank where I am going. They will think I am somebody special when they see you with me." But she declined, repeating what he had told her about this being a business trip. He didn't insist, relieved for having asked her.

---

Thrilled by this new adventure, Julie dashed for the airport exit when they got off the plane, leaving Molu to fend for himself. She got into a cab with a couple, tourists who had been waiting for someone to share the fare to the famous souk, while Molu looked for the car that was to take him to the bank. After ten minutes, he jumped into a cab and gave the driver the name of the bank. The drive to the center was as long as the one from the Abu Dhabi airport to the Mussafah industrial zone. Fortunately, no labyrinth enfolded the financial institutions in Sharjah's center.

Chatting with cab drivers was one of Molu's better habits; sometimes cabbies had inside information that would surprise even the most sophisticated. A few minutes into the drive, he struck up a conversation with the taxi man, who had seemed reluctant to turn on the meter when he got in. This man was not as uncommunicative as the merchant had been on the drive to Mussafah, but Molu had to prod him. He was in Abu Dhabi because it was a Moslem country, welcoming to Pakistanis like himself in search of work. From what he had observed, there were about as many Africans as Europeans in the Emirates.

"Could an African marry a Pakistani?" Molu asked. To that, the man did not reply, and Molu thought he had offended him. Perhaps the driver had taken his question to mean that he was looking for a certain kind of excitement involving Pakistani women. Such things offend because they are born of bigotry. Europeans argue against being "too sensitive;" that there is no implied meaning in these remarks. Molu knew differently.

"I am here with this woman, her parents are from Southern India," Molu said simply, when the driver didn't answer, "and I am concerned that this society may not look with favor on her being with me. That's why I asked you the question I did. It's only after I asked it that I realized that my question might have offended you. If that's the case, I apologize."

"South Indians can be very black; still, I am sure that in India it would be bad," the driver said, seemingly having given Molu's question a great deal of thought. "Racism is part of their religion. I don't know that it would be as bad someplace else."

"What about here? How would it look here?" Molu pressed.

"I have not seen anyone like that here." After that answer, Molu asked no more questions.

———  ———  ———

He sat waiting in an anteroom twenty minutes before being ushered into the bank's president's office. During his wait, no one came into the bank, and he wondered if it was a bank at all. He would have said no, except that the Dictator had said it was.

There must have been a conference, for men, all wearing the national dress, were walking out of the office. None looked at him directly, seeming to Molu to be embarrassed by his presence. The president stood at the door to greet the visitor. He showed him to a chair in front of his large desk. "I was hoping you would not come; that perhaps you had changed your mind —"

"Why would I do that?" Molu interrupted. "You spoke to President Motutu. He is the one who set this in motion. He didn't tell me to cancel; that's why I am here."

"Yes, well, of course. I was referring to the situation in your country. I thought that… well you had other things on your plate." The banker spoke in a subdued tone. Molu wasn't sure whether he was being solicitous.

"I don't understand what you mean by the situation in my country."

"I am not a diplomat; I am a businessman. The solvency of this institution is my only concern. When I spoke to your president, we agreed on payment for articles to be delivered periodically in the future. Well, we are not sure that the deliveries will be possible any longer."

"You're questioning the president?" Molu said, incredulous.

"The international community is. Our shareholders would not expect anything else. I spoke to our agent in New York earlier. There is doubt — expressed doubt — in the international community regarding the sustainability of the current Kinshasa government. Under the circumstances, a delay in the transaction seems recommended."

"And what about the president?" Molu said, becoming angry.

"If the situation changes, we'll be interested in reconsidering."

"You are not reliable. Why would he reconsider you?"

"I am sorry." The insincere apology had a finality that stung the way only reality could. The banker must have pressed a button, for the door was opened from the outside. He stood at the same time. Molu glared at him and at a man at the door and walked out. He had been in the banker's office less than ten minutes.

The Dictator had been clear that he should not haggle with the banker. But he had been angry that the man had impugned his country. If this were the best he could do when he was following a script, how would he handle hostile governments against which his wits would be his only asset? He shook his head, wanting to dismiss the thought, but it did not leave him.

He had to call the Dictator immediately to tell him there was no check. His sense of failure — and, yes, of betrayal — tortured his spirit. If the Dictator might think he had pocketed the check, that thought, at least, did not linger.

The cab that had brought him in swung around to pick him up for the trip back to the airport. In the VIP lounge, he would call the Dictator to inform him of the failure in Sharjah. He argued with himself against mentioning what the banker had said regarding the sustainability of the regime.

He wished he could discuss with Marcel what the banker had implied. Was it buyer's remorse that had prompted him to back out of a lucrative deal, or had rot in Kinshasa become visible to the financial community? He was loath to believe in the latter, unconvinced, as he was, that Kinshasa might be lost. But trust was the acknowledged hard currency in the diamond business. And moneymen were never averse to making deals with less than AAA-rated countries, so why had the banker backed out? He did not yet have the answer.

Molu, absorbed in his thoughts, listened only now and again to the driver who had noticed the change in his passenger and sensed his distress. The generous tip earlier had loosened the driver's taciturn inclination and made him more talkative. "The climate in the Emirates is not as harsh as people think," he told Molu who was looking out of the window. "November to April is the best time for the tourists here; it's much cooler. The notion that heat is not as bad when it's dry is nonsense. When it's 110 degrees, it's hot, dry or not. If you have the time, go to Al Ain; it's an oasis in the middle of the desert. It even rains there. Al Ain is what Eden must have looked like; it will astound you, it's so green there. The entire area is a garden — two hours from Abu Dhabi. I can make the arrangement for you, if you so desire."

Molu thanked the driver. "I may have to leave right away. We'll see. When we get to the airport, give me a telephone number where I can reach you. If there is time, I am sure my companion — I told you about her earlier — would like to go for a visit. She is a real tourist. We'll see."

Danielle had never made him wait this long, and when the Dictator finally came on, Molu didn't recognize the voice. It was more than frailty, Molu acknowledged, when the Dictator also failed to react to his report. Uncertainty had replaced vigor in his boss's tone. The hypnotic voice was a throaty murmur now.

Molu told him word for word what the banker had said, repeating points he considered significant, hopeful that the Dictator, who always had an answer, would be able to provide some direction to the business at hand. Molu said he was going to Al Fujayrah to see Sheikh Mustapha bin Omar at the bank there. Perhaps the Dictator would recall that he had told him to fly to Geneva if it had not gone as planned in Sharjah; but he didn't react at all to that, instead said weakly, but without hesitation, "If you think it's best." Then Danielle came on, perfunctorily asked if there was anything else, and when Molu said no, hung up without further ado.

Molu had very much wanted to ask her about the Dictator's state, but he dared not. Danielle's imperiousness always intimidated him. Before hanging up, he looked at the receiver that he still held in his hand, as if hoping the equipment, that had heard everything, could explain what it all meant.

I have to call Marcel, he repeated to himself, as he dialed his friend's home number. Surprisingly he was not as lucky as in his attempt to call Kinshasa. After several tries, he left the booth to consult with the pilot of his chartered plane and sat down to wait for Julie to return from the souk. Then he went back to the phone booth to call his wife.

Again he had to wait, this time for the maid to get his wife out of the bathroom, where she was every weekday at 7:00 a.m.

"Mokonzi, you have landed. I am surprised to hear from you. What did you forget?" she asked, sarcastic as always.

"I just talked to the president and wanted to discuss something with Marcel, but I think he is still sore at me. He didn't pick up the phone when he heard my voice on the answering machine. You know how selectively he answers —"

"Well, I am not surprised. You didn't exactly endear yourself to him the last time you had him over. But that's not why you called here —"

"I want you to call him for me. He'll pick up for you. Ask him to call me at this number." He gave her the number written on the underside of the receiver.

"Are you alright? You sound — how shall I put it?"

"I think something is wrong with the president," Molu whispered. "I don't know… maybe something has happened… It was like he was drugged or something. I never heard him incoherent before. The U.S. embassy in Kinshasa must have reported if anything is amiss with him… if he is incapacitated… and Marcel would know."

"Well, from what I have read, Nundu is steadily advancing. From what you've told me of Nundu, if I had him at the gates of my capital, something would be amiss with me. It looks like there is no effort to organize a counteroffensive. *Le Monde* reports that the French will intervene. Have you given this some thought?"

"I don't think it's as bad as all that —"

"That's what you always say, God damn it. But is it possible that he's got no more tricks up his sleeve, eh? Maybe he is suffering from dictatorial narcosis. He is human, you know. No, maybe you don't know. Let me ask you this? Is it possible that this time he's run out of whatever he's used in the past ten years to —? Maybe this is it. No more of the Houdini stuff, eh? Is it possible? You will never give up on him —"

"Please, call Marcel," he interrupted. "I need facts. I cannot know anything until I have facts. Marcel can tell me if there has been any report of anything untoward in Kinshasa — that's what I mean. I know he is not immortal. I never said he was. But they have written him off before —"

"Ok, I'll have Marcel call you. If need be, I'll go to his house to get him to answer the phone. Shouldn't you think about staying out of Kinshasa until this clears up? Talk about facts. You said Nundu was a hoodlum."

"A crisis of this kind — a foreign minister is essential," he interrupted her. "I am the honest broker there. That's what I am, and I implied that to the Rwandan ambassador. They'll want to speak to me. She must have gotten through to Kagame already. If I could talk to Marcel, he would tell me if there has been any change in our situation over there."

Julie walked into the waiting room. The pilot, an annoyed look on his face, was standing at one of the glass panels watching the planes on the tarmac. He saw her and pointed to the open booth where Molu was sitting, a phone receiver to his ear. After a moment Julie looked back at him, shrugging a question. This time the pilot gestured 'telephone' with his fingers and irritably pointed again in the direction of the booths. She saw Molu and walked behind the booth where he was sitting and playfully planted a noisy kiss on his forehead. "*Chérie, je ne savait pas ou tu étais —*" Molu covered the mouthpiece. There was a moment of silence from the receiver; then he heard his wife say, "Nef wants to talk to you."

"Mokonzi," he heard his daughter's contralto voice "*Mboté? Sángo níni?* What did you tell Mama? She looks like she swallowed a fish again." She was referring to a gold fish her mother had swallowed on a dare at a King's Dominion amusement park when Nef was about six.

"*Malámu, melesí. Na yo?*" He answered. "Have you missed me?"

"*Malamu, melesi.* Missed you? I didn't even know you were gone," she teased him.

"Tell her not to forget to call Marcel. Tell her that I'll wait fifteen minutes for him to call me. Hang up now, so she can call him. I'll call you back later." He would have liked to have instructed Nef, "Tell Mama I love her," but Julie would have heard.

He stood up to hug Julie. "I was talking to my office in Washington. I've to wait a few more minutes for a call."

"The pilot doesn't seem too pleased," she told him.

"He is being paid for his time. What does he have to be un-happy about? How was the Gold Souk?"

"It's the most extraordinary place I've ever seen. You should see the people — there are tons and tons of gold there. I bought you an African bracelet; you know, the one they make with elephant hairs in Tanzania. But in gold." He looked at her, surprised. "Could I give it to the president as a gift from Sharjah? That would be fitting; he is called the Great Elephant."

"No! I bought it for you to wear in remembrance of Abu Dhabi and what we meant to each other here. You can always get him another. This one is for you. Please!"

"Alright, it was a thought. I am sure he has one already. The gifts he gets from all over the continent!"

The phone rang.

"Wait for me over there, will you, darling? I won't be able to concentrate if you are too close."

"Ella said you called earlier." It was Marcel. "I went out for an early breakfast. I have an 8 a.m. meeting this morning on the Hill. What's up?"

Molu told him what the banker had said and about his conversation with the Dictator. "I don't know what to make of it. He didn't sound like the same man. It was as if he were drugged. Do you know anything?"

"Our embassy in Kinshasa has not issued many reports. Mosley runs a tight ship. Everything has to clear his desk. I haven't seen anything about the president being sick, though. The newspapers are full of reports about the advance from the east, but nothing about his health. Talking about the way the president sounded, what did you tell Ella? She sounded — how should I put it? Dis-traught. I don't mean pissed off, the way she usually sounds, but troubled."

"She reads the newspapers and thinks the sky is falling —"

"She asked me about the international calling code for this telephone number," he interrupted. "I told her I would have to check. She is not exactly a high school drop out you know. She has the answer by now. She knows 971 is not anywhere near Brussels."

"I realized that, Marcel. But after I couldn't get hold of you, I chanced it. I'll deal with Ella later. Do you know anyone at the embassy in Kinshasa who can enlighten you as to what is happen-ing? The newspapers can only give you so much."

"You are wrong there. Most of the time reporters have more accurate information than that person who hardly ventures outside the embassy walls, or who listens to just one local who may or may not know anything. Our intelligence is perfunctory because of that. But I know a guy there now who is known for his up to the minute reports. Oddly, he hasn't reported anything. I can try to give him a call and see what he says. Where will you be later?"

"OK! It's worth a try. If that banker is right — and I must tell you I doubt it — then we have a problem of a greater magnitude than I envisaged. I have to fly to Al Fujayrah. It'll be easier if I call you. How about every hour or so?"

"That's fine; I should have something later today. Regarding that banker, he is not exactly Alexander Hamilton. For him to turn down that diamond deal says everything that you fear now. How long can you stay in Abu Dhabi?"

"Why do you ask?"

"You should consider staying put until you know for sure that you are going to a country that will welcome you."

"I am the foreign minister, Marcel; my place is there."

"You haven't been sworn in yet. Until you do —"

"My place is there! I am going to be foreign minister and go on to do the best I can for my country."

"If you have a country! But I hear you, I'll try to track that guy down and get back to you."

"Thanks man!"

"Yeah! I'd like to be the fly on a wall when you thank Ella."

<hr>

That day, Marcel spent every free moment phoning Kinshasa. The press officer was in bed when at last the lines cleared, and Marcel, surprised after so many failed attempts, heard the phone ring its long, soft international signal at the other end. Pleased to unburden himself to a kindred spirit from headquarters who wanted information from him, the press officer was happy for the call, regardless of the late hour.

"I have to brief someone about the situation in Kinshasa," Marcel said without too many greeting preliminaries. "But there haven't been many reports from the embassy I can use —"

"No report, you mean," the press officer interjected heatedly. "Mine are stuck in the ambassador's in-box."

"Why? Is it because he disagrees with what you're reporting?"

"Who knows — I don't know; he hasn't said diddly to me. But he told the deputy they were written in Ebonics."

"Ebonics? He actually said Ebonics or —"

"It's from the mouth of the deputy. That's what she told me when I wanted to know why my reports had not cleared."

"Mosley is known for his antipathy to blacks, but this is kind of sick."

"Don't I know? From the moment this guy stepped down from the plane… You know, I read somewhere that anti-Semitism was the snobbery of the lower class; well, I think that the snobbery of the Mosleys of this world is antipathy toward blacks like me. But I am not going to take it lying down, Marcel. I am working on an angle that will see me through this. I'll take care of Mosley. You heard that he found his wife with her driver?"

"Take it easy, Ken! I heard that she had a location-stress break-down. I didn't hear about a driver. Do you really want what sounds like shit to splatter you? If it's the reports you are worried about, I'll take care of that for you. Send me copies through the diplomatic pouch, and I'll pass them around; make sure the right people see them."

"That's fine with me. I'll put them in the pouch first thing in the morning. I'll have something else in there with a note that you should read first. I can't say more over the phone."

"I understand… but can you comment on the papers' accounts of what's happening in your area?"

"Sure! The report from the New York Times two days ago was comprehensive. I told the correspondent everything I had wit-nessed. He got it right."

"I saw the piece you're referring to. But it doesn't say anything about the president's health."

"The president's health? I didn't know that was an issue. The security chief is someone I know; I can ask him. He may not tell me, but I will note his reaction to my question. He may be listen-ing to us right now."

"The security chief ? — You know the security chief ? He is the guy who pulls the strings over there! If you can find out from him that would help. He should know. If something is not right with the president that would give the situation a perspective it currently doesn't yet have."

"Know might not be right — he is someone I talk to from time to time. We have a kind of relationship —he's helped me in the past. I saw him the other day and asked him about the troops I had seen in town. He didn't say much, but I could see that was something weighing on his mind. I ended up answering more of his questions about what people were saying in regards to the soldiers than he did about what the government was up to.

"We talked about the new foreign minister. Before coming out here, I went to see Sakeseba for a briefing at their embassy in Washington. His wife was my daughter's pediatrician. I learned that he was arriving Thursday. The security chief made some remarks about him that I didn't understand, something like 'the beggars do indeed need a foreign minister.' I thought that it was a peculiar thing to say, but he didn't elaborate. He just smiled; it was the first time I ever saw him smile."

"The beggars need a foreign minister? What does that mean?" It was on the tip of Marcel's tongue to tell him that it was on behalf of the foreign minister that he had called, but instead said, "Could beggars mean Kinshasa? A country pleading for help would conceivably fall in that category. Sarcastically, it could! But what a morbid thing for a security chief to say!"

"I wouldn't say more over the phone, Marcel. You know what I mean. Have no fear, I'll get back to you. On a very different subject, the word is out you're going to Burundi as ambassador. Should I say congratulations?"

"No congratulations are in order; I would be just another African American appointed to another African country. The truth is, I am tired of the crap we have to put up with here; and, between us, I am leaning toward retirement to make some money and do what I please. If the best they can do for me is Bujumbua, I may not be interested in being another African American statistic. I'll let you know if I take the job; you may want to come there as press officer."

"No thanks, I am tired of being a statistic myself. Africa is not getting better; progress here, as they say, is uphill. Every minute I wonder what I am doing here; I can't stand just being a witness to decline. And malaria is kicking my butt — the only place I'd consider is London."

"London? I couldn't help you with that one; Africa is the best I can do. I understand that Mosley's deputy is — how should I put it, on intimate terms with Matthew Greeson, the Fatman, the manda-rin of barons at the Department. Now, if Matt Greeson gives the word that it's London for you, you got a handshake. Talk to Mosley's deputy."

"I told you I was working on an angle — I can't say more over the phone."

"What about that boat of yours? The last time we talked, that's all you had on your mind."

"I would love to be on the boat right now, man, top gallant to Saint Lucia. It's the boat if they don't give me London — I have had it with being a constant place-seeker — that's it."

"You know what the Invisible Man said, *'the dumbest black bastard in the cotton patch knows that the only way to please a white man is to tell him a lie!'* Talk to the deputy!"

"Is that right? The Invisible Man said that? I'll remember it, I promise you."

"Thank you, Ken."

"You're the man bro."

———

It was even later that night that Molu in Abu Dhabi spoke again to Marcel who told him, his tone brittle and urgent, what the press officer had said.

"He told me that he saw government troops streaming in from the front and spoke to the security chief about it. The security chief was very interested in what people were saying about soldiers coming in like that."

"The president is concerned what the people think," Molu said, by way of explanation. "Fear of an imminent collapse would frighten the populace. Heads of state are always concerned about people's fears; it's obviously something to worry about."

"He, the security chief, said something about you being the beggars' foreign minister. What is that about? The only thing I can think of is that the government is seeking — the way beggars might — assistance to meet the challenge from the east. Does it mean anything else to you?"

"Mgonu must be quoting an author no one has ever heard of. He is a sort of a literature enthusiast — I don't know what the beggars reference means, or where he got it from. It's obscure, like Maka. What else did you find out?"

"It's the press officer I spoke to. He said that he met you at the embassy in Washington when he was there for a briefing. The phones are not reliable over there; he was reluctant to talk openly. He is pouching his reports — Mosley has refused to clear them — to me. I think Mosley looks at these reports as exaggerated rumors. And as is his wont, he doesn't think much of the press officer who is also black."

"You trust this source?" Molu asked. "You told me yourself that guys like your press officer over there have little contact with people. Isn't this like Rwanda? They don't know what's happening! Maybe there is a good reason for Mosley's refusal to clear your guy's report."

"No, this man is different; he is not another innocent in Africa; he is one of the few who ventures outside the embassy and who talks to people. He is a sporty type and has a knack for this kind of work."

"What is his name? I don't remember a press officer at any briefing."

"Ken Taylor!"

"Short? Bald? I remember him. He was married to a woman from Rwanda. She had gone to visit her family — she was killed. They had a daughter. He wanted to know if there were boats for rent on the river."

"He is the one. He's been posted in every country in Africa — has had malaria and everything else each time."

"How long will it take to get his reports in the pouch?" Molu asked. He was now concerned.

"It could be a couple of days, maybe more. If you haven't already, you should read the piece about Kinshasa published two days ago in the New York Times. The press officer told me that he had talked to the reporter. I read it several times, as have the policy makers here. What you make of it is up to you. I agree it's comprehensive."

"What are you suggesting?"

"I told you before, stay put or return to the States. If I were you, I wouldn't go near Kinshasa. Unless the French intervene to stop Nundu, the Motutu era is history, and it's everyman for himself after that. The feeling here is that the United States has washed its hands —"

"I've been thinking about what you said earlier. If the reception in Al Fujayrah is similar to the one in Sharjah, I'll consider all options. That's as far as I can see right this moment. I don't want anyone to construe that I am running away if I don't go on to Kinshasa. Abandoning the president is not part of the options; I have to live with myself too you know."

Marcel said good-bye, feeling queasy, like a bout of malaria coming on. He knew that regardless of how dire the situation in Kinshasa, his friend would end up there. He made a mental note to call Molu's wife to warn her.

# Chapter 24

When he realized that he would have only one passenger for the flight to Al Fujayrah, the pilot said, "The view is more rewarding than all the gold *souks* in Arabia." Julie, who had walked Molu to the hotel's entrance, didn't wait for his acquiescence but ran back to retrieve her pocketbook and passport. Molu looked at the pilot grimly, but the man smiled, pointing at the blue sky, whether to invoke God or to repeat what he had said, Molu didn't know, certain only that two passengers cost twice as much as one.

The view was one they had never seen before. Creation unfolded below them with a sweep of the panorama from a cloudless sky. From Abu Dhabi they flew east across the desert and mountains of the United Arab Emirates, and over Al Ayn, the garden oasis, then north to Al Fujayara, the one member of the UAE to face east toward the Gulf of Oman. Al Ayn's green vitality lay like an emerald in the brown field of the desert. As if in a desperate denial of the desert beyond, the people had left no particle of oasis unplanted. The pilot passed over it twice to satisfy his passengers. Then he flew north, where Al Fujayrah sits below Khawr Fakkan underneath the northern part of Oman, the peninsula jutting into the Gulf of Hormuz. Through the view, they  glimpsed themselves cleansed of all pretension. As the plane taxied onto the holding area of the Al Fujayrah Airport, they smiled, reflectively to reassure one another they had not seen a mirage.

---

A man in an ill fitting western suit was at the airport gate waiting for Molu. He introduced himself as a driver from the bank sent to meet the visitor. To Molu's dismay, he seemed to recoil at the sight of Julie, staring at her for a long moment, debating whether to say something, finally turning toward the exit in silence. Julie looked at Molu, made an unmistakably French face, and laughed. He kept his glum face on, passive to what was unfolding around him.

Decidedly eager to finish his assignment, the man left the air terminal and directed them to a large black German sedan in the parking area. Julie and Molu sat in the back seat, holding the straps above their heads, eager themselves to be off. But it was twenty minutes before they stepped onto the downtown sidewalk before a hulking gray and green building. Molu asked the driver if he was to be the one to take them back to the airport. Before the man could answer, Molu told him "No" several times, wagging his finger for emphasis.

An employee of the bank then opened the door. The men in the bank looked with curiosity at Julie; however, there was more amusement and appreciation than hostility. She stayed behind with her cup of menthe tea, while Molu was ushered into a narrow side office furnished only with a conference table and three chairs. A television set was at the corner, below the window facing a small patio. To Molu, it was like a patient examination room in America.

Presently, a very large man, wearing a khandura, hardly able to lift his feet off the ground, entered the room and locked the door behind him. He held a brown envelope on his protruding stomach. "I want to make sure we are not disturbed," he said in a well-modulated British accent, as he reached for Molu's hand. "They have a habit of bringing tea at most inopportune times. The locked door means no thank you; go away." Sheikh Mustapha bin Omar laughed, exuding confident joviality. He pointed at a chair for Molu to sit at the table. He then heaved himself around slowly to a seat across from the visitor. The envelope he put in front of him. "May I see your passport, please," he asked softly. Molu hesitated, "I showed it to one of your employees."

"I understand," said Bin Omar. "Please understand that our business is personal; this is strictly between your president and myself. The bank is only a venue. Your passport is for my own peace of mind. Please! I am surprised you haven't asked to see my document."

"I didn't think that necessary," said Molu. His voice carried annoyance. "The president's word is enough for me." Molu handed him his passport. Bin Omar looked at the first two pages of the document carefully and put it next to the envelope.

"In this envelope," he said pointing "is most of what I need to discuss our business this afternoon. Missing is an account number in a third country where I would deposit the payment for the stones."

"My instructions did not include such information Mister Bin Omar. The president asked only that I ascertain —"

Bin Omar interrupted. "As long as the durability of your government was not in question, a third country account was not needed. I must consider that your president may have to reside abroad —"

"What are you talking about, sir. What does abroad mean?"

"I have information that your president is making plans —"

"The president has no intention of living abroad, Mister Bin Omar! I don't know how I could make it plainer."

"My information —"

"Mister Bin Omar," said Molu, shaking his finger in wide negative arcs, "the president does not intend to reside abroad. Now, if you are referring to our current impasse, know that we have had them in the past; and given the geopolitics of the region, we will unfortunately have them again. The president will be there to handle these transactions. I hope I am clear, and we can move to discussing procedures; that is if you agree to do business with us. But have no fear, I will advise him of your request regarding accounts in a third country; but I'll not do so in the context of his living abroad."

"Very well, Mr. Ambassador, you know your capability better than anyone. But forgive me; we must understand each other, our transactions will have to be payment on delivery. That's another reason a third country account would have been practical."

Molu laughed. "I was hoping that trust would be the basis for our transactions. If it is payment on delivery, we probably could get better rates in the Gold Souk."

"Not if you are talking about millions of American dollars, you can't."

"I understand that. What I meant to say is that a simple payment and delivery transaction can be had anywhere. Without credit, or should I say trust, we would be operating with one hand tied behind our back, as the Americans might say."

"Your Antwerp transactions are payment on delivery."

"You will pardon me if I do not go into details, but — I can tell you that you're misinformed. I opened the Antwerp *comptoire*. I know."

The banker studied his visitor for a moment, then looked into the envelope and took out a check. He lifted Molu's passport as if to show it to him and put the check facing up between its pages. "This is, as the Americans might say, a goodwill gesture." He put the passport back next to the envelope. "I couldn't help noticing the young woman you came in with. No one failed to notice her. How should I put this? She wouldn't be looking for employment, would she?"

Molu glared at him, seeming not to have understood the question. He then glanced at the passport, the check for fifty thousand dollars protruding from its pages. After a while, he leaned forward, his eyes asking the man in front of him, what kind of pig are you? Bin Omar blurted something in a language Molu didn't understand. He removed the check and threw the passport at Molu. After slapping the table, he lifted his enormous bulk from the chair, moved with surprising alacrity to unlock the door, and doddered out without any further word. Molu followed quickly and ran to where he had left Julie. She was still sitting there, a cup in hand.

The large German sedan was parked in front, the reckless driver at the wheel. Molu rushed Julie into the back seat. The driver whipped the car in a U-turn, his passengers holding on to the handles overhead. They were back at the Al Fujayrah airport in even less time than it had taken for their trip to town.

Julie kept her eyes on Molu, her request for an explanation urgent. Molu didn't say anything in the car, pointing at the driver with his chin. "Let's go inside, I think we should leave right away," he told her.

Instead of following him inside, she went around the car and from her pocketbook took out a hundred dirham bill for the driver. "Thank you!" she told the man, handing him the bill. "You should be at Le Mans." The driver looked at her blankly, and she made a driving gesture, and said, "*vroom, vroom.*" Comprehending, the driver smiled. She then joined Molu who had come back outside to wait for her.

"Now what was that about?" she asked, but with less annoyance.

"Let's go inside, and I'll tell you while we walk," Molu answered, urgency in his voice. Julie fell into step beside him.

Exiting a side door, a square shouldered man, disfigured by varicella, garbed in a khandura, a man in shadows, who seemed never to have made eye contact with anyone, slammed into her, deliberately they were sure. She spun and shrilly cursed him in French. The man continued walking and lifted his arm in the gesture of dismissal. Molu pulled her by the arm, "It's your dress," he said. "Some people here are more conservative than others and frown at your seeming indifference to their custom. Are you alright?"

"I am alright! What happened back there that we had to leave as if you had robbed the bank?"

Molu laughed nervously. "The president of the bank — I guess he was the president of the bank — wanted to buy your services. He offered fifty thousand American dollars."

She looked at him not believing her ears. "Oh my God! What did you say?" she asked, walking faster.

"I told him double or nothing… No, I said nothing. I just walked out to get you. I think we'd better be off. Who knows what he might do? He may accuse me of having robbed the bank."

Holding hands, they ran toward the terminal where the charter pilot waited. Impatient to be off the ground, the airport formalities that were cursory before suddenly seemed laborious. In addition, late afternoon departures made the queue of planes waiting their turn to the runway long — intolerable to Molu who expected the tower to refuse his plane departure clearance at any moment. He imagined Bin Omar waving checks at the controllers.

Once up, the view from the air awed them anew. The sun was setting, a universal conflagration unfolding west above Abu Dhabi. They kissed to affirm each to the other and to savor another scenic blessing. They were awaking to a unique moment at a crossroad in their unique lives.

"There will never be another moment like this to say I love you," she shouted over the engine's drone, while she caressed his thigh.

"I agree," he mouthed, bringing her hand to his lips. The setting of the sun had shrouded the desert. That distressed them; they had looked forward to seeing Al Ayn one more time.

"We have seen it all. I think the sooner we get out of here the better," he said in her ear. She nodded approval.

Night had fallen when their plane reached the Abu Dhabi airport. "What if we change hotels tonight?" Julie asked him, pointing at the Airport Hotel sign as they walked up the stairs to the terminal. "That may give us a layer of security. We'll tell them at the Continental that we have booked a flight out for this evening. But I doubt there'll be anymore flights to Geneva tonight."

"OK," said Molu. "I'll dismiss the pilot while you find an Etihad Airways counter to make the reservations. My flight to Geneva is around noon tomorrow. If they have an earlier flight anywhere in Europe, take it. We'll go from there."

Counters for Etihad Airways, the Emirates' national airline, were throughout the doughnut-shaped terminal. Julie was walking toward the one next to the Golden Class Club when Molu called out to her, "Anywhere but London." She turned and gestured, uncomprehending, and he came to her, "I wouldn't want a stop in London," he said shaking his head. "I'll tell you why later. It has something to do with the way they look at my diplomatic passport."

"OK," she told him, her serious frown on. "I'll wait for you here."

After looking for him, Molu found their pilot in the next to last hangar of the airport, a fuel truck next to the plane. How long would they have had to wait, Molu wondered, if, as planned, the pilot had driven them back to the Continental Hotel. Instead of giving him a five-hundred dirham tip, he gave him three hundred. The man looked at the bills then at Molu, said something Molu didn't understand and walked back to his plane. "Thank you," Molu called after him.

"I had to walk to the far end of the airport to find the pilot," he said when he found Julie, seeing the impatient concern in her eyes.

"There is a flight to Geneva at 8:55 tomorrow morning. I made the reservation."

"Reservation as in one reservation?" Molu exclaimed.

"You have to go to Geneva —"

"Come with me," he interrupted, panicked. He took her hands and, coming closer, repeated, "Come with me." She heard the words, but the relief in his eyes made the decision for her. She had felt Molu's apprehension their first day here; the words and the lovemaking could not disguise that she was an encumbrance to him — at this time. He did not want her to follow him; being along was a burden. That was understandable, she told herself; there was uncertainty to where he was going. Uncertain, he didn't know where she fitted in his life.

"I'll tell you what," she answered. "We'll make Paris our hub. I'll go there after I visit my parents."

"My business here is finished," Molu tried to explain. "I don't need to go to Geneva. I can call to tell them what happened here. Let's talk about what we can do at the hotel."

"Alright, but let's check in here first, and then we'll go for our bags at the Continental," Julie suggested.

"OK! While I am here, let me see if I owe anything for rebooking my flight. That will save us time tomorrow. Check in and I'll meet you in the lobby."

"Sure," Julie answered, turning toward the entrance, her eyes downcast.

Instead of checking in, she sat on a leather chair in the hotel's lobby, her shapely legs crossed, her presence leaving no one there indifferent.

He didn't want to be seen walking in here with me, she thought. What a paradox he is, a thoughtful man driven by fear.

He wasn't bullshitting me when he said, come with me; but outside of four walls, Africa is the only place where he is comfortable being with me. And I'll never go back to Kinshasa.

Julie had begun reciting verses from the Bhagavad-Gita when Molu came near and saw her deep in thought. He knocked on the top of her chair. "May I come in?" he asked. "Did you get the key for the room?" Julie smiled, shook her head, no. "Have you read The Bhagavad-Gita? My parents taught it to me." He shook his head, no, the way he did when annoyed. "I will make you a gift of it," she said lightly, smiling inside. "Let's go see about the room here."

Molu was sure that "the hotel is fully booked" verdict was due to their having gone to the desk together. Julie thanked the clerk amiably. This was the only hotel at the airport. Molu would have to come back early in the morning for his flight to Geneva.

Waiting in line for a taxi to the Continental, Julie asked suddenly.

"How old are you?"

"Huh? Why? You know how old I am."

"I am thirty-two, and I know that racism is a fact of life. Why don't you?"

"What brought that on?"

"You did. You mope like that hotel person stepped on your soul. Maybe there was no room. You're not a little boy whose ball strayed —"

"You enjoy racism?" Molu interjected.

"That's a stupid question!"

"Well, I don't," Molu said with finality, as if that should explain his view on the matter.

"What I mean is that you should get it off your chest. Don't flay yourself like a victim. Express your disapproval — do something."

"What are you talking about?" he said.

"That I am here with you. That I see you. It doesn't become you; your eyes are too expressive."

"What doesn't become me? I don't understand."

"Masquerade! That's what. You have an open face — too open for masquerades. I didn't book the room because your staying behind to make sure you didn't owe anything to Etihad Airways was a pretext for not going into the hotel with me."

Molu smiled. "I am sorry! Now that you can read my thoughts, I will have to love you with even greater diligence if that's possible, until you are too deeply affected to lecture me."

"Be serious!"

"I am! I have to reassert my prerogative. No?"

"What prerogative?"

"A man's!"

"A man's?" she asked in a voice that reminded him uncomfortably of his wife's. "You can't walk into a hotel lobby with a woman you say you love, but you can talk about a man's prerogative."

How would the Dictator respond to her salvo? Molu asked himself. He hunched his back in one of the Dictator's poses as if putting his weight on the cane with the handle carved in the shape of an elephant. "You have a private vision of the truth?" he asked in the Dictator's voice. "… The answer to the absurdities of the world? And you can walk without your feet touching the ground?" She looked intently at him. And he laughed. "I don't know what I can do," he said in explanation.

"You love the president," she said finally, shaking her head in the 'who can understand-this-madness' gesture.

"You know," Molu said, "not all choices are the same; some are luxuries not even the man who has nothing to lose can make."

"What does that mean?" Julie asked.

"That I love you more!"

"Yeah, but he is the light in your future like that sun we saw setting over the desert."

"I hope not," he said shrinking back. "The sunset heralds the time of whispers and shadows. To us Ngbandis sunsets mark the hour when a shadow can be a banana leaf dancing in the moonlight with the wind, or an ancestor retracing the steps of his youth. Sunset is also the time death opens the door of his establishment to welcome the living. Until the sun rises again his door stays open. We prefer to close our eyes until the sun rises again. But some of us are not so fortunate.

"So you will understand when I tell you that I hope there is more to the president than a setting sun, regardless of how majestic over the Arabian desert it looked to us this evening."

She looked at him for a while in silence and then said, "If the sunset we witnessed foreshadows ruin, Judgment Day has no herald with more panache."

"It's no wonder Maka Mgonu stares at you; he has something for poets."

"That's not funny. That's not funny at all," she said shaking her head.

"I just wanted to shut you up," he said. "Hearing about me makes me uncomfortable. But I am grateful for you in ways I am afraid I will never be able to express.

"This is the first time you have said anything about your tribe. I may have to say, I am proud of you, sooner than I thought."

Julie now spoke of the view they had experienced to and from Al Fujayrah, saying that it had somehow purged them of their conceit. "It would take a lot to cleanse me," Molu answered. And Julie searched her memory for what that meant.

Molu watched her undress. She was so perfect, he shivered at the sight of her. She was the only woman of the many he had known who achieved real orgasms every time they made love. She would perspire and, at the height of ecstasy, frissons would electrify her. Her passion had become his addiction. His mouth watered. He was sure she could hear his heart. He didn't know where to touch her first. His embarrassment of riches enhanced his desire for her, as he saw again that, unlike his wife's, her hips were as luscious in as out of the black panties she favored. She made the decision for him, lying on her stomach to show him where to start. Their last night in the desert brought them to the gate that lovers swear they pass through but once.

# Chapter 25

It had been a long day flying from Geneva, and the nine other passengers had been asleep when the aircraft entered Kinshasa's airspace. The cabin had fallen quiet over Ethiopia, soon after the service of warm Swiss croissants and Norwegian smoked salmon, followed by French miniature pastries and the ubiquitous chilled Perrier-Jouët's Champagne rosé.

The wine was not the cause of Molu's lassitude. Giving him pause was the sense that his good fortune was like the clouds he was flying over. A cloud standing straight against the sky attracted his attention; it looked like an idol there waiting to receive offerings from passing aircraft. Molu kept his eyes on it until he could no longer distinguish it from the others that had joined it. The clouds would dissipate, hopefully into rain for a drought-cursed continent. Are there enough clouds on the planet to undo this life-choking drought? If I had a coat of arms, he told himself, it would have a cloud of that shape in it. When asked what it meant, he would answer that, man's future being mutable, he wanted to express through the picture of a cloud his determination that Africa's current history not be its future. At that moment the aircraft's wing on his side lifted, and the sun as if to convey its blessing displayed a phantasmagoric scene of orange-fringed clouds as far as the eye could see. The wing came back down and, as it did so, covered the fiery ball that was blinding him.

He feared for Kinshasa's future, but more about his ability to influence the events currently flooding the country. The bankers' dim views of the regime's future, expressed so spontaneously, had affected him the most. Having concluded that the president would be removed, the money men were, he was sure, looking to trade elsewhere. Perhaps ahead, if not right behind him, a Nundu emissary was in the Emirates to shake the bankers' hands on Kinshasa's diamonds. How long before the Pakistani merchant in Abu Dhabi came to the same conclusion? He swore that if he came through the current difficulty, he would do everything in his power to see that the merchant acquire a monopoly on the president's diamond trade, to reward the Pakistani for his faith.

"You are my reward for what I did to protect the village. I am sure of it." And when Julie said, "What did you do," the urge to unburden himself to her was overwhelming. It was as if telling her would bind her to him, succoring him from his lonely vigil over his conscience. A moment of reflection and, "I helped kill a man," he answered in a flat voice. She put her serious face on to look at him, her forehead still moist from her earlier effort to give him all he wanted of her.

"He was a Belgian priest, Father Brabant. I liked him, actually; he was progressive in that, unlike the others, he showed a bit of interest in us children. He built a schoolhouse for us to go to three times a week. And on Sunday he tested us. He learned some Ngbandi to teach us letters. I guess he thought it would be easier in our own language, or perhaps he saw that we would never need French or Flemish. He even liked women. He was always in the stands when the bare-breasted maidens were performing at harvest time. And he was curious about the village. Curious in a good sense — he wanted to understand us, whether to convert us, which he was good at, or out of his personal commitment — unlike the curiosity of the others who came to measure us like specimen in a zoo.

"Those, we call them *Zóbas*. They called themselves anthropologists, searching for proof that nonindustrial societies were irremediably primitive. Some of them came to the village for the sole purpose of practicing their racism. Africa attracted them the way Southeast Asia attracts pedophiles. They behaved with the mean resolve of men protected by the colonial authority. They liked watching the women working. And they looked for environmental stimuli to match with the village's behavior. Instinct, you see, not intelligence motivated us; and they wanted to measure it.

"The president experienced this much more than I did; the practice had waned by the time I was born. This is laughable today, and it was then, too. Their measuring drove us to escapades the whole village had fits of laughter about. Our parents would send us to other villages to stay with relatives until the *Zóbas* had moved to a different area.

"A *Zóba* saw no difference between an African and a beetle. God they loved beetles! I am sure if the choice were between a beetle and one of us in a life or death situation, they would rescue the beetle. And there are as many types of beetle as there are mangos on a tree. They paid us for the beetles. The bigger the bug, the bigger its horn, the more money they gave us.

"Through Father Brabant, I became a stamp collector. He used stamps to teach us a bit of geography and more about his native Belgium. Stamps fascinated me, made me dream of other places, where I had an idea they didn't measure people. I remember his showing of one from Cameroon. We laughed and looked at one another. The Cameroon stamp had a naked African archer on it. A savage! Not a Pygmy, or as the president decreed we should call them a few years ago, a Bambuti, or a Ba.

"As long as it was the Bambutis they considered savages, we didn't mind. It even made us feel better about ourselves; gave us a certain importance. Eventually we accepted that the naked archer could not be other than a Bambuti. You see, seeing an African depicted in a savage state on a stamp embarrassed us; we preferred to be seen as *evolués*, literally, improved or advanced Africans, not monkeys, the Belgians' name for us.

"I would do anything for a stamp — disobey my mother and let *Zóbas* measure me for stamps. One *Zóba* wanted beetles even more than I wanted stamps. For my beetles, he would steal from a colleague's stamp collection to pay me. Instead of coins, I got stamps. And beetles were my hard currency.

Then came another drive to suppress the village customs. The president called them the ISSMC, the 'International Society for the Suppression of Monkey Custom.' He said he had made it up after reading about the 'International Society for the Suppression of Savage Custom,' Joseph Conrad mentions in his *Heart of Darkness*. Members of the society cursed and damned the village for its un-Christian practices. They even cursed the people who went to the church because they were not zealous enough. I guess they had expected that the village churchgoers would collaborate in the suppression efforts. But the villagers knew that collaboration would mean being ostracized. That would mean having a fate worse than leprosy to befall them.

"Father Brabant was caught up in the drive. His superiors must have prompted him. I cannot think of another explanation. Mildly, shyly, at first, he spoke of the anti-Christian nature of masks. Then, although he knew it was not true, he began saying that we wor-shipped ancestors; that we were as savage as the Bambuti; that it was his and the *Zobas'* and the *evolués'* and every civilized person's duty to impound the masks to save us from ourselves. He must have studied masks; he knew more about them than even the elders did. That's why I said his superiors pushed him. He was too familiar with the masks' significance to speak against them the way he did.

"The elders were alarmed, but they had heard Belgian and other priests clamor against the village's customs for as long as tradition could recall. If they were concerned, it did not show, until the first harvest's initiation ceremonies, and when men in nearby villages reported that masks were disappearing and that the Belgian army would come to take them all away.

"Mokonzi Waza Kabasu had eyes made to stare. In fact, he had won every staring contest held in the district by forfeit; no one would stare against him, not even Belgians. Had they dared, *Zóbas* would have loved to measure him, I am sure. Scars lining his narrow forehead distorted his brow and made his eyes open wider. I don't think he could ever close his eyes. He slept with them open. And, of course, the scars and the staring eyes gave him a look of permanent annoyance. But I never saw him angry only thoughtful. Sitting in a circle around him outside his house, we youngsters listened to him speak of the ancestors and were transported to an unrecognizable land. Tradition he gave us. It was something, we, a conquered people, could venerate. Memory and reverence are what he gave us. We had something to dream about and carry with us all the days of our lives, like the people who carry the blessing for their homes around their necks.

"His talk about the river captivated me; his river had such exciting adventures. When he spoke of the river, he would stand, throw his head back and move his torso and hands to pantomime the river's motion. When he came to the cataracts he would jump up, and you thought he would stay in the air. His voice would accompany his movements, mimicking the river's hushes, growls, and swooshes. The women would all come out to watch him perform. But they remained behind the trees. Only their laughter gave them away. Whatever appreciation I have for the land and the river I owe to Mokonzi Kabasu, the great *raconteur* of my youth. And he was my mother's older brother and the Mokonzi na Bakonzi of the largest village in our district.

"After a while Father Brabant was always drunk. He couldn't digest the palm wine. He thought it was like white wine. He never appreciated that, unless consumed fresh, palm wine spoils, and by eleven o'clock he was sick. We have a saying, man is like palm-wine: when young, sweet but without strength; in old age, strong but harsh. In my mind's eye, I can see him bent over retching, outside his house near the little church, his hand on the wall for support.

"When he was delirious, he would utter his mother's name and a Fatou-Anne; I am sure the current foreign minister of Senegal is that woman. I suppose he had met her during a trip to Paris before the Second World War. As fate would have it, I met with her recently at the United Nations. I was going to tell her about Father Brabant, but I would have had to tell her of his death. I didn't know how to manage that.

"We have a weed growing along the riverbed. It has wide eight-point green leaves. Its seeds resemble large, shiny coffee beans enclosed in a spiny pod. My mother would purge me twice a month by making me swallow one of those foul-tasting seeds.

"It was simple really. All I had to do was to put a handful of crushed seeds from the riverbed weed Mokonzi Kabasu had given me in Father Brabant's palm-wine clay jug.

"It's only when I went to Brussels many years later did I find out the properties of those seeds. Walking through the *Jardin Botanique*, I bumped into it, our riverbank weed. I laughed; it was like meeting a pauper you knew dressed in a tuxedo. Then I remembered Father Brabant. At the Jardin Botanique, the weed had its own bed with expensive cedar mulch around it. At its feet, it had a plaque with its name in Latin, looking important. It wasn't spindly like ours on the riverbank are, but lush; its leaves were greener and its seed pods heavy and a healthy red. It was well fed. I grew embarrassed, as if meeting a poor relative who had become rich. I read that it was ricinus communis, the castor bean plant. The poison ricin is one of its by-products.

"We thought Father Brabant had died in his bed. No one had seen him, although some people walking by his open door say they heard his prayers; but of course, no one would go in. Then one afternoon, three days after I put the seeds in his wine, Mokonzi called me. Father Brabant was seen staggering toward the river. I was to follow him and make sure he would not return. The village's ways were at stake.

"I followed him with a club in my hand. I don't know what I would've done with it. I had never hit even a snake. But Mokonzi had gestured forcefully that I should strike him with it if necessary.

"Part of the river's outer bank was sucking mud like quicksand. We caught birds, huge capitan fish and other things there. It was a natural trap. Mokonzi Kabasu pulled a boar from there once; but it escaped, and the whole village ran after it. They managed to bar its route into the underbrush and it returned to the mud. Mokonzi roasted it for the village to eat that night.

"Father Brabant was wearing the white cassock he used for mass, not the threadbare pants and shirt he wore habitually weekdays. He seemed to be looking for a shallow area to walk into the river but was confused. Several times, he stumbled on the riverbank and lay still on the pebbles. Each time he lifted himself up after resting a long moment. That must have disoriented him more; the last time, he turned back toward the village, but tottered into the mud. His legs disappeared, as if he had fallen into a hole; and he remained there, not moving, praying loudly, '*Agnus Dei qui tollis peccata mundi miserere da me.* That was his favorite, I think; I heard him say it many times. He made us say it, to ask forgiveness for being ancestor worshipers. I still remember it, *Agnus Dei qui tollis peccata mundi miserere nobis.*

"I watched, crouched, at the edge, wondering if I would help him or finish him off. Then he began removing his cassock. '*Retire moi de la boue que je n'y reste pas enfoncé,*' he muttered. It must have taken hours, and the sun bleached the disturbed mud around him. And when he had finally lifted the white garment off, he reached sideways for the bank and pulled himself onto the sun drenched pebbles. For a while he remained there bent over, naked, his hands on his knees. Then he arose and staggered, crossed himself, and embraced the river.

"That afternoon the sun seemed to be no higher than the treetops, so violent were its rays. That occurrence must have attracted every simian in the area. I had never heard such screeching before; it was as if every ape in the region had come there that afternoon for a bout of madness. It was deafening. The river also was different. The water shone like a cut Angolan diamond.

"The river took Father Brabant, and I ran to tell Mokonzi Kabasu. He made me recount every detail of what I had witnessed Father Brabant do that afternoon. He listened with his head bowed, sitting on his stool, scratching his neck. I stood sideways to him. He seemed surprised when I mentioned the congregation of monkeys in the treetops. He didn't care for them, except as stew with a plate of plantain or yam. He mumbled for a while. I didn't understand what he was saying. Then I heard him say, 'That's what we have to do — you saved the village, Molu. The ancestors are in your debt. How many of us can say that?' The sun was setting when I finished telling him all. The large bats were already aloft, darkening the sky. Hungry like they were, I ran to my house."

Molu had expelled the lump that had been suffocating him. He lay staring at the ceiling, looking dazed. Julie's hand was on his chest. She had not said a word nor moved while he spoke. She understood that he had to pull himself up from his soul to tell her his story.

"How old were you?" she whispered after he was silent for a while.

He did not answer at once. "Eight or nine," he said at length.

"After Father Brabant went into the river, what happened?"

He moved closer to her. "I told you, I went to tell Mokonzi Kabasu."

"No, I mean — was he found?"

"Later — down river, some people found him on the other side, near Mpouya, where the river is at its narrowest. I know that another priest from a nearby village went, but our village never heard. That priest went into his house to remove his things. But no one said anything."

"You blame yourself for his suicide," she said. "That's a bit much!"

"Tradition says that no one tests the depth of a river with both feet. I think he knew he had been poisoned. He wasn't going to recover; he knew that. That's why he gave himself to the river."

"You've been telling yourself that all these years? You have no way of knowing what was on his mind. On the other hand, it just may have been that spoiled palm wine — or who knows? From the sound of him, he was a sensitive man. He may have apprehended that he and his church were a destructive force in your village. Going to the river was his way of doing penance for the sins of his order against Africa. I am not talking about a messianic complex or whatever — just that he may have been honorable."

"He was! I think he was."

"Then?"

"Castor beans — a deadly poison. I read everything about their properties. A handful — he should not have lasted three days."

"That's what I mean; you don't know what caused him to do what he did that afternoon. He may have thrown up and cleansed his stomach out with the spoiled palm wine. His system may have been spared."

"I don't think you understand. I feel remorseful for what happened to him. He was a sort of friend; he wasn't a persecutor like the other priests. But I still think that what Mokonzi Kabasu did was right — protecting the village was right. At independence, I was one of the boys who threw rocks at the other priests; they were functionaries, promoting their Belgian colonialism. They were not in Africa by consent; no, they were there by their imposition, our misfortune. But Father Brabant was not one of them.

"We were fortunate that Mokonzi Kabasu was the elder, especially at that time. The Belgians had him on their payroll, sure. But the village meant more to him. And he wanted to be in good standing when he became an ancestor. Had he let the village become more foolish than it already was, the ancestors would not have welcomed him in their midst. That's why he did away with Father Brabant. Given the magnitude of the Belgian colonial enterprises, it wasn't much, but it was something. If we had had more like him over the ages, we would not have ended — well you were there, you saw for yourself how we ended.

"My remorse is that it was Father Brabant who died, not that I played a part in his giving himself to the river."

"What was the problem with your masks?" she asked her voice now louder, her demeanor almost cheerful. "What could it have mattered? The few I saw in Kinshasa were small and unassuming. The priests also worship images… We Indians say that truth is one; wise men call it by different names."

"I haven't given it much thought. I remember that the priests tore down whatever distracted from the promotion of their religion. Belgian paternalism didn't admit that Africans could have a viable set of religious beliefs."

"And you think that's why your village's masks were targeted?" She sounded unconvinced.

"Must have! Even Father Brabant, who looked at them as culturally significant to the village, turned against them."

"Because they worshiped them in the village?"

"Well, not like I worship you," he whispered, caressing the curve of her side.

"That's the way all men worship," she said in a low voice, half jokingly.

"Africans do not worship masks," he answered. "Masks are for spiritual —"

"It will soon be time to dress for the airport," she said moving his hand downward. "I've been rationed enough, and I want a taste of real worship and spirituality before it's time to go."

He thought the request reasonable and obliged, whispering, *nalingi yo, nalingi yo.*

Julie was accompanying him to the airport. In the back seat of an Al Ghazal taxi, she chatted as if Molu's departure from Abu Dhabi was an everyday event, as if she would see him later that evening upon his return home from the office. But in the early morning, the desk at the hotel had booked her a flight on Etihad Airways to Guyane.

In the taxi, Molu held her hand, and crossing the circular terminal he held her hand, proud, his prize on display. The world should notice his flaunting her, as he had wanted to do in Kinshasa, but where she had been, he agreed, rightly so, very cautious. He held her hand all the way, until at the gate they checked his passport and took his ticket. He embraced her, holding on to her for a long moment. She only heard a few sobbing words, but she understood. For an hour, she stood by the gate, watching the aircraft.

In the duty free shop, a man in a khandura recognized the couple. He had bumped into Julie in Al Fujayrah, and she had roundly cursed him. He followed them and watched them embrace. Anger crept into his features, turning his face into that of a stern avenger.

Julie did not leave the gate until the plane had left the ground. Her golden brown face pale, she walked with short, reluctant steps. Feeling Molu inside of her, she then smiled enigmatically. Do your work little Molus, she urged.

The man in the khandura followed. It was easy; she walked so slowly. The airport speakers announced that the Etihad flight to Geneva had taken off on time. She turned to look where the sound was coming from, and the man saw that she was smiling. That enraged him. He opened the knife in the wide front pocket of his khandura and moved closer to her.

Julie walked to the information desk in the main concourse. She had remembered the taxi queue and wished to avoid it. But there was no one at the desk. She turned toward the shopping area, where she had seen a customer service desk. They could call Al Ghazal Transport for her. Near the Golden Class Club, the crowd parted.

Julie heard a man behind her shout words in a language she didn't know. She felt a sudden burning sting in her left side under the ribs that made her gasp. She tried to put her hand where the pain was, but she recoiled when she saw the gushing blood. Spinning, she saw Golden Class Club painted on the door.

A passenger told the police he heard a man shout, "Slave's whore," and he had also heard the woman cry "Molu" several times. Then she lay still.

246

# Chapter 26

Molu pinched himself, and, if he were asleep, he prayed that he would awaken at least where he had been and not where ill fortune may have set its trap for him. As the aircraft entered his country's airspace, the lethargy lifted and his mood improved. His spirit was buoyant when the plane touched down at Ndjili airport.

---

At the evening briefing two days earlier, the Dictator had come up with a new idea to bring Molu, whom he now referred to as the "wretch," safely home.

"My plane is flying to Geneva. My wife and her sister have a few things to pick up in Europe. I can kill two birds with one stone by getting the wretch on board. He will be thankful not to have to spend a whole day getting here. I looked at his itinerary — all that time out of touch. He flies to Rome, lays over, flies to Addis, changes planes, his time between flights is nine hours. This gesture will eliminate any suspicion he may have picked up along the way."

Actually, it was the call from Molu in Sharjah that had prompted him to send the plane to Geneva. He was afraid that what the banker there had told his foreign minister about the loss of the regime's rating would inspire flight. Molu had sounded flustered, incoherent, when he spoke about reports from Wall Street regarding the government. Might he decide not to come to Kinshasa on one pretext or another? A former prime minister was pleading illness as an excuse for staying in Brussels. Like Molu, this man had his immediate family abroad and had no incentive for coming to Kinshasa, except for the new position he had promised him.

He was debating whether he should clamp down on the media. The New York papers had infuriated him with their reports of soldiers surrendering.

Reluctantly, he had not told his security chief the true reason for sending the plane to Geneva, fearing that Mgonu also would begin preparation for the flight of ignominy. Mgonu was fiercely protective of the people who worked for him and would do the unimaginable to keep them from harm. Where could the security chief find a welcoming exile? For the first time, he gave the question some thought.

As long as he thinks he has no place — that's what would keep him upholding the regime at all cost. But that's unethical, he told himself. The man has dedicated his existence to you. One more shame you don't need. If it comes to leaving, you should call your friend in Togo to take in Mgonu. If I start making plans of this kind, how long before — I wish Bisengimana were here; he is the most suited to be my intermediary with the Ugandans, he acknowledged, in great sorrow for himself. Or Molu! But forgiving Molu would mark me as a dead man. My responsibility is to be uncompromisingly ruthless. If it were for myself — but why think of what is not possible. I need someone I can trust. My wife and her sister would acquiesce to nothing else but remaining here. She wouldn't even talk about the possibility of leaving. I wonder how long before I tell Maka that I, myself, have to go to Geneva. Doctors should have vultures as their emblem; snakes are too good for them.

"I would think that such attention would add to any suspicion he may have," Mgonu had answered, taken off guard by the Dictator's new line of thought.

The Dictator was distracted, and Maka had difficulty finishing his second briefing that day. He urgently wanted to return to the question regarding the troops drifting from the front that he had addressed at the morning briefing. They were alarming the people, and as importantly were affecting perception of the government. His agents had reported that people were writing off the administration, and a sense of inevitability was setting in. He wanted to muzzle the press that was turning the Tutsi power into a superpower.

One reporter even compared the Tutsi progress to the 1967 Israeli advance in the Sinai. "They are disciplined, methodical — they surround fortified areas, but leave an escape route for our obliging troops to take — entire battalions surrender over the telephone. Fax is used for a similar purpose."

"They have been most generous," the Dictator intoned. "I can even say they have kept me alive. I don't know another woman who would so understand."

The security chief had heard the Dictator refer to his wife and her sister as though they were a single individual before and had not given it a second thought, but listening now, he experienced a sense of alarm, of events spinning out of his control, of doors shutting. Not knowing what to make of it and stunned by the flood that engulfed Kinshasa, he wondered if the twins were not the answer to his now very real dilemma. How would he approach them though, singly or together? He could hardly tell them apart. And what would he say to them? Your husband is handicapped. Unless you help me prop him up, an evacuation is not out of the question. The Dictator was observing him with a shrewd eye, quizzically, unblinking, seemingly reading his mind.

"Talking about her settles me," he said contentedly at length. "It's like that tea you drink to help with your digestion. Talking about them does the same thing for my state of mind. But what are you thinking, Maka? I hope it is not that the Molu business is no longer a priority. Because if you are, think again."

Mgonu became defensive, "I understand the importance of making an example of Molu —"

"An example? Maka? After all I have told you, you call what we are going to do to him an example? It's not an example, my friend, it's our reality — the whole thing. But if you insist on saying example, add paradigmatic to it, so that everyone understands what you are referring to. I am sure somewhere in there an example has a place, and I may have used the word myself."

"I thought we should also discuss the reversal our troops have experienced lately, Mokonzi," Mgonu said.

"Yes, the reversal! Let me worry about that. Truccard called me. They are concerned. It's their investment after all. You see Maka, the French have a duty not to allow our destabilization here. When they see that our troops are being pushed, they will do what's necessary to protect their investment here. It's very simple really. But I also must do my part to illustrate that it is I who is the force to be contended with here. You heard what Jood said. I am still in shock at what he said. How can you understand the Americans having fallen for Nundu? He was Patrice's bagman — he couldn't read or write. Thank God for the French.

"People know I have favored Molu. When they see what has befallen him at my hands, they will look at betrayal through different eyes. And they will appreciate that I am not a marginal, propped-up autocrat relying on the French to keep me in power. I will brook no betrayal. Maybe we should hang a sign with that on it around the wretch's neck. If you want you can add, 'example' on the sign as well. I am in deadly earnest, Maka! As events are demonstrating, it is even more important that I do my part to show them out there that I am not to be trifled with."

"As you know it's all arranged for him to have his spot in Gombé near the American ambassador's residence," Mgonu said. "The new guards there work for us. Their job will be to watch over Sakeseba, to make sure he doesn't wander around. You know! What I wanted to ask you next has to do with the ambassador's schedule —"

"Schedule?" the Dictator exclaimed. "Hasn't finding his wife with the driver made it impossible for him to function here? The humiliation has made him persona non grata. What schedule?"

"Well, he has taken the offensive, Mokonzi —"

"The offensive? What're you talking about, Maka? How can he take the offensive with something like that hanging over him? Isn't he in a hole, hiding? The man across the river in Brazzaville is shameless, but if his wife were found with a driver… What are you saying, Maka? He wasn't humiliated? Is that what you are telling me?"

"I am sure he was humiliated, Mokonzi; how can he not be? But he didn't fall apart. He put her on the first flight out, the one to Brussels. He even accompanied her to the airport, by all accounts very solicitous to her, not upset at all. He then called his staff together to say that conditions here had unbalanced his wife. She is now under doctor's care — those are his exact words. He has been telling everyone he meets that she is in a hospital at home. At a reception in Gombé, an informant reported that some people there suggested that Africa was to blame for unhinging her. I understand that Washington is letting him decide how to handle his family situation as he sees fit. They have accepted that hardship was the cause of what they call her breakdown. I have begun an information campaign that should put things straight, using the video the agent made."

"Molu has a lot to answer for," the Dictator intoned.

He got up from the sofa and slowly walked to his desk. He lifted the cane with the handle carved in the shape of an elephant and lovingly passed it through his left hand. He then caressed it with his left cheek and then his tongue; thereupon, he smashed it against the desk.

---

He came home to the muted reception the regime reserved for its royalty. Citoyen Nganga, who had known him since his army days and called him by his first name, stood at the foot of the steps, smiling broadly the regime's welcome.

Nganga had waited in the background before stepping in to greet Molu after the sisters and their retinue had left. Their antics bored him. He could no longer bear them, for it meant making an effort beyond his forbearance. Not even resignation would help him with them now. Moreover, they had failed to renew cheer in the Dictator. Nganga's assistant had met them at the plane; the man was glad for the opportunity to play a role, if only for a brief moment, in the twins' rocambolesque lives.

The foreign ministry heads of sections, lined up behind Nganga, standing at attention. The foreign minister's black limousine, newly washed and polished, gleamed a few steps to the side. Molu looked at the limousine next to the aircraft and pictured a man in a blue silk suit being met the way the world's important CEOs expected to be met. Nganga bowed deeply when Molu stepped down onto the tarmac. "Welcome home, Minister Sakeseba," he said solemnly, pride in his voice. Molu reached out and took his hand.

"Does it mean what I think it means, to have the great Petit Pierre Nganga meet me at the airport this way? The plane, the limo and Citoyen Nganga for me?"

"Fitting, yes," Nganga said. "The foreign minister is the cabinet's most important member. I asked the ancestors the moment I heard of your appointment that it might lead to even greater things. Mokonzi, if you look at him closely, is tired. Even a genius, if he has been in harness all these years, gets weary. You are his favorite. You are like a son. In my memory, you are the first cabinet member to have received the courtesy of the presidential plane to come home. You didn't know that, did you? You thought the plane was for his wife and her sister.

No, it was for you. They went for the ride and, of course, to shop. Fitting? Yes, very yes!"

"No, I didn't know about the plane. Shedul told me only after I had completed the president's business that the plane was at Cointrin. I would have had a long layover in Addis if I hadn't caught it.

"But what do you mean, tired? The planets would leave their orbits if anyone thought of taking his place. Let's not even imagine such a thing."

He spoke to the protocol chief to ensure that not even a *soupçon* of disloyalty would attach to him. The regime did not permit a touch of doubt. You were for, your life offered as security, or you were against. Reflexively, Molu had refrained from saying more about the Dictator to Citoyen Nganga who may have been testing him.

<hr>

Maka Mgonu was to have been at the airport to satisfy himself that his men were following his directions exactly. Thorough as always, he feared that conditions had not allotted enough preparation time for the operation the Dictator had ordered against his new foreign minister. At their last meeting, a worried Dictator had wistfully reminded him that the smell of blood had a way of pushing men to behave out of range, the way men must have when they hunted to live.

"Please Maka! Watch carefully," he had almost pleaded. "Do not let your men get out of range; blood has a primeval hold on all of us. Watch, or it will not be a success. A disaster we cannot suffer at this time. But I desire it to be a full thing; and for that, Molu has to realize that he is powerless to change anything that has befallen him, that his collaborators will not help him. It has to be complete, Maka, physically and mentally, it has to be complete. If he dies, we have failed."

To stalk the prey, he would have stood at his post in the shadows, below the terminal's portico, spying on his men's conduct. Dreading being a prey himself, he appreciated his predator's role. There was security in that: he would not be a quarry as long as it was he who played the killer.

He was not at the airport because the army chief of staff had barged into Maka's office just as Maka was leaving for Ndjili. Everyone heard the general's vehicle screeching to a halt. The security chief was at the door of his office when the general entered the building unannounced, shouting that Kisangani was about to fall. Mgonu slammed the door shut. The capture of the eastern capital, a center for the diamond trade and a major transportation hub, including an international airport, and with strategic assets on the river would scissor the country in two.

"You are a fool Luc!" Mgonu told the general in his most infuriated voice. "Mokonzi has ordered reinforcement for Kisangani. Why aren't you holding on to your courage with both hands? And why aren't you in the field with your men shouting orders instead of running in here like Abelard with Fulbert, knife in hand, on your tail?"

A short, neat man, acutely aware of the stars on his epaulettes, General Luc Mako Liekungu stretched his height as high as humanly possible. "I just left Mokonzi," he said.

"So, you saw the president," Mgonu said, his voice curled with derision.

The general stared at him, as if his eyes and ears had misled him, questioning, which head of state he had just seen. "He was incoherent," the general said, speaking in a strangled voice. He spread his hands and dropped them to emphasize his despair at the disastrous end.

"He was tired," Mgonu said in a louder voice. "Wouldn't you be tired if you had a five-foot two frightened rat pestering you?"

"He was incoherent, Mgonu. Lost. He didn't know what day it was. You can sneer, but you and I are pillars to an edifice that has collapsed. Instead of sneering at me, what do you say we do?"

"Edifice, General? Edifice? You now use words whose meanings you don't know. Is that what fear does to a general?"

"He was incoherent. Babbling," Liekungu repeated, trying to make his cracking voice convey urgency, jabbing his finger at the Dictator's picture behind the security chief's desk.

"I told you he was tired," Mgonu said, turning around to look at his boss's picture. "And since when do you point fingers at Mokonzi?"

The general just looked at him, his lips moved, but no word came.

"Scared generals are gyrating generals," Mgonu continued, his tone bitter. "You are not about to turn traitor, are you? We are watching you!" He gestured to show what he meant. "Kisangani was your reason for barging in here like a hen with an egg sticking up its ass? What happened to 'the great counter-offensive' you were bragging to us three days ago?"

# Chapter 27

Mgonu hated General Liekungu. He hated himself more than ever. He hated the world, for Julie was dead. The Continental Hotel in Abu Dhabi had notified her husband that someone had fatally stabbed his wife at the airport. Upon getting the news, Mgonu had rushed to see the husband. In his grief, he implored every divinity he knew that the agent overheard wrongly what the husband had said to an assistant. But prayer was in vain, Mephistopheles had said in Faust, he recalled.

At the hotel the husband told him in the French accent Mgonu despised what his Abu Dhabi colleague had reported, why Julie was there and with whom. The hotel manager shrugged, telling Mgonu that his wife had made herself available to the highest black bidder. "*C'est bien fait pour sa gueule.*" She got what she deserved.

Lost in grief, his skin more grey than black, his brown eyes lifeless, Mgonu stared blankly at the manager. Grief eviscerated his mind. After a long while he repeated the hotel manager's words so softly the Frenchman could not hear them, "*C'est bien fait pour sa gueule.*"

He took out the square-top brass knuckles that he always carried and deliberately, as if not to panic the manager, put it on the four fingers of his left hand. He took off his dark glasses, as if desirous that the manager be able to give a full description of his killer. Maka turned his head slightly to the right to look at the Frenchman, a mongoose eyeing a venomous snake. The hotel manager gaped at Maka's hand, then into his anguished eyes. Indignation flushed his face.

Maka's eyes remained focused and did not blink. Fright suddenly blazed on the manager's face, as he realized death's eyes were upon him. Unable to speak, he moved his shoulders, as though to ask what he had done to deserve such fate. He then ran to the window facing the street and looked below. Running past the security chief was preferable to jumping, he decided. At the last second, Maka took a step into his path and swung, striking the Frenchman full force below the heart. The chief's five bodyguards outside rushed into the manager's office. One of them said importantly, automatically, dumbly to the body on the floor, "*les gorilles vous saluent bien,*" the gorillas say hello.

Mgonu stalked out.

---

The grief soon became a physical pain; acute, it took away all measure of life itself. What was the good of breathing?

At his desk in the dark, he waited for the hour when the man who had caused Julie's death would step into his grasp. What he had in store for Molu lessened his anguish, and he massaged the thought with all sorts of imaginary contrivances that would prolong his nemesis' agony. Torture was for life, he told himself. That helped him cope somewhat. Molu's ruin would quench the desperate need to avenge having lost Julie — the one thing that would make her live again.

Once he was comfortable with that thought, it drifted. Remembrance that he had suggested to the Dictator that Molu be kept on the move to lessen contact with collaborators replaced it. He screeched and hit his chest uncontrollably, as if that would shut up the thought.

What-ifs swamped his mind. What if he had kidnapped her and taken her to live in the forest? What if he had arranged for Molu's wife to witness her husband's pestering Julie? And what if he had disregarded the Dictator's order and had had Molu assassinated like Letelier on a Washington street. At that, he experienced a new awareness. It was as if his mind had cleared like dark clouds parting to let the sunshine through. The Dictator was responsible. Had the Dictator followed his advice, Julie need not have died. Then the clouds closed over the sky.

Molu had seduced Julie. As a seduced woman that she had gone to meet the rake in Abu Dhabi. Why couldn't he have left her alone? Why this innocent woman? Now more solitary than ever, without even an imaginary sweetheart, Mgonu was abandoned to suffer what Molu had wrought. He would use Molu's carcass to make a pyre for Julie.

Upon this promise, the security chief went to kneel in front of his desk, holding the corner so that he wouldn't fall. Julie stood in front of him. She had on a dress of tangerine and green colored silk. He intoned Wilfred Cartey's verses as if reciting a dirge,

> I hear ranchitos calling
> Calling you and me
> I hear ranchitos calling
> Begging to be free
> I see them
> Scale the mountain tops
> And mingle with the clouds

---

Far away, he heard the engine of a Land Cruiser as it came closer and halted in front of his building, and Julie vanished, replaced by the army chief of staff bending at him across the desk. This whimpering cretin was very alive, while Julie was dead.

"He had peed on himself," he heard the general say. The man's croaking irritating him. "He was sitting in a pool of urine, who knows for how long, gazing at his cane. I asked him for help for Kisangani. He babbled. He talked of memoirs he was writing so that his historical life would be understood better than his lived one was."

"How can that be possible?" Mgonu asked.

"Possible?"

"Yes, how can his documented life be greater than his lived one?"

"The man is a wreck, Maka. Rubble. That's what I am telling you. And Kisangani is falling."

Mgonu took off his dark glasses, startling the general who had never seen the security chief without them. It was an unrecognizable face, the dead brown eyes like Dude's, his pet lion, when eyeing a joint of zebu.

"Kisangani is falling, March 15, Kisangani is lost."

"Are you a soothsayer come to tell me to beware the Ides of March?"

"But don't you understand what this means?"

"I know what it would mean, if that's what you are trying to ask. The president has sent reinforcements — food and weapons. Generals are supposed to use such materiel to make war."

"Yes, but the soldiers didn't eat the food. It was stolen before it reached them. And yes, he sent guns, but no ammunition."

"And your Serbian mercenaries, they lack food and ammunition?"

"Those terrorists?" The general shouted. "All they have done is to turn the people against us. It is not my place to remind you that you were the one to suggest them to the president. Brutality is not always the answer, Mr. Chief of Security. Doesn't one of your fables say that?"

"We have a prime minister, you know," Mgonu said. "Why aren't you in his office? He can do more than I can. Go see him! I have to leave for the airport."

"The fake prime minister?"

"You supported him. He is your creation."

"Kando is on an island in the middle of the river."

The security chief put on his glasses to conceal the dread that had replaced his anger. But his lips formed a questioning "oh."

"And the people are helping the Ugandans, leading them through the forest so that they can maneuver around and behind our flanks." The general sensed that he had the security chief's full attention.

"You have been outflanked? You told Mokonzi that you were outflanked?"

"Yes."

"You are telling me the world has turned over? You told Mokonzi the world had turned over?"

"I tried to tell him, Maka. I stood in front of him in that *urinoire* stinking room. He just mumbled something about his memoirs. He writes his memoirs while the capital is becoming more defenseless by the hour. Listen to me! The end is coming at us faster than he can eat grubs from sapelli trees. What are we going to do? You always have plans. What's the one for this?"

"Yes, I have a plan."

"Well? What's the one for this situation, or is it personal to you alone?"

"What does that remark mean, General?" Mgonu said in his deliberate, menacing voice.

"Exactly that," Liekungu answered, unafraid. "Are you making plans for yourself alone?"

"You mean am I going to abandon you, General?"

"Oh, I know you'll abandon me. Are you also going to abandon YOUR Mokonzi?"

"If you weren't such a nonentity, General, I would be in my right to shoot you, especially since I need bodies for a pyre. Calling a man a traitor in this country is a capital offense; unfortunately so is killing nonentities. As much as I want to do the latter, it revolts me more to do the former; so you live for others with less discernment to rid the race of you."

(History would later reflect that General Liekungu left the meeting with Maka Mgonu to tell his men Kinshasa was now an open city. One of his men shot him. They said he had betrayed the president. Accounts later reported that the president's son had murdered him.)

Liekungu gazed at the security chief, fear back on his face.

"This would be a good time for madness," Mgonu told him; "but I am not so fortunate. So I am stuck with you. There is money! Money shoots straighter than guns. Why don't you use it?"

"There is no money," the general said. "I have not been able to pay the men in months. Most is stolen before it gets to them. And in any case the market women don't accept it; they say it's not genuine. Listen to me, Maka; you have to understand, I have no way to defend the capital. Capitulation is a day distant. Every man must care for himself now."

Mgonu looked at the general, deliberating whether he should confide in the army man. At length, he said, "The twins!"

Liekungu gaped at him.

"The twins would never leave. They'll make him stay; he will take all the necessary measures then."

<h1 style="text-align:center">Chapter 28</h1>

Danielle hovered at the office's door, a harpie imposing her prerogative as the Dictator's personal secretary. Citoyen Nganga, jauntier than usual to hide his disappointment and his ill will towards the secretary, stood reluctantly to the side, bumping up and down as if a drugged marionette. Molu looked at them, with understanding, but without conceit, the way a parent would disobedient, quarreling, siblings. He walked in with an eager step.

———————

As he had ordered, the Dictator was now alone with his foreign minister. The room had the pungent smell of a tomb. The Dictator sat forlornly in a high-backed chair. Molu felt the need to move closer, as though no matter how loudly he spoke the man in front of him would not hear. *"Mbote Mokonzi! Ozali malamu?"* he greeted the Dictator hesitantly in Lingala.

The Dictator looked up slowly, reproach in his rheumy eyes rimmed in red. The pupils were a blurred gray.

Molu repeated the greeting in Ngbandi. The Dictator acknowledged him and lowered his head again. He looked at the door as he did so, as if expecting someone to walk in. He seemed to be waiting. And Molu sensed anxiety in the wait. Hurriedly, Molu thanked him for the use of the aircraft that had flown him from Geneva and began the brief he had memorized about the trip to Abu Dhabi. The Dictator stared at his feet. His head bobbed. Molu was not sure whether he was listening. Then from deep inside him, the Dictator said, shaking, "I am angry with you, Molu."

"I understand, Mokonzi. I am sorry it didn't go so well. But the Pakistani is —"

"It has nothing to do with that," the Dictator interrupted, his voice gaining strength. "You think you can still play the fox — why isn't Maka here yet?"

"I don't know what you mean, Mokonzi. The fox?"

"You think you can get away with it?" the Dictator asked as though arguing with himself. "Conspiring with them to humiliate the nation — for my overthrow. You thought you could pull it off like a thief in the night. Well — you can't!"

Molu stared in silence.

"Maka wants you dead," the Dictator said, shaking his head as he looked up for the first time. "Besides, you took a woman he wanted. I

259

ordered them to stop her from flying to Abu Dhabi. Danielle can tell you about it. Maka had one of his men disgrace the wife of your friend, the American ambassador. We will not let you and your conspirators assume we are no longer of any consequence."

"I don't understand Mokonzi?"

"I found you out. Betrayal has a stench. It wasn't difficult."

"Betrayal?"

"Sending that Jood Mosley here was the signal for them to start their offensive, the indicator to begin dismantling my work. You gave in to that — my work — my work to shape a country out of the colonial swamp. My life's work."

The tears came as if to deepen the dictator's grievances. Molu looked on, uncomprehendingly, suspended between sorrow at the ruin of his Mokonzi and fear at witnessing the end of his future.

"I could have been the Nasser of Africa," he said, pride in his bassoon voice, "if I had not sold out." His long fingers pulled his hair. Directly, he shouted: "Cretin, I gave in to them to safeguard the country. Nasser had a civilization waiting for a Nasser. Who was waiting for me? This is all about Patrice, isn't it? Patrice is on a pedestal today because he is dead. Had he lived they would have lynched him like they have lynched me. Who doesn't know that?"

He looked at Molu from the corner of his eye and moved his head as if listening to himself argue. But he answered himself, "He was no match for them. No idealist is a match for them. It's tooth and claw against tooth and claw. He had will, I give him that; but it was a stubborn will — a will untempered by knowledge or understanding. He was a man who ran around the world without leaving his house. He was a paraplegic trying to throw himself on a moving train. It took a pimp to play in their league. That's right!

"I was the right man for the time; I was one step ahead of survival, Patrice was always one step behind." Molu nodded in agreement.

"A balkanized country isn't a country; it's a brothel. There, only vultures feed." Again Molu nodded.

"How many Africans were interested the way the Arabs were in getting back their dignity after the colonial rape? They did not colonize them the same way they did us Molu. Maybe the desert and God protected them. I was right to say that, they did not colonize the Arabs the same way. Could anyone here have said no to the Western Consortium, the way Nasser could? With what? Sekou Touré did, he answered, and the people — the women — followed him. De Gaulle respected him for having told him what to do with himself." He paused. "My memory is not so reliable," he said. "Sekou Touré had Nkrumah to back him. Whom did I have? I won't say Patrice!

"Sekou Touré was a tyrant," he answered, with an odd forcefulness. "He had people bring their relatives to the jail when the announcer read their names at the end of the noon news broadcast. Oh? And what have I planned for my boy Molu?" he asked. "One thing is certain, I have not learned."

"Could I really have been the Gamel Abdel Nasser of Africa, Molu? Even the sound of his name connotes respect. I would even be satisfied if they say I was a Nasser manqué. It seems so long ago that I thought of being the hinge in the history of Africa. Then, that's all I thought about. You've heard me speak of Nasser, Molu?" he asked.

"If I knew then what I know now, it would have been possible to be the Nasser of Africa. Sure! But then I thought the Western Consortium was all-powerful. It was their swagger — I didn't know their weaknesses, Molu. I couldn't even imagine that they had any."

<hr>

"How can you call God just after He gives you Belgians for colonial masters? What could the ancestors have done to deserve such a fate, Molu? God didn't do it, you might say. But He let it happen! What is the difference?

"God, if I had known! What I could have done! Nasser! It took me a long time to see they had fears. Now that the end is near, I have to look to them for still more help. Where is the justice in that, Molu?

"I should have built the army, made it invincible. If I had, I wouldn't be in the fix I am in now, you will say, Molu. And I'll be smug for the last time and tell you that in the nation that I built, you couldn't have strong leadership in a country as diverse as ours and have a strong army. The army and the leadership couldn't have coexisted. I don't have to tell you that, Molu.

"Leading this country is one of the most exhausting in the canon of governance. Why do you think I made my pact with the devil? The Western Consortium, I mean. I did, so that I wouldn't inflict on the country an army coup every six months and a civil war every five years.

"If we, I mean our ethnic group, Molu, had been larger, I could have tried to staff the army with them, or enough of them to keep the balance in my favor. However, it was not to be.

"If that were the only reason for my pact with the Consortium, I'd have no regret. But it is never that simple. One need created another and another, like dominoes. Today? Today I cannot tell you what those needs were. Does that mean they were not important? Who can say? You? I can only swear that they must have been important.

"For a long time it was I who pulled the strings, and I could be as bourgeois as I wanted about everything. It was a simpler time, Molu, a time when it was not yet necessary to make up ignorance with mindless circumspection. But the years pressed. I was busy. Unaware as I was, I also began to slow down. These aren't excuses, Molu, just a tally of faults that are now demanding payments.

"The Consortium grew resentful of my smugness. Why should I answer the phone when the vice-president of the United States rings when the president answers the phone when I ring? I wasn't judicious enough. Remember, Molu? It was I who had to stand next to the president of France at our yearly Francophone summit. Me, no one else! Me, Mokonzi na Bakonzi to stand next to the president of France at a meaningless enclave. It's not the big enemies you have to worry about, though. Keep small enemies on the other side of the river. Remember that, too, Molu.

"Having love is not the antidote to everything: I knew that. There is too much risk of people hating you when all you want is love, for no one loves you unless they know you. That's a risk I didn't know how to take. But is there anything I wouldn't give to be in Patrice's shoes? Maybe they know how much I resent wearing the same shoes as Pinochet, Abacha, Marcos, and the illustrious others they have put me with. How could they have done such a thing? No one can say those names without including mine in the same breath. Once they initiate you into that pantheon, they can say anything about you.

"And don't forget, Molu, it's those I gave in to who put me there. 'Unless you do what we tell you, we will put you in the Duvalier pantheon. Crown you the Zeus of it all, the Chairman of the Board. And when you do we will put you there just the same.' They can push my button with that anytime they need a service, Molu. 'You do what we ask, and we'll see to it that your name is removed from the granite where it is enshrined on the pantheon's wall.'

"They can compare me to Kurtz, put me in the Grand Guignol, or say I have billions in Swiss banks. If anything, it's Quixote that I am, Molu, not Kurtz. But Kurtz is what I am stuck with every time there is a heart of darkness story and not necessarily in Africa. I am proof that, 'it is easy to carve a dead elephant; but no one dares attack a live one,' as tradition says."

"You are not in any of these pantheons, Mokonzi. It's the media —"

"The media? Yes, Molu, the media! They even criticized me for holding the Muhammad Ali championship bout in Kinshasa. I could have invented the polio vaccine, and the media would have criticized me for that. They never reported that the event succeeded in putting the country on the world map — my goal. Was it my fault if rumble rhymed with jungle? The only person to benefit from the Ali show here was Joseph Conrad, dead sixty years. His *Heart of Darkness* was on the best seller's list in Europe and America for months following 'the rumble in the jungle.'

"I was tall, I wanted distinction. Nothing felt as exhilarating as walking into a room and hear people stop breathing. I could never tire of hearing that sound. But I would see the country cut up into hostile portions to be thought in the same breath with Nasser. There is nothing I wouldn't give to be in the Nasser pantheon. I would even forgive you, Molu, for that.

"I gave you everything, Molu, but that was not enough for you. I made you my son." Molu glanced downward, taking a deep breath, his mouth opened. "You were the pillar on which my legacy rested. So what do you do? You let them humiliate me, and with me, the country and everything else we worked for. Yours was the most nefarious crime, letting them humiliate me! I had to name you foreign minister to revenge myself on you.

"Was all my scheming worth it? Now, I don't know. All your life, study men! Gain an instinct for them. That will serve you well in everything you engage in. It did with you, Molu. Hadn't I known that ambition was your liability, I never would have snared you where I could revenge myself on you. I thought women were your handicap, especially foreign women. I even ordered what's her name removed to get my hands on you. There is no obstacle from hell or conceived by man that you wouldn't have gone through to get here. I wished it hadn't been so easy to tamper with your destiny, Molu. I mean that! But it should not be said that you didn't have a way out.

"At first that was not true, but once I saw how little effort I needed to manage you, I left an opening for you to slip out. It's important for me to be able to say that cruel I am not. But like the crabs I used to trap in my youth, the lure was all there was — to the detriment of your life, the lure was all you could smell.

"You may say that a leader is too far removed from day to day operations to concern himself with revenge. Look again! If you are not in the game, you look at revenge with a dilettante's eye. But if you are, no slight can remain unrevenged without imperiling the whole edifice of your power. Man's fear will drive him to unimaginable feats of imagination, including dreaming of unseating you."

Once again Molu breathed deeply. Motutu's words had reminded him what Colonel Freeman had advised he do — that Molu should replace the Dictator.

"If you fail to correct a wrong done to you — you is, of course, the country, the regime, the government, the family — imaginations are stimulated to dream what otherwise should never be dreamed. And don't forget that by killing one, you warn a hundred, as the Chinese say. You may choose to be Job, and I suppose there is some advantage in that. Me, I thought it proper to be Jacob; and not only because I inherited a land, unbelievably, of milk and honey.

"I never think of China's enduring its humiliation at the hand of the Consortium without ruminating about us. The Consortium lusted after no land to the degree they did after ours. The scramble for Africa revolved around us. And if today Africa is a senseless congerie of borders, it is because the Congo served as the converging point for the inside-out contest for our land. I have heard from many what happened, but no one has enlightened me as to why. It was so comical that day in Addis; little Zengher tried to explain in his vile hiccupped accent how beneficial French colonialism had been to him. I have not laughed like that since. I thought the Nigerian delegation was going to hang him. He ran! I had no idea he could run. He never came back to Addis after that. What I know is that it was our misfortune to be where the sun rose and where the sun set.

"Around the time of the 'rumble in the jungle,' Maka gave me a copy of Joseph Conrad's story, having highlighted several passages. One that I still remember should explain what I am telling you. Conrad said it with a clarity I envy. *'They were conquerors,'* Conrad explains, speaking of the Consortium. *'And for that you want only brute force — nothing to boast of, when you have it, since your strength is just an accident arising from the weakness of others. They grabbed what they could get for the sake of what was to be got. It was just robbery with violence, aggravated murder on a great scale, and men going at it blind — as is very proper for those who tackle a darkness. The conquest of the earth, which mostly means the taking it away from those who have a different complexion or slightly flatter noses than ourselves, is not a pretty thing when you look into it too much.'"*

"You memorized that passage, Mokonzi?"

"Yes; what is there for me to do? Responsibility! Is there a responsibility here, in what Conrad says? That's what I wanted to know. Institutions are not made of mortar and steel. They have a soul, men's soul, a country's soul and they have memories. Historical memory is as real as the sun setting right at this moment over the savanna. If someone tells you that institutions are guiltless of the crimes individuals have committed in the institutions' name, hide. Man's way of shirking his obligations is to absolve institutions of liability for the crimes committed in his name.

"Molu, there is paper in the second drawer. Take some. I should write my memoirs. I must guide those who follow me. It is a tale of immeasurable accomplishment, not as I lived it, of course, but how in time someone will write it. If I must brood about the future, let's write it. We don't want clichés or caricatures to replace Motutu. A seer must first be a poet. Sit Molu and write this down — in a clear hand, please. It will help that someone, give him — let us say her; women are much more truthful — a head start if you will. What would I say? WHAT WOULD I SAY? My fellow Africans, be as single minded as they are? Civilization their style means obsessive single-mindedness that the end justifies the means? Trust them only after you have acquired what it takes to be like them, not before? Whatever I say would not include be like them. Are you getting all this down, Molu?"

"Yes, Mokonzi."

"Good! Keep writing. Everyone wants to be like them. Mallets. Distrust all those who cry out to be pegs. But let the pimp caution you — what's the matter, Molu?

"You want me to write 'pimp,' Mokonzi?"

"Of course! If you don't write it, someone else will. Remember, I didn't invent the term. As I was saying, I had to hang my mind on the idea that if I couldn't beat them I would be one of them. If you succeed in becoming like them, you will dry up; there will be nothing left of you. You will be without essence. You will be hollowed to invisibility. Is any wealth worth that? That's what I want you to write down, Molu. In every paragraph of my memoirs, that's what I want to say.

"And, of course, I would have a chapter on the Consortium's relationship to God; for I often wonder if their indifference does not come from the abstraction they have made of the Almighty. Have you noticed, Molu, that they put God wherever they have a need? God planned the scramble for Africa, I heard them say. God has retribution for everyone except them. Retribution never concerns them. What do they know that we here do not, Molu? Maybe it's abstraction that I have wrong. If I say rationalization, I may get closer to the truth and be clearer. I could not write a memoir and not be clear!

"In my memoir, I'd also discuss greed; I have no choice. Everyone thinks I am the authority, when actually greed is something I know very little about. I can hear people laughing when they'd read that. But it's true!

"Alright, what is greed? It's the accumulation of wealth for its own sake, right? Did I ever engage in that? Not once! Is it greed if you use wealth to do good? I understand the Chinese use the same character for friend and enemy. Maybe I have that wrong; it's for something else they use the same character. In any case, both my friends and my enemies misinform about me. Or is it disinform? I did use the wealth. All of it! But I lived the way a man of my station should. I was head of one of the largest and richest countries in the world. Should I have lived like a pauper, or acted as if my country was of no consequence? I would have done it an unpardonable disservice if I had done such a thing.

"I should say in a whisper that being African and therefore poor causes people to look askance to my use of the Concorde. What is there about an African or his history that he should be the constant penitent? They fawn over humble Africans, as if humility is penance for our guilt. I will not say guilt for being African; that would mark me a radical.

"About greed, I can say very little. I just don't know. I can't tell where profit ends and greed begins. My supporters always demanded 1,000 percent profit. Why wasn't five hundred enough? I asked that of one pharmaceutical man who was cleaning us out. He said, because he didn't know how long making a profit here would endure. Doubt about us and our stability was widely accepted.

"You are what you appear to be. If you look destitute, people will assume that you are — no second look necessary — and behave towards you accordingly. But if you look prosperous, that's what they will go by. The same man will experience different reactions from people depending on his looks alone. So what if I used the Concorde to go to Cannes to have my teeth cleaned? It meant that my country must have been doing well, inducing the moneyed set into investing in Kinshasa. I became accustomed to fooling people with appearance, and it never stopped.

"Did you get all of that, Molu? Make sure you do; I will not be able to repeat any of it. There is more, much more.

"Run when they tell you about having a convergence of interests. You converge; they profit. It's an axiom. Letting your mind wonder from that axiom is the ticket to the poor house that's present-day Africa. How can your interests be theirs? If it is that simple, then why didn't I know it? Since these are my memoirs, and we are talking about truth, I will tell you. I didn't because the picture of a tall African entering a room breathless silence in his wake seduced me. Breathless silence, that's the drug that gave me the high I couldn't do without! First, not to exhale, were the gullible; I understood them, I was one of them and didn't take them seriously.

"And don't let them fool you with a gold watch. I should talk. My watch cost less than five dollars —"

Feeling the seat's cushion getting wet under him, he stopped the dictation. It was warm and it stung his genitals. Ignoring Molu, he cursed repeatedly sotto voce in his native tongue. Molu's reeling mind tried to discern how this interview would all end. Insanity! The Dictator had him trapped in this tomb of a gaudily furnished office that could be his grave at any moment. What was there to do? What would Marcel recommend? He sat frozen at the end of the dictator's desk, afraid to move, even slightly, or to say anything that might jar the Dictator and produce another crisis. From time to time, he looked from the corner of his eye at the door. Danielle was on the other side, keeping watch, two of the Dictator's bodyguards in front of her waiting.

The Dictator resumed thinking in French, and he swore he would remain in the chair until it dried from his body's heat. No one should see his deterioration. But perhaps it was an accident, a temporary occurrence, and not the loss of a function, not incontinence; earlier he had had much wine to lessen the pain in his abdomen, and there was the Ethiopian coffee he loved but that always created urgencies.

Having reassured himself, he took up where he had left off, having warmed to what he would say in the memoirs that his bewildered foreign minister was writing for him. "I am sorry for the interruption, Molu. It's that I was thinking what else to say. Let's take up where we left off. This is important. I have thanked the ancestors often for agreeing to make me tall. Revulsion strikes me, when I think that I could have been like that wretch Zengher of Senegal, the one African I know for sure who had confusion for a mind.

"Do you know what Zengher's favorite saying was? 'Reason is Greek as emotion is African.' Now I ask you, what does that mean? Greeks don't feel, Africans don't think? Zengher wanted the world to think him a French intellectual — wrote inane poems with the help of a French dictionary. He was a runt of a man. He never laughed, equating being serious with being brilliant. De Gaulle looked down on him, but looked up to Sekou Touré. Although it was Zengher who sought every opportunity to kiss de Gaulle's ass, it was Sekou de Gaulle looked up to, even though Sekou told him in a most spectacular way what to do with himself. Certainly, too, I would warn against arrogance, Molu. I would not be ashamed to speak of myself in that context. I will say without reservation, openly, that I became arrogant not out of pride for what I knew, but out of stubborn ignorance. If there is a comic aspect here, it's that I was fully aware of how little I knew. Arrogance I used freely in lieu of knowledge. I thought it dangerous to display the most mundane ignorance. In me, arrogance and fear had the same head. The mob is partly to blame. I would mention that with a degree of humility, for I owe it all to the mob. The more arrogantly I behaved, the higher the mob carried me. This is not something I understood; I just sensed it and took advantage.

"Speaking of ignorance, I don't think the Consortium meant us this much harm. Man is not this deliberately cruel. Nevertheless, through insistent arrogance, they made ignorance a determinant for everything. Stubborn ignorance ruled and it is us who were left with the results, while the Consortium moved on, leaving us once again to clean up after them.

"Certainly, too, I will not forget to say, stay away from illness. Doctors are vultures —"

Danielle's voice intruded like a sentry's on the other side of the door. Then, "The president is expecting me," echoed from the deep, minimalist voice of Maka Mgonu. The Dictator floated between wanting to be done with his burden and seeing his legacy live. The denouement of his reign at hand, he made his choice. He wanted something of himself to remain; whether Molu personified that possibility for him, he could not readily have said. He only knew that he wanted to go on, carry forward, as it were. So he pointed at the barely-visible door, flush in the wall. "My wife will show you out," he said. "They are meeting in Kisangani. Apologize for me. Buy time until Paris makes a decision." He was gratified that Molu took the beginning of his memoirs with him.

# Chapter 29

If Danielle thought the security chief had an innate subservience to her, his manners that evening dissuaded her. She had always imposed her way, as custodian to the Dictator's gate; but that evening, Maka, haggard, like a man staggering under a mighty burden, ignored her arrogant injunction to wait until she had announced him. He shoved her against the fake antique bureau by the door, toppling the vase of yellow roses she had so carefully arranged there that morning. He barged into the Dictator's office, followed by the two bodyguards who had stood in front of Danielle like two postulants while Molu was closeted with the Dictator.

One glance and he realized that Molu was no longer in the room. He looked at the Dictator sitting behind the desk, then at the cane with the handle in the carved shape of an elephant by the Dictator's right hand.

"If you had not sounded like a salad seller in the Grand Marché, Maka, he would not have fled."

"He killed her — you killed her," Mgonu said. "I told you to kill him outright. But no, and she is dead."

"The country is more important than any woman, Maka," the Dictator said, as was his habit, as if to a simpleton. "It is not my fault."

"You are to blame," Mgonu said, finality in his voice. "It is you who is to blame."

"I am sorry you feel that way, Maka. I have to make decisions that no one who does not sit here can understand." He looked at the security chief as if he were being patient with a fool. "If you listen to me, you will see that not all is lost; there is still time; we can still have our revenge; it is not the end. We need Molu to buy us time with the Ugandans. Yes, I told him about the conference in Kisangani," he nodded, a hint of a conspiratorial smile on his drooping lips, his eyes reaching out to his faithful servant. "The French will come in; but until they do, we need to steal a bit of time from the Ugandans. Molu cannot escape, here or there; it makes no difference."

Mgonu was a cynic about the French. "I don't care about any of that — the French, you. Her pyre, you are the carcass for it."

"You don't care," the Dictator said, disdain now in his voice. "I am not asking you to care. I am asking you to consider that the country needs for us to look beyond … What carcass are you referring to,

Maka? Is this something from one of your books? This is no time for escapism."

The security chief looked at his Mokonzi for the last time and put on his dark glasses, severing the bond between master and servant. He turned to the two men who had accompanied him into the dictator's office and pointed at the door in the wall. The Dictator tried to shout an order, but he gave up before he could say anything, as the security chief, now a stranger, moved closer to the desk as a mud crab approaches a rotting fish.

"Listen Maka," he said at length, forcing the security chief to listen, the tone of his voice reminding Mgonu of his loyalty oath. "I can talk to Eyadema; we have too much in common for him to refuse me this favor, or to Bongo in Gabon. We are of a kind. They will take you in. You will like Togo, Maka. The German cultural center in Lomé plays Goethe all the time. You will be safe there, too."

But he no longer had the security chief's ear or heart. Had the Dictator offered him the old Alexandria Library, Mgonu would not have heeded him. Having tasted the limit of sorrow, he was beyond reach. "She was innocent," he said, his yearning, a sudden outburst. "Even Girolamo who converses with God would approve of her. For what did you sacrifice her? *Know that unheard-of times are at hand.* Kisangani has fallen, and Liekungu is dead, a carcass for her pyre. In the sky, she will see it; the country in flame, she will see it. She deserves no less."

He looked up when he heard the door in the wall open. The Dictator's wife and her twin, Ides of March crows, walked into the office with Mgonu's men behind. Molu was not with them. Mgonu gazed at the two women, as a lion would when disturbed at its kill. Then, he drew back his left arm and in an enraged motion slapped the Dictator across the face with all his strength. The Dictator's thick-rimmed spectacles shattered upon hitting the outer wall. The Dictator lay underneath the large desk still as a corpse.

Mgonu and his men walked out. His face set, his task clear, the buoyancy he felt at being freed from the Dictator's grasp added lift to his stride.

# Chapter 30

Molu spent part of the night sitting in garbage, mostly rotten mangoes, his back against a stall in the Grand Marché, facing Avenue du Commerce better to keep an eye on the main entrance. The marché was the hideout of choice for deserters, criminals, men on the run from the authorities. Maka's men drove by in their trucks and SUVs, scarabaeid beetles circling a dung pile. Dreading the lepers and paralytics, who spent the night in the market, along with sorcerers and repulsive creatures men fear instinctively, no security agent on foot came near the vast obscure commercial area. The market beggars were strewn about the fetid grounds as if it were a battlefield. Singly or in groups, they chattered in urgent undertones.

———

A man Molu could not see, but was sure was mad, addressed him with an earnestness he had seldom heard. Afraid of what the man might do if snubbed, Molu listened: "I have been on the streets for two years," the beggar said unexpectedly. "When Jonas died I took his place. I was able to claim a spot at the tall wall of an American family's house whose husband was an official at the Embassy in Kinshasa. It was a choice place. God only knows what I'd do to get it! Jonas was stingy; like the fattened ox in the proverb, he gave up his fat only when he had been deprived of his life. You know the saying.

"I did not always have God in my vocabulary, you understand. But after what happened to me, a day, a minute doesn't ticktock without a call to God. Sometimes though, I only think about Him, and don't ask for anything. I am always afraid that His divine intervention, as limited as it is, will go back where it came from if I appear greedy. I go for days without saying 'God help me.' I fear that if I indulge too much in calling Him, He will get annoyed, and the first thing He will do is take away my spot, and, to spite me, give it to Zali, the stinking tramp whose envy of me is another reason for the fear I live with. I know I am going to die of fear, not hunger or anything else. So the last thing I need in my life is another angry God. When I feel this way, I remind myself — quickly, I have to tell you — that He did help me once. And with that proof in mind, I tell myself that He must not be a bad God, the kind that gets angry and does things to you. My illusions like my fears have only the horizon for boundary.

"Look at Zali. How can a two-legged man smell the way he does? When his leg began to rot, his uncle made him a beggar, he told me. He tried begging near the Continental Hotel, but his smell was unbearable, even to the white patrons who seem to like having beggars around. So every day he comes to see if I am at my spot. Thankfully, his smell warns me of his approach, like a gun shot; I am sitting, my back against the wall, by the time he crosses the alley, pretending to be just passing by.

"I fear Zali because it wasn't that long ago that I was like him, coveting the spot then held by Jonas, the beggar whose cousin was a guard for the American family. Jonas after years of street begging got lucky — his cousin was hired as a guard and arranged for Jean-Claude, who had held the spot for as long as people could remember, to be taken away during one of the Motutu's no-more-beggars-in-Kinshasa week. In return, Jonas gave him his coins. That was their understanding: Jonas would scour the town for coins to pay for the spot at the American family's house.

"In the morning, Jonas would always be the first in line at the market, where, to lure God's benevolence, the women would give their coins — the smallest ones — to the beggars, hoping that God would then recompense them with a good day of selling what we are sitting on. At first, the coins from the market women were enough for the cousin; but, as he acquired two wives to go with his new guard job, he asked Jonas for more. Jonas had no choice but to go in the diamond business."

"The diamond business?" Molu almost shouted, at this time listening attentively to the beggar who no longer sounded so mad.

"Friday is diamond day in Kinshasa," the beggar answered, his voice stronger, confident, now that he had someone who listened to him. "Over a hundred cripples take the ferry from Brazzaville to Kinshasa in the morning. Battling for position the entire thirty-minute voyage across the river, the cripples then race their wheelchairs throughout the city to reach the back doors of the Continental Hotel in the center of Kinshasa. Each has a preferred route and for forty minutes it looks like a hundred tomcats chasing one female in heat. Even the taxis get out of the way during the cripples' race to the hotel.

"Upon arriving at the Continental, the cripples throw themselves on the ground and scurry frantically to disassemble their wheelchairs. Thrashing about like vipers, they race to point the mouth of the largest tube-like part of their chairs toward the stern Lebanese who stand at the hotel's door with the diamonds. These men don't care for the wriggling in front of them. Until all the cripples are motionless, the Lebanese do not start filling the tubes. There is seldom a shortage of diamonds, and they usually fill all the tubes. But when there isn't enough for every tube, only the cripples who arrived first at the hotel's back door receive the precious stones. Then, with amazing speed, they put their chairs back together, and with a deliberateness full of tension, wheel back to the ferry for the return trip to Brazzaville.

"Even for Jonas it was easy. On diamond day, he dragged himself to the river and waited for the cripples to get off the ferry, taking a position behind the collector's booth. The first one who came by the booth, Jonas threw a towel around his neck, sending the man flying to the ground. He got in the wheelchair and raced for the Continental Hotel. He had spied on them and knew he had to fall on the ground to dismantle the wheelchair. But Jonas was a fool; like a drunk guinea cock, he forgot about the hawk. He had not taken the time to learn about the wheelchair and didn't know how to take it apart; nor could he tell the Lebanese men why he was there. I won't make the same mistake. I only need someone to help me knock over a cripple so that I can get my fill of diamonds behind the Continental Hotel. If you help me, you'll have half."

"I may have to do that," Molu said, keeping another option open.

The din in the Grand Marché continued until half past two in the morning. The noise from voices softened until the market became a club where men go for polite company. Then suddenly, the sound of rattles in sleeping throats replaced words in voices and no one stirred as if death itself had ran through the Grand Marché, spreading tranquility there.

Unlike the others, Molu could not close his eyes. As exhausted as he felt, he was too stunned to sleep. He did not worry over where the next coin would come from. He wanted to hear again the Dictator's last words to him about Kisangani, rest his mind with thoughts of Julie, prepare for Maka. His mind, however, insisted that he concentrate his thoughts on his village. And there he returned. It was as though he had never left; that the village had been a symbol for his whole life. It was as though he had no urgency to preoccupy him currently, and no concern outside of the first years of his life.

His village?

Molu could not understand it. Why was it that, until he came to rest this night on this pile of mango refuse, he seldom thought of his village? Now, full of remorse at not having kept faith with the place of his birth, he was certain that his ancestors had in turn not kept faith with him. His ancestors had agreed among themselves that he, Molu Sakeseba, he of titles, connoisseur of pomp and colorful rituals, should expiate his many offenses by ending one night with beggars in the Kinshasa Grand Marché.

The village overwhelmed his thoughts, transporting him back to hear his mother's voice once again. A slight, good natured, very dark skinned woman, a second wife who sold peppers in the market.

Like all African children, he belonged to the entire community; but it was his mother's presence that was so vivid and immediate that it frightened him. She was more alive now here in his mind than she had been in person. Even his father who, typically, had as much contact with him as everyone else in the village while he was growing up was there, too. Molu acknowledged that his destiny was now in the hands of his disappointed ancestors.

No thought of his village was complete without remembering in the clearest of detail the story of the Belgian cleric who had frightened the elders. Curé Roger Temple had come uninvited from the Belgian city of Louvain to Molu's village in the Equateur region of the Congo, when Molu was seven years old. Molu learned about Temple from Waza Kabasu, the elder, the Mokonzi who delighted the children with tales of the village's ancestors' heroic feats.

"It did not take me long to determine that this Curé Temple was trouble," Mokonzi Kabasu would always begin when speaking of the man the other elders called 'oyo mondele,' that white man. "I had never met a priest like him before," he would say, lifting his arms to emphasize 'never.' "And I perceived that the village's ancient beliefs were about to sustain an assault never before experienced at the hand of this immaculately dressed priest. I knew as surely as anything that I would have to shake this tree to make the dewdrops fall. You see, the Belgian priests who lived beside us on our land were men who seemed to gain comfort from their proximity to us Africans. Then I saw that in a perverse way these priests were appreciative of the Africans for being what Belgians considered inferior beings."

(What Mokonzi Kabasu could not know and that Molu discovered during his personal and professional dealings with the Belgians is that these Flemish-speaking priests, exiled in the middle of the vast Congo, were grateful to Africa for having rescued them from the inferior status they held at home. Either in spite of or because of that they were the most fanatical colonialists. Seldom with outright cruelty, the priests treated the Africans like mongrels in the streets. Their deference to the elders their first day in the village was soon replaced by an indifference that left no doubt as to where the Africans stood in these priests' understanding of the colonial social ladder.)

"With these priests," Mokonzi Kabasu would say reflectively, "it was possible to employ delaying tactics to protect the village's ancient ways. When they would shout their incomprehensible obscenities and threaten to stop the distribution of cooking oil and rice or to withhold the medicine to cure our illnesses, the elders would proffer apologies to make things right. Again, there were even more personal ways to keep the priests pacified." At that, he would open his eyes wide and snicker loudly enough for the ancestors to hear.

"This Temple was a different kind of man and priest. I had seen him in my nightmares, and I could tell how unsettled the ancestors were by his coming to our village. Bees that never worried about anything but finding the next flower turned their vigor into stinging everyone without provocation. The birds became mute. Monkeys went mad as if a ghost was haunting them from dawn to dusk. It was another troubled time. Clearly, his arrival had perturbed the ancestors.

"Unlike the corpulent priests who passed through, Temple was a sparse looking man, with a narrow face mounted by a prominent very thin, almost translucent nose on top of which were unblinking eyes hiding in immense holes. Although young, he walked with a bow, seldom raising his head, giving the impression of being in conversation with his God at all times, even when in motion. During his short stay, the villagers never came near him, as though they were reluctant of getting too close out of fear he would do bad things to them."

---

(When he arrived in the Congo in 1956, Roger Temple had just turned twenty-six. He had studied with the Jesuits at the Louvain Seminary. He had then attended the Seminaire des Missions in Saverne, and the Seminaire des Peres du Saint Esprit in Alsace. His father had been a mail carrier so punctual that the people of the district he served for twenty-seven years had nicknamed the church's clock, "Père Temple." His mother was a primary school teacher who also taught catechism at no cost to the church on Wednesday afternoons and Saturday mornings to the coal miners' children outside of the town of Mons. Like her husband, she approached her duties with a seriousness that no one could fail to notice if not always appreciate.

Roger, their only child, lived to please his parents. By the time he was five he knew the entire catechism by heart, which he would recite at breakneck speed to entertain them. They did not praise him for his diligence when he did this but would look at each other and nod appreciatively. For Roger that was enough. He soon memorized other church books to his parents' obvious delight.

The sons of civil servants followed their fathers in occupation and career, and everyone expected that in time Roger would work at the Mons's post office. But after the Germans occupied Belgium in 1940, the schools were closed for the war. And for four years, Roger's classroom was his mother's tidy living room. There, she encouraged him to memorize every breviary her priest, Father Jacques Brabant, could loan her. Brabant also arranged for Roger to spend two afternoons a week at the town's diocese, to read and translate Latin church texts into French.

Roger was the priest's favorite altar boy. Brabant liked him because unlike the other boys Roger was dependable to a fault. But more importantly, it was Roger's view of God that appealed to the priest. To Roger, God was wrath and conquest — a God who demanded unquestioned adherence to His world order.

When Father Brabant asked Roger to join his corps of altar boys, the young man said he did not think much of the Mass. "There are better ways to serve God," Roger told him certain of his views. Only the threat to cease his Latin lessons had convinced Roger to become an altar boy in Brabant's church. In time, Brabant would also convince Roger of the importance of the Mass. "Unless death is knocking at their bedchamber's door, people have more immediate priorities," the priest explained. "Unless you give them color and mystery, they sleep late on Sunday and stay away — the socialists and the Anglicans love these people."

In time, under Brabant's mentoring, Roger recognized that extermination of African superstition in Belgium's colonies was the most rewarding way to serve God. And here he was, Mokonzi Kabasu's nightmare in the flesh, armed with the mission to rid the colony of the practices of ancestor worship. He had made this long voyage to take the Africans into his hands and save them from themselves. Aware that many before him had left Belgium for the Congo with the same mission, he arrived in the village with a plan conceived with Rector Jules Renquin of the Louvain Seminary eight years earlier. That so many others had failed to pry the Africans from their ancient beliefs did not dim his fervor; his plan assured him success. He had no doubt he would achieve his objective, a triumph for the church and greater Belgium.

As early as 1936 Father Brabant understood that Belgium's empire was ephemeral, fated to disappear without leaving an imprint, unless men like himself intervened to bring it to the ways of the church. The clamor for decolonization had a deep, heartfelt resonance, the sound men make upholding a cause greater than themselves. This clamor aroused the consciousness of the world. After a while, its sound ceased, and revolt replaced the last song sung on a distant African shore. Revolt was the elixir that accorded its participants rediscovered dignity. Even some heretofore-fanatical colonialists found themselves drinking of it. And by the time Brabant's favorite pupil arrived in the Congo twenty years later, the French and the English were packing their belongings to depart the continent and would be leaving in a few years as fast as they could find ships home.

Brabant followed with alarm the Algerian struggle to the death for independence and was shocked to hear of the natives' unspeakable acts, going to any length to remove France's tutelage. He thought a malevolent spirit had inculcated the natives with a strain of madness and barbaric ideas that would not be still until the people had tasted victorious independence.

Roger Temple blamed the European governments for colonization's demise. In his first letter to Father Brabant from the Congo, he complained, "Had these governments not let lapse the appreciation for the church's contribution to the colonial order, self-rule would have been checked. It has been a long time since they have given the priests the first stab at converting the natives before the colonial army moved in. The French are the great sinners here, having gone so far as to make Africans citizens of France, even paying natives to attend the Sorbonne where the communists trap them in gossamer webs of deceit. France deserves the Battle of Algiers." As a young priest in Flemish Ostende, Roger Temple had spoken out publicly against the Belgian government educating the Congolese.

"Two days after his arrival here, Temple ordered that I come to see him," Mokonzi Kabasu was taking up the tale again. "Time seemed precious to him, and he did everything hurriedly. Aghast at the suddenness of the order, I answered that I would set foot in that man's jurisdiction only if the other elders came with me. 'Come alone,' his *Zóba* interpreter repeated; 'the priest wants to talk to you alone.' I told the others, but they shrugged. It was my problem alone. They were tired of grappling with the Belgians — fatigued. The Belgians had stripped them of strength by destroying their perspective as elders. They could no longer look the village in the eye. If the Belgians' purpose was to do away with ancestors, they were succeeding, for how can you have ancestors unless you have respected elders? What's the use of being an ancestor if you are not remembered? I was worried; I had a stake in the old belief. An old man is soon to be an ancestor. My influence in the village came from the fact that the people did my bidding because I was soon to have absolute power as a living spirit, an ancestor.

"Dignity was no longer synonymous with being an elder. The old men were sure the Belgian's summon was a demand for another corvé of labor. I said it couldn't be; the order was from the new young priest. He would not be involved in demands for laborers from the village. Like mad men they shouted at me that he was an enforcer of the Belgian colonial order.

"Rebellion has a pungent smell, similar to a rotting forest. I had been sniffing it; but until that day, I didn't know its source. This discovery concerned me greatly; for I didn't know where it would lead, other than to the disaster we had always experienced in our confrontations with the Belgians. I did not doubt the practical truth of our customs, nor did I underestimate the sustaining strength of the old ways in the face of Belgium's aggression. Yet, I had become aware that the world was changing since the first cry for independence. Instability stalked the old ways. The army men came from Kinshasa caring nothing for the ways of the village. And the young women had thrown themselves at these men with terrible consequences.

"I spoke no more, signaling that I would answer the order and go alone. And I went. Temple was as polite as people like him knew to be with old Africans. Hurriedly, he told me that the church was making little progress in this part of the colony. I thought of quoting him the saying, 'if you have one finger pointing at some-body, you have three pointing at yourself,' but I did not. Instead, I said, he who does not cultivate his field will die of hunger. If he didn't know why converts went elsewhere, I wasn't going to tell him. As you know, a fool is thirsty even at a river's edge.

"These are his exact words: 'You are driven by superstition, and bringing the light of the Lord to you may be a climb up Calvary.' The main reason was our dependence on masks for our ceremonies. He was going to confiscate the masks from the entire area and put them in warehouses that men from the village would build. I made the mistake of telling him that the masks were ours, and as we respected the symbols of his culture, so he should ours.

"The *Zóba* must have interpreted what I said wrongly, for the young priest lifted his head and rudely stared at me the way my father would when I was a boy. 'There is only one culture,' he said as if talking to a pupil in the back row of the class, after he had stared at me enough, 'Europe's. There is only one church, the Holy Catholic and Apostolic Church. We have come a long way to bring you the light of that church. You should be grateful. Saving you from the darkness of yourselves is our mission.'

"Speaking to me as if to a dunce in the back of the class is something I never got used to in my contacts with the Belgians. Because of them, disgust crowned my life. Nothing experienced by men anywhere could compare to what Belgians did to us. I thanked him for his generosity and said we were just fine with what we had. He could go back to where he came from, carrying our thanks. He laughed good-naturedly, the way one does at a prattling child and remarked he would save me in spite of myself. I was surprised he could laugh, and that gave me the confidence to repeat that no one had asked him to come to impose his ways on our village. That made him laugh even more. 'It is a duty,' he said. 'We have to bring you the light of the church. For this, He created His church, His church! When you are in heaven, you will thank us.'

"I said that we did believe in God, if that was his objection." 'Only through His church, His church can you speak to God,' he proclaimed. "I asked, isn't God, God? 'Yes, but only through His church will God hear you,' he repeated before dismissing me like a servant. "I said in Lingala, when I turned around, *Nzambe ezali Nzambe*, God is God, more to remind myself than to make a point.

"I went back to tell the others what the priest had said. When everyone understood the consequences of what the priest proposed to do, no one said anything, except for a Lissala man who said needlessly as only a Lissala man would, 'tradition has it they arrived here with only a book. Now we have the book; they have everything else. And they want to take away the masks too.' No one said anything to that; it was an unnecessary comment. Everyone there was aware of how much we had lost. Lissala men alone do not know that two waterfalls cannot possibly hear each other. We departed quietly. Whether anyone was deliberating with his own mind what to do, I cannot say. But all knew what the ancestors expected of us.

"When they told me the young priest had drowned while crossing the river, I didn't ask any questions. But that did not stop the Belgians; as you know, a single bracelet does not jingle. A few months later another priest, Father Brabant, wise in the art of subtleties and conversions, arrived to take the place of the one who had drowned."

# Chapter 31

At 4:00 a.m., Molu headed for the river, his blue silk suit in a bundle under his arm. He fell in with the market vendors who, every morning, made the trip to Inongo on the shores of Lake Mai-Ndombe in the province of Bandundu for the dried fish, cassava, fresh vegetables and fruits Kinshasa was so fond of. The city looked like a crushed termite nest. Men mostly, a few in army uniforms, gloom of face, rushed about, fleeing to where, Molu could not tell. They were dashing about aimlessly, fearful and morose, pushing well-dressed frightened children in front of them. The few women at their side had angry curses on their lips. They no longer bribed with worthless coins; their lives merited the green, blue and pink-colored hard currencies they threw about to pay for transport.

Others, conceited in their hope, taking no notice of an unenforceable curfew, enthusiastically if mindlessly rode the excitement's crest, which like the fog from the river had seeped into every pore of the now open city. Some from this group looked for like-minded companions for reassurance in smiles of class recognition or for agreement that a new era was dawning with the new day. Others just sat by the road — tree branches, symbol of freedom, at their side — waiting for the show to commence, for the parade to pass. They had the best seats under the tent; they would not move until the circus had folded its canvas.

Cataclysmic change swirled at Kinshasa's door, awaiting the sun to rise before entering the city. The group at the side of the road, answering to their hunger pangs, were there seeking the new Big Man's acknowledgment that they were the first, the most dedicated ones to welcome him to his newly minted reign of patronage power. Their allegiance had always been for sale; at roadsides, they waited for the new buyer. Their fortune was just one Big Man away. The noise of trucks, mopeds, ruined Mercedeses was deafening.

Molu was about to regret having left the enclave of the Grand Marché when a vendor at his side said, "You must be the mango man — we all smell of what we sell." Molu nodded indifferently, the way a man desperate to rest would. Before the sway of the craft made of two fishing boats tied together, an outboard motor astern, lulled him almost immediately to sleep, Molu recognized in the darkened river a reflection of Mokonzi Kabasu. In his dream he heard the story of a young Belgian priest who had come uninvited to his village to drown in the river all his masks, totems and other village artifacts. The young priest with Father Brabant's face was lurching drunkenly toward the river, yelling, "*Agnus Dei qui tollis peccata mundi miserere da me.*" Molu came behind to bash him with an unfinished mask, but the monkeys in the treetops shrieked and both looked up laughing.

In Inongo, vendors and buyers mingled in a sort of dance to the tunes of the latest news from the capital. Two opposite allegiances divided the people here, and each sought the information that sustained their hope. Those who resided in Inongo and environs were the supporters of the current Dictator; he was born only one province away and was one of them. During his reign, they had benefited from his largess toward his home province. If dethroned, especially by a man from another region, especially one from the Luba south, they would lose all favors and would be taxed for having received them in the past. The second group was of two minds. One was that the transforming power of a new regime would turn the society they knew on its head. Change would be a charitable foundation that would put farms, boats, houses, cars and stores in their laps. What was there to lose? So, they hoped the hope of the impotent. Those in the other group had drifted to the shores of Lake Mai-Ndombe in Bandundu from other parts, and the people here looked on them as likely thieves, strangers from the other side of the river. A thief always came from elsewhere. After a robbery, an entire village would mobilize, shouting frantically, to run down the thief. Mad with fright, the man, certain that mutilation awaited him, would dash in a merciless effort to put distance between himself and the village he may have victimized. Bitter at their outsider's status, this group had developed an ideology founded on their resentment. Northerners enjoyed too many privileges, they claimed and eagerly awaited the day a regime would make northerners outsiders too.

A Ngbandi speaking army man, as eager to be of service to a regime high official as he feared the change that would see him dead or running for his life, readily acquiesced to Molu's request for assistance to reach Kisangani. Molu had the face of hope. The army man gave him his ear, anxious that someone, a foreign minister at that, would act to arrest the debacle. Molu said, his face resolute, his manner determined, that the president had asked him to go to Kisangani to parley with the rebels —

"Ah, I knew it," the man said, grabbing Molu's arm and letting it go as if he had touched an electric wire. It didn't matter that Molu had nothing but what the Dictator had told him to take him forth on such a journey. But the man did not need more. His excitement was great, but as hollow as his hope. "I told myself, the president must have a plan," he said expansively. "He wouldn't just let these people come here without doing something."

"Yes," said Molu, uncertainty in his voice. "But with all this mayhem around us, how do I get to Kisangani?"

"I think I can get you a flight to Mbuji-Mayi. The commander of the base is sending a transport to get his in-laws out. From there, you are sure to catch a flight to East Province."

"The Mbuji-Mayi in east Kasai?" Molu said, incredulous.

"Yes," said the man, shaking his head and lifting his arms as if such gestures would make obvious Mbuji-Mayi was Molu's only option. "The other way would be to find transport to take you north to Mbandaka in our province, then to Boende, Yanganbi and then to Kisangani. That will take days. You should get on the commander's flight," he said, a desperate plea in his voice. "You could be in Kisangani tonight," making another gesture of certitude with his arms.

"Well, I don't have days," concluded Molu, remembering his village saying, "Two men in a burning hut must not stop to argue."

———

"Can it fly?" Molu said when he saw the AAC.1 *Toucan,* a seventeen-seat antique, the round blue, white and red emblem of France painted on its side, revving up on the tarmac.

"It does," said a European whose French quivered under his Slavic accent. "And it drops bombs as good as a B-47 does except more accurately."

"Yes, but will it make it to Mbuji-Mayi?" Molu said.

"We'll see," the mercenary said, excusing himself, as he turned for the plane. Molu remained at the door of the commander's office, considering other alternatives. The pilot returned after a moment carrying a flying suit, new in a sealed plastic envelop, which he handed to Molu. "That should be your size. My commander said you are the foreign minister; what is there for you to do in Mbuji-Mayi? You have family there, too?"

Molu was reluctant to speak to a mercenary. However, besides the straight back of a European military officer, the man had an air about him, the air possessed by all the trustworthy diamond dealers Molu had done business with over the years on the Dictator's behalf. "My final destination is Kisangani," Molu said. The mercenary whistled and shook his head, a gesture conveying the difficulty of the mission.

"Finding transport to Kisangani," the man continued to shake his head, "will not be easy." It was a matter of fact statement; not one meant to impress. "For a price, I'll drop you there after I've picked up my commander's family. They won't know the difference." The mercenary held Molu's eyes. "What do you say?"

"What's the price?"

"You tell me. What is it worth to you?"

"I don't know," Molu said at length.

"Five thousand American dollars — I have to give something to my mate." He nodded toward the waiting aircraft.

Molu unfolded his blue suit with care and took out two stones from the jacket's inside pocket. The mercenary whistled. "So, it's true! I heard this was the place. This is the first time I've seen one; and I've been here five months. Is the yellow one a diamond?"

"Yes, an Angolan gem."

"If I swallow it, will it — you know."

"No, it's perfectly safe."

"Ugh, I hope you don't mind parting with it — I'll let you have my civvies, as well; that suit will not open any door for you."

# Chapter 32

Had Molu not gotten off the old French airplane at the Mbuji-Mayi Airport, they would not have spotted him. He had his last meal on the Dictator's plane, and three hours into the slow and uncomfortable flight, hunger was a torment. What's more, he could not stretch his legs in such an aircraft. He would have jumped to the tarmac once the AAC.1 *Toucan* touched down had the pilot not cautioned him to wait. The pilot shouted and cursed from the cockpit for stairs, but no one approached the aircraft that had just landed. He jumped out. The stairs he found were too short by a couple of feet, but it was enough.

The radio message crackled in the security chief's armored Chevrolet Suburban. When he heard, Maka jumped from his seat as a flame fed by a sudden blast of air would. Molu was at the Mbuji-Mayi airport.

Mgonu spared neither himself nor his agents in the search to find Molu. His agents and their hangers-on scoured the city in wider and wider circles looking for the foreign minister whose betrayal, Mgonu told them, had caused the disaster the country was reeling under. His pockets were also bulging with Angolan diamonds. Whoever found Molu would be rich.

The Dictator's son lent Mgonu a hand in hunting his father's foreign minister, while a cruiser, its two Honda BF90 horsepower churned at a private pier ready for a fast passage across the river to Brazzaville. Before escaping, the son had his squad, "The Invincibles," assault the Continental Hotel during a noisy, rage-filled interlude.

The Gombé beggars also joined in the search; they had much at stake besides better living conditions when Molu came to live among them. In addition to the payment for keeping Molu boxed in outside the American ambassador's residence, the security chief promised them even more if one of them found him. And after twenty-four hours, he added another steep price on Molu's head.

It was senseless many thought. The regime's exodus was underway, and what difference would it make now if Molu was caught. Regardless of the *sauve qui peut* in progress, locating Molu was what completely engaged the security chief. "When a man has lost his senses, he can walk on water," a beggar quoted a proverb. But most of them deduced that such dedication was proof that he must be communicating with the ancestors — a conclusion that strengthened their dedication to find the traitor.

---

As they had done elsewhere, the insurgents had left an escape corridor for Kinshasa's troops to withdraw west that resembled the sprout of a gigantic funnel. Informed that enemy forces had opened their corridor out of Mbuji-Mayi, Maka and his two lieutenants lifted off in the interior ministry's *SA 330 Puma*, his gestures assured, precise, as though he had divined the triumph of his mission. His mood and the bonus he had promised them carried his men along with renewed confidence.

They were flying to the town of Mwene-Ditube near the Angolan border, and would use arranged ground transport for a stealthy entrance into the Mbuji-Mayi airport. One .45 Magnum revolver's bullet behind the foreign minister's left ear and the chief could exult in contended peace. Further plans were only for the benefit of his associates.

They would land the helicopter and abandon it; if necessary, they would remove across the border where the Dictator's Angolan allies would provide safe conduct to reach Boma on the Atlantic coast. But really, what happened after the revolver had its way with Molu was of no concern to the security chief.

Like all men, life imposed itself on Maka Mgonu; and as long as he could settle this score, he would go along. The bargain: kill the regime's new foreign minister. That was the condition for his acceptance of life; and life agreed, permitting him to take the measures he saw fit to fulfill his stipulation. His men heard him pray, and took heart from his words, *"may He never allow me to die until I have taken due vengeance upon him."* Mystification obliging, they nodded approvingly — the chief was conversing with his patron saint.

Manically he hunted Molu to satisfy Julie's spirit. In shadows and in beams of light, dressed as he had first seen her, she put her golden-skinned hand lightly on his arm and smiled at him knowingly. He put his hand in her hair as he always had dreamed. He could do no less for her.

---

He knew the Mwene-Ditube area well, having gone there in person to raze a village thought disloyal to the Dictator. It was during the regime's consolidation period, the period of lesson teaching. There, they had mythologized his ferocity, his cruelty, his invincibility and the spells that protected him. They spoke of the aura that proceeded him to light his way. They spoke of him in this manner in the tales of their oral tradition in subdued fear, and in the hatred the Lubas were known for.

***

Immediately upon setting down west of Mwene-Ditube, an ominous voice, deep and broad, echoed the rumor that the Dictator's evil one was in the area. The hum was electrifying; it was more powerful than the invasion from the east that had dislocated the region. The elders here made every effort to divine the ancestors' intent behind this occurrence. "Disaster, what else?" They all nodded agreement. Fatalism was a comfort their hearts could not do without.

The Ugandan troops sensed that a change had taken place in the area around Mwene-Ditube. The wind mellowed and the rain ceased, the trees became still, the birds silent, and the monkeys in the treetops became watchfully thoughtful. It was as if a maniacal being had entered the area and the forest awaited his purpose in silence. That it was a living thing would have been reason for optimism any place else; here, where fatalism ruled, it was cause for fear and many departed hurriedly for higher grounds. Unable to pin point the disturbance's cause, the Ugandans spurned "another Congolese superstition" and kept the Mbuji-Mayi escape spout opened. Their forces ran unabashedly to capture the capital where much loot awaited the conquerors. It was only a single bridge away, and they focused on no other objective.

***

There was a large, very handsome, much courted woman in a village near Mwene-Ditube. She had many names, not all of them flattering. A shoemaker who had taken up the trade upon the death of her husband at the hand of the incendiary security chief, she lived to take the sort of revenge on him only an embittered imagination could make possible. She would suffer any outrage to revenge herself on Maka. On hearing he had returned, she raised the alarm, shouting as if a thief had been through her village. The elders, however, thought it wise not to interfere with one so well provided for by the ancestors.

"Rain beats a leopard's skin, but it does not wash out the spots," they reminded her.

"Yes," she agreed, "but though the axe forgets, the tree remembers."

"Myths are made of more than imagination," they cautioned.

"Thirst for revenge is stronger than myth," she answered.

"Between fear and hatred, hatred is stronger," they agreed.

The shoemaker offered herself to whoever isolated Maka for her. A cause had come to the village, a reason for looking beyond the world-altering turbulence of Ugandans, Tutsis and others. The villagers, moved by a newfound meaning in their chaotic lives, hoisted their machetes to their shoulders and joined in the hunt for the security chief.

The Puma helicopter that landed in the area drew the attention of the Ugandan troops as a new car would young men everywhere. The passengers, the indifferent troops left to the villagers to locate.

As Maka walked to the vehicle to take him to the Mbuji-Mayi airport where salvation awaited him like a lifeboat a drowning man, a tall villager ran behind him and struck him an oblique blow on the back of the head with his machete. Mgonu only slightly injured, nevertheless stumbled. He fell on his hands but would have stood, if a throng had not fallen on him like a cascading deluge on an uprooted tree, smothering him. His men, dumbly, looked on, shocked at seeing their chief incapacitated, as though the river had suddenly dried up leaving them stranded. Without the chief, they were mindless, lost in a desert, a dead guide at their feet. Although they were armed, they did not shoot, moving backward away from the crowd that had swarmed from the bushes. Had they fired a few rounds, even in the air, the crowd would have scattered the way crowds always do. Mgonu's men backed away, turned, and ran for the welcoming underbrush.

Like a flower opening, the mob peeled itself from the body of the security chief lying face down on the ground. After a moment, he regained his senses and turned around to see the setting sun, the clouds, and then the faces and eyes looking at him as they would a supernatural being. Only his shirt they had left to cover him.

Around him, men formed a circle, standing as close to one another as possible like bars on a prison wall, as if to prevent his escape. Two feet behind the men, women waited in their circle in quiet resolve. Mgonu recognized the formation; knew what that ritual called for next. *Un battement de mains*, and the women's circle would swiftly change place with the men's. A blade would appear and one of them would mutilate him, as all thieves were. He had feasted on tales of such rituals. The last was about the man who frantically ran to catch what his assailants were discarding of his body. As he bent over to pick it up, they kicked it out of his reach. Life gone with his blood, he fell down grateful for oblivion. "Thieves menace traditional order," the security chief had adjudged in the clinical way he had of settling the affairs of men — "they deserve such time-honored punishments."

They thought he was about to stand, and the man behind him pushed his shoulders roughly down. He tried again, this time remaining in a sitting position. They seemed to be waiting, and he guessed it was for the Ugandans or the Tutsis to take him away. It would be best if the Ugandans came; to them he could explain, and he was persuaded he would get to the Mbuji-Mayi airport. The Tutsis would regard him as a *génocidaire* and take him away or execute him here. If the Tutsis came, he would not have Molu's carcass for Julie's pyre. That was the most terrible fate he could imagine at that moment.

Hunger gave the vultures' croaks a strident persistency, and, as they assembled in the treetops, moved their heads and bare necks in and out, the way they did when anticipating a fierce struggle for scraps. A green anole was taking in the last of the remaining sunshine; suddenly, it jumped into a hollow in the trunk of a tree, as a yellow hawk swooped to catch it. For a moment, the hawk's angry screech as if daring the lizard to show itself masked the vultures' croaks. Like in a fable all the characters were present either to witness or take part in an unfolding drama.

The villagers waited impatiently, their excitement a gnawing pain, uncontrollable, exasperating. The most determined ones reproached the security chief for being here, for undergoing a degradation, and for stirring the children to such frenzied excitement. People were arriving from the surrounding area as if invited to a chief's feast. Witnessing a man's degradation was a great event, an ultimate moment. Eyewitnesses real or imaginary would speak of it as the highlight of their lives. Maka mumbled to himself. For an instant, all conversations ceased, and the mob bent to him, seeking to fathom his words. They looked at one another, questioning, and resumed speaking, an incomprehensible drone.

The men no longer stood as close to one another, and Maka heard the one who had pushed him down earlier speak loudly and, for a moment, the circle was tight again, prison bars again. Fifteen minutes later, the man again brought back order to the tattered circle.

Mgonu sat on his bare rear end eyes shut, his muscular arms holding his knees close to his powerful chest. He seemed not to breathe, and the mob thought terror had suffocated him. He continued to mumble, rocking to and fro. For a moment, he sat still, thinking. Then he resumed muttering to himself and swaying. The crowd didn't pay attention; words they did not understand did not concern them. The agitated voices droned ceaselessly, as the crowd's perturbation swelled like a balloon. As dusk settled on the field, the rabble's enthusiasm for the security chief's degradation increased beyond human endurance.

"He is saying, 'burn me,'" someone announced. 'Burn me,' "that's what he is saying," the explanation shuddering through the minds of all the bystanders. Softly at first, an imperceptible whisper, as though praying, Maka's voice became louder and the mob quieted to the resonance of "BURN ME" from the security chief . When they had all heard him, they jeered, "Is that what they do in your part of the country? Don't tell him what Balubas do to thieves here; he might die of fright."

"Lubas are colonial whores," they heard Maka say in Tshiluba. "Tradition is right, Lubas are Belgium's whores."

He could have stood up and walked away; and so shocked were they, that they would not have moved to stop him. The mob remained silent a moment better to experience the anger his words had caused. Lubas had suffered massacres under the current regime; and those in the crowd who knew who Maka was shouted for his immediate degradation.

The elders finally arrived, and the mob reluctantly opened a path to let them through. Words of remonstrance were exchanged; the bystanders had had enough of waiting. The elders reached the clearing where Mgonu sat surrounded by the men and the women in the circles, keen for the ritual to begin. Each walked to him for a look at a man who was not a mere man, staring at him with expressionless faces. They then conferred briefly and nodded, as if saying in unison, "I told you so." Unbelievably, two went to Maka and lifted him up. The mob shrieked its disapproval, as if the elders had repealed an ancestral right; but the elders imperturbably marched the security chief out. The sky had turned dark blue — a *supplizio* blue.

The shoemaker stood at the periphery of the crowd, holding at her side a long metal instrument she used to cut the leather for the soles of her shoes. The handle was dark gray, the color of iron hewn by sweat, its well-honed cutting tip shining silver from a recent sharpening session on a riverbank rock. Maka was speaking to one of the elders at his side, his manner urgent. The shoemaker waited for them to go through the uncomprehending, jeering crowd that fell behind them, wanting to know where they were taking the security chief. One of the elders turned around to speak to a colleague. The man vehemently shook his head like a bird gulping a large fish and pointed in the direction of the village. At this, the shoemaker ran toward the village, stopping at a clearing. Standing erect, she waited, her right hand at her side, eagerly readying the instrument by twirling it with her fingers. The elders walked faster now, urgency in their steps, keen to leave behind the jeering crowd still following them.

Maka gazed at the woman standing at the side of the path to the village. As if sensing what she was to do, his eyes bulged. A latent will to live took his mind and held it, gripping it. And he lifted his right arm then his left to free himself from the hands of the elders supporting him.

The crowd behind surged, their hands outstretched as if to catch a rooster that had gotten loose. Her assignment desperate, the woman on the path ran to Maka, her bare feet mashing the ground, sounding like drums on judgment day, resonating the assurance of her purpose. In one exuberant stroke, she pushed the blade down Maka's entire torso, slashing him from sternum to scrotum. The elders supporting the security chief had stood transfixed as if caught in the light of the coming horror, in effect propping Maka up, an offering for the shoemaker's blade.

Maka thrashed on the ground, his entrails lifting up from his body as if from a boiling cauldron and spilling on the ground like foam on a shore. "*La médiocritée du sort, la médiocritée du sort,*" the mediocrity of fate, the mediocrity of fate he repeated. It was his end and he wanted to think of something meaningful to mark his passing. Only a prayer came. It didn't matter, he realized, as suddenly as his mind had reached out to the will to live a minute ago. Nevertheless, he thought it proper to remember the Père Blanc who had baptized him Girolamo.

For a moment, he looked at a figure in the distance, and whispering put out his hand as if to touch it. One of the elders asked, "Is one of the twins named Julie?" They looked at each other.

"There was more to this man than hard speech and a shaved head," one of them answered. "Would that his brain had gotten in the way of his heart."

"He behaved as if he were a character in a story told to teach through entertainment."

"Does someone like him occur in nature? I mean naturally?"

"He was what he seemed to be, no more."

"But I can't figure it; he was as skittish as a hyena, what could possibly have made him come here at a time like this?"

"It was written — the ancestors willed it."

"He was a vulture! Let his brothers have him."

———  ———

They resumed their march to the village. In the time it took to get there, the forest had made Maka its own. He would not be an ancestor. His *vita* argued against membership. He was not a man who had harmony in his vocabulary; and he had no descendant to link the living to the ancestors with entreaties and offerings. To compound his unfitness, he did not have a fine death. Besides, he could not claim the prerogative of a firstborn son. He was satisfied to be a spirit haunting the woods and the neighboring village, declaiming incomprehensible musings, another malediction in a region that knew nothing else.

# Chapter 33

In spite of Molu's urgent entreaties to take off for Kisangani, the pilot went looking for his commander's in-laws. The roads were crowded with refugees, and with the Hutus who plunged into the woods to elude pursuers. The pilot's was an impossible task. Ugandan soldiers helped him get through, but the in-laws were not at the agreed pick up point. The pilot came back to the plane — "fuel it," and they would be underway to Kisangani.

An avuncular Ugandan colonel, a smoldering pipe at the corner of the mouth and a short swagger stick under the arm, matter-of-factly observed that there had not been fuel at the airport for more than five days. He offered to radio Kananga, in the next province, for a fuel truck. Crowd obstruction would make it difficult to reach Mbuji-Mayi, but he was sure one would be at the airport in a day or two. Meanwhile, the pilot, the copilot and Molu could share in his men's meals and sleep in the hangar where they would tow in the plane for the night. He would post guards there as well.

"He is accommodating, isn't he?" the pilot remarked to no one in particular. The colonel was indeed behaving as if hostilities had ceased, enhancing Molu's apprehension. Except for the refugees streaming westward, relations had returned to normal. Getting fuel for a plane with a French emblem on its side was commonplace, an everyday occurrence. Molu went to speak to the colonel.

"You're a long way from home," he said in the voice he used with taxi drivers.

"Yes, Kasese is a few kilometers from here," the colonel said, puffing nonchalantly on his pipe. He was eager to be gracious in the country where his troops were gobbling up territory as fast as they could say Mbuji-Mayi.

"Kasese? Is that near Kampala? I was there two years ago."

"Kasese is just across Butembo in north Kivu."

"I was also in Butembo once."

"We drove down from Goma in north Kivu, then Bukavu, and Mokobola," the Ugandan said.

"You must have been at this for a while."

"A bit less than ten days. Except for the Hutu militiamen, there was very little opposition. There was no door to push against really," the colonel said. His tone expressed surprise. "We would have reached Kinshasa already if it had not been for the crowds along the way. We were not prepared for that." Molu could not think of the word, the antonym of arrogance, to describe the colonel's demeanor. The Ugandan spoke as if his drive to Mbuji-Mayi had been a stroll in the woods of Molu's youth and not the occupation of territory the size of Europe. Molu would have preferred to hear unadulterated arrogance.

"How do you explain this conflict?" Molu asked, looking down, following a moment of reflection.

"Motutu's support for the Hutus, that's how I explain it. The Hutus, they are driven to wipe out the Tutsis from east Africa. That's what it is. It's an easy one for us! Unless we put the Hutus in their place, they'll go on killing. Had they no support from such a state as this one, it would not be so urgent to act."

"And East Kasai's diamonds?" Molu said. "They mean nothing to you?"

"Exactly! Diamonds have nothing to do with it. Nothing! It's what I told you — to offset the Hutus. There is also Motutu's support of Sudan, but that's a secondary factor. Now, I will not say that we are so different that the saying 'to the conquerors the spoils' doesn't apply to us. Diamonds are helping us keep boots on the ground. The campaign may be easy, but it's not cheap. But they are the industrial kind," he smiled; "a few kilometers from here, in Angola, there, you have real diamonds!"

"I think this is an unnecessary conflict," Molu said, taking a deep breath. "The man you are imposing on Kinshasa is a terrible choice, a man of no faith. Who knows where he will lead us, you, and everybody?"

"That should be up to the people of this country to decide."

"The people are not allowed to choose," Molu said, glad to have found a point in dispute with the colonel.

"Uganda is not imposing Nundu here," the colonel said. "Had Motutu not subsidized the Hutus, we would not be having this conversation — certainly not in Mbuji-Mayi. But I can tell you from what I have witnessed since I came into this country, the people seethe in their desire for change. As I told you, we would be in Kinshasa if so many didn't crowd around us. Of course, our leaders make alliances on the usual lines of interests."

"The disinheritors of the colonial legacy support vanquishers, whoever they may be," Molu said, eager to puncture the Ugandan's poise. "They will crowd behind the next man who comes along standing in a jeep. Uganda is not different; you have at least three population groups there that would welcome the first man to wave at them from a jeep."

"You are referring to Joseph Kony's Lord's Resistance Army. My oldest boy — he abducted him — while he was visiting his grandparents in Gulu. How can anyone support Joseph Kony, a man who trades in children? But Motutu is supporting him."

"I am sorry about your boy," Molu said. "We are sitting on the most unstable colonial fault line in Africa. Generations will feel the shock of all these conflicts."

"I don't disagree," the colonel said wearily. "As for me, I live for the day Africans make their own decisions. But I apologize for not asking what your interest in this is?"

"I am the foreign minister."

"The foreign minister? Well, then, that's why you're going to Kisangani. But — at the last briefing, they told us President Motutu was ill. He is in the hospital. They have moved the negotiations to Pointe Noire in Congo-Brazzaville."

"Pointe Noire?"

"Yes! The Serb can take you, once he has fuel. I can call along the line to expect you."

"I am in your debt. And when do you expect to reach the capital?" Molu asked.

"By the end of the week. Once across the bridge over the Bombo, we are in Kinshasa."

"One other request, please. Can you patch through a telephone call for me to your foreign minister."

"I am sure he is on his way to Pointe Noire, too. Once your plane is fueled up —"

"There is no time, Colonel. The fuel truck may not get here, stranding me in Mbuji-Mayi for days. Please, Colonel!

"You'll be safe here. You have my word."

"I'm grateful. But you said a moment ago — I thought you understood. Africans were once the children of harmony. We don't have to end up like this."

"I don't know," the Ugandan answered.

"I am Kinshasa's foreign minister, and I need to speak to the foreign minister of your country. He is a thoughtful African; I am sure he will welcome my call."

After some moments of silence, the colonel said, "I will have to pass on your request to my superiors in Kananga. May I have your papers?"

Molu handed him his diplomatic passport and the cable the Dictator had sent him, appointing him foreign minister.

"The president delegated me to go to Kisangani," Molu said. "The venue has changed. It's urgent I speak to your foreign minister."

"Wait in the hangar."

Molu stared at him.

"I have other matters to discuss with my chief. Wait in the hangar, please."

Molu left.

Twenty minutes later the colonel emerged and walked to where Molu waited. He handed Molu his papers. "My chief said he will do what he can to get your message to Dr. Mananga."

"Thank you," Molu said. "I met Dr. Mananga in Kampala two years ago. A thoughtful man. How long do you think it will take to patch me up to him?"

"I would say quite a while. Your message has to go up the chain of command. This will require patience."

The Ugandan and Molu walked out of the storage area and gazed at the line of refugees streaming by the airport. Molu said, pointing, "Can you ask these people to be patient, Colonel?"

The Ugandan sighed. "It would do no good to say it to them. Escape has a mind of its own. But you… you have a choice."

They heard the phone. "It's for you, Colonel," a corporal shouted.

"That was my chief," the Ugandan said when he returned. "He wants you to know that he has sent your request to headquarters."

"As I was saying, I have no choice," Molu said. "Africa is begging for a reprieve from the likes of Jean-Luc Nundu."

"You mean to stop Nundu from taking over in Kinshasa?" the Ugandan asked. His studied casualness slipped for an instant, and he pulled the meerschaum from his mouth in a gesture of astonishment.

"You look at me as if you were measuring me for a rope," Molu observed.

"Not at all, not at all. I am just surprised. Privately, I don't like my army to be associated with the likes of Nundu."

"I once stopped a Belgian from robbing us of one of our traditions," Molu said. "The Nundus of Africa and their supporters are the thieves now."

"Well … Yes. But powerful forces carry Nundu forward," the colonel cautioned.

"That's not what you said earlier. You said it should be up to the people of this country to decide. That's what you said."

"Yes!"

"I am like you, Colonel," Molu said. "I'd like to see Africans decide."

A deafening hubbub rose from the throng moving west outside the airport's perimeter. Between the Uganda colonel and Molu there was a long silence. The Ugandan glanced at his companion. The glow in Molu's eyes almost blinded him.

"I only ask that you help me put the case of the people to fellow Africans," Molu then said. "Only that."

"What can I do?" the Ugandan asked. The movement of his shoulders expressed that from Mbuji-Mayi there was little he could do.

"Let me use your satellite telephone," Molu said. "You could patch me up to anywhere in the world."

The Ugandan's eyes questioned Molu."

"I need to talk to the Senegalese foreign minister."

"I've heard of her. She is famous," the colonel said. "It won't be easy to get through. But I'll try. If I am questioned, I'll say I am doing a Senegalese reporter a favor. My army is keen to support journalists."

"Thank you," Molu said.

After multiple connections, the Ugandan heard the ring in the ministry on Place de l'Indépendance in Dakar.

"My French is poor," he told Molu, handing him the receiver.

———

"Trying to contact you has become a tradition with me," Molu told Fatou-Anne Cerusu. His voice carried his delight at hearing the warm Senegalese accented French of the minister. "If it hadn't been for the aide who was with you in New York, your operators would not —"

"Where are you, Mr. Sakeseba?" she interrupted him. "I've been looking for you."

"I am at the Mbuji-Mayi airport in Kasai Oriental. The Ugandan army is here. I am able to speak with you thanks to their colonel who has given me access to his satellite phone.

"Ugandans are known for their broad mindedness," Mrs. Cerusu said. "But what are you doing? You're not a prisoner allowed a phone call, are you?"

"No, I am not detained. They are not interested in prisoners — But let me tell you why I called. I may not have much time. The president sent me to represent Kinshasa at the Kisangani meeting . It's now in Pointe Noire. I need your help to contact the Ugandan foreign minister. He knows me. The colonel here has put in a request for me with his superiors. But I am afraid that will take too long."

"Yes, I can call him, of course, but… what do I tell him?"

"Tell him I need help to get to Pointe Noire. A safe-conduct for myself and two pilots and fuel for a plane.

"Certainly, I will do that," Minister Cerusu said.

"I ask nothing for myself, you understand — nothing," said Molu, as if talking to himself. "Give the people a chance to choose their government. Don't impose someone by fiat."

"Isn't it too late for that, Mr. Sakeseba? Nundu's backers are at Kinshasa's gates."

"No, it's not … too late. It's up to the Ugandans and the Rwandans to say where Nundu is. With your help, I can put the case of the people to them. They can permit Kinshasa to have a new start, with a peace settlement followed by the people's opportunity to decide for themselves."

"Let me see what I can do. Call me if you need anything else."

---

Fatou-Anne Cerusu's appeal opened the sky for Molu. He spoke twice to the Ugandan foreign minister. The first time he told him of his Kisangani assignment and requested help in getting fuel for his plane. Molu then pleaded that the people not be taken for granted. Politely, the Ugandan minister replied that Minister Sakeseba had very little say in the matter now.

Two hours later the Ugandan called to say that his "Kinshasa colleague" had a safe conduct to travel to Pointe Noire. Molu had again entreated him to vote for the people, not for another dictator. "Let's make Pointe Noire memorable as the place where you say 'we will do right for our fellow Africans,'" Molu told him. Hurrying to hang up, the Ugandan minister answered that he would do his best.

The fuel truck arrived late in the night.

Molu had been watching the long lines of refugees streaming outside the airport — thousands of Edvar Munch's wretched ghosts, misery loose in the land of the Lubas.

The colonel came to him. "I wish you luck," he said, taking his hand in both of his.

"There is nothing capricious about the ancestors," Molu said. "You are the proof. It could have been a jailer here instead of a believer."

Molu hugged him.

"Take care! A voice crying in the wilderness is a magnet for arrows," the colonel warned.

"I am committed, Colonel," Molu said. "I will not quit before I give it my best."

"I'll tell them you are on your way" said the colonel. "I have put some sandwiches and water on board for you. Remind the Serb not to fly under eleven thousand feet."

# Chapter 34

Except for the one-hour wait for permission to enter Congo-Brazzaville's airspace, which the pilot warily spent circling the southern town of Matadi, a few miles north of the Angolan border, the flight had no delay, skimming the dark littoral forests. The AAC.1 *Toucan* landed in Pointe Noire, a sleepy town on the South Atlantic coast of Congo-Brazzaville early enough for Molu to see the fishermen putting out to sea. Pointe Noire's deep sea port services the country's oil industry ran by Elf Aquitaine. Cargo ships, plying the Gulf of Guinea's and other trade routes, find large berths there.

Molu completed border formalities quickly; however, the pilot and the copilot were not allowed to leave the airport. An official told Molu to come back during office hours. They would then give the pilot and his mate transit visas to go to a hotel in town. The two flyers were shown a bench in an area where people lay sleeping on the ground. Molu promised to return.

A wheezing taxicab took him to Hotel Azul on Boulevard du General de Gaulle in the district named for Patrice Lumumba where Molu had stayed years before.

Pointe Noire's neighborhoods have memorable names. The old quarter is named *Ndji-Ndji;* the largest residential quarter *Tie-Tie.* The driver suggested a hotel on Avenue Marien N'Gouabi in *Mvou-Mvou,* but Molu wanted to be in the center of town. The driver warned him off *foula-foula* — the buses.

The night clerk was still on duty. She had been asleep in a chair behind the counter when Molu pushed the door. A large woman, wearing a red apron covered with drawings of blue-colored sea shells, she stood the instant the door was opened. In her state between sleep and wakefulness she had an odd look in her eyes.

"I am sorry I frightened you." Molu read her name tag, "Angélique."

Angélique giggled, "That's alright. You're looking for a room?"

"I need two. For how long, I don't know."

"You have a reservation?"

"No."

"That's alright. We still have three left. We usually have more, but there is an important meeting in town."

"*Mwaramutse, Amakuru,*" Molu said.

Angélique replied, "*Mwaramutse, ni meza.*"

"I thought so," said Molu. "You speak French with a *Kinyarwanda* accent. Rwanda is one of my favorite countries. Before I quit smoking, I used to be crazy about its cigars."

Angélique, her manner more guarded now, gave the new client a *fiche de séjour* to fill out. Then keys to room 103 and 208. The two flyers would fill out their own *fiche.* Molu asked where there was a *pharmacie,* to get some toiletries. Angélique did not hear him; she was staring at his *fiche*, her lips moving.

"Something's wrong with my name?" Molu asked.

"No," she giggled. But the blood had drained from her face. Molu stared at her. What's with this woman? he wondered.

She unfolded a map of the city and pointed to a *pharmacie.* Also to Hotel Novotel where Dr. Mananga said the conference would be held. The *pharmacie* was on the way to the Novotel on Boulevard Pierre Savorgnan de Brazza. Going back to the airport, he would stop at both.

He asked to be awakened in two hours and thanked her, "*Murakoze, muramuke,* Angélique."

She nodded, not looking at him. Something is definitely the matter with this woman, he told himself.

---

In his room, Molu asked Angélique to connect him to a shop on Rue du Faubourg Saint Honoré in Paris. Julie would leave her phone number there for him. An elegant woman's voice answered that Julie had not been by and had not called. Could she take a message for dear Julie? Molu gave her the number of the hotel in Pointe Noire and ask that Julie call as soon as she checked in.

He then asked the operator for a connection to his wife. He was falling asleep, beginning to dream about the lines of screaming figures in Mbuji-Mayi, when the phone rang. Speaking quickly, he told his wife where he was and why. Her voice, which he hardly recognized, was cloaked in sadness. No, she was not sick, she answered.

She pressed him to return to the United States. With the president incapacitated and the security chief dead, the regime was a shell. She had read the news of Mgonu's death in a back-page story in a New York paper, she said. Molu absorbed the news during a long silence broken by his wife's sobs. He then asked that she call Marcel to tell him what he had told her. Molu would call him after the first meeting with the Ugandan foreign minister. They talked about the children. "Hang in there," he told her, before he hung up. He had never heard his wife cry before.

After a shower, he took out his suit, removed the Dictator's "memoirs" from the breast pocket and wiped the suit with a damp wash cloth. He washed his underwear and his shirt in the lavatory. He hung everything and turned on the shower's hot water and closed the bathroom door.

He lay down, hoping for a few hours of sleep; but his mind was like a movie screen, showing his family, his village, the Dictator, the incomprehensible Maka Mgonu and Julie saying good-bye at the Abu Dhabi airport. Garbled images rushed at him, swamping his mind. He dressed quickly in the damp clothes and left the room.

A new clerk was on duty. A pretty, vivacious woman, she gave him a look of undisguised approval. He said good morning and gave her the key. The sun was hot, and the sky bright, a shining ode to living. He looked toward the ocean, remembering the last time he was in Pointe Noire, the endless beach, the cold water. That was in another life.

Another gasping Renault taxi took him to the Novotel. The town was not yet fully up, making the trip for the sideways-moving cab an easy one. Even at this early hour, onlookers were beginning to crowd the sidewalk across from the hotel. Access will be restricted totally in a few hours, he thought. Perhaps he had been wrong not to have taken a room here.

The lobby swarmed with burly men in dark suits. It looked like a coffee break at a reunion for security men. Molu became more apprehensive. Then he spotted a short, bald man, who did not belong in this gathering. He looked at him fixedly, trying to remember where he had met him. The man noticed, and, after a moment, smiling broadly, walked to Molu, his hand extended.

"Minister Sakeseba, you don't remember me? Ken Taylor. You were kind enough to brief me yourself, when I came to your embassy two years ago."

"Yes, yes! I was trying to recall where I had met you. My friend Marcel Garinaldi has spoken of you very warmly. It should have come to me; but I'm too tired, I guess. And you've lost weight. But what are you doing in this crowd?"

"This is my Kinshasa swan song. I'm giving the embassy a hand on figuring out what's going on here."

"You're celebrated for being the best man for the job."

"I get out more than most. That's true," Ken said.

"What's the situation, Ken?" Molu asked intently in a whisper. "My wife told me that Maka Mgonu was killed."

"Yeah, I heard that. Apparently he was caught by a crowd with a grudge."

"That's hard to believe. Maka was the most cautious man in the world."

"But not cautious enough! I heard that he went on a rampage. One of the people he killed was the Continental Hotel's manager."

"Let me ask you this, Ken. Where is the U.S. on this meeting?"

"What do you mean?"

"Would they support President Motutu?"

"President Motutu? President Motutu is flying to Morocco in a day or two. He is too sick to hold on. You don't know that?"

"I've been out of touch. We need to talk. What's your room number? I have to go to the airport now to get my pilot. I'll come back to see you. Are you the only one from your embassy here?"

"I'm staying at another hotel, but I'll be here all day. Brenda Bleding is here, too. She is the chargé d'affaires."

"What happened to Ambassador Mosley?"

"Brenda happened to Mosley. But mostly, Mosley happened to Mosley."

Molu stared at him a moment. "Will she talk to me, you think?"

"Brenda doesn't do anything she doesn't get something for."

"She'll figure President Motutu is out: She doesn't have to talk to me. Is that it?"

"Ahhh. Brenda instinctively sniffs only the side of the bread where the butter is spread. But I'll talk to you!" He grinned. "A friend of Marcel is a friend of mine."

"I'm grateful, Ken. I'll be back within the hour. I'll look for you."

<hr>

Molu hurried out. His taxi driver spotted him and shouted, "Airport."

More people were heading for the Novotel. For sure the authorities would not allow a crowd to gather. They would prohibit anyone not part of the Pointe Noire conference to enter the area. Molu told the driver to hurry.

But the pilots were gone, and the plane too. No one knew or would say what had happened. Finally, Molu went up the control tower, and when he refused to leave, a controller disclosed that the pilot was ordered to move the *Toucan* to the Brazzaville airport five hundred kilometers away. They needed space for the planes of conference delegates. For ten minutes he gave Molu a tutorial on the limits to the number of aircraft at the airport, named for the first president of Angola, Agostinho Neto. Molu was trapped in Pointe Noire.

He then remembered what Ken had said about Mgonu killing the hotel manager and knew it had something to do with Julie. The onslaught of dread told him that something terrible had happened to her. He heard Mokonzi Kabasu intone a saying, "There is no one to share a path with when a companion dies."

————

At the Novotel, Dr. Mananga had still not arrived. Molu wrote him a note, giving him the address and telephone number of his hotel. He then asked a bellhop to show him where the meeting would be held. No guard was at the door. It was a large square room with bare walls; an oversized basket of flowers was at the center, surrounded by a conference table. He went around the table, reading the participants' names. His was not one of them.

He sat on Dr. Mananga's chair, looking around the room, taking in every detail. He sat until a gray haired, stout man and his aide entered. Molu stood to greet them.

"August Mananga. Good to see you again." The Ugandan looked at Molu with twinkling eyes, his hand extended.

"Great to see you again, Minister," Molu said, shaking the Ugandan's hand with feelings.

"Should we go to my room, so we can have a moment in private? This room will soon be a bazaar."

"By all means," Molu said.

————

On the way to the elevator, Molu spotted Ken Taylor, leaning against a table, reconnoitering the lobby. He excused himself.

Pulling the American behind a potted palm, his manner urgent, he asked, "Ken, do you have any idea why Mgonu killed that hotel manager?"

"This is rumor, you understand," Ken said, his voice low. "It seems that Mgonu had something going with the manager's wife. She was killed in Bahrain somewhere, and Mgonu blamed the manager for it. I don't know if that's true. A beggar in Gomé told me that."

Molu stared at his hands gripping the back of the sofa. "Thank you, Ken. I'll see you later."

"Sure! Let's do lunch. I've never had lunch with a foreign minister."

Molu turned toward the elevator. The tears in his eyes were pools of pain.

"Is something wrong?" the Ugandan asked.

"I just heard that someone I cared about very much was killed."

"I am sorry. My wife passed away last year. I know how you must feel. You can unburden yourself in my suite."

---

Molu stepped onto the balcony. He stared at the ocean in the direction of *Côte Sauvage*. Sobs shook his tall frame, as if the sun was making him shiver. The Ugandan watched and murmured what a poet friend had said about the reality of a man in pain, "A man who cries is not a clown at an amusement park." He sat on the living room sofa to wait.

After a while, a composed Molu came in, faced the Ugandan minister. "My grief is nothing compared to what is happening to us," he said.

"Motutu was a fool," the Ugandan said, heatedly, pointing at the space next to him for Molu to sit. "His mistakes have had their way with him. Would that they had stopped there!"

Molu waved a hand, as if to say, let's not waste time on blame. Then said, "As I was telling you on the phone yesterday, Minister, if you and the Rwandans throw your support behind the people —"

"Minister Cerusu spoke to me yesterday," Dr. Mananga interjected, "and again this morning. I promised her that I would do everything to get you a hearing."

"I don't intend to give just token remarks, Minister," Molu affirmed.

"Nor am I asking you to," the Ugandan minister said.

"Then you can level with me."

The Ugandan look at Molu as if debating whether or not to confide in him. "We are not comfortable with this fellow Nundu. No sensible person is. But I am afraid your country might have to make the most of a President Nundu."

"It's decided then?"

The Ugandan shrugged.

"All you have to do is to temporize a bit," Molu urged. "You and the Rwandans hold all the cards. Nundu cannot spit without you."

"He knows how we feel about him," the Ugandan said. The minister had a tone of disbelief that Molu didn't understand fully the man they were contending with. "Nundu has others waiting in the wings to back him. I am afraid we are inheriting a dreadful future in the Great Lakes region."

They sat in silence.

"Minister Cerusu and other friends spoke on your behalf. We will not summarily dismiss you, Mr. Sakeseba, if that's what you are worried about."

"Thank you," Molu said.

"But they are concerned about you. Minister Cerusu even suggested we offer you asylum. We agreed. You need not remain here."

Molu stared. "My daughter has a little song she sings. It's from Black Sheep," he said. "You can get with this or you can get with that. I think you will get with this, for this is where it's at." Pointe Noire is 'where it's at,' Dr. Mananga."

The Ugandan minister smiled. "I grant you your point."

"I'm glad," Molu said.

"But Nundu and his party look upon you — shall we say — differently. They see you as a rival.

"Even in my ministry I have to contend with a faction that argues it's not in the interest of Uganda and Rwanda to have such a large country as yours stable. Stable, your country dwarfs us, like the United States does Mexico.

"They want Nundu because he is a bull at a red-flag convention. He will keep Kinshasa impoverished for the foreseeable generations. The president and I are strongly opposed to this view. An unstable Kinshasa spills unrest into Uganda and Rwanda. It's senseless to promote permanent chaos in the region. But this bloc has momentum on their side.

"They are aware of the appeal you intend to make. The man you saw me with is here to make sure you don't get too much of an ear. Leave Pointe Noire, I beg you."

"They sent my plane to Brazzaville. Something about needing parking space here," Molu said.

The Ugandan looked at Molu, alarmed.

"They have bribed the airport officials," he said, drawing a long breath. "Use my aircraft. The president won't object. They'll let you leave in my aircraft."

"You can hold your army in place," Molu said, impatiently. "Don't enter Kinshasa. That's the best solution."

"You don't appreciate how far down this road we've gone. If we tell the army to halt now, we'll either have a mutiny on our hands or others will step in to further Nundu's cause. We'd lose all influence. You wouldn't want that, would you?"

"Of course not."

"Then, leave now."

"I came to Pointe Noire to ask for an opportunity for Africa. As I told the colonel in Mbuji-Mayi, I won't quit until I've done that.

"The head of my village used to say 'There is never a choice: you either stand for something, or you go down for something.' In the past few days, I've found out the importance of standing for something. You see, most of my life, ignoring that early wisdom, I thought I had a choice."

The Ugandan minister shrugged again. "Have you written down what you want to say? It's important that you be clear. Passionate but clear!"

"No, not yet."

"You can stay here to do that, if you like. I've got to go to the lobby to talk to my Rwandan counterpart. Earlier, I caught scent of danger."

"Thank you. I accept your offer. I'd also be grateful if you let me use your telephone."

The Ugandan pointed at the desk. He then left the room. Molu could hear him outside argue with the man who had walked in the meeting room with him earlier.

---

Molu asked the operator to connect him to Washington. It was 12:30 p.m. in Pointe Noire, 7:30 a.m. in Washington.

After a fifteen-minute wait for the connection, he heard Marcel's voice.

"Sorry to wake you, Marcel."

"I've been awake since Ella called. How is Pointe Noire? I was there, once, when oil was discovered."

"It's still a drowsy little town. The port is busy though. Lots of ships."

"Ella said you were delusional as usual," Marcel said. "What is she talking about?"

"She may be right this time," Molu said, chuckling. "Ken Taylor is here. He told me the old man is flying out in a day or two. To Morocco, he said. When I saw him, a couple of days ago, he looked done in. Man, do I have a story to tell you."

"Ken would know."

"Yeah! And he said that Maka Mgonu was killed —"

"The security chief? I read that," Marcel said. He, too, was subdued. "It looks like Nundu is in."

"Well, we'll see. I had a long talk with the Ugandan foreign minister a short while ago. Nundu's so-called allies are going to let me put the case of the people —"

"The case of the people? What are you talking about?"

"What I am talking about is a chance for a fresh start in Kinshasa, Marcel."

Marcel was silent.

"Why not let the people choose? That's my case before the Ugandan minister. A new start, Marcel! Sooner or later, they'll have to go to the people. Why not do it now. The end of the Motutu era is a dramatic moment — the timing couldn't be better."

"But it's a castle in the sky, Molu. It's too late, whether they like Nundu or not."

"That's up to the Ugandan army, Marcel. But somebody should put the people's case on the table. No one at that meeting will do it. It's up to me.

"What better way to end my tenure as Kinshasa's foreign minister than to speak on behalf of letting Africans decide for themselves. It's not for myself that I am asking anything."

"Man, they'll brand you as Motutu's lackey and everything else in the book: From Johnny-come-lately to a sore loser."

"Yeah, I thought about that. What is important is for a voice in that room to say — enough! If name calling is the best the opposition can manage, that will speak for itself."

"You're one stubborn dude!"

"You think I am stubborn?"

"Is the Congo River long?"

"Ella thinks I run from responsibility. I think it's because I told her that when I was a kid, I was afraid to die. One day, I asked my father how to tell I am alive. 'If you can hear your heart beat that means you're alive,' he told me." Molu laughed. "So I'd run to hear my heart. Ella thinks I've been running ever since. Don't ever tell a woman anything, Marcel; she'll make a book out of it."

What was Molu saying? Garinaldi tried to decipher his friend's rambling.

"Is there anything you want me to do for you here?" he said.

"Keep an eye on Ella. She is not as tough as she talks."

"Yeah, I'll do that. I'll call her now to let her know I've spoken with you."

"Thanks, Marcel. I'll talk to you later."

"OK. When you see Ken, say hi for me and congratulations on the London assignment. He is going to be one of the very few African American men posted in Europe. That's progress.

"But he's going to be so bored after a few months there; he'll ask to return to Africa, malaria and all. Don't tell him that part." Marcel didn't sound like he was joking.

Marcel would know what Ambassador Mosley's story was. But Molu didn't ask. The question was too trivial, he thought.

―――  ―――

Molu went back on the balcony. He looked again at the sea and the moored ships, waiting to unload their cargo. He felt a serenity. It was a brand new feeling. He went back in; pulled hotel stationary from the desk and began to jot down what he proposed to say at the meeting. A rush of optimism flooded his mood.

He placed a call to Fatou-Anne Cerusu. The hotel operator was new. The afternoon shift, Molu thought offhandedly.

After a twenty minute wait to be connected, he heard the minister, "Are you in Pointe Noire?"

"I am."

For ten minutes they talked about the reality on the ground. Molu argued that it was still fluid. Fatou-Anne countered that *les jeux étaient faits.* She repeated the phrase several times, apologizing for sounding like a teacher in her dotage. "Not at all," Molu assured her, a bit patronizingly. The Senegalese minister gave him her home phone number, in case he needed to contact her urgently. Molu promised to call following his first appearance at the meeting.

After he hung up, the minister smiled. At the UN she had heard someone say that a particularly effective diplomat drew on a "combination of naiveté and cunning" to get things passed. Molu's Pointe Noire gambit was a blend of naiveté and cunning, she thought. No one was enamored of Jean-Luc Nundu. Molu was gambling that his appeal would reinforce the doubt they all felt toward the warlord and slow down the rush to recognize him as the next strong man in Kinshasa. But more importantly, the old minister told herself with renewed respect, if Molu could make the delegates look upon the ideal — freeing Africans — as an imperative, he would score the most telling point Africa had experienced since the formal ending of colonial rule.

―――  ―――

Molu folded the four sheets of paper lengthwise and put them in his breast pocket, next to the Dictator's "memoirs." He looked at the blue stationary, remembering. He treated me like a son, he thought. Better than a son. How could he have believed that I had betrayed him? Sickness, old age, Mgonu, madness?

Someone should write the memoirs. Molu doubted that anyone but the Dictator would be held responsible for the calamity that had befallen the country. "Mokonzi had no associates, no one, not even a cheerleader," he said aloud to himself, before opening the door, shaking his head in disbelief. He left the Ugandan minister's suite, closing the door softly behind him.

The lobby was crowded with delegates, aides, family members and hangers-on. Molu paused as he grasped that at least half of them were diamond and other mining companies' operatives.

The mood was jovial; laughter screened the piped-in music from the in-ceiling speakers. English and Swahili were the languages of choice. Where was the musical Lingala that Molu loved? He stood in one corner to scout the area. Three Asian men were talking to a white woman. Perhaps the chargé d'affaires Ken Taylor had told him about. What could she be telling these men? Molu wondered.

Those who recognized the old dictator's foreign minister made furtive looks in his direction and moved away. He was the losers' representative at a meeting to divide spoils. He had nothing for them. He resolved not to be marginalized, calling first on dignity not to fail him now and on Mokonzi Kabasu's lessons on staring.

To alleviate his discomfort, he looked for Dr. Mananga. He found him in conversation with a tall angular man whose face reminded Molu of someone he had met. He approached the two men with a look of confidence he did not feel. Dr. Mananga turned to his left, pretending not to see him. Molu came right next to him, their sleeves touching. At last, Dr. Mananga acknowledged him and introduced the man he was talking to, Bernard Damuya, his Rwandan counterpart. Dr. Mananga's affability had vanished.

Bernard Damuya smiled easily, exuding insouciance. It would take more than a high-level meeting to ruffle him, his bearing told Molu. He extended his hand. "My sister told me about you," his tone conveying familiarity. Molu had a questioning look.

"Our ambassador in Washington," Damuya clarified. Molu heard the same accent as the Azul's night clerk's — and that of the operator who had placed the call for him to Fatou-Anne Cerusu.

"Ah yes," Molu said, amazed that the stern woman he had met at the coffee shop in Chinatown was a relative of this easygoing man. "Meeting her was a great education."

"You should have listened to her," Damuya said.

Molu didn't know what that meant — didn't ask, preferring to take the opportunity to tell the Rwandan what he planned to say at the meeting.

"There is a question whether or not you will be able to address the delegates," Dr. Mananga interrupted. "Nundu's people are against your presence here. They tell us that President Motutu is about to leave the country and thereby step down from office."

"Nonsense," Molu said angrily, in a dull voice. "Have you seen any legal document of resignation? No! Even if the president were to go abroad, African heads of state go abroad regularly for medical —"

"You didn't let me finish," Dr. Mananga said, taken aback by Molu's vehemence. "Minister Damuya and I have consulted on this. We agree that you have a right to speak here. However, once President Motutu leaves the country — and everything points to an imminent departure — you will be without a platform. I am sorry. Personally, I don't think you should remain here. I told you that upstairs."

"And I told you that my course was set. That it was the least I could do."

Surprising them, Minister Damuya declared, "Good for you, Minister Sakeseba! Your words should set the cat among the pigeons, as my Australian wife likes to say. Not a bad thing. I'll make sure you've your say, so help me God."

Dr. Mananga raised a finger, whether to object or assent, his words were drowned out by an uproar in the street and at the hotel's entrance. The lobby crowd parted for a slight man dressed in a *grand boubou* who, as loud as his lungs could manage, boomed out declarations in a language of a far away land. Molu realized when he heard "Nundu" with every shout that the warlord had brought in a praise professional, a *djeli*, to extol him. Molu laughed at the absurdity of this public relations ploy. Then, the crowd's renewed roar strangled the *djeli's* exaltations, as Jean-Luc Nundu walked into the Novotel.

Jean-Luc Nundu was a short, round man in his early fifties. Upon seeing him for the first time, most people in the Great Lakes region assumed he was in diamonds — the illicit side of the trade. Unsure of his luck, he made no firm decision and trafficked with all sides in a conflict. He was an impossible ally. Consequently, his partners mistrusted him and used him, until someone more reliable came along.

The *djeli* before him, shouting his praise, the warlord strutted into the lobby. Bodyguards swarmed protectively around him. They were weary of his choleric outbursts; shyness and public self-consciousness set him off unexpectedly. People pressed to get close. Nundu walked slowly to give himself an imperious look — to appear presidential. Instead, the royal rolling stroll enhanced his mobster's air. Molu smoldered. This is Kinshasa's next president? he asked himself.

Nundu stopped to shake some proffered hands, desultorily, as if rehearsing for a future performance. Ken's chargé d'affaires was one who took his limp grasp. They chatted; then Nundu stepped into the meeting room to boisterous applause and shouts of "vive Lumumba, vive Nundu."

<hr>

Molu was one of the last to go in. Pointing at him, an aide spoke in Nundu's ear. The warlord shifted his glance. And for the first time since he entered the hotel his expression changed, and his lips stretched into what might have been a smile, as he took in the hatred in Molu's eyes. Nundu turned to his aide and whispered intently. Molu was left with alarm bells ringing in his head.

Nundu continued to walk around the table in his deliberate manner, greeting only selected delegates. He didn't shake hands with Dr. Mananga nor with Minister Damuya, the Banyamulenge representative, or the Burundi delegate. Molu could not tell if that was an oversight or a deliberate slight. If the latter, the Tutsis were Nundu's target of displeasure. Nundu on the other hand lingered with the Angolan, the Zimbabwean, and the Sudanese delegates as well as the Hutu representative. The lines were drawn then. Molu's hopes soared.

His presence in the meeting room having conveyed the intended blessing, Nundu moved toward the door, waved to more shouts of "vive Lumumba, vive Nundu" and processed out. A guard closed the door behind him.

Presently an aide to the Ugandan minister came in, and spoke urgently in his boss' ear. The minister followed him out. A few minutes later, a hotel employee, holding a placard with "M. Sakeseba" written on it, stood at the door. Molu followed him. An annoyed Dr. Mananga was waiting for him.

"A message from the president's office just came in," the Ugandan minister said, with undisguised irritation in his muffled voice. This Sakeseba was a nuisance! "Minister Cerusu asked that you call her."

Molu ignored the demeanor; he understood. Politely he said, "Thank you. I told her that I would call when the meeting was over," intending to go back in.

The Ugandan grabbed his arm. Perhaps Molu had not heard him correctly. "This is from the president's office," he said, frantic, his voice low, startling Molu.

"Alright," Molu answered, at length. "May I use the phone in your suite? I can have privacy there."

"No," Dr. Mananga said. "I don't know what this is about, but the message has a codicil: we should not use the hotel's phones. We have one in our security detail's room. You use that one."

Molu looked at the Ugandan questioningly.

"It is a secure line," Dr. Mananga said.

Dr. Mananga took Molu to his delegation's secure room. The phone, a bulky KVH Trac 25, was on a bare desk in a suite workspace. A Ugandan agent followed Molu, dialed the number Molu gave him and stood by as if waiting for further instructions. Molu's "thank you," and look to the door told the agent this was a personal call. The man left with the door open. It was 4:45 p.m. in Pointe Noire.

When he was sure it was Minister Cerusu on the line, he hastened to say that he had gotten her message. He asked that she not say anything. He would call her back within the hour. She said, "Hurry" and hung up before he did.

He stepped out of the little room, forcing himself to be calm. Only the man who had placed the call for him, and who now looked at him intently, was in the suite. Where was Dr. Mananga? The minister had gone back to the meeting, the agent answered.

Molu hurried to the lobby to look for Ken Taylor. He found the American in the hotel's main restaurant in conversation with two African journalists. Molu approached the trio and casually asked Ken for a word in private. The press officer expertly excused himself to his companions.

"Ken I need your help —"

"What?"

"You told me you had a room at another hotel. I need to use the phone there."

"Sure! I gather you also need to get to my hotel as inconspicuously as possible," Ken said lightheartedly. "The embassy has two cars for our use here. They're in the back. Let me say good-bye to my friends here. I'll meet you there in ten minutes."

"You don't need your chargé's permission, do you?"

"Man, the only thing I'd tell Brenda is that a brother from another planet had landed in Washington, DC, just to scare the shit outta her. Come on!"

————

The press officer was behind the wheel of a new Citroën when Molu came out. "How do you want to do this?" Ken asked. "Lying in the back seat or sitting behind me like you were a delegate going somewhere?"

"I saw the crowd outside the hotel when I came in earlier," Molu said. "I think it'd be best to crouch in the back."

"Let's hurry up," Ken said, "before Brenda starts looking for me. Being surrounded by brothers makes her nervous. You should see how she locks up her room. She has gadgets for the door, the window, the bathroom. I am her security. She wouldn't give me the time of day any place else."

"Marcel spoke to me about the hazards of being black in your service," Molu said. "You should write a book about it. Marcel calls you a natural. But let me tell you off the record, Ken, why I need your help."

Ken listened attentively; saying only when Molu, bent down in the Citroën back seat, had finished, "Man, will I have something to tell my grandchildren?"

The press officer was an expert driver. From the hotel parking lot, he came out leisurely, not to attract attention. But once on Boulevard Pierre Savorgnan de Brazza, he sent the Citroën flying. Even hard-nosed *foula-foula* drivers were startled. From *Tie-Tie* to the old quarter of *Ndji-Ndji*, where he said he stays when in Pointe Noire to indulge in his passion for sailing, took him less than ten minutes.

"Where'd you learn to drive like that?" Molu asked when they arrived.

"In South Carolina, running from peckerwoods."

"Like Brenda?"

"Yeah," Ken laughed, "like Brenda. But it's Brenda who got me a handshake for London. I'd never have gotten that, not in a thousand years, if it weren't for her."

"I'd forgotten," Molu said. "Marcel asked me to congratulate you. He said you'll be one of the few black men from your service in Europe." Molu chuckled.

"Yeah, I don't know if I can stand it," Ken sighed.

They entered the hotel by the back door and took the stairs to the second floor.

"You have to be connected by the operator downstairs," Ken explained when they were in the room. "There's no way around it. I'll place the call. She knows me. When it rings in Dakar, I'll go downstairs to distract her. She won't listen in, if that's what you're worried about."

"But won't that make her wonder who is using the phone?" asked Molu.

"I'll tell her about boats," replied Ken. "She loves that. The most important thing is not to have the operator listening in."

It was a Fatou-Anne Cerusu Molu had not heard before. Speaking in a tone that made disagreeing not an option, she told Molu, her voice sudden, "A friend called to report that one of their people at the Novotel has intelligence concerning you. Nundu's people intend to get rid of you. And I don't mean putting you under house arrest. It's that simple. And they can do it. There is a ship leaving Pointe Noire for the Cape Verde. *Le Cayor*. You should get on it."

Molu said, "I felt something like that coming. I'll make my statement and go from there."

"Time for statements is passed. Get on that ship now," Mrs. Cerusu entreated. "There'll be plenty of opportunities for statements later. Fighting another day does not include suicide. Get on board, while there is still daylight."

"I take your meaning. I'll get on."

"They'll let me know when you're on board," Mrs. Cerusu said.

———  ———  ———

Molu went to the window. Already dusk was shading Pointe Noire. In less than an hour, the tropic's night would descend on the city like a sudden pall. Ken came in. "She didn't even notice that I was in two places at the same time," he said, jovially, to a subdued Molu.

"Thanks." Molu took out blue-colored sheets of paper from his breast pocket. "When you write your book about Africa, use this!"

"What is it?"

"A few things the president told me the last time I saw him. He was rambling. But you may find something useful in them."

"OK. You're sure you want to give them to me?"

Molu nodded.

"Thanks! I'll definitely write something about Africa. I've seen so much on this continent.

"You need anything else here? A drink?"

Molu shook his head.

"Let's blow this joint then."

———————

Out of sight in the back seat of the Citroën, Molu spoke to Ken about what he intended to say at the meeting later. He wanted the press officer to report his comments to his journalist friends. His voice fervent, although muffled by street and engine noise, he said, "In that room, I am going to talk about resources, Ken. How we use them in Africa. You've seen enough in your postings to know that what I am going to say is true.

"Because the man in power gains control through violent means, he must use all the country's resources to stay on top. He is on a tiger. Now, if he comes in through the approval of the country — the front door — he doesn't have to worry about getting knocked off. And instead of using the country's resources to protect himself from those who want to do to him what he did to his predecessor, he can use the wealth in the country's behalf. He stays alive and the country benefits. We all win —"

"What do you have, a death wish?" Ken cut in. And he slowed the Citroën down, to pull to a curb, to face Molu, better to tell him what he thought of his sentiments. Molu reminded him they had to get back to the Novotel.

"You shocked me," Ken exclaimed, getting back on the road. "Man, are you out of your mind? They'll kill you for saying that stuff. I've had friends killed and many in jail for saying less than that in Africa. You can't rock this boat with impunity. There are too many who benefit. It's a system like any other."

"But it has to be said, Ken. That's where it begins. Will you tell the journalists what I said? Please."

"I don't have a problem telling the journalists. That's my job. But I can tell you what they'll say. I am being frank with you. They'll say, 'President Motutu wrote the book on defrauding Kinshasa to stay in power. Who is his foreign minister to talk now?' Mammy Yokum at this shindig is like Mosley at a civil rights rally. Why didn't you talk before?"

"Because I was part of it, Ken, and we were not in the chaos we are in now," Molu said. "But I hear you. I'm not offended."

"This will make journalists I know shake their heads in amazement. *Se sera du jamais vu*," Ken exclaimed. "They'll think you've lost your marbles. Being sanctimonious or messianic won't play well at all. Not at all."

"I am counting that a few will pay more attention to the message and not as much to the messenger," Molu said.

------

When they reached the Novotel's parking lot, Molu said in heartfelt gratitude, "Thanks Ken! You're a true brother. You don't know how much I owe you. Can I buy you dinner later?"

"Sure!"

"The last time I was here, the best restaurants were near the port. What about your chargé friend?" Molu asked. "You think she would join us?"

"Brenda?" Ken exclaimed, taken aback by Molu's invitation. He turned around to look at Molu, who was sitting up now. "What do you've in mind? I told you how she was."

His tone solicitous, Molu answered, "Ken, circumspection is not an option. That call at your hotel — It was about what the Nundu people plan to do with me. I have it figured out. They'll never do it in public nor with a white American official around. It's as simple as that. My escape is a ship in port. If I can get on it, I'll owe you for the rest of my life."

"Man, ain't you something?" Ken, incredulous, said.

"I am sorry Ken. I can't think of another way out. You're the person I have to trust. If you can't do it, I'll understand."

"But I like a challenge," Ken said, grinning, trying to find his footing in what was being asked of him. "I don't know about Brenda's part, though. Brenda doesn't do blacks."

"You told me she was an opportunist," Molu said. "The bait is what I'll tell her about my last meeting with the president. If she's as ambitious as you say, she won't want to pass on that. I bet she'll ask you to listen carefully to what I say for a report to Washington."

"If she says okay, which is a big if; she'll ask that we eat here."

"You tell her that there are too many eyes here. She doesn't want the whole world to know she's meeting with me. Try Ken. My life depends on it."

"I'll try," Ken pledged. "Once you get out of the meeting, I'll see you. The safest thing is for us to go in an embassy car. What's your plan at the restaurant?"

"The restaurant will be my jumping point," Molu said. "I am banking that as long as the chargé is around they won't do anything. I'll go from the restaurant to the ship.

"I'll talk to your chargé for about half an hour. Then I'll excuse myself. That'll be the signal to you that I'm gone. I'll give Marcel a ring. He'll call you with news of me."

Ken said, "OK. If there's anything untoward, I'll speak in Lingala. '*Malamu*' is the only word Brenda knows.

"You go in the hotel first. I'll follow in a few minutes."

———

Molu carefully opened the back door and entered the lobby. It was as crowded as when he had come in this morning. Delegates and their aides surrounded by dependents and others were taking a break from what must have been a querulous first session. The din in the lobby was no longer tinged with joyful expectation, as people stood in fours and fives arguing loudly. Contention heated the air.

Making his way through the crowd, Molu looked for Dr. Mananga or his Rwandan colleague. The morning's furtive looks in Molu's direction were now neutral glances and even smiles, albeit timid ones. He saw Minister Damuya coming towards him.

"Mananga thought you had left Pointe Noire," the Rwandan said with a snicker.

Molu ignored the comment. "I detect a change of mood," he said.

"The mood has changed alright," Minister Damuya said, distaste in his voice, his unperturbed demeanor no longer prevailing. "No one seems interested in the direction your country is taking," he said. "Mining rights is what's on everybody's mind. And you know what that means. It's now everyman for himself. Don't be surprised if enemies are now your friends and vice versa. This has taken a dangerous turn. I am considering suggesting to my president that he not attend the session for principals the day after tomorrow.

"But what about you? We are going back in the room in a few minutes. The first day is loosely structured to enable everyone to have his say. I will recognize you. That has been the procedure. Mananga or someone else will second."

"I am ready," Molu said. His heart roared.

———

A few minutes stretched into almost an hour, as hangers on and mining companies' agents gave last-minute advice to delegates, delaying the start of the session.

As the door closed, Minister Damuya rose. He made a striking figure, reproaching the delegates' behavior during the earlier session, reminding them that millions had died in the Great Lakes region, and that more carnage was on the way, unless they took their obligations seriously. And then he bellowed "PEOPLE are on the agenda here, NOT MINERALS." He then looked around and ascertained the impact of his words. Only a few had paid attention. He shook his head, as if to say, what can be done if they don't listen. He was about to sit, when he remembered and rose again.

His tone formal, he said that theirs was a meeting among Africans. Extending courteous hospitality to everyone was not only a tradition in Africa but an obligation here. He asked that they welcome *Monsieur le ministre des affairs étrangères du Congo-Kinshasa*, Molu Sakeseba. There was an intimation of disapproval around the room as Molu who had been sitting next to the minister rose to speak. As he sat down, the minister whispered, "Say what you have to say very quickly."

Molu thanked the minister and repeated what the later had said about the millions killed. *I say mea culpa and accept fully the responsibility my government may have in these crimes. But mea culpas are only a beginning. What is vital is for the people here to send a message to the four corners of Africa that brutality has no place in the way Africans take power from Africans. An African in a presidential chair should not be there through coups, killings or military movements. He should be there only because Africans have rights, which do not include sound of boots drowning a market woman's voice.* Molu heard laughter of derision.

When he began, few paid attention to his words. As his passion radiated to etch his meaning on the consciousness of the delegates, more listened. He had learned to speak from a master. Concern showed on the face of some in the room. He was too convincing. Some were even forgetting that he was Motutu's ambassador. One gave him the finger by the throat sign. Defiantly, he pressed on.

*A great friend told me that the one thing he regretted in his life was to have led a coup. Among the people they killed was the wife of the man he overthrew. He would say, 'why should this or that colonel or general, or whoever not do what I did? Why should it stop with me or with them? I must spend most of the country's resources to remain in power. Why is that fair?' He was convinced that the catastrophic drought of the '80s was the ancestors' punishment for what he had done. He was probably right. He would sit for hours with his prayer beads, chain smoking, staring at the sky, praying for rain. Why, indeed? Everyone here speaks on behalf of progress in Africa. What kind of progress includes killing to gain and stay in power for forty years?*

*A contraband head of state has a crooked system for a government. That government sucks all the resources of the country to keep the paramount leader in power. Nothing is left for education, health, transporta-*

*tion, clean water, and other services governments are supposed to provide. Such systems require — demand in fact — that there be no functioning institutions.*

*My fellow Africans, how much underdevelopment and chaos are enough before plundering and selfishness give way to the good sense of survival — our continent's survival?*

*My country is pivotal to what happens in Africa. The center of gravity as it were is literally there. Inflicting another illegality on Kinshasa is the last thing Africa needs. It need not be this way, my fellow Africans. Eschatological catastrophe awaits us if you do not say enough.*

*Your voice on behalf of giving the people back their voice will reverberate throughout the continent and will give Africa the start it didn't have forty years ago. Resolve not to leave Pointe Noire until there is a peace settlement contingent on the people being allowed a voice in how they are governed!*

*The Mututu era is over. The next man who sits in the presidential chair in Kinshasa should not be there because of foreign interests or because he was carried to the National Palace on the shoulders of armed men from either distant or nearby shores. I thank you kindly for your attention.*

Molu heard applause and a few shouts of "vive Lumumba, vive Sakeseba." Minister Damuya congratulated him for being passionate and succinct. "They may bag you but that was bonzer, as my Australian wife would say," he told Molu. Dr. Mananga came over to pat him sheepishly on the back as well, and, with a worried look, ask what he was going to do now. Molu had angered Nundu's people to wrath. The man who had given him the finger by the throat sign gazed at him as if considering him for a box. Molu walked out of the room to shouts of vive Lumumba, vive Sakeseba.

***

Ken stepped out of the elevator and saw Molu, an apprehensive look on his face. He smiled as he approached him, "You're out already? How did it go?" Molu grabbed Ken's arm as if to make sure it was really him. "Yeah," he said, letting out a sigh of relief, anxiety had been choking him. "I was told to make my remarks succinct. And there was a guy gesturing the cut throat notice. I am anxious to get going. But what about your chargé? Did she buy it?"

"Yeah, she bought it. She assumes that what you tell her about your president will put her in the big time. She imagines she'll be made ambassador to Germany. Ambition is an incredible thing!"

"The president told me just a few days ago," Molu said, "that ambition had led to my downfall. He may have been right."

"There comes Brenda," Ken said. "Oh Lord!"

Molu saw a tall, attractive, deep bosomed woman, in an evening dress, forcing herself to walk straight the way inebriated people do. He went to her and bowed deeply. "I am privileged to make your acquaintance, Madame l'Ambassadrice."

"Well, aren't you gallant?" Brenda said, her voice stiff, doing her best to keep her words on a certain course. The smell of mouthwash perfumed her.

Ken was convinced she would add, "For an African."

Molu turned to Ken. "Let's get out of this lobby, Ken," he said urgently from the corner of his mouth. "If they see that she is drunk, it may be the same as not being here."

"Yeah, I see what you mean. But tread gently with her."

"May I offer you my arm Madame l'Ambassadrice?" Molu offered. "There are steps to the parking area."

"Thank you, sir," Brenda said, taking Molu's arm. She looked at the press officer, as if to ask, why can't you be like this gentleman? Ken rushed ahead to open the door for them.

Ken dismissed the driver for the evening and got in behind the wheel of his embassy's car himself. He expected Brenda to sit next to him; but she went in the back seat and asked Molu to join her. Ken did not like being his chargé's chauffeur, Molu saw, and demonstrated his displeasure by leaving the dark parking lot as hastily as the car would go. Brenda pitched into Molu's lap, cursing. She grabbed the strap above her head, screeching for Ken to slow down. But he paid no heed.

From Boulevard Pierre Savorgnan de Brazza he sped north on Avenue N'teta Kouilou until he reached the Rond Point. He then turned west on Avenue Makelekele toward Bord de Mer and the port and restaurants. Molu looked back to see if they were being followed. No one could have kept up with Ken, he was sure.

When they reached Bord de Mer, Ken looked in the rearview mirror at Molu, questioningly. But he had been driving too fast, making it impossible for Molu to spot *Le Cayor* and point to the restaurant closest to the ship. After several passes, Molu caught snatches of letters that may have said *Cayor* streaked with rust on the side of one of the vessels. However, the port was dimly lit; he couldn't be sure. Nervously, he nodded. Ken turned the car around to park behind the restaurant, *Le Homard.*

Molu got out quickly to open the door for Brenda, hoping that the gesture would mollify her. Still, she berated the press officer for driving like an inconsiderate maniac. Ken looked in Molu's direction as if to say, London can't be this bad. He winked.

The restaurant was a standard Pointe Noire beach eatery for foreigners. Brenda was still fuming at the press officer. Molu sat next to her, and under his thoughtful courtesies she relaxed and toasted their meeting. He invited her to share a bottle of *Château Neuf* with him; instead, she ordered an eau de vie, *marc de champagne,* her latest find in liquor. She downed several aperitif glasses to accompany grilled fresh sardines. Molu glanced at Ken questioningly. He shrugged. Soon Brenda would move from intoxication to incoherence. When Molu was ready to go, he could excuse himself. He would take care of his chargé.

As the moment to make the journey from the restaurant to the ship approached, Molu's trepidation mounted. Ken waited, saying nothing. Brenda, on the other hand, chatted expansively but disjointedly about her experiences as a diplomat. Some people grow quiet when under the influence; Brenda did not. Molu made out vaguely the name of the capitals where Brenda said she had been posted; he could hear nothing else but his heart, like a funeral bell pealing in his ears. As to the reason Brenda agreed to meet with him, the 120 proof *marc,* on top of what she had before, had drowned her memory. Molu could have spoken about his river all night, and she would not have noticed.

He wasn't sure he could move his legs. He considered giving up, of going back with Brenda to the Novotel and staying in her room. Ken looked at him as if he knew what he was thinking. Finally, with a head gesture, Molu said he would pay for the evening, and turned to his right to hide from view the bills he was taking out of his wallet. Under the table, he put them in Ken's hand, but the press officer shook his head. He would take care of the tab himself.

Molu stood and said he was leaving, telling Brenda it had been a pleasure to meet her. By then she was fully inebriated and shook his hand perfunctorily. Molu turned to Ken and nodded his thanks.

A stocky man and a large woman, holding what to Molu looked like long-barrelled handguns at their sides, were standing about three hundred meters from the restaurant's parking lot. They were looking at the ships, arguing in the *Kinyarwanda* language. Molu knew a few words and phrases like he knew them in all the languages of the nine countries bordering his. He heard the woman say "*umugore*" and "*ambasade*" — a woman from the embassy. The man told her, "*itonde*" — be careful. She answered that they still had to check whether or not the party was still in the restaurant. Molu thought that he had heard that voice before. He remained face down on the sand, in the darkness, steps from the restaurant's kitchen door.

A car was lurching from the parking lot, its driver in a hurry. It must be Ken, Molu thought. The stocky man sprinted uselessly towards the car. The woman followed, shouting, "*urihe?*" — Where are you? She tried to hurry, but her size made running too taxing. And when an object fell from her hand, she yelled, "*attends moi.*" The effect would have been comical during the day. She settled for walking, shouting again "*urihe?*" Then it was "*alihe?*" She was assuming he had left the restaurant, perhaps in the fast car. The pair began to argue again. Molu heard the man ask, "*Urashaka iki?*" — What do you want? To follow them, the woman answered. After a moment, Molu heard a car's engine.

He stayed on the sand, immobilized. Then he looked toward the loading area, a pier that extended a hundred yards into the black waters. The pair might return when they realized he was not in the car. After a long while, he ran to the loading area.

Some dim lights from battery lanterns helped him in his search; however, he saw no vessel named *Le Cayor*. His unease oppressive, he walked up and down the dock, reading the names, not daring to ask about the ship he was looking for, taking cover behind a container or a large box whenever he saw someone.

Between two medium-sized vessels was nestled a little cargo ship. He had dismissed it as too small for a voyage to Cape Verde; now, he stood beneath its stern, praying it was *Le Cayor*. A man on deck had been observing him. Presently, the man walked from mid-ship to the stern and looked down. Molu waited, not risking a question that would identify him unnecessarily. "Are you from Minister Cerusu," the man asked in a low voice, after a moment of uncertainty. Molu could hardly open his mouth, relief having overwhelmed him. "Yes, yes," he said, finally. "Wait a moment!" the man told him.

After what to Molu was perpetuity, the man came back accompanied by another carrying what looked like ropes that he swung over the side. Molu went to the Jacob's ladder and warily climbed up.

The man who had spoken asked to see Molu's papers. He then introduced himself as Kane Diallo, Captain of *Le Cayor*, a Senegalese 22,000-ton cargo ship, powered by a four stroke diesel engine. While unloading cargo in Port Gentil, Gabon, he had received a call from the foreign ministry in Dakar, requesting that he come here and wait for a passenger. Minister Cerusu had helped him in the past; he could not refuse a request from her ministry. But he had agreed to do so only until midnight. Molu asked if he had observed a large woman and a man watching his ship. No, the captain told him; there had been no one. Perhaps it was his overwrought mind that had imagined the pair, he thought.

---

Kane Diallo had read the exhaustion in the passenger's eyes and hurried the tour of the ship. At the bow, he paused to tell Molu about sea sickness, explaining that on a small ship, a squall was a tsunami for the sufferers. He thought it wise to show Molu where the heads were at the bow and at the stern. While there he pointed at the cuddies in case the passenger was caught in the open during a storm.

Molu bumped into several crew members who paid little attention to him. He did not ask about the crew but noted that the galley could accommodate only twelve. When the captain was satisfied, he took the passenger to his cabin. "You'll use my cabin during the four-day voyage," he said. Molu looked at the bunk appreciatively but thanked him — a cot anywhere would do, he said. Diallo lifted a hand to gesture that Molu should not be concerned, and showed him where he kept books and a bottle of rum. Before he closed the door, he asked that the passenger stay in the cabin until they were at sea. Molu wondered if he could watch the ship leave the dock. The captain said that he would send someone to get him. But Molu had scarcely taken his shirt off that he was asleep.

The sun was overhead, when the captain noticed his passenger. He was holding the grab rails at the bow looking at the flat sea, which at that hour twinkled like diamonds. He sent one of his men to bring him to the quarterdeck. When Molu came up, he greeted him in the understated manner Molu had noted last night and told him, "When I reported you were on board, I was asked to tell you to call the minister. She has news for you, I was told. Bakary will show you how to operate the phone system. Also, it's lunch time, but you can have breakfast if you want."

"Thank you. I'll have some coffee," Molu said. "I don't think I can eat yet. Where are we?"

"Off Gabon."

---

Bakary took Molu to the communication room and showed him how to use the sea to land server. Minister Cerusu must have been waiting for his call.

"Have you heard the news," she said, her voice subdued. "Nundu was assassinated last night." Molu immediately thought that was the reason he had gotten out of Pointe Noire so easily.

"At what time?" he asked, seeking to make the connection.

Minister Cerusu ignored the question. "The Ugandans and Rwandans want you to be president," she blurted out.

Molu was silent.

"You say nothing to this?" She thought she heard sobbing sounds.

After a moment, Molu said in a sober voice, "Perhaps what I said at the meeting in Pointe Noire was not reported to you. I meant every word. No one should be brought to power on the tiger's back. I am surprised you think that I would want to be a contraband head of state. We've had enough of Nundus and even of Mututus."

"What I am surprised of," said the minister in an unusually sarcastic tone, "is that I forgot what a dreamer you were."

* * *

Except for a few hours gazing at the ocean, Molu spent the days listening to a powerful multiband radio in the captain's cabin, and, through Radio France Internationale, followed events in his country. As Minister Damuya had said, friends were now enemies and vice versa, in the free for all that Kinshasa had become. Hope and uncertainty raced to and fro in Molu's mind, as he tracked the positions of the parties engaged in a conflict that seemed to have lives without number.

On the third day Captain Diallo informed him that *Le Cayor* would dock in Dakar before proceeding to Cap Verde. Something about a new consignment of crab shell flakes was the reason, he explained. Molu would get off in Dakar, where Minister Cerusu's people would process him to his next destination. He thanked Captain Diallo profusely for what he and his crew had done for him. The captain lifted a hand to acknowledge Molu's thanks; he was a man of few words who preferred to keep a weather eye open at all times. Molu went astern to gaze at the water as if performing a ritual to exorcize the regrets consuming him.

Minister Cerusu came personally on board to thank Captain Diallo. When it was his turn to greet the minister, Molu thought her distant, but accepted that he had disappointed her. But perhaps it was the beard he was letting grow that had put the minister off. She could be hermetic when she had a mind to. So he spoke only of how well Captain Diallo and his men had treated him.

They got off the ship using a gangway, and Molu told her how he had gotten on. "Jacob's ladder," she repeated, and looked at him as if to adjudge that he had little to show for the many opportunities the ancestors had put in his path.

Then he heard, "*Nayebi bino te. Nabo sani nkombo na te, Mokonzi na mandefu,*" and his daughter Nef was in his arms. His wife too had made the trip to Dakar, and they wept together. Fatou-Anne Cerusu was pleased.

———

Before getting on the flight to New York, Molu told the minister about Father Brabant. Fatou-Anne was not surprised that Brabant had gone to Congo-Kinshasa. But when Molu told her that the priest had killed himself there, a sad look passed over her beautiful face, like a Harmattan storm over her native village. When the storm had passed, she remarked, nodding reflectively, as if to certify the truth of what she was about to say, that Molu reminded her of the Belgian priest. As to that time in 1936, she recalled how much it rained in Paris then — "*Ah, les pluies du temps jadis,*" the rains of yesteryear," she sighed, paraphrasing Villon. Molu was certain she was referring to her youth and not to the year.

———

In February, Molu's wife had another daughter, Fatou-Elle Sakeseba.

Fatou-Elle's father took a job as an adjunct professor at a university in the District of Columbia, teaching the history of coups d'état in Africa. He spends many hours telling skeptical students about Lumumba, Motutu, Nundu and others. His daughter Nef thinks he chose that particular university only so that he can see the river on his way to work.

Having sworn that he would not shave until he returned to Africa, his beard is now very bushy.

Marcellus Garinaldi told a childhood friend who congratulated him on being named Assistant Secretary of State (ASS) that if it were not for Africa he would not be anything, least of all ASS. He asked the friend not to forget to add African affairs when giving his title; explaining that where he works, African Americans are favorites for assignments in Africa. "But thank you, Jesus," he told the friend.

Using what Molu had given him of the Dictator's memoirs, Ken Taylor drafted a report for Brenda that he said reflected what Molu had told them at *Le Homard.* Brenda sent it to Washington.

It was her achievement that the Dictator's "revelations" included no mention of the U.S. government's decades of shoring up his regime. Washington, reeling from disclosures of support to unsavory dictators, was grateful. To recompense her, Brenda received what she calls a "grip" to be ambassador to Berlin. Unfortunately, a presidential campaign contributor asked for Germany, and the White House obliged. Brenda settled for Austria.

She made sure Ken Taylor heard of her appointment; she was hoping he would call. When he didn't, she called him. "Deputy to the ambassador to Austria is a great job, Kenny; you'll be the only little black twit so assigned." Ken laughed. "Braunau is in Austria, isn't it? The last time I checked it was." Brenda didn't know what he was talking about. "In ten thousand years I'll consider your offer, Brenda. But thank you for asking. Have a nice tour," he told her before he hung up.

Three months after taking residence in London, Ken was bored. He was going to resign, to go ply the Caribbean Sea, when he received a late-night call from a friend in higher places with another offer of a handshake. Ken is now the American ambassador to the C.A.R., the Central African Republic. His deputy is a fellow African American.

# About the Author

A lifelong student of the oral tradition and the literature of Africa, Christian Filostrat has resided in several countries on the continent, immersed in the culture while studying languages, socioeconomic and political trends unique to the region. He had the opportunity to observe and meet several heads of state. He draws on this experience and on his compilation of tales, proverbs, and traditions of the African peoples, as well as on his appreciation for the African narrative.

In his writing of this story, tradition, paranoia, and machination entwined the exigency of survival. Mr. Filostrat resides in Washington, DC.